BAD SISTER

SAM CARRINGTON

avon.

AVON

A division of HarperCollins*Publishers*
1 London Bridge Street,
London SE1 9GF
www.harpercollins.co.uk

A Paperback Original 2017

1

First published in Great Britain by
HarperCollins*Publishers* 2017

A catalogue record for this book is
available from the British Library

ISBN-13: 978-0-00-820021-3

Set in Minion by Palimpsest Book Production Limited,
Falkirk, Stirlingshire

Printed and bound in Great Britain by
CPI Group (UK) Ltd, Croydon CR0 4YY

MIX
Paper from
responsible sources
FSC™ C007454

BAD SISTER

Sam Carrington lives in Devon with her husband and three children. She worked for the NHS for fifteen years, during which time she qualified as a nurse. Following the completion of a psychology degree, she went to work for the prison service as an Offending Behaviour Facilitator. Her experiences within this field inspired her writing. She left the service to spend time with her family and to follow her dream of being a novelist. *Bad Sister* is her second psychological thriller.

Readers can find out more at http://www.samcarrington.blogspot. co.uk and can follow Sam on Twitter @sam_carrington1

For my sister, Celia – who is not bad at all.

Then

The heat pressed against her face.

On it. In it. Her cheeks felt like they were burning inside as well as out.

The little boy stood motionless beside her, his scorched pyjama bottoms trailing the pavement. His dark unblinking eyes stared up at the leaping flames erupting from the upper floor, then his attention turned to the bedroom window.

At the man screaming there.

She watched too, unable to drag her gaze away.

The man's face seemed oddly distorted; like the famous painting she'd seen once: *The Scream*, wasn't it? He banged against the windowpane, his mouth opening in a large *O* shape. The howl coming from the dark hole didn't sound human. His hands were either side of his dripping face. Was it melting?

He disappeared from view.

The boy's small hand slipped into hers. She snatched it away, and finally turned from the burning scene to look down at him.

'What have you *done*?'

CHAPTER ONE

Connie

Monday 5 June

'All right, Miss. Didn't think I'd bump into you on the outside.'

Connie froze, the voice behind her instantly cooling the blood in her veins, despite the morning's warmth. Her head dropped involuntarily, her bobbed, black hair falling forwards, creating a curtain on either side of her blanched face. She could pretend she hadn't heard, carry on walking, but if she ignored him he might follow her. Slowly, she turned to face him.

The man – wiry, thin from heroin addiction – leant against the wall adjacent to the train station entrance, cigarette in mouth, his eyes squinting through a cloud of smoke.

A thin wisp of air expelled from Connie's lungs and pushed its way through her pursed lips. Her shoulders relaxed a little. It was only Jonesy. She could cope with him.

'Oh, hello, Jonesy. How are you doing?' Connie instantly regretted the open question. She gave an exaggerated look at her watch, then smiled, hoping he'd get the message that she was in a rush.

'Well, you know how it is, Miss. It ain't easy, they got me on a short leash, like – but it's better than being in that shithole I s'pose.'

Connie raised her eyebrows. She was inclined to agree with the last part.

'What you doing with yourself now you've left, Miss?'

She hadn't expected that question. How did he know?

'Oh, well . . . I've gone for a change in direction.' She turned away from him, her attention shifting to the small group of people heading into Coleton station, the low hum of their early morning conversation drifting on the air. She wished she could slide in step with them, get away from Jonesy quickly. She didn't want to give him any details about her new job, or get into an awkward conversation. He might have done his time, but someone who'd been convicted of aggravated burglary wasn't a person she particularly wished to converse with right now. She checked her watch again. 'I've got to go; I'm going to miss the train. Sorry.'

'Ah. Okay.' He shrugged, his voice clipped. 'Another time, then.'

Connie hoped not. 'Good luck, though.' She turned and walked towards the entrance.

'They were wrong, you know,' Jonesy said, his voice carrying after her. 'To treat you like that. It wasn't just your fault.'

Her steps ceased for a few seconds, then, without turning back, she ascended the stairs to the platform, her heels clicking rapidly on the metal.

Her heartbeat matched her footsteps.

CHAPTER TWO

DI Wade

As murder locations went, this was up there with the ones categorised as 'unusual'. Detective Inspector Lindsay Wade had seen bodies dumped in all manner of places, and wasn't easily rattled. This case didn't have the shock factor in terms of it being off the wall, or weird – it was that the body was clearly meant to be found. Already this had put a bad taste in her mouth, and a cramp in her stomach. The killer wanted people to know, wanted the press coverage, the limelight. Murders like this were usually thought out, planned. And they also didn't tend to be one-offs. These were the alarm bells ringing in Lindsay's mind as she and Detective Sergeant Mack turned off the road in the dark blue Volvo Estate and on to the driveway leading to HMP Baymead, the local prison four miles outside of the market town of Coleton.

'How long ago did uniforms get here, Mack?'

Fifty-two-year-old Charlie Mack had always been known simply as 'Mack' even at school. No one used his forename, bar his mum. Humming an unrecognisable tune, he flicked through his black pocket notebook. 'The first got here at 7.35. Call came in from the Operational Support Grade in charge of the front gate at 7.20. Said he'd heard the screeching of tyres, saw a white, unmarked transit van drive at speed back up the road leading out of the prison. Thought it was just some idiot messing around; with the driveway being accessible to anyone, he said they often get vehicles that aren't official – not relating to employees – coming in and out. There's also a public footpath that runs along the top of the grounds, popular with dog walkers apparently.'

'Christ, you'd think it'd be more difficult to get to, more secure.'

'Yeah, but it's a cat C prison, out in the sticks. The fencing is high enough, and it's not like you're going to get some nutter trying to scale it, in or out, not with that roll of wire on the top.' DS Mack motioned out the car window at the perimeter fencing as they drove by. The red-brick walls of the prison buildings could be seen beyond the fence. The site had been used as an army camp in the run-up to World War Two. The buildings were now a mix of old and new, with a new larger cell block being more visible than the older 'H-style' living blocks that housed the majority of the inmates.

'So, who found the body?'

'A Carol Manning, prison officer. First one of the morning shift to arrive at approximately 7.10. She had to walk past the victim to get to the entrance. She raised the alarm with the OSG.'

'Why did he wait for another ten minutes before he called it in?'

'They were pretty shaken, you know, the way the man'd been killed . . . and the fact they knew him.'

'I guess. Did uniform ask them whether they'd touched anything, messed with the scene during that time?'

'Yep, and if they did, they didn't own up to it. And apparently more employees arrived for work before uniform got here too.'

'Great. So it's a possibility then.' Lindsay parked alongside the other police vehicles, sighed and pulled her long, red hair back into a ponytail, deftly looping and securing it into an elastic band before she got out of the car. As she usually did, Lindsay stood and took in the surrounding area, her hands firmly in her trouser pockets. Mack hung back, waiting for her to complete her routine scan. Lindsay's eyes settled on the tape cordoning off the area, then shifted to the white tent erected over the body. A pale-looking PC stood at the entrance to the scene, clipboard in hand. She breathed in deeply, the mugginess of another humid day already saturating the air, then exhaled forcefully. 'Right.' She turned back to the boot of the car, lifting it to reveal the items they'd require. 'Let's get in there and see what we've been left.'

CHAPTER THREE

Connie

It took Connie ten minutes of winding through side streets and a brisk walk halfway up the main road of the historic town of Totnes to reach her building. She wiped the sheen of perspiration from her forehead – it was the reason she liked to get the early train, to prevent this kind of exertion first thing in the morning. The hill was a killer at the best of times and didn't suit her size-16 frame – a consequence of months of late-night snacking on salt and vinegar crisps, and her consumption of takeaway and convenience microwave meals for one. She much preferred to amble up it. Still, she'd made good time, despite her unexpected encounter with Jonesy.

She stopped and looked at the shiny gold-plated plaque which adorned the wall to the left of the entrance: MISS C SUMMERS CPsychol FBPsS, like she'd done every morning for the past five months. She'd probably tire of it at some point, but for now, seeing the plaque flooded her stomach with a warm sensation; she was proud of her efforts in setting the practice up, of gaining a client base. She'd considered getting a consulting room with one of the counselling psychologists she'd met when she trained seven years ago – to keep the financial outlay down. Melissa had a successful practice in Coleton – she'd gone straight into her counselling role, whereas Connie had made the choice to do a post-graduate qualification in forensic psychology. It would've been more convenient for Connie to take a room in Melissa's building. But having the autonomy and freedom of being on her own outweighed the pluses of sharing workspace and costs.

Her new place of work was tucked in between a jewellery shop and an estate agency. It was a narrow two-storey building: a small room on the ground floor with a kitchenette and toilet off it, and another upstairs which she used as her office and consulting room. It was compact, but sufficient for her needs; a far cry from the vastness of the prison environment. A shudder passed through her. She disregarded it; the feeling would go in time. She had a lot to look forward to now: she had a new name – she'd changed it from *Moore* and taken her mother's maiden name instead; her own consultancy; only herself to answer to, and she was no longer bound to working with criminals. Connie really had changed direction. It was time to concentrate on helping the victims of crime, not the perpetrators.

As Connie stepped through the blue wooden door into the room she'd designated as a client waiting area, a voice – high-pitched and shrill – assaulted her ears from behind.

'Hey. You're late. I've been hanging round here for ten minutes, people watchin' an starin' at me, like I'm some weirdo nut-job.'

Connie gave a tight smile and stepped aside to let the young woman and her four-year-old child through. 'I'm sorry, Steph.' She didn't point out that Steph's appointment was at 9.15 a.m. and actually she was early.

'Well, you're here now. Let's get on wi' it.' Steph roughly tucked some long strands of wispy hair behind her right ear, then pulled at the boy's arm, half dragging him towards the stairs.

'Um . . . If you could give me a few minutes, please. Time to fire up the computer, sort the room . . .' Connie indicated for Steph to sit in the floral-print tub chair. Steph stopped, glared at her for a few seconds, then huffed and pulled the boy away from the stairs. She sat down heavily on the chair, lifting the child on to her lap.

'It's tight time-wise today. As you can see, I got Dylan.' She looked down at the boy, ruffled his mass of curly blond hair and then glared once more at Connie. 'I got no one to 'ave him, his pre-school won't take him 'cos he's got a rash.' Connie wondered if Steph had noticed her eyebrows suddenly lifting, because she quickly added, 'It's not contagious. He gets bouts of infected eczema, I've told 'em that, but they don't listen.'

'Perhaps a note from your GP might help.'

'You know what I'm like with *them*. Don't trust 'em.'

Connie would bet that Steph didn't really trust her either. She seemed to put little faith in anyone.

Connie ascended the stairs and turned right at the top, swinging her consulting room door open. The smell of freshly cut grass wafted to greet her. She'd strategically placed the room diffuser so that her clients would feel relaxed by its refreshing fragrance. Everyone loved the smell of cut grass.

It didn't usually have the desired effect on Steph, though. It would take far more than fresh cut grass to relax her. This was Steph's third session. The other two had begun in a similar way and had ended the same – but in the middle, it seemed anything could happen. It was a surprise, like opening a box of chocolates and realising the menu was missing, so having to pop one in your mouth and hope that by the time the chocolate's centre revealed itself it didn't turn out to be Turkish delight. Today's centre, Connie thought, was very likely to be Turkish delight. Apart from anything else, how was she going to carry out her session with Dylan in the room?

Once her computer was on, suit jacket hung up, comfy chairs arranged, and paper and pens placed on the floor under the window for Dylan, Connie called for Steph to make her way upstairs. She didn't take notes during the sessions, worrying that doing so would give the impression it was some kind of test, or that a report was being written about the client. Connie preferred to let them talk, have a proper conversation, full eye contact throughout. It made for a more relaxing atmosphere, showed them she was genuinely interested in their problems. Following the hour-long session, Connie wrote up the main points straight on to the computer: any developments, issues for further consideration – and a plan of action structured to the individual for their progression.

Steph's needs were complex; Connie had yet to penetrate the tough outer shell she'd constructed over the years, in order to expose the source of her current fears. Perhaps today might bring a breakthrough. But, as Dylan sauntered, head bowed, into the room and slumped to the floor beside the pens and paper, she realised it was unlikely. He seemed small for a four-year-old – not undernourished, but delicate, like a strong hug might break his bones. As much as Steph's exterior was hard, and to the outside world she might appear to be an overly authoritarian parent, Steph was fiercely protective of her son, which meant she'd be guarded, hesitant to open up in front of him for fear of causing him worry.

'Please, sit down, Steph.'

'What we gonna talk about today then?' Steph jutted her square chin forwards. 'How coming to this place was a bad idea? How that copper assigned to help me integrate – or whatever posh word he called it – has basically given me the brush-off? How last night I was scared to sleep 'cos the dreams have got so bad I can't bear to shut my eyes, just in case I see him again? Up to you, Connie. You choose.' Steph threw herself back in the chair; head tilted upwards, a deep ragged breath escaping her open mouth.

Connie's stomach tightened. Today was different. Steph seemed agitated from the off; no slow build-up. Where should she start? How could she approach her needs in this one-hour session? She decided to give the control back to Steph; clearly the lack of it in her own life made up a large part of her anger.

'Which of those issues do you think is the main one troubling you at the moment?'

'They all are. And them are just what've immediately sprung to mind right this second. Trust me, there's a load more to add to that collection.'

'It's a case of untangling them, Steph – one by one. At the moment they're all bunched together and it can be difficult to separate those that are founded, that are actually worthy of concern, and those that can easily be dispelled by just a few moments thinking them through. Seeing if they're logical; real.'

'They're all fuckin' real.' Steph turned quickly towards Dylan. He was deeply engrossed in drawing a picture; she sighed and returned her attention to Connie. 'Okay. I'm dead angry at Miles. He's dumped me in this town, so bloody far away from my home, and expects me to just get on wi' it. I know I had no support in Manchester, not really, but I knew people. Knew the places. Knew the dangers. Here, in this weird hippy-Totnes town, I know nothin'.' Steph waved her arms around, supposedly mocking the town's residents.

'Okay. It's good that you recognise where your anger is directed. We'll start there.'

Connie relaxed a little. As a starting point, this was actually a good one. Steph had been relocated under the protected persons scheme two months ago. Her assigned constable was Miles Prescott, an old-school police officer – and one who was nearing retirement. Connie had met him a few times; she'd taken on two of his relocates: Steph and Tommy. Those in the scheme were always given access to a psychologist – often they had issues of trust, but mainly they were afraid. And having been taken from their family and friends it meant them starting over again, completely, with different identities, new names. From what she'd learnt of Steph, her sense of identity had already been on rocky ground. She was unsure who she was any more, and the only constants were Dylan, Connie and Miles.

Connie's input was ten sessions, with an option of monthly catch-ups after – so, soon enough, one of Steph's three supports was going to go. If she felt Miles wasn't being as supportive as she'd been led to believe, then she'd feel alone – just her and Dylan. Connie had to try and encourage her to make friends in Totnes, help her to 'become' Stephanie Cousins. Put her old name and identity in a separate compartment. Not that anyone could forget who they were; where they came from. And nor should they – but if she was to succeed in integrating Steph here, Connie would have to help her build a new life.

'So, what is the current situation with Miles?'

'I think he's fed up wi' seeing me. Got better things to do wi' his time. He told me he can't babysit me and Dylan all the time, said I gotta be the one to make positive changes and *embrace* this new life.' She whispered the next bit: 'That fucker – I put my life at risk to help 'em out. I went to that court and helped put a lowlife drug dealer away. He won't rest until he's made me pay for that. He'd have killed me then an' there, I could see that in his eyes. They still could, if they find out where we are . . . Miles is meant to protect me, ain't he? Not abandon me when it suits him. When I've outlived my usefulness.'

'Is that what you think he's done? Abandoned you?'

'What would you call it?'

Connie leant her elbow on the arm of the chair and rested her chin in her cupped hand, contemplating the question. 'Well, abandonment is a strong word. I wonder if what he's actually trying to do is reduce his support in an effort to encourage you to go out of your comfort zone—'

'Er . . . I think you'll find coming to this poxy town was already out my comfort zone. Dropping my boyfriend in it, testifying against one of the most powerful gangs in Manchester – *that* was out my comfort zone. But it's not just that. What I want now is . . .' Steph turned away. Connie saw dots of blood appear on her bottom lip, her teeth clamping down hard and grinding the thin skin.

13

'Yes, go on. What is it that you want now?'

Steph wiped at her mouth with the back of her hand, and then looked directly at Connie, the light from the window highlighting the unusual amber shade of her eyes. 'I want someone to protect *me*. Make me safe. Stop *him* getting to me.'

'Okay, that's part of the reason you've been relocated – to prevent your boyfriend, or any of the gang members, from harming you. Miles has ensured—'

'No. Not them. And Miles has ensured nothin', apart from his stupid conviction. He might think he's protected me by setting me and Dylan up here. But if he leaves me to it now, leaves me to fend for myself, then he ain't gonna stop him from getting me.' Steph's face darkened, her expression fearful, frozen in time. Another time? Some other place?

'Steph. If you aren't talking about your ex-boyfriend, or the gang members, then who?' Connie leaned forwards. 'Steph.' She placed her hand on Steph's knee. Nothing. Steph remained stuck, transported, as if she was in a trance. 'Stephanie.' Connie spoke more firmly.

Steph's eyes returned to Connie's. 'Sorry. I was gone then.'

'Where? Where were you, Steph?'

'Back.' She shivered, drawing her unzipped hoody tighter across her chest. Her voice lowered, her tone hard. 'Wi' him.'

'Who? Who are you with?'

'Brett.' She spoke the name as if it hurt her to say it.

The silence following the mention of this name stretched. Connie waited for her to elaborate. But she seemed to have gone into a daze again, her eyes penetrating the walls and beyond. Without warning, Steph bolted up and out of the chair, striding towards Dylan. She scooped him up. He thrashed briefly in her arms, trying to reach down for the paper scattered on the floor before she shouted at him to be still. Then she headed for the door.

'Steph, we still have half an hour of the session. It might be good to carry on, don't leave now,' Connie shouted after her as she got up and followed Steph out.

She watched as Steph descended the stairs, Dylan bobbing up and down with each step. As she reached the bottom she turned. Her eyes were wet with tears.

'He will come for me. He'll finish what he started. I know it.'

'How do you know it, Steph?'

'Forget it, Connie.' Her voice was flat. 'You can't help me.'

Connie was still on the top step as the front door of the building banged hard in its frame. She ran down, and outside. Steph was already disappearing into the crowd in the market square opposite. What was that all about? She'd assumed Steph's fear of being found was related to the gang that her ex-boyfriend had been a part of. But now she'd thrown something new into the pot. She'd have to write it down while it was fresh in her mind. There was no mention of a Brett in Steph's case file, the one Miles had given her, she was sure of it. Connie had read the file thoroughly; it hadn't taken long. It detailed her ex-boyfriend and the known gang members, and family-wise it said that her mother was in a nursing home, her father's whereabouts were unknown and she had no siblings.

As Connie returned to the consulting room to note down her questions, the security buzzer for the front door sounded. She exhaled and stretched across her desk, pressing the button to release the lock without asking who it was. It'd be Steph, hopefully, coming back to finish her session. But the noise on the stairs suggested more than one adult. Connie marched across the room. She let out an involuntary yelp as she flung the door open to find two people standing on the other side.

CHAPTER FOUR

Connie

'Morning, sorry to arrive unannounced.' The petite red-haired woman, who looked to be in her mid-thirties, didn't seem at all sorry and squared up to Connie as she thrust a badge in front of her face. 'I'm Detective Inspector Wade. This,' she threw a thumb in the air, indicating back over her shoulder, 'is Detective Sergeant Mack.'

Connie raised her gaze from the short female detective to the tall man standing directly behind her. The disparity in their heights was almost comical. 'Right, um . . . okay. Come on in.' Connie, flustered due to Steph's shock exit and now the sudden arrival of the detectives, allowed them in and shut the door behind them. She'd met DS Mack before, she was sure – couldn't place where right now, though. She was used to dealings with the police, but they were usually planned meetings. This was unexpected. It was likely to be something relating to being an expert witness, or profiling. Occasionally in the past she'd consulted independently on cases that required profiling criminals. She hadn't done this kind of work since leaving the prison service. Somehow, though, this felt different. She'd always got a call first.

'What can I do for you both?' Connie sat in the office chair behind her desk as if having that barrier gave her an element of control.

DS Mack had taken a seat, the one Steph had occupied moments before, his long legs reaching the desk. But DI Wade paced the room, her hands in her suit trouser pockets. She settled in front of the array of framed certificates hanging on the wall adjacent to the window.

'You used to work at HMP Baymead,' DS Mack said as he flipped through his notebook. 'As the Head of Psychology.'

'Yes, that's correct. I officially left at the beginning of this year.' Connie shuffled in her seat.

'Can you tell me the reason for your departure from your position there?'

Really? She was going to have to go through that?

'Personal reasons, Detective Sergeant. I'd been on long-term sick for six months and the job no longer held the . . .' she looked up and to her right, trying to think of the right word to use, '*attraction* that it once did.'

'I can't imagine that working with criminals could ever be classed as attractive, Miss Summers.'

'Well, *you* work with them, DS Mack.' Her eyes penetrated his. She wasn't having her career choice, or the reasons for it, coming under fire.

'Ah, well I don't work *with* them; I work to put them away. And I've never thought it's an attractive job. I'd like to think it's more to do with my duty to the community.'

Of course, Connie thought, it was the standard answer many police officers gave. She'd put money on it not being entirely true for DS Mack.

'Are we going to debate who has the best reason for working with criminals,' Connie said overly sweetly, 'or are you going to get to the point of why you're here?'

A snigger came from the other side of the room. DI Wade turned her attention from the certificates and drew the remaining

17

comfy chair across the beige carpet to sit next to DS Mack. She smiled at Connie before asking, 'Your reason for leaving the prison service, or rather, an instigating factor I believe, was to do with an Eric Hargreaves, known to most as Ricky. Is that right?'

Connie gripped the arms of her chair almost as tightly as the anxiety gripped her insides. What had he done now? More to the point, what else was *she* going to feel responsible for – another offence? An attack, or worse, a death? Connie's breathing accelerated; the wave of panic threatened to spill over. *Relax. Breathe.* Her grip loosened, her heart rate steadied. She was overreacting; her thoughts weren't based on any actual evidence. They were unfounded. He was still in prison. *Wasn't he?* Connie attempted to work out how long he'd got left to serve, but her mind scrambled around, unable to do the maths. Both detectives were staring at her, waiting for her to speak. To tell them about an experience she was trying so hard to forget. Ricky. That name unlocked so many painful memories.

'The circumstances surrounding Ricky's case certainly had an impact, yes. It's not exactly ideal, is it? To recommend a prisoner's release only for him to rape a woman days later.' She averted her eyes. Didn't want to think about it, much less talk about it. What that poor woman went through, how she must've felt when she found out her attacker had only just been released. How much she must hate those who allowed him back into the community – hate Connie for reporting to the parole board that he was safe . . . Connie rubbed at her wrist absently, a raised red mark appearing.

'No, Miss Summers, it's not,' DS Mack said gently. Although to Connie, there was a hint of distaste in his words. He probably blamed her too.

'Please, call me Connie.' Him saying 'Miss Summers' was beginning to grate on her nerves.

'The reason we're here,' DI Wade's blunt, monotone voice cut through, 'is because we have a murder scene—'

'Oh, no, no. How? How has he committed a murder?' Connie put her head in her hands.

'Sorry, you don't understand. He hasn't *committed* it.' DI Wade narrowed her eyes and moved forward in her chair. 'He's the victim.'

CHAPTER FIVE

Then

Blue lights reflected in the puddles of water that had formed on the pavement, spilling into the gutter and down the drain, taking with it lumps of black debris. The show was over; the flames extinguished. Life as she knew it extinguished as well. The door of one of the ambulances banged. The girl jumped – she'd been so focused on the scene. A hand touched her shoulder, a paramedic spoke to her as he guided her to another waiting ambulance. The sounds were muffled, as if she was underwater. She snapped her head left and right, trying to clear it. He'd disappeared from her side. Where was he? Had he already been taken?

'Where's my brother?'

The man looked down at her, his eyebrows drawn together until they touched in the middle. 'What does he look like?'

'About this high.' With a shaky hand, she indicated up to her shoulder. 'Black hair. He had blue pyjamas on. He's ten.' She swung around, eyes flitting over the scene, darting between the many figures that scattered the area. 'Where is he? He was with me.' The pitch of her voice elevated. The paramedic shouted to his colleague, asking if a boy had been taken to the hospital. She saw the shake of his head, the rising of his shoulders in a shrug.

'Don't worry,' the man said, 'I'm sure he's safe. It's scary for a ten-year-old, perhaps he's got out of the way. I'll ask the police to look for him.' He made a move to bundle her into the ambulance, but she forced her body weight back against him, stopping his attempt. 'Are you all right, love? Come on, you need to be checked over.'

'No.' She turned and glared at him. 'I need to tell them. I have to find him, and make sure they know.' She struggled against his grip, pulling away from him, and the blanket he'd placed around her shoulders fell to the ground.

'Wait, please, you need to be assessed!' His voice trailed after her as she fled.

There were at least four police cars. Why did they need so many? She ran to each one, pushing past bystanders as they lazily watched the scene, checking to see if he was in any of them. Where was he?

'Hey, hey. Slow up.' A policewoman gently placed both arms around her shoulders. Why did everyone feel the need to touch her? 'What are you doing here? You should be on your way to hospital.'

'No, no. I need to find my brother.' She didn't make eye contact with the woman.

'Ah, I see. It's okay, he was frightened, he's with one of the PCs over there.' She pointed at an unmarked car, up the road on the right.

'Did he tell you?' The girl raised her wide eyes to meet the policewoman's.

'Tell us what?'

'That it's his fault. Did the little *creep* tell you?' She tore away, and ran towards the car. The policewoman followed. As the girl approached, she saw him in the back seat – with a blanket wrapped loosely around him, as they'd wrapped it round her. He looked small; innocent. The screech came from deep within her, filling the night air. 'You little shit, you murderer!' she shouted, banging both fists repeatedly against the window. The boy shrank away

21

from it; from her – moving backwards, scrambling to the other side of the car. The policewoman was with her now, holding her arms; holding her back. 'He did it. He started the fire. He's a weirdo, always playing with fire. He killed him.' Her determination gave her strength to break free. She launched again towards the window. She didn't bang on it this time, but pressed up against it, squashing her features. It cooled her face.

The boy inside cowered. Tears had made clean tracks down his blackened face. He shook his head, his whole body seeming to tremble. His mouth opened and closed like a fish gasping out of water. Finally, he managed to say, 'Don't be angry at me. I'm sorry, sis.'

CHAPTER SIX

Connie

'I don't understand.' Connie released her hands from the arms of the chair, gripping one in the other instead. 'How?' Her gaze darted between DI Wade and DS Mack, searching for clues while she waited for a response.

'Mr Hargreaves was on ROTL – release on temporary licence—'

'Yes, I know what ROTL is, Detective Inspector. But, *why* was he? He'd not long been reconvicted.' Connie felt heat flushing her face. 'How had he possibly been assessed as being safe to leave the prison?'

'No offence, Miss . . . sorry . . . Connie. But hadn't *you* assessed him as safe to return to the community?' DS Mack said.

'None taken. Because, yes, I recommended his release – along with other professionals, I might add – but at that time he hadn't committed a further offence. Now he has, and so it would be ridiculous to allow him ROTL now, wouldn't it?'

'Calm down, Connie,' DI Wade said, as she shot DS Mack what appeared to be a warning look. 'DS Mack hasn't really explained it properly. Hargreaves was granted permission by the prison governor to attend his mother's funeral last Friday. It was meant to be for a few hours, under prison-officer guard. But somehow, following a commotion at the graveside, the full details of which we've yet to discover, he made a run for it. It's assumed he had help on the inside as well as the outside so that he could orchestrate the whole thing to coincide with the funeral.'

Connie sat back, forcing her shoulders down into their natural position. 'So, now he's dead?'

'Yes, that's right. Three days following his escape. His body was dumped outside the prison gatehouse this morning.'

'Well, that's unfortunate for him, I guess. So what's any of this got to do with me? Why are you here?'

'Well, that's the interesting part.'

Nothing about the case so far was in the slightest bit interesting as far as Connie was concerned. She didn't want to have anything to do with it. Her upper body slumped. What the hell was coming next?

'Eric Hargreaves' body has been mutilated, the type and detail is not being disclosed for obvious reasons, but let's just say it's been done in a . . . *particular* way—'

'And you think I can help establish the type of person who would do this, give you some clues as to their motive?'

DI Wade scrunched her face a little and gently shook her head. 'I'm sure you could help with that, yes, but we're calling on you for a different reason at present.'

Connie's stomach dropped. 'Oh?'

'You see . . .' DS Mack took over. 'On closer inspection it was noted he had something written on his hand.' He paused, a smile playing at the edges of his mouth. He was enjoying dragging out the details; making Connie squirm. She rubbed at the raised red mark that was still on her wrist. It was stinging. She closed her eyes to block out DS Mack's smug face. Although she couldn't remember where she'd seen him before, she hoped after this that she'd never see his face again.

'Am I meant to guess?' Her tone sharp.

DS Mack shifted sideways slightly in his seat; his feet kicked the corner of her desk. He reached inside his jacket pocket and pulled out a see-through evidence bag containing a photograph. He held it out towards Connie between the thumb and forefinger of each hand.

She blinked rapidly a few times, then frowned.

She stared at the words: 'CONNIE MOORE' written in black on the palm of the bloody, grey-tinged hand.

Connie's face tightened.

'It's a conundrum for us, too,' DI Wade said. 'But we're hoping you'll be able to shed some light on it?'

CHAPTER SEVEN

DI Wade

'Wow, Mack, what was all *that* about?' Lindsay slid into the seat and slammed the driver door in one smooth movement, then stared at him.

'What?' He kept his focus forward.

She recognised that tone. He knew exactly what she was referring to; it wasn't as if he could've missed her sharp glance when he'd spoken to Connie Summers.

'Do you know her?'

'No,' he answered quickly. 'Why do you say that?'

'Oh, you know – the weird atmosphere as soon as we walked into her office, the underlying tension, the sarcasm; signs people might show if they've got history.'

'Wow, you've got one hell of an imagination. Don't you think she's a bit young for an old codger like me?' Mack ran a hand through his grey hair. Lindsay stared at him for a moment, taking in the mix of dark and light grey tones. She actually liked his hair; it was still thick, if not a bit unruly – if anything, it was his stubbly beard that aged him, made his face appear more weathered. She smiled.

'Good point.' Lindsay turned the ignition. She and Mack had worked together long enough for their working relationship to feel comfortable. Even as his superior, she could be herself, have a laugh. It was important in their line of work, and had become even more so since their last murder case; it'd taken a long while to regain her confidence after that one. To trust her judgements; instincts. Thankfully, the force still believed in her ability and skills as a DI.

'Oh, cheers, *Boss*.'

She grinned. She'd get to the bottom of it at some point. She'd never seen him conduct himself that way before. There had to be a reason for it.

'So, your personal stuff aside, what did you make of Miss Summers?'

Mack shook his head gently, tutting. 'Not sure, if I'm honest. She was a bit hostile, short.' He raised one eyebrow. 'You know, personal stuff aside . . .'

'Hah! Yeah, I thought that too, though. It could just be because she'd been slammed for being instrumental in his release, perhaps she still has guilt issues – and now her name is on Hargreaves' hand she's worried the past will rear its ugly head again. I get that.'

'Or?'

'*Or*, she has an idea of why her name's on his hand and is hiding something.'

'So, we're not thinking she's a target? If the killer wrote her name, you don't think it's because she might be the next victim?'

'Well.' Lindsay raised her shoulders in a half shrug. 'We can't rule that out. But it didn't seem threatening, just a name – not *you're next, Connie Moore*.'

'I can see what you mean, but I'd feel pretty uncomfortable if it was *my* name on a dead man's hand. How do you wanna play it then?'

'I think get her onside in a professional capacity – as an advisor. She's worked for the police before, so should be easy enough to cut through the red tape and get her cleared. That way we can keep an eye on her, keep her close, in case we do uncover any evidence that she's at risk. And we need to get as much info from her on Hargreaves and his associates as we can, see where that leads us. I'll give her a call later to set it up.'

'Okay. Hope she lightens up a bit then if we have to work together.'

'If you apologise for the fact you never called her before we arrived, then perhaps she will.' Lindsay gave him an exaggerated wink.

'For heaven's sake. You aren't going to let it go, are you?'

'I don't know what you mean.'

'Just drive.'

CHAPTER EIGHT

Connie

Connie had left her office early. The bitter taste left by the detectives' visit, followed by a phone call asking her to be an 'advisor' for the case, meant she hadn't felt like doing the admin she'd originally planned for the afternoon. Now, with the sun moving behind the house and dulling the interior of her lounge, she snuggled on the two-seater sofa with Amber, her long-haired Ragdoll cat, who was lolled across her lap. She felt herself relaxing as she stroked the cat's long white fur. Careful not to disturb Amber, Connie reached to the other end of the sofa for the controls and turned on the television.

She pitched forwards in shock, unintentionally slumping Amber on to the sofa.

The place was uncomfortably familiar. Connie's neck flushed, the way it did when stress or nerves took over her body, her left hand unconsciously moving to it, touching the heat. She didn't want to look, but her eyes refused to shift from the TV – the red-brick walls, the high perimeter fence, spread across the screen as if mocking her. Not again. Why was this happening now?

The reporter's voice blended into the background as Connie scanned the picture for clues. A white tent covered the area where Ricky's body had been, nothing to see there. To the side of the reporter, a small crowd gathered. She recognised a couple as her former colleagues: officers, a woman from admin. The others were probably rubberneckers, the draw of a major crime too great an opportunity to pass up; their morbid curiosity outweighing any sense of moral integrity.

'Although the victim's identity hasn't been officially confirmed, an inside source has spoken to *Spotlight* and it is believed that the deceased may be the same man released in December 2015 following an assessment by psychologist, Connie Moore.'

Connie's head snapped back. Did they just say her name? Stabbing at the controls, she rewound the programme and let it play again. The room darkened. Connie's head felt light, her hands clammy as not just her name was expelled from the TV, but her picture flashed up too. Connie's jaw slackened. Why link her with this? They didn't even know the man's identity for sure. Her full attention now gained, Connie stared at the reporter. Skinny woman, early twenties, pinched expression, a nose too big for her face. She now had ridiculous purple-coloured hair, not the chestnut brown it had once been, and it was shorter – but it was undeniably the same person. Kelly Barton. What a bitch. Her dubious reporting skills had gone a long way to triggering the depression and anxiety that caused Connie to go off sick last year, following the aftermath of the Ricky incident. She'd fixated on Connie's involvement over and above that of the other people who'd also had a hand in Hargreaves' release, which made it appear Connie was solely to blame. She hated this woman. How dare she drag her into this.

The ringing of her mobile made her jump. She snatched it up from the table beside the sofa, knocking this morning's coffee mug as she did, the curdling milky dregs splashing out. She shook the droplets from her hand, then rubbed it on her jeans.

The mobile display read *Unknown caller.*

Great. Was it starting again? One previous mistake. She'd thought it was over. But clearly others weren't going to allow it to rest. And what would happen once his identity was confirmed, once they found out the police had come to her for help? When they knew her name had been found on Ricky's body? A shudder rocked her. She got up from the sofa, paced the room, arms crossed tightly. The ringing stopped. Connie sighed. It was her work mobile, she'd purposely got a new one solely for her new business – she didn't want to give her personal number out to clients. The unknown caller could be a prospective client responding to her advertisement.

The phone gave its sharp ring into the silence. Unknown caller, again.

Leave me alone.

Connie set it to silent. Hopefully, if they were clients, they'd leave a message and she'd return the calls tomorrow. She watched her hands. The tremor. *Please don't let it start again.* She switched the TV off. A low buzzing sounded from her handbag. Her personal mobile. She rummaged in the pocket of the zipped compartment.

Her mum.

Inhaling deeply, Connie pressed the accept button.

'Hey, Mum.' Already tears pricked her eyes. How sad was it that her only ally was her mother? No boyfriend. No *friend.* She had some friends, but they were mostly linked to the prison. They weren't close, more like acquaintances. And they certainly weren't ones she wanted to speak to just yet.

'Have you had a good day?' Her mum's concerned tone exposed her attempt at naivety. She'd definitely seen the news.

'You saw it then.'

'Oh, darling. I'm sure it'll blow over. Again. They don't even know it's the same man.' The hope was evident. Connie was about to crush that.

'It is, Mum. It's him.'

'They—'

'Mum. The police came to see me. It's definite.'

31

Silence.

Her poor mum. How could Connie put her through it all again? It had almost destroyed her watching Connie fall deeper into the void of depression. She'd been scared. Scared that Connie might do something 'stupid'. An image of her brother flashed through her mind. However low she'd sunk, Connie had always kept the knowledge within her sights that she had to come through it, for her mum if not for herself.

She couldn't let her lose another child.

'It'll be fine, Mum. Don't worry. And at least I changed my name, my consultancy won't be affected . . .' A thought crossed her mind. 'Have you spoken to Dad?'

'Er . . . well, I was really worried when I saw the news . . .' Her voice was flustered. So, she had called him. Connie knew they still used each other for support. Years of marriage, a shared tragic loss – their joint histories brought them together during challenging times, despite their separation. But Connie wished he didn't know of this latest development. He'd see it as a negative; an inability to handle herself – to stay out of 'trouble'. She'd regularly disappointed him when she was growing up. He'd made it very clear that her brother had been the one who had the shiny, promising future ahead of him. The one he was proudest of. The one who would go into the family business. Nothing she could do would ever compare to the success her brother would've had, if he'd been the one who'd lived.

'And what did he have to say?' Why was she asking? She didn't want to know.

'He said it was probably a flash in a pan. Told me not to worry unduly, that it was just another blip . . .'

Connie snorted.

'Just another blip,' she repeated quietly. She took a deep breath. 'He's right, Mum. Honestly, you should listen to him. It's a murder enquiry. The focus of the police and media will be on the person who did it, not so much on the victim. He was a criminal; no one

32

will be interested in his life – or in me. It's bigger than that now.'
Her voice held more conviction than she felt.

'You sure?'

'Look, I'm working with the police on this. It's not my fault and I can't be blamed for anything this time. I promise.'

The call ended with her mum in a more hopeful place.

But Connie shouldn't have made a promise like that.

A nagging, anxious voice crept through her skull.

Are you sure *it's not your fault?*

CHAPTER NINE

Connie

Tuesday 6 June

Connie's night had been restless; the shock of the situation, the worry of the repercussions sinking in and taking up residence in her tired mind. There'd been no hope of solid sleep.

The 6.00 a.m. alarm rang out for the third time. She reached across, smacking it into silence. Connie stretched out, her body at a diagonal on her double bed. She could do that. With no one else to take up the space it was one small joy she could relish. It was one of the few pleasures of being single. A string of short-term encounters, some failed blind dates set up by well-meaning colleagues, and a more recent, and more complicated date that had unexpected results, didn't add up to any kind of satisfaction in that area of her life.

After a hastily taken shower, Connie took a sachet of ready-made porridge and tipped it into a not-so-clean bowl from the side of the kitchen worktop. It'd do. As usual she overcooked it in the microwave, the sludge-like consistency spilling over the top of the bowl. She attempted eating it before it'd cooled sufficiently, and the roof of her mouth bubbled in a painful blister. *Get it together, Connie.* She'd worked so hard to get to this stage in her life; independent, having her own business, she couldn't allow a lowlife criminal and an annoying reporter to ruin her success. And then there were the police.

She'd told DI Wade that she wouldn't be of any help – past the fact she'd written a report twenty months ago – but they felt that as she 'knew' Eric Hargreaves, he might have disclosed something from his background, associates that could be critical in the investigation. Why couldn't any of the other psychologists from Baymead help with their enquiries? And there were other employees from the offending behaviour programmes department that'd had dealings with Ricky. They had access to her report, her notes and emails. The police didn't need her. Not really. Why were they so keen for her to be involved? So they had a scapegoat if things didn't go their way? She'd been that before; she wasn't willing to be one again.

How much weight were they giving the discovery of her name on Ricky's hand? Did they think it was related to his murder or just a coincidence? They obviously had to follow any lead, and a name on the body was bound to need investigating, particularly when that name had been instrumental in the prisoner's previous release. Although they seemed to have found that out very quickly, given she'd changed her name since then.

The words from last night's report spiked her memory. *An inside source.* DI Wade and DS Mack had known about her past with Ricky before she'd mentioned it, so someone must've jumped right in and told them. Did the police think she was involved in Ricky's murder? Some kind of revenge attack, payback for messing her life up? Surely not. Maybe they were concerned that the murderer had put her name on Ricky's hand as a warning and that was why they were so keen to pay her a visit. Admittedly, she'd had a flash of panic that it was a sign that she was 'next' as soon as she saw the picture of Ricky's hand, but she'd dismissed that as paranoia. It was too subtle, and by all accounts, the person who killed Hargreaves was far from that. No, it didn't fit. There had to be a different reason her name had been found on a dead man.

These thoughts clouded her mind for the entire journey to Totnes, the weight of them seeming to make her head heavy. When DI Wade had asked her to be an advisor, she'd been reluctant, not wishing to commit. She'd said she'd think about it. Connie's assertion to her mother that she was working with the police had served to allay her mother's fears – but for Connie, the thought made her stomach contract. The Hargreaves mess had caused her enough trouble and Connie was doubtful she'd be much help now that he was dead – she probably wouldn't be able to tell DI Wade anything she didn't already know. If she didn't get involved any further, then she could forget all about it. No harm done. No further damage to her career. Or her well-being.

The earlier weight lifted as she walked through the side streets. All would be fine, she'd decline the invitation to be an advisor. She finally raised her head as she crossed the road to her office.

Steph was sitting on the steps, slumped against the wall. Had she come back to finish yesterday's session?

'Sorry, I know I haven't got an appointment . . . but I'm worried.' Steph dipped her head, fiddling with the zip on her hoody.

'No problem, Steph. I'm free until ten.' Connie unlocked the door and walked through, waiting for Steph to follow. Pulling herself up from the steps, Steph turned to face Connie, but didn't make any move to cross the threshold.

'I think I'm gonna 'ave to change shrinks.' She stared into Connie's eyes. 'Sorry, but you've drawn attention to yourself – your face on TV for all to see. You're too dangerous to me now.'

CHAPTER TEN

Then

It took a whole month to rid herself of the smell. The stench of smoke: the taste of it, the memory of dripping, burning flesh clinging to the tiny hairs on the inside of her nostrils. Things had moved on quickly from that night; even before the reality of the situation had time to hit home. Her life had changed completely, snatched from her in an hour of fire and fear. She'd gone from her cosy three-bedroomed terraced family home – to a run-down, hellhole of a flat rented from the council by her good-for-nothing uncle. Or that's how she remembered her mum talking about him. Good-for-nothing-Jimmy. Layabout. Scrounge. Druggie. Criminal. No one ever asked anything of him unless they were desperate. As she was now. Maybe her mum had got the better deal – even a shitty nursing home was preferable to this.

Because she was sixteen, there wasn't much the social could do about it. And she was *not* being put under some do-gooder's care. She could look after herself. And besides, her boyfriend had promised she could move in with him any day now. Things would get better then.

At least *she* wasn't inside a secure unit.

But he'd got what was coming to him, hadn't he? He had to

be punished. He'd be safe inside there; looked after properly, by professionals. They'd sort him. Perhaps even help him.

And if he was inside . . . it meant she was safe too.

His face, pale, innocent, looking up at her from inside the police car, appeared every time she closed her eyes for more than a second. His voice – pleading, apologetic – sounded in her ears whenever there was a quiet moment. It snaked its way inside her brain and spread like a disease.

Damn him.

If you play with fire, you'll get burnt.

CHAPTER ELEVEN

Connie

'I can't afford to be found, you know that.' Steph remained on the top step. She was alone, she must've dropped Dylan off at pre-school today. Connie looked up and down the street; no one was taking particular notice of them, but she felt the need to get inside, have the conversation in privacy.

'Please come on in, Steph.' She smiled, hoping to coax her. Steph gave a furtive look around too, and then bolted inside. Connie let out a lungful of air and gently closed the door.

'This shouldn't affect you, Steph. It's something that happened over a year ago, before I began this consultancy. My involvement was reported at the time, then it all went quiet – it wasn't even really to do with me, it was the justice system. And I changed my name . . .' She trailed off. Without going into the whole sorry tale, she wouldn't be able to make Steph understand. And it was unlikely to ease her concerns anyway. What would, really? She had every right to feel vulnerable. If the press began digging into Connie's life again, there was a real risk that Steph's new identity could be compromised. She prayed this would blow over. A few hours and she'd be telling Wade she was out; didn't want to be involved. Although, the fact her name was written on the dead man's hand complicated matters. How was she going to safeguard Steph?

'But you can't guarantee it, can you?' Steph's pupils, wide and accusing, bore right into Connie's. Her shoulders dropped.

'You're right. It is a risk and, even though I think it's a small one, I'll contact Miles, let him know the situation and he can refer you to a new psychologist.' Connie knew it was the sensible option. The safest. But she hated that she needed to do it. Hated that stupid bitch of a reporter. Hated Ricky Hargreaves. Even dead he was causing her problems.

'So you're givin' up on me? Like everyone else? That was quick, Connie.'

Connie's brow furrowed. She shook her head. She wasn't expecting that reaction.

'I don't understand, you said you needed a new psychologist, that I'm a risk?'

'Can we just have another session; I got something in the post this morning. You're the only one I can talk to about it.'

'You shouldn't be getting post.' Connie's hand flew to her chest. 'Who knows your address? Only utility companies should have it.'

'It's okay. It was forwarded to me at this address by Miles. They go into my Manchester place and pick up stuff now and then. They normally read it, 'specially if it looks suss, or they think it's from any of the gang, but this was unopened.'

'Oh, good.' Connie released her hand from her chest.

'But it's not good. It's from *him*.'

Connie's interest was renewed. Was she going to find out the real reason for Steph's current anxiety? The immediate situation with Ricky, and Steph's threat of finding a new psychologist, melted into the background.

'Let's go on up, shall we?' Connie started up the stairs, confident Steph would follow.

Steph took her usual chair; Connie pulled her own up close, just in front of Steph. She had to be careful here, let her talk, not jump in with questions. *Be patient.*

'Tell me about the letter.'

Steph's body shuddered, then she took in a deep breath. 'It's from Brett.' Even though Steph was naturally fair-skinned, any hint of colour she'd had drained slowly from her face, like water being let out of a bath. It looked to Connie like she might faint, but she recovered; taking a few rapid breaths, she appeared to compose herself. Connie bit the inside of her cheek to prevent herself talking, from pushing Steph into going faster. It had to be in her own time. *She* had to have the control, not Connie.

'He used to write all the time. Well, monthly. From the YOI.' She paused. It stretched. This was going to take a long time. Connie glanced at her watch; her next client was due at ten and she'd hoped to have made progress with Steph by then, but at this rate she'd have to cut her short. She'd have to prompt her. Steph had dropped her head and was twisting her fingers in the bottom of her oversized hoody.

'So, Brett is in a Young Offenders' Institution?'

She looked up again and sighed. 'Yep. Has been for years. Was in a secure home before that.'

'Okay, so hadn't you heard from him in a while then?'

'I'd ignored his letters. I guess he gave up trying 'cos I never wrote back. I think it's been two years since I got one.'

'You mentioned Brett the other day. It sounded as though you were afraid of him finding you? Why is that?'

Steph's eyes widened. Her words rushed out: 'He's a murderer.' She wiped her hands on her thighs, up and down, up and down. Then she looked up. Tears had appeared, bulging at her lower lids; her face had taken on a cold, hard, mask-like quality. 'And he's my brother.'

Connie sat back in her chair. Had she heard right, that this 'Brett' was her brother? How could that be? The background information she'd been given couldn't have been wrong, surely?

'Steph, I'm a bit lost,' she said tentatively. 'I didn't think you had any siblings.'

41

'Well I do. Spent a long time wishin' I didn't, but I do have a brother.'

Connie shifted in her seat. She'd have to go over the file, check this out with Miles Prescott. She was Steph's psychologist; Miles should've given her all the relevant information required to carry out her job. Why leave out significant details pertaining to her family. What else had been omitted?

Connie suddenly had a dozen questions she wanted to fire off, but held back. Steph obviously wanted to talk, or she wouldn't have shown up today. She allowed the silence.

'He was ten when he did it. The fire.' She screwed up her eyes tight, her lips were drawn in a straight line. One knee bounced as if on a nerve. 'The little weirdo torched the house while we slept.'

Poor Steph. What a terrible event.

'How did you escape?'

'I hadn't been asleep long, could hear him padding down the stairs, wondered what he was doin'. After he didn't come back upstairs, I went down to check what he was up to. He was always messin' around wi' matches, lighters and the like. Weird thing wi' fire. Didn't trust him. I thought I smelled smoke as I got outside their room. But it didn't sink in.' Steph tapped her temple with her forefinger. 'I assumed he was up to no good downstairs. I'd no idea he'd set the fire in their room. Stupid. If I'd just sussed it then . . .'

'You couldn't have known. It's normal for us to think about what we might have done after any situation. It was a traumatic event for you, Steph. Don't blame yourself.'

'I could've warned them earlier. Stopped him dying like that.'

'Your dad?'

'*She* got out, somehow. Don't know how, she was badly burned. Has never spoken since. Not a word. I think Dad panicked.' Her breathing shallowed. 'He was at . . . the . . . window . . .'

'Take some deep breaths, Steph.' Connie leaned forwards, put her hands on Steph's, breathing in slowly, out slowly, along with her.

'I watched. I watched him burn. And that murdering creep watched too.'

'I'm so sorry, Steph. To witness your dad dying, it's a terrible thing to have experienced.'

'Well, it wasn't quite like that, I mean – it's not as bad as if he'd been—'

A tap at the door stopped her. Connie jumped up, apologising for the interruption, and strode across the office. She hadn't buzzed anyone in – was the damn thing broken? She poked her head around the door, it was her next client. She told him she'd be five more minutes, asking him to wait downstairs. She'd have to wrap things up with Steph. Unfortunate timing.

'Sorry, Steph. Look, I've got my next client waiting, but I could see you again tomorrow so you can continue?' Connie raised her eyebrows, but carried straight on without waiting for Steph to answer. 'Unless you don't want to risk it. I mean, I understand your position, but you could be a while waiting for another psychologist . . .'

'Um. Well, I don't know, really.' She looked lost, her eyes darting about. 'Yeah, okay. I'll come tomorrow.' She got up and headed for the door. Before she left, she turned. 'But I am gonna need to swap as soon as poss, if you don't mind.'

Connie nodded. Hopefully she'd be able to get to the bottom of the letter tomorrow. And if the reassignment to another psychologist took as long as she assumed it would, then it might be that she could complete all of the ten sessions anyway, so she'd still have the opportunity to unravel Steph's story. But she'd be able to continue only if her connection with the Ricky murder didn't bring any further media coverage to her door. She'd have to do everything she could to make sure it didn't.

CHAPTER TWELVE

DI Wade

Lindsay Wade blew out air slowly from her puffed cheeks. That wasn't a conversation she'd been planning on having this early in the investigation. Had she convinced her?

'That sounded heavy.' Mack wheeled a chair towards her desk, sitting the wrong way on it, leaning his head on his crossed arms over its high back.

'Yep. Connie Summers. Running scared, I'd say.'

'Oh? How come?'

'Said this situation and her perceived involvement has already impacted negatively on her practice – one of her current clients is in WP and is freaking out about the publicity her shrink is getting, threatening to change psychs. Miss Summers obviously doesn't want her client to be put at further risk, so doesn't want any further involvement.'

'But you persuaded her to continue, by the sounds of it?'

'Only if we contact her via phone. No more visits to her consultancy.'

'Ah well, that's better than nothing.'

'Hmmm. But you can tell so much more by watching body language.'

'Skype her then.'

'Hey, Mack. That's quite clever for you.'

'Sarcasm is overrated.'

Lindsay checked the time on the laptop. 'Right, let's get to the briefing.' She grabbed the files piled on her desk and pushed up from her chair. It was the second time in as many years that she'd been in Coleton police station, using their rooms as incident rooms. Her base was Middlemoor, in Exeter, but she'd been keen to take the lead on this case. Make up for before. So, back to Coleton it was.

'The pattern of mutilation is interesting.' The slides moved across the huge white screen projected on to the back wall of the incident room, gruesome shots like those in the god-awful *Saw* movie that Lindsay had never been able to sit through. She was surprised that any of the prison staff had even recognised this guy when he landed on their doorstep. She pointed to the next slide. The most horrific. She cast her eyes around the room. Some of the team had turned away. 'Yeah, not good, is it?'

'T'was some angry crackpot who did that,' a voice from the back declared.

'Actually, I'm not so sure.' Lindsay took the pointer stick and placed it over the enlarged picture of Eric Hargreaves' torso. 'I know it looks a total mess at first glance. But look at the way the body has been quartered. It's precise. I don't think someone with anger issues did this. It's too controlled. They had planned how they were going to do it. This was carried out carefully.'

'So, they had time then, no rush,' Mack said.

'Precisely. Must've had Hargreaves somewhere they considered safe, somewhere they wouldn't be disturbed for quite some time.'

'What about the writing on his hand – "Connie Moore"? What's that about?' DC Sewell asked.

Mack turned in his chair to direct his response to her. 'Well, there are various possibilities, but at this early stage we really can't be sure about any of them.'

'Like what, sir?'

'Depends on who wrote it. If Hargreaves did, then we are never going to really know, but we *could* assume he had an obsession with her, perhaps. People don't generally write names on themselves, more likely you write something you don't want to forget – a number, an item you want from the shop.'

'Or a name you didn't already know, so that you remember it's someone you need to speak to, or something?' DC Sewell said matter-of-factly. 'And if it was written by the killer?'

'That's where it becomes tricky,' Lindsay said. 'If the killer wrote it, do we assume it was for us? The body was deliberately left outside the prison, a place where it'd be found and police called quickly. So, was the killer leaving it as a clue – ensuring we follow up the lead and interview Connie Summers?'

'Or,' Mack added, 'was it to make sure *she* knew? Knew that Hargreaves had been murdered, that he could no longer do harm to others.'

'Like some kind of gift to her? The guy that ruined her career, served up cold on a platter?'

'It's a possibility.'

'So our killer potentially knows her, wants to do this *for* her – a revenge killing, but for someone else's benefit? Weird,' Sewell summarised.

'Well, they can't know her that well. They used Moore, not Summers. They don't know she changed her name.'

'That's a possibility, Clarke,' Mack said, 'unless they used Moore because that would make us believe it was something to do with her past – her role in the prison.'

'Going back to revenge,' Anika, the team's new DC interjected, 'Hargreaves raped a woman when he was released. It could be that his victim, or her family, decided to hand out their own justice.'

'That's a line of investigation we'll be following up, Anika,' Lindsay said.

'Could he be in love with Summers?'

'Careful, Lloyd. "He"? We don't know it's a he.'

'Must be, Guv. Surely. To overpower him, he's not small. Then inflict that much damage and then move the body. And dump it quick as lightning at the prison gates before anyone can stop him?'

'Could be more than one person involved,' a voice piped up.

'Could it also be a warning – that Connie Summers is going to be next?' another DC asked from the back – the whole room was beginning to buzz with questions; possibilities.

'Hang on, hang on, guys.' Lindsay stood up, both hands held out in front of her. She looked to Mack, wondering if he'd voiced his earlier concern to any of the team. He didn't meet her gaze. 'Let's keep calm; focused. We don't want to jump the gun – talk serial killer just yet.'

The room fell silent. Lindsay continued.

'I want us to concentrate on the *most likely* first. We won't rule anything out, but let's not get carried away either.'

'We need that psychologist in here, so we can interview her. Get her to tell us everything she's ever known about Hargreaves,' DC Sewell offered. 'And about any attention – male and female – that she's had over the last year or two. That could lead to names we can check out, Boss.'

'Okay. Yes, that's more in line with how I wanted to approach things.' Lindsay rubbed the back of her neck. 'I was hoping to get her in as an advisor.' She perched on the edge of the long table and crossed her arms. 'I feel she'd open up more, talk freely, if we gave her a role rather than treat her as a person of interest.'

'She's worked with the police before,' Mack said. 'She's given independent expert witness evidence, profiled criminals, that sort of thing; I think she'll be helpful in that capacity. It's just getting her here. Whatever route we take though, she's the person who knows the most about the victim at this point, so we need to tread carefully.'

Lindsay was silent for a moment, then she nodded. 'Agreed. Let's sort a game plan then, shall we?'

CHAPTER THIRTEEN

Connie

So, she wasn't as 'out' of the investigation as she'd planned. Connie closed her eyes, shutting out the faces of the other passengers. She failed to shut out the voices though. The ones in her mind – warning of danger to come. Her head lolled, until it touched the coolness of the window. It bumped gently against it as the train rumbled along the track towards Coleton.

It had become very clear during her conversation with DI Wade that one way or another she wanted her to be involved. Even if she'd point-blank refused, she knew Wade would get around it by bringing her in officially – as a suspect probably. Her name had been implicated – literally. There was a chance Ricky could have written it on himself, but her gut told her otherwise. For whatever reason, the murderer wanted her attention. It was the job of the police to find out why. There was no escaping it, she was already involved whether she liked it or not. It'd been naively optimistic for her to think she could just 'opt out'.

She would have to find another psychologist for Steph.

The blur of green and brown fields suddenly changed to buildings – the short journey ending. She couldn't wait to get home, have a long bath, eat the last remaining chicken and mushroom pizza, then snuggle on the sofa with Amber and watch a DVD.

She wasn't even going to entertain the idea of watching news, or any other normal programme. No. It was Ryan Gosling in *Crazy, Stupid, Love* all the way tonight. And she'd switch the phone off too.

She'd be in her own bubble. The one without Ricky Hargreaves. The one without a murderer who knew her by name.

She heaved herself from the seat and nudged past a few people standing in the way of the exit door. Why did people stand there when there were plenty of seats? They weren't even getting off. She smiled tightly at a man who grunted as she moved in front of him. *I just want to get off the train,* she wanted to scream at him. She refrained.

Her heels clacked up the steps of the bridge to the other side of the station. Reaching the top, she hesitated. A figure stood at the other end of the footbridge, leaning against the side. She looked back over her shoulder. No one else had got off at this station. She continued, more slowly, squinting as she went, trying to make out some features. Man? Woman? Teenager? Trainspotter? As she approached, the figure surged forwards. Connie's heart quickened. Should she turn and go back? No. She was being ridiculous. It was probably someone waiting to meet a friend, a lover, a family member, off the train.

It was a man. Definitely. He wore a trench coat, dark grey. Yet the weather had been hot. No showers. No need for a coat like that.

Unless you were hiding something within it.

Connie cursed her prison background. It'd made her ultra-cautious. Untrusting. Her imagination didn't need much stimulation to become hyper-sensitive.

Keep walking. Keep walking. It's nothing. He's nothing.

She lowered her chin, subtly inching her way to the far side of the bridge, farthest from the man.

Ten feet.

Five feet.

He walked towards her. Moved to the same side of the bridge as her.

Quick. Phone. Get your mobile out.

Too late for that now. It was deep inside her handbag somewhere.

He was almost upon her.

He reached inside his coat with his left hand.

Connie let out a gasp.

CHAPTER FOURTEEN

Then

Barton Moss Secure Care Centre, Manchester

Hey sis,
Why don't you come visit? No one comes. I don't understand
what happened, how the fire killed Dad. I don't remember.
Please come see me. I don't like it here.
   Brett x

Brett,
Why aren't I coming to see you? Are you serious? You set a fire.
You killed him. You could've killed me as well. You can't get
away with this 'I don't remember' crap. You know full well how
it happened. The real question is why. Why did you do it?
   What did you think would happen to you? Of course you
were gonna be sent away, who the hell would want you in their
house after that? NO ONE would feel safe. Ever again.
   You need to stay in that place forever.
   I can't forgive you. I can't come see you 'cos I never want
to look at your face again.
   Jenna.
   PS Don't expect any other family to come either. They all
feel the same way.

51

CHAPTER FIFTEEN

Connie

The man propelled his hand forwards.

'I've gotta give you this.' His voice, gritty, like something was caught in his throat.

Connie felt the warmth of his hand as he pressed it against hers, too shocked to move it away as he shoved something hard into her palm before striding off in the direction he'd been walking, across the bridge.

She expelled a short, sharp breath – it hurt her lungs, her trachea, as it burst out of her. Her ears rang. She was close to fainting. Her mouth opened to speak, but nothing came out, her vocal cords paralysed with fear.

She grasped the handrail. Her upper body folded over, her chest touching her thighs. By the time she'd recovered enough to right herself, the man had disappeared.

'You all right, Miss?' the voice in front of her asked. She felt a hand steady her.

'Yes. Yes, thanks. I'll be fine.' She looked up.

Jonesy. She removed her arm from his grip.

'You looked like you were about to pass out. Been drinking, Miss?' He laughed.

Connie feigned laughter, but averted her eyes. She gripped the unknown item the man had given her in her right hand, afraid to open her fingers and reveal its identity with Jonesy there. The shakiness of her legs passed so she moved away from the handrail and carried on down the steps towards the exit. Jonesy followed. She jammed her right hand into her suit-trouser pocket.

'You sure you're gonna be okay, I can get you a taxi, if you like?'

She was about to say no, that she was fine to walk. Then a thought sneaked into her head. *What if he follows me to my house?*

'I might do that, yes. Don't worry though, I can manage, they're right there.' She pointed with her free hand to the taxis waiting at their rank. 'Thanks.' She moved quicker now, making her way to the first car in line. 'Bye, Jonesy,' she shouted over her shoulder.

She waited until she was safely inside the taxi before giving the driver her destination. Even then she gave the road just down from hers, not her exact address – just in case. Was Jonesy at the station because he was catching a train, or meeting someone coming off one? Twice now he'd been there when she had. Did he know the times of the trains she usually caught? Was it coincidence he appeared just after the mystery man?

The object.

She wriggled in the back of the taxi, the seat squeaking as she retrieved the object from her trouser pocket. She slowly unfurled her fingers. A small, black memory stick, with the word 'SanDisk' in red printed on it. Why the hell had that man given her this? What was on it? Was it a mistake – meant for someone else? He'd shoved it in her hand and said . . . what was it again? The sheer panic that had washed over her now rendered her memory inadequate. She squeezed her eyes. *Come on, come on.* 'I've got to give you this'? Was that it? Yes, that was right. She opened her eyes again, stared down at the stick which lay in her clammy palm. I've *got* to give you this. Did that mean he had a burning need to hand it to her? Or that someone else was making him give it to

53

her? Perhaps the answer lay in whatever resided in the memory of the two-inch piece of plastic.

The mugginess inside the back of the taxi threatened to suffocate her. She wound down the window, it stopped halfway. With her face turned slightly and angled so she could push it out as far as possible, Connie sucked in the cooler evening air. The taxi driver was talking. She withdrew her head.

'You all right, love?' His eyes, reflected in the mirror, found hers. She smiled weakly.

'I will be. In a minute.' *When I'm home*, she thought. 'You can drop me at the end, just up there by the park. Thanks.'

She rummaged in her bag for her purse.

Connie waited for the taxi to drive out of sight before turning the opposite way and walking as fast as she could back down the road they'd driven, then ducked through the alleyway between Park Road and Moorland Street. Her house came into sight. She relaxed.

The front door key took a few attempts to find its home, her fingers trembling and preventing the easy action. Once inside she locked and bolted the door and flung her handbag at the banister, the long strap wrapping itself securely around it. She kicked off her shoes and called for Amber, breathless from all the exertion. A white bundle of hair hurried towards her. 'Hello, baby.' Connie scooped her up and fussed her, comforted by Amber's ecstatic purring.

The day's heat had been trapped within the walls of the house, so Connie went to the kitchen, letting Amber scramble down from her arms, and opened the small window. Then she went to the lounge, her feet moving soundlessly over the thick, soft carpet. New. The smell still lingered in the room even though it'd been two weeks ago now. She reached to open the large bay window, but stopped herself. She stood looking out on to her street.

The opposite row of houses, all converted to flats, were bathed in a yellow hue from the street lamps. It still wasn't properly dark

– the sun not setting until around nine thirty. The street was quiet, no strange figures hanging around. She yanked the curtains across.

What was she going to do with the memory stick? She'd be mad to insert it in her laptop; it could upload a virus. But could she hand it over to the police, even though she didn't know what it contained? Who had given it to her – and why? She'd have a bath, then something to eat before she decided what to do with it.

Wrapped in her fluffy cream dressing gown, Connie shoved her frozen pizza in the oven and retreated into the lounge. Her laptop lay on the rectangular coffee table in front of the TV. She paused, staring at the memory stick which she'd placed on the closed lid, as if it might pounce on her if she got closer. She really should hand it straight over to the police, to DI Wade, and have done with it. But while she'd been relaxing in the bubbles of the bath, Connie's curiosity had been piqued. She wanted to be prepared, no surprises.

She had to look.

But not on that laptop. If there was a virus, or spyware, she didn't want to risk it destroying her new device. She had another laptop – had used it during her degree work. It'd been redundant for some time, due to its age and bulkiness – it wouldn't matter if she plugged the stick in and it screwed it up.

Now, where was it? She'd still got boxes in the second bedroom; the spare room, which she hadn't got around to sorting yet. She'd moved in two years ago; laziness had prevented her dealing with them. That and becoming too busy with setting up her consultancy. It took half an hour of rummaging through containers filled with junk – an old video box-set of *The X-Files* she'd been obsessed with when she was a teenager, puzzles she used to do with her mum, old *Vogue* magazines from a time when she'd cared about fashion, Stephen King novels she hadn't got around to putting on the bookcase – to find the laptop and charging cable. She carried it downstairs and plugged it in. It still worked. Connie's stomach contracted. Should she do it? Her hand, the stick clenched in it, hovered over the port. What was she worried about? What could possibly be on it that would cause her to be nervous? *Come on, Connie. Just do it!*

The high-pitched alarm jolted Connie back into the moment, a painful sensation shot through her heart like a knife piercing it. She dropped the stick and jumped up, running to the kitchen. Smoke billowed from the oven. The pizza. She grabbed a tea towel and recovered the blackened circle from the oven, blinking her eyes to rid them of the stinging. She threw it into the sink, hearing a loud hiss as it touched the water. She sighed. It'd have to be baked beans on toast then. After. She'd have to do the deed first otherwise she'd likely burn the toast too.

Kneeling on the floor, laptop open, she finally placed the stick in the USB port.

Two file names appeared.

And both took the breath from her lungs.

She stared with a mixture of disbelief and curiosity. She had to open them now.

One click and the news article from 1995 filled the screen. And the sadness she'd felt back then returned automatically. A single tear began its journey, surging over her cheek and landing on the keyboard.

Who wanted to give this to her? It's not like she needed a reminder of the incident that had rocked her world. It was part of her.

Connie clicked on the other file. She read the document, her curiosity slipping into anger, and she slammed the laptop shut.

Why the hell was someone dragging this up now?

CHAPTER SIXTEEN

Connie

Wednesday 7 June

Having been sleep-deprived for the second night in a row, the journey to her office was slow, her legs leaden. Connie was heavy – with resurfaced grief and anger. She was glad she'd looked at what the memory stick held though, before handing it blindly to the police. It had nothing to do with their investigation. Just her. And her family. But the who and the why were questions she needed answering. Another burden she didn't need.

The fresh cut grass wafted from the room as she opened it, and for the first time the scent made her stomach churn, like the queasiness of early pregnancy. For a moment Connie stood, hand placed over her belly, and thought. *No.* She couldn't be. Dates were completely wrong. She let her hand drop and carried on over to her desk. The memory of her unsuccessful pregnancy lingered even once the queasy sensation had disappeared. Last year had been a tough one. She wasn't sure if she could cope with another like it.

She fired up her computer and hung her suit jacket over the back of her chair. Steph should be arriving soon, she wanted to run through all the information she held on her first, find out if any of yesterday's story checked out – the family history, the names. It didn't. Very strange. She leant back and stared at the screen, then retrieved the paper file from her desk drawer. She frowned. Both said the same: mother in a home, father's whereabouts unknown – not dead in a fire, as Steph had described – and no siblings. *No* brother. No one named Brett. How could it be so wrong? It was likely that Steph had lied. But why? What could she gain from making it up? Attention? Continued input from the services she was so afraid would abandon her? It made some sense. In Steph's mind, if she came up with a story in which she or her child were in danger, then Miles would offer further protection and Connie would offer more sessions. Could that really be what Steph was trying to do here?

The intercom buzzed. Hopefully, she was about to unravel whatever was going on.

'Morning, Steph.' Connie opened her door to let Steph in. 'No Dylan this morning?'

'I took him to pre-school, I had to. Needed to see you on my own.' She looked drawn, a deep line ran from one side of her forehead to the other, her lips were tightly closed and her nostrils flared. 'He's out.' She brushed past Connie and sat heavily in the chair.

'Brett?'

'Yes, Brett!'

'How do you know?'

'Got this.' Steph held her hand out, in it a piece of folded paper. 'Another one. This morning.'

Before Connie got into this, she needed to retrace a step, or twelve. She hadn't found out what the first letter had contained yet.

'Okay. Try and keep your breathing steady.' Connie flinched as Steph shot her an angry glare.

'Are you for real?'

58

'I just want to understand what's going on, Steph. And for that to happen, I think being calm would be best.'

Steph snorted. 'Fine.' She took a deep, exaggerated breath in, and slowly out.

'Can you tell me about the first letter?'

Steph sighed, slumping her shoulders. 'I wasn't gonna read it, but somethin' made me. I had this feelin' that it was gonna be bad. Bad for me and Dylan.

'It started off the usual – *Dear sis. I need to see you. Why didn't you write or come see me?*' Steph shook her head gently. 'But then it changed. His letters usually blamed me for some stuff, like abandoning him when he needed me, being a bad sister, that kind of bull. But this one was different. Seemed even more angry than usual.'

'Angry in what way?'

'Like in that he threatened me and Dylan. Said he'd finish what he started.'

'Oh. He said those exact words? Have you brought the letter?'

'Oh, right, so you're questioning me, don't believe what I'm tellin' you?'

'No, it's not that, Steph. I thought reading it would help me to interpret his words.'

'What's to interpret? He'll finish what he started, Connie. He started the fire, he killed his dad, Mum's as good as dead, and his big sister is the one that got away. It's pretty simple, eh? He's wanting to kill me and Dylan now. Finish whatever weird, psycho fantasy he's got going.'

'Sometimes, when we're scared, things that are meant one way are taken another. We read things into it, and can blow things up, out of proportion—'

'I don't scare easy. I grew up learning how to cope wi' being afraid, I dealt wi' it every day just crossing my own estate.' Steph glared at Connie, and huffed. 'You wouldn't know. You got no idea, you and your cosy sheltered life down here . . .'

'Actually, I grew up in Manchester, too,' Connie snapped. She closed her eyes, pinched her nose with her thumb and forefinger and took a deep breath. 'I know more than you think.' She spoke without looking at Steph, not wanting her to see the pain in her eyes. 'Anyway, go on.' Connie straightened, was back on track. This was Steph's session, possibly her last if she didn't consider it safe to visit any more; she couldn't let her own past creep into it.

'Well, perhaps this'll show you that I'm not making it up.' Steph thrust the piece of paper into Connie's hand. She was reminded instantly of DS Mack doing the same on Monday. She hesitated. Once she opened this paper and read its content, she was involved. She opened it. The writing was a scrawl, barely legible:

It ends with fire. We should all burn together.
I'm coming to see you.

For a moment, Connie didn't know what to say. It seemed pretty cut and dried – if *she'd* received this, she would've taken it as a threat as well.

'You're going to hand this to Miles?'

'What's he gonna do about it?'

'He can find out where Brett is, if he's been released. Keep an eye on his movements?'

'*If* he's been released?'

'Well, isn't it possible that someone else could have posted this to you. For him?'

'I guess. But now I think about the way he worded the other letter, he said why *didn't* you come see me? Not why *aren't* you coming to see me? I think he must've been out then. And the older letters from him were all postmarked from the YOI. But not these.'

'And you're sure this is Brett's handwriting?'

'What are you getting at?' Steph's brow furrowed.

'Could it be possible it's from one of the gang members connected with your ex-boyfriend, not Brett?'

'Well, that don't make any sense, does it? It ends wi' fire. Only one person who'd say that, Connie.' She was shouting now, her face reddening.

'It's okay.' Connie reached across and touched Steph's shoulder reassuringly. 'When did you get that first letter again?'

'Yesterday. But Miles must've got it before then, to be able to send it on to me.' She played with her hands. 'I'm thinking Brett's already here.'

'I doubt that. He wouldn't know where to start looking for you.'

For a second or two those words seemed to calm her. But then she shook her head, her eyes wide and glaring. 'I'm looking for him. At every turn, I'm expecting to come face to face wi' him. On the street corner, in the local shops. In my house. But I don't even know what he looks like any more, haven't seen him for eight years. What if I don't even recognise him? He could kill us before I even knew it was him!'

Connie inhaled deeply. This was getting difficult; the intensity of Steph's fears were increasing rapidly. She wasn't sure how she could reduce her perceived danger without appearing as though she wasn't taking her concerns seriously.

'We really need to speak with Miles—'

'He won't believe me.' Steph got up, heading for the door. She turned, shaking her head. 'Like you don't.'

Connie remained in her chair. Chasing after her would be futile; nothing she could say would change Steph's current anxiety state. Miles was only person who could do that.

CHAPTER SEVENTEEN

DI Wade

Lindsay read through the transcripts again. The interviews with prison staff had yielded a list of Hargreaves' known associates. The security team informed them of the SIRs that had been handed in relating to him; these security information reports mostly detailed the names already given to them, but also contained overheard conversations between Hargreaves and other prisoners – some drug-related, and some from staff members who'd been on the receiving end of a veiled threat or remark, or intimidating behaviour. All relatively normal stuff as far as the staff were concerned. A lot of the prisoners had similar reports. None of the information flagged up any major warning signs, and there was no obvious individual who might have been instrumental in his escape at his mother's funeral. Lindsay tasked a small team to check out the names on the list.

They'd questioned the officer Hargreaves had been handcuffed to when he escaped, and, as yet, he was holding up under pressure, giving nothing but the original story. He'd been dragged to the entrance of the cemetery, where bolt cutters and a knife were hidden, and threatened by Hargreaves to help him release the cuffs. Despite another prison officer coming to his aid quickly, it still appeared that Hargreaves had had time to get away. Somehow that didn't make sense to Lindsay, but everyone was sticking together and there was no other evidence to the contrary at this point.

'So, what are we up to today, Boss?' Mack flashed her a toothy grin.

Lindsay considered this for a moment. The pathologist was due to carry out the post-mortem this morning. Although they'd got a lot from the preliminary findings, it would be interesting to discover the not-so-obvious. Hargreaves' wounds were externally gruesome, in-your-face mutilation obviously meant to shock, but she wondered if there would be any surprises – what might be lying beneath the surface waiting to be found.

'Fancy a trip to the mortuary? I got us an invite.'

'Oh, how could I resist such an invitation?' Mack drew himself up to his full height. 'I bet you're a bundle of fun on a date, aren't you?' He grabbed the keys and headed for the door. 'Come on then, Ms Macabre. Let's get over there.'

It was Lindsay's first time in the morgue since Erin Malone. The smell as she entered through the double doors instantly brought back the memory of the murdered teenager. Was this post-mortem going to be any easier to watch because this victim had been a criminal, not an innocent like Erin? He was a person, after all. Like Erin, he had had a family, friends. Had he been a good man once, and then merely taken the wrong path? He'd attacked women. He'd shown no remorse. Was this his punishment? But did anyone deserve to be hacked up, spread open and left on display?

'You okay, Boss?'

'Yep. Fine. Just eager to find something out about our murderer. I'm hoping he's left us a bit of himself behind.'

'Yeah, that would be helpful.'

The pathologist greeted them, all smiles and joviality. He'd been equally jolly on the phone, telling Lindsay that he'd recently taken up the post following his predecessor's retirement and was eager to be of assistance in the murder case. 'Welcome DI Wade, DS Mack. I'm Dr Lovell. You can call me Harry.' He swept up to the metal gurney theatrically. 'A fine morning for it!' He waved an arm, indicating around the windowless room.

Lindsay cringed.

'Putting on a bloody show for us, then?' she whispered to Mack, who looked to be suppressing a giggle behind his hand. Laughing in the morgue wasn't professional. Still, Harry had lifted the tension; the anticipation of the event was now quashed a little.

Eric Hargreaves' body looked fake; like a dummy someone had made for Halloween, or one carefully crafted by the special effects teams for TV shows like *Silent Witness*. His skin appeared pale and waxy until you took in the injuries. They had a purple-red tinge to them. The flaps of flesh hung to the sides of his torso like chunks of meat hanging off a slaughtered pig in a butcher's shop, exposing his bent ribcage – a structure meant to protect his heart – now broken and useless. The whole scene looked surreal. That was the only thing that enabled Lindsay to distance herself – if she didn't think of this body as a man, a once living, breathing man, she could get through this. As tough as she considered herself to be, no matter how many times she'd been to the morgue, it was one of her least favourite parts of her job. There was something unnerving about silent, still bodies. And her mind always conjured her dear dad, and unwanted visions of him lying on a slab in this very morgue.

Lindsay took a deep breath and turned to Mack, his height blocking the strip lighting. 'Wouldn't you be better sitting?'

'Hah! No, I like to be able to see right inside, can't take in all its glory if you're sat.'

'As long as you don't faint. I'm not attempting to catch you if you do.'

'I'm good. Thanks.'

Harry conducted an external examination, calling out measurements to the path assistant as he travelled around the body. Lindsay noted that Hargreaves had extensive tattoos but her ears pricked when she heard Harry say a few of them appeared to be new.

'Oh? How new?'

'I'd say, given the colour of the ink and the absence of swelling or scabbing . . .' He paused, bending closer to the cadaver. Lindsay felt her upper body move forward, eager for him to carry on. 'That three of these were acquired post-mortem.' He looked up, raising his eyebrows in their direction.

'That's interesting. So, mutilation through cutting *and* through tattooing? Why bother with both?' Lindsay wondered out loud. 'Can you take pictures of those, please.'

'Perhaps that wasn't part of the mutilation,' Mack said. 'Could be a message?'

Lindsay's blood pulsated loudly in her ears. A tingle of excitement travelled the length of her spine; that familiar feeling of adrenaline coursing through her.

'A message for who?' she asked quietly and the question hung, suspended in the room like oil on water.

CHAPTER EIGHTEEN

Connie

Connie watched Steph from the window of her office. She was weaving her way through the throngs of people, seemingly the only one moving down the street; Connie could see her small frame being buffeted as she attempted to go against the stream. She looked so slight; vulnerable. She was strong though, Connie felt sure of that. She had fight in her. But was she also full of lies? She pulled her gaze away from the window and sat at her desk. She needed to have a conversation with Miles Prescott.

It took a while before she was put through to him. Getting the right department was clearly an art form; pressing the right buttons to be connected to the right people. Finally, Connie heard a deep, gravelly tone – one of a man with a forty-a-day habit – that she recognised as Miles.

'Miles, it's Connie Summers, Stephanie Cousins' psychologist.'

'Ah, yes. Been expecting a call from you.'

'Oh, really? How come?'

'Well, she's been getting a bit jumpy lately. Coming out with all sorts, so I figured she'd be speaking about it with you. A matter of time before you needed to cross-reference facts with me.'

Connie was taken aback. If he knew this, why hadn't he

contacted *her*? Perhaps Steph had been right about him, that he wanted to pull back from her, withdraw some support.

'Right, well now that it's been established that she's currently going through an episode of anxiety, perhaps together we can come up with a plan of action.'

'To be honest, Connie, there's not much more I can do. She's had input from the witness protection team for four months, we've given her everything required to make a new life, but she seems to be trying to sabotage her own integration with this latest lot of anxiety attacks—'

'No disrespect, but you've been the one who has given her reason to be anxious.'

'Er . . . I don't know what you're talking about.'

'The letters? Forwarding them on to her without even knowing who they were from.'

'Oh. I see. Well, I need to put you right there, I'm afraid. I didn't forward her any letters. Every so often, one of the team will check her old address, and her uncle's, to see what post, if any, is there. There's been nothing of note for the entire time she's been in Devon.'

'Well if they haven't been sent by you, that means someone has got hold of her address; her new identity must've been compromised?'

'You're assuming someone *has* got her address. I think what you *should* be considering is that no one has written or sent any letters. That this is a figment of Stephanie's imagination.'

'No. You're wrong.' The quiver in her voice came as a surprise to her. Having Miles question the reliability of Steph's claims was somehow causing Connie to waver too; she couldn't entirely dismiss the possibility. But she'd *seen* the letter: plain paper, not headed with an official address. Not created in Steph's mind. Although it was paper anyone could have got hold of. That Steph could have got hold of. Connie tutted, berating herself for doing exactly what Steph accused her of: not believing.

'Next then you are going to tell me that her own brother is also a figment of her imagination?'

There was an audible silence. Then Connie heard a slow out-breathing of air.

'Look. I don't know what's going on. You've seen Stephanie's file as well as I have. There is no brother.'

'How . . . why would she make up a brother? An entire story about where he is, and why he's there?'

'And is it this brother who is supposedly writing to her?'

'Yes. He's been in a YOI but she thinks he's been released. She got the first letter on Tuesday.'

'You're going to have to leave this with me, Connie. I'll go back through her case files, see what I can dig up. If there is a brother, I'll find him.'

'I'd be grateful. And whilst you're at it could you also find out about the fire, the one that happened when she was sixteen? The mother survived it, but Steph is saying that her dad didn't.'

Miles sighed loudly. 'I really think I'm going to be wasting my time. As far as we know, Steph's dad's alive but his whereabouts are unknown, I—'

'Yes, yes,' Connie interrupted. 'I know what the files say, but I want you to check this story out please. If you wouldn't mind.'

'Fine. Fine, I'll get on to it. I'm busy though, you understand, so it might take a few days.'

It wasn't the way she'd imagined the conversation going. But at least Miles had agreed to delve further into Steph's family history. She'd failed to mention that Steph wanted a new psychologist. She would tell him. Perhaps when he'd returned to her with the information. In the meantime, she'd keep a check on the news to see if any further reports on the Hargreaves murder mentioned her name. The police should keep quiet about the writing on his hand, they liked to hold such information back from the press. So as long as she didn't gain any further media attention, the risk of exposing Steph's new identity would be minimal.

For now, at least, she wanted to continue with Steph as her client. She wanted to get to the bottom of her fears, because whether they were fact or fiction, there was no doubt in her mind they were very real to Steph.

CHAPTER NINETEEN

Then

Uncle Jimmy spent his days lying like a big fat pig on his couch, a beer in one hand, TV remote in the other. Empty cans surrounded the patch of floor in front of him. Her mum had often told her stories of how he'd wasted his life, how he could have been so much more. Instead he'd chosen to be a lazy good-for-nothing and sign on the dole, pissing his giro money up the wall. Or these days, it seemed, into his pants. The stench of stale urine made her retch.

She had to get out.

A roof over her head was one thing, sharing it with a disgusting pervert was another. Her mum had failed to tell her about his fondness for young girls. Before she'd moved in he'd been unable to do much about his urges. Now though, when he wasn't passed out, he gave her far too much attention – ogling her, trying to catch her in the bathroom, touching her at every opportunity. She'd had enough of that kind of behaviour; she wasn't going to accept it from him.

It was time to force the move to Vince's. He'd been keen for her to move in when he found out about the fire, but his eagerness had dwindled recently. Suddenly he had lots on, friends camped round at his, no space for her. But he'd promised. And she wasn't about to let that go. Promises were promises. You can't go back on them.

She hadn't.

CHAPTER TWENTY

Connie

Despite attempting to clear her mind, Connie struggled to fully concentrate on her last client of the day – thoughts, questions about Steph's story periodically pierced through and she found herself lost at times, having to ask Paul to repeat himself. She'd annoyed him, his tutting following each request to 'say that again', giving away his irritation.

She was relieved when the session was over. It was only four thirty, but she didn't want to catch her usual train. She'd get the later one, at six. Be unpredictable. Just in case. Connie made herself a cafetière of coffee, then, enveloped by the peace of her room, sat and allowed the questions she'd been trying to repress flood her mind. How could Steph's family – her brother, dead dad – be unknown to the witness protection team? It was their job to know everything, to ensure their witnesses' safety. How could it be possible that Miles didn't know about Brett? Had they merely concentrated on the gang and Steph's boyfriend when carrying out risk assessments? But surely background info was key to covering every base, ensuring no one knew of Steph's new identity, her new home. There should be no loose ends.

Something wasn't right. Had they screwed up? Perhaps in their eagerness to get Steph to testify, they'd missed vital background checks. Although why Steph hadn't just told Miles about her brother was strange.

Connie let her head drop into her cupped hands. These questions forced her in another direction, and her thoughts drifted to her own brother. To the memory stick she'd been handed. Hadn't she spent the last twenty-two years burying the memory of Luke's death? She didn't talk about him. Her brother dying when she'd only just turned fifteen impacted on her more than any of her family ever realised. More than she'd let on. Even to herself. The only people she ever spoke his name to were her parents. And even then, it was sporadic: his birthday, the anniversary of his death. She didn't like to bring him up in case she upset her mum.

Someone wanted her to remember him though – the article and the document had suddenly thrust his life, his death, in her face. Where she had to take notice of it. She and Steph seemed to have that in common: a lost brother. Very different circumstances, and Brett was still alive physically, but still – they'd both suffered, both experienced the grieving process. They both had unresolved issues about it.

But how could Connie guide Steph through her anxiety, her problems, when she'd never got her head around the event that changed her own life? After Luke died, her father had moved them to the other side of Manchester. But not content with upending them all once, her parents had then dragged Connie away from big, bad Manchester to the idyllic coastal town in Devon, peeled her away from her friends, her support network. Just like Steph. The similarities had gone unnoticed until now. Until the memory stick had found its way into Connie's hands, she'd buried her past. Buried Luke. But, like Steph, the past was now forcing its way into the present.

It had been a random attack, they'd said. He'd died quickly, they'd said. Wrong place, wrong time. As simple as that.

But then why had someone gone to the trouble of searching her past to bring it all up again now?

73

CHAPTER TWENTY-ONE

Connie

Getting the later train had been a good call. There were no sightings of Jonesy, and more to the point, no further 'gifts' from strangers. Connie's muscles had begun relaxing once she'd got home, showered, had a lasagne microwave meal and sunk into the sofa with a glass of wine.

Her personal mobile jumping into action interrupted her evening. Sighing, she pulled herself up and placed the glass on the coaster. For a moment, she froze. The caller ID showed as Niall. What did he want? Her finger hovered over the accept button, then moved to decline. She hesitated. He'd been a good support during the initial shit-hitting-fan stage of the Hargreaves cock-up. He'd popped over to the psychology block for coffees and chats, been very vocal about how none of it was her fault, how Ricky was an evil manipulator who'd pulled the wool over everyone's eyes. Then he'd taken her out for a meal – to console her, cheer her up. Help her forget the horrible situation. They'd got on so well, and he had made her cry with laughter. He'd been exactly what she'd needed. And then of course there'd been sex.

There'd been no communication from him since she'd gone off sick last June. She hadn't told him about her pregnancy, which had been a relief once she'd realised it wasn't his. But regardless, she'd obviously become too needy in his eyes. So, the question was, why was he ringing her now? Was he the leak – the person who'd spoken to that sneaky reporter, Kelly? The thought made her cheeks burn. *The arsehole.* She jabbed the 'accept' symbol.

'Yes?'

'Connie. It's Niall.'

'Yep, what can I do for you?'

'Uh . . . well, I was just wondering how you were doing, really.' His delivery was unsure – a slight stammer evident. Connie assumed it was his guilt showing. Or hoped it was.

'You haven't wondered enough to call me in, what – the previous *twelve* months?' Her voice was clipped. It wasn't even intentional, in fact until now she hadn't realised how annoyed she was about his total abandonment.

'Of course I've wondered. I've thought about you a lot, but, you know . . . men aren't great at this stuff . . .'

'This *stuff* being?' Why did men think if they pulled the 'we're not good at this stuff' routine that women would roll over and accept it and forgive them their inadequacies?

'Difficult emotions. It was hard for me to know the best thing to do . . .'

'Oh, it was hard for *you*? I'm so sorry about that, Niall. How selfish of me to have put you through that.'

'Okay, I can see this was a bad idea, I'll leave you to it.'

'Oh, you're not enjoying the conversation? What a shame, I have so much to fill you in on.'

'I'm sorry I've upset you by calling.'

How did he do that? One sentence, spoken in a quiet whisper oozing sincerity, and already she was regretting her abruptness.

'No, no.' Her voice softened. 'It was brave of you to make the effort, finally.'

'Can I pop over for a coffee sometime? Catch up properly?' His tone was suddenly bright.

As much as it irked her to admit it, she would quite like some company. She would also like to do a bit of digging to find out what had gone on in relation to Hargreaves' escape, and which employee had been responsible for giving her name to the media. To the police too.

'I'm pretty busy with my consultancy, but I'll check my diary and give you a text.'

'Oh, okay.' The pause lengthened. 'You won't text me though, will you?'

Connie sighed. She didn't want to make this easy for him, why should she? But she found herself caving in on hearing the disappointment in his voice. Perhaps she was more desperate for company than she'd thought.

'I *will*. More likely an evening though, I don't get back from work until six-ish.'

'Great. Thanks, Connie. I know I don't deserve another chance, really.'

'It's just a drink. Don't go getting any ideas, it's not another chance like *that*.'

'Loud and clear. I'll look forward to your text. Night, love.'

He hung up before she could make further comment.

Her moment of relaxation had passed. Her shoulders felt tight, her neck stiff. From one telephone conversation? She rotated her head and massaged her neck. How had this week become so stressful, so quickly? It most definitely wasn't part of her plan.

CHAPTER TWENTY-TWO

DI Wade

Thursday 8 June

Lindsay Wade spread four photos across her desk. Each enlarged image showed a different tattoo.

'What do you make of these?' She directed her question at Mack, who, coffee in hand, was staring at the monitor on his desk. He put his mug down and scooted over, the wheels of the chair squealing in protest. He picked up one of the photos.

'The murderer likes birds?'

'Helpful. What kind of bird does it look like to you?'

Mack tilted his head, squinting, then shrugged his shoulders.

'No idea. I'm guessing it's not one specific species, more like a mixture – seems muddled. Perhaps our killer is a crap tattooist?'

'Quite possibly, as the other three are similar – they're pretty muddled too.' Lindsay handed Mack another picture.

'I thought there were only three new tattoos. Where's the fourth come from?'

'We left a bit too early. When Harry was sewing Hargreaves back up, he found this one on the lower half of the torso. It revealed itself when he lifted the flap of skin that had been sliced and left hanging.'

'Nothing else hiding in the flaps?' Mack sniggered. Lindsay silently raised one eyebrow. He dropped his head and stared at the photo, his features suddenly serious. He gathered up the others. 'Okay, so we've got four tattoos that have been created post-mortem, we're assuming by the killer—'

'Highly likely I'd say.'

'He obviously had a clear reason for creating these, took some time over them, even though they're pretty rough. So, we've got a bird – of unknown species. A code of some sort?' Mack continued to sift through the photos. 'Then, a word – I think, although I can't make it out, and finally . . . lines and crosses, a pattern?'

'That's about as far as I got too.' Lindsay took the photos from Mack and placed them back on her desk. 'Do you think they could be prison-related? Or some gang code?'

'It's possible, I guess. Tattoos are more prevalent in the prison community in Russia and USA, though, I'd say.'

'Okay then. We still need to look into the possibility, but . . .' Lindsay bit on the inside of her cheek, thinking. 'You suggested in the morgue they could be a message. One that only the person it's intended for could interpret?'

'Yes. I was thinking Connie Summers?'

'Well, given that her name is on the dead man's hand, I suggest we should ask her. It could be that it's because she's the one who'll be able to tell us what they mean?'

'Only one way to find out. I'll give her a call, get her to come on in.' Mack propelled the chair back to his desk.

'Actually, Mack – make a copy of these pictures and go see her, will you?'

He replaced the phone, frowning. 'But she doesn't want us to turn up at her office, remember?'

'Yeah. I remember.'

'You playing some kind of mind game here?' Mack sat back in his chair, crossing his arms.

'No. Not at all. But I don't want her in here quite yet. I want her independent from us until she's given her thoughts on these tattoos. I don't want anyone else to . . . *contaminate* her thoughts.'

'I think you want to make her uncomfortable.' He smiled. 'Which is your way, I know. But won't that jeopardise you making sure she doesn't believe she's a person of interest?'

'My way? Don't know what you mean. And no, I don't think it will make her uncomfortable – she'll be in her own, safe environment. I think it'll wind her up a bit, but I also think she needs to know who's in charge. Don't you?'

'Sure. I'm on it, Boss.' Mack put two fingers to his forehead in a salute and took the photos from her.

'Good. Make sure you only do one copy of each and bring these back to me before you go, yeah?'

'Ah, I was hoping I could make a dozen copies and distribute them to my mates at the local tattoo parlours.'

'That's a good idea, actually. But just the one copy for Summers at the moment. We'll look into showing others when we have a bit more info.'

'Okay.'

'And when you get to hers, keep it business, eh, Mack?' Lindsay winked.

'Ha. Ha. You're *so* funny.'

'Seriously, though, don't act like you did before – we want her to assist us, not clam up because you're rubbing her up the wrong way.'

'Yeah, yeah. I'll be on my best behaviour. Promise.' He winked back.

Lindsay casually looked through the photos of the tattoos, her mind flitting from one thing to the next, the low hum of the computers and buzz of her colleagues' discussions dissolving into the background. Her thoughts had no structure – they were erratic, not settling on one concrete idea or theory. She needed other people's input. Raising herself from her desk, she took the pictures to the back of the room and began sticking them to the large whiteboard. Sensing the room quietening, she turned. The team had stopped what they were doing and eager, keen eyes were now trained on the photos.

'Right, well it looks as though I already have your attention.' Lindsay moved to the side of the board. 'Gather round.'

The squeaking of chairs and the shuffling of shoes followed her invitation. The group of officers stood shoulder-to-shoulder in front of the whiteboard. Lindsay waited for them all to settle and then turned to the board.

'Four pictures: each depicting a tattoo left on Hargreaves' body post-mortem,' she said simply. 'Thoughts?'

There was mumbling; some hushed interchange between officers.

'Now, now, don't be shy. Spit it out, people.' Lindsay picked up a dry-wipe pen and drew a line downwards at the side of the photos. 'Brainstorm time.' She smiled. 'Let's have some ideas on photo one. Go.'

As brainstorms went, it had been a productive one; not too many ridiculous ideas, and some solid possibilities as to what they were and what they could mean. None of the ideas correlated with the victim himself, or Connie Summers. Currently, they were random tattoos.

'Guv.' DC Clarke raised his hand from behind his desk as he replaced the receiver. 'Got a hit on one of the names on that list of Hargreaves' prison associates.'

'Go on.'

'Oscar Manning. Was released six months ago from HMP Baymead. Had links with Hargreaves on the inside. He's the only one on the list that's not still banged up, so could be one of the outside sources. Someone who'd be able to help orchestrate an escape attempt from the funeral.'

'Good work. We got an address for him?'

'No, not yet.'

'He could still be on licence.' Lindsay rubbed at her temples. 'Get hold of the local probation, see what they can tell us. We need to get him in for questioning, pronto.'

Lindsay swept past the rows of desks, working her way back to the whiteboard. The amount of time she'd spent staring at the photos of the tattoos meant she'd probably never get them out of her head. It would be far worse if she couldn't figure out their relevance – they'd forever taunt her. Hopefully, Mack would get something to go on, something that might link the tattoos – either to each other, or to the victim, or Connie herself.

CHAPTER TWENTY-THREE

Connie

At some point during Connie's walk from the train station to her office, drizzle had laid a fine film of damp on her. Once she emerged from her thoughts and realised, she welcomed the coolness and lifted her face to meet the droplets. The forecast hadn't given rain. The last few weeks had been unremitting heat and a humidity she wasn't used to in the West Country. Connie paused halfway up the hill, readjusting her shoulder bag and stretching her back. It was aching more frequently these days, she really should get it seen to. She'd add it to the list of things she was unlikely to ever get around to.

As she stood in front of the Narnia shop – her favourite place to browse during her breaks from counselling – Connie looked through the East Gate Arch that spanned the narrow street. Beyond it, she could just make out the steps of her building, and a tall figure beside them. She groaned. It better not be him. Her stomach twisted. Of course it was. He couldn't have seen her yet, though, so she still had time to turn tail. She'd sit in a café for a bit, he'd give up waiting soon enough. Wouldn't he? Why hadn't he called to let her know he was coming? More to the point, why was he there? She'd insisted to DI Wade that if she was to assist them with the case that they should not come to her consultancy. Wade had agreed. Her face burned. That obnoxious, lanky man was going to mess up her hard work; ruin the progress she'd made – what if Steph saw him? She turned to walk away.

Three paces.

Damn that man. She cursed. She couldn't. He'd only come back anyway.

Connie turned, and stomped towards DS Mack.

'Ah, there you are. Morning, Connie.' DS Mack greeted her with a smile; each corner of his mouth seemed to stretch to the sides of his face, like the Joker's grin. There was a familiarity about that smile. She grimaced. Didn't respond. Nudging past him, her eyes averted, she unlocked the front door and walked in. The urge to shut the door on him almost overtook her good judgement.

'What do you want? You're not meant to come here.' She purposely made her tone sharp.

'Sorry. Yes, I'm aware you spoke to DI Wade about that, but I'm afraid this was important, and, well, I couldn't really afford to wait for you to come to us.' He appeared awkward, nervous even – the arrogance he'd displayed the other day not apparent now he was on his own. Perhaps it'd been for the benefit of his DI.

Connie checked her watch. Forty-five minutes before her first client of the day. 'Make it quick then.' She let him into the waiting area and stood, staring at him. His hair was ruffled, giving him a dishevelled appearance despite his smart suit. The shoulders were a darker grey due to the drizzle. She imagined he'd have to buy specially tailored suits because of his height.

He cast his eyes warily around the area. 'Shall we go up to your office?'

Connie tutted. 'Fine.'

Upstairs, he stood by the wall of certificates and waited while she took her suit jacket off, watching as she shook the drizzle from it before hanging it up. Only when she sat, did he take the chair opposite her. Was he being polite now to make up for his previous poor manner? He really must want her onside. Despite wanting to give him a hard time to make up for his behaviour *and* the fact he'd ignored her request, Connie softened.

'What is it that I can help you with, Detective Sergeant Mack?'

'If I'm calling you Connie, I'd feel more comfortable with you calling me Mack. All my colleagues do.'

She raised her eyebrows. The buddy-buddy approach now, was it? She wanted to point out that she wasn't his colleague, and wasn't particularly fussed about making him feel comfortable, but instead she let it ride. She didn't have time to be dramatic, or awkward. It'd be quicker and more painless if she cooperated fully and got this done so she could carry on with the rest of her day.

'Okay, Mack – I'll do what I can to help.'

'Thank you.' His face brightened, transforming his weathered-looking appearance into one that seemed younger than it had before. Connie couldn't confidently put an age on him – he could be anywhere between forty-five and fifty-five, she presumed. He opened a large envelope and pulled out its contents. 'These were tattooed on to the victim, Hargreaves, post-mortem.' Mack placed the pictures on her desk and fanned them out. 'Obviously we're looking into these independently, however, I'd like your thoughts on them.'

Connie sat forward and straightened the A4-sized sheets. She studied them one by one in silence, giving each tattoo about ten seconds of her attention before going back to the first and picking it up.

'Being copies, it's difficult to be sure, as the detail is lost some-what.'

'I know, but any ideas are welcome – perhaps you could come into the station soon and see the originals.'

'Hmm.' Connie gave him a thin smile. 'Well. They're quite

crude. All of them are roughly done with just dark ink. Although I'd bet this wasn't standard ink a tattooist would use, more likely an improvised ink.'

'Like that used by prisoners?'

'Certainly I've seen many that are similarly etched while I worked in Baymead, yes. And Hargreaves had a number of tattoos that were done in that way. He'd had a few adjudications for having them and giving them to other prisoners. He'd been on basic regime loads of times because of it. He had an obsession with them and didn't care about punishment, always had stuff confiscated but seemed to get his hands on new gear easily. Are you sure they were done post-mortem?'

'Pathologist confirmed. So, first picture – what would you say it is?'

Connie looked at Mack and frowned. Was he serious?

'It's a bird.'

'What type?'

'How should I know. I'm not a twitcher!'

Mack snorted. 'Ha-ha. All right, but I want your perspective, your idea of what it might look like. We have our impressions about each of these tattoos but wanted your opinion. And as you worked in a prison, and with the victim, I . . . we, thought you might have something different to offer?'

'Okay. Fair point, we can perceive things differently so it's worth gathering other people's views.' Connie looked back down at the bird. 'It's odd. Not sure if it's just bad drawing, but the top and bottom of the bird are disparate – like two separate halves of different birds. I haven't seen anything similar in the prison.'

'We had the same feeling on that one. Can't say which species they are?'

'Nope. You really do need a twitcher for that. All I can say is they look to me like your common garden variety.'

'Next?'

'Hmm. All I can say is that it appears to be a pattern of lines and crosses. Code? Or perhaps it represents something – a sign or symbol? It does remind me of something . . . not sure what, though. I feel like I've seen it, like on a shop sign, maybe.'

Mack was writing furiously in his notebook, his brows drawn close and tongue protruding through his lips in concentration. He looked like an overgrown child.

'And this next one I'd say *is* a code.'

'Can you make out what the letters are?'

Connie reeled off the letters and numbers: 'U, 2, X, 5, 1. The five might be an S though, difficult to tell because of the blurring.'

'Sure. Any ideas as to what they could mean?'

'Part of a number plate? That's all I can come up with off the top of my head. Can I take these?'

Mack hesitated, seemed to be weighing up the options. 'Er, no. My DI would string me up.'

'Can't have that now, can we?' Connie gave him a wry smile and handed the picture to him, storing the code to memory, to recall when he'd gone.

'Last one, then I'll get out of your hair.'

'Looks like it should be a word, but it doesn't look English. I can't make it out. If anything, I'd say that could be a prison tattoo, one meant to affiliate the person to a specific gang. I can't say I've seen it before though, but there will be prison officers who'll know if it's gang-related – they might even be able to tell you which gang.'

'That's great.' Mack gathered all the pictures, patting the edges to make a neat pile, then replaced them in the envelope. 'You've been very helpful—'

'I don't think I have, Mack. I've probably not told you anything you didn't already know.'

'Next time, I'll ask you to come into the station. In fact, we could do with you as soon as possible. We need to compile a profile of the killer, and your track record is pretty good.' His face flushed. He'd avoided a direct response to her statement and gone for the 'we need you' approach, again.

'Sure. Is tomorrow good enough? I was only going to have an admin day, so I can free myself up.' Anything was better than police showing up at her door again.

'Great. Yes, I'll arrange it and give you a bell to confirm,' he said as he left the room.

Connie heard his heavy footsteps dash down the staircase. She stood at the window and watched him weave his way across the street; he crossed the market square and disappeared, presumably heading for the car park.

Grabbing a piece of paper, Connie scribbled down the code. U2X51. By the time she saw Mack tomorrow she wanted to give him something better than 'number plate'. Despite her initial reluctance to get involved, Connie's intrigue was drawing her into this case. Besides, it would keep her mind occupied tonight, keep it from straying to Luke. And what resided on the USB stick.

CHAPTER TWENTY-FOUR

Then

Her uncle gave her a tenner and a pat on the backside when she left his flat. Said: 'Be careful, missy. You don't know this lad from Adam.' She'd given him a forced smile, muttered her thanks for letting her stay the past couple of months and left without a backward glance. She *knew* Uncle Jimmy, but that hadn't been of any comfort – the fact she didn't know Vince very well was neither here nor there. At least it got her away from Jimmy the letch.

Vince helped lug her bags up the four sets of concrete steps to his flat. She'd only been there once before, after a party where she'd been drunk out of her skull. Looking at the state of the flat now, she realised her memory of it had clearly been wrong. Either that, or he'd been burgled. He gave her a lopsided grin, cigarette hanging from one corner of his mouth.

'Where can I put this lot?' She indicated her bags.

'Only got one room other than this, so knock yourself out.' He winked.

There was nowhere to put them where she stood. It was an L-shaped open-plan room with a battered three-seater sofa, a TV on a crate, a cluttered coffee table, and clothes strewn all over the place. Her eyes travelled over to the tiny kitchen area and to what she assumed were work surfaces, but couldn't be sure because of the piles of takeaway containers, pizza boxes and dirty plates. She closed her eyelids tightly. What had she let herself in for?

'The other room then, I s'pose.' She shrugged.

Vince waved an arm towards the other room. She took small steps, to avoid tripping on discarded items – what exactly she was treading over, she didn't care to know – in the direction indicated. She pushed the door open with her shoulder. A smell, sweet, sickly, wafted out to greet her. It wasn't much better than the first room. She tried to quash her feelings of disgust; her disappointment. This was a move she'd been looking forward to, one she'd obsessed about and that had got her through the darkest days at Uncle Jimmy's. The reality of it fell far short of her expectations; her hopes. How could she have gone from a decent three-bed house to this in such a short time? This sucked.

Her mind conjured Brett's face. This was all his fault.

CHAPTER TWENTY-FIVE

Connie

Tiredness swept over her. She'd only seen two clients since her visit from Mack, but her energy was zapped – the effort of actively listening and responding appropriately to them leaving her weak.

A brisk walk down the hill to the bakery for a calorie-filled treat would sort her out. She got her purse and keys, planting them in her suit jacket, and headed out. The drizzle had been replaced with sun again – the sporadic clouds light and fluffy now. It was one o'clock so the cafés were full. She glanced at the faces of random people sitting at the tables in the windows as she passed. Busy. Chatty. Social. She made a mental note to text Niall later. She didn't feel the need for company quite so strongly now, but she knew she *should*. She might have to force it, but in the longer term it would be better for her. She didn't need her mum to tell her that; she knew it only too well herself.

While standing inside the bakery contemplating which pastry to have, she felt a tap on her shoulder. Assuming she was in the way, or had failed to move up sufficiently in the queue, she stepped back and apologised.

'I thought it was you.'

Connie straightened at the sound of the voice, whipping her

head around to face the opposite direction. Her pulse pounded in her ears. *Ignore her.*

'Connie, isn't it? We met last year?' Her voice, every bit as slippery as her nature. The other customers in the queue turned to look at her. Or perhaps that was her imagination. Her neck burned, the prickling heat travelling to her cheeks.

'Interesting developments at the prison, don't you think?' she continued, craning her head around Connie's side to get back in her eye line. Kelly Barton knew what she was doing; she was waiting for a reaction.

Connie closed her eyes and drew in a deep breath. *Go away.* Seeing the woman on the news, listening to her say her name, knowing she was eager to link Connie to Hargreaves' death, had been bad enough. Meeting her unexpectedly, face to face like this, was enough to cause a wave of anger to pulsate through her tense body.

'It's been confirmed. It's Eric Hargreaves. How ironic that he escaped then wound up back at the prison, dead. Bet that wasn't his plan.' She laughed; a light, bubbly giggle as if she'd been told a joke.

This woman needed taking down a peg. Connie's fists clenched. The weight of people's stares dragged her shoulders downwards. Let the horrible woman blabber on, she wasn't going to engage.

'How do you feel about it? You know, seeing as you got him released then he raped that poor girl.'

Connie heard a gasp from the woman in front of her. Great. Why wasn't the queue moving? The heat in her cheeks spread. She shivered as a bead of sweat ran down her spine. *Don't give her the satisfaction.*

'Yes, you must be so relieved. At least he can't hurt anyone else now. And you can't be blamed for anything more. You're off the hook. Pretty convenient for you really.'

The woman who'd gasped turned to face Connie full on. 'I hope you can sleep at night!' she said before bustling out of the shop.

Kelly grinned. 'I'm sure you will now. The person who almost ruined your career has had his comeuppance. Must feel pretty good.'

That was it. All she could take. She finally whipped round and confronted Kelly Barton, put her face as close to hers as she dared.

'I think you'll find it was *you* who ruined my career, you ignorant woman.' Connie's words forced themselves through her gritted teeth. No longer feeling like anything to eat, she pushed past Kelly and walked out, leaving the echo of shocked whispers behind her.

Connie took big strides, getting back up the hill more quickly than she'd ever managed before – adrenaline fuelling her ascent. She didn't stop until she was securely behind her door. She leant back against it, her breath coming in rapid pants. Her hands and legs shook. Kelly must know where she worked. If Connie remembered correctly, Kelly worked from the news studio in Exeter. Far too local for her liking. And now she seemed to have set her sights on Connie again. How many more times would she 'bump' into her from now on? She was after a story, and she wouldn't stop until she got her teeth into something substantial – something to get her noticed nationally. If that woman dared to cause a major upset in her new career, she'd better be prepared for the consequences. She'd got away with it once but Connie wouldn't let it happen twice.

CHAPTER TWENTY-SIX

Connie

It'd taken the best part of half an hour for the shaking to fully abate. She was able to put the incident to the back of her mind while she saw her afternoon clients; now, though, as she finished typing the notes on her computer, Connie sat back in the chair and allowed it to replay in her head. Where did Kelly get off following her into a shop and harassing her? She should call the news broadcasting house, put in an official complaint. She felt fairly certain that Ms Bloody Barton wasn't acting on her employers' request. This was all her. Her attempt at gaining a reputation for herself; a leg-up the journalistic career ladder into the gutter tabloid press. At anyone's expense.

The ring of the phone pulled her abruptly from her thoughts. She picked it up, grateful for the distraction.

'Miles Prescott, I've got some of the information you requested on Stephanie Cousins,' the gruff voice stated.

'Hi, Miles. Thanks for getting back to me so quickly.'

'I'm not sure what I have is that enlightening, but I've done my best.' His tone hinted at indignation. Like she'd asked for something over and above his duty.

'Okay, well anything more than what I have has got to be useful.'

Connie took a pen and poised her hand over her pad of paper ready to write notes.

'There's nothing about a brother.'

Connie's shoulders slumped. 'Really?'

'Really. I did find out about the fire at her family home, though.' Connie heard the clicking of computer keys. 'I've got a psychiatric report here from children's services, dated October 2007. Makes for interesting reading.'

'Can you email it to me?'

'Sure. I'll have to send you a redacted version though, you understand, for security.'

Connie sighed. 'Fine. Anything else that might help me in untangling this story?'

'I don't know if it's a help, but her mother was diagnosed with severe dementia shortly after the fire. She has apparently never spoken a single coherent word since.'

'That's sad. Must've been so traumatic for her. And Steph.'

'The report certainly points to Steph never forgiving her mother. Loads of issues are attributed to the mother's lack of support – feelings of betrayal and abandonment are discussed – following the devastation of losing her home and her father.'

'So it mentions her father? He died in the fire, as Steph said then?'

'Guess so. Don't understand why this wasn't known to us. As far as we knew, her dad was merely unreachable – alive, but at an unknown location.'

'The information you have is clearly inaccurate. Begs the question how it could be so wrong. Seriously, Miles, this is basic stuff – background info, family history. How have you done your job effectively if this information was missing, or patchy at best? How safe is Steph if her own witness protection team don't even know the full picture?' Her rant extinguished itself. She loosened her grip on the receiver, unaware until she felt the tingling in her fingers that she'd been holding it so tight. Her anger at Kelly and now the incompetence of Miles' team had come spilling out.

'We've done our job, Miss Summers.' His voice, curt.

Connie felt she'd said enough on that point. For now. 'If there's no mention of a brother, who did they attribute the blame of setting the fire to?'

There was a long pause.

'Says here that it's unsolved. Fire investigators reckoned the fire's source was inside the hall, the accelerant was petrol. It was suspected to be a firebomb through the letter box. No one was in the frame for it.'

'That doesn't fit Steph's account. She said Brett started the fire outside her parents' bedroom.'

'As I said before, I'm afraid you can't rely on her accounts. Post-traumatic stress was suggested in the report. I think she's fabricated it all, if you want my opinion.'

She didn't.

Why hadn't this come to light before? If Miles' team could get his hands on the reports now, why not while they were compiling their file on her? Had they just not bothered, and concentrated on the gang they wanted behind bars rather than the well-being of their informant? The system had let Steph down. Perhaps now Connie knew the extent of their shortcomings, she herself could help Steph properly. She *did* believe her accounts. Steph had no real reason to lie. Her initial concern that she was fabricating the story to ensure her continued support from Miles was now banished.

'The fact that some of the things Steph has talked to me about have turned out to be true, Miles, means it's quite possible others are too. I'm prepared to believe Steph is being threatened by her brother, Brett, via letters being sent from the YOI he is, or was, incarcerated in. So I suggest you look into that please. If there's a Brett Ellison being held, or having been held in the past, the records will prove it. Then you have to take her concerns seriously and up her security level.'

Miles mumbled something she didn't catch and then said he

would contact the YOIs in Manchester and the surrounding area. The call ended with his promise that he'd get back to her as soon as he had any further information.

In the next session with Steph, Connie was going to blow this whole thing wide open – tell Steph she believed her story and ask her to tell her everything she remembered about the threats Brett had made. If her Protected Persons Constable couldn't offer enough protection, she'd have to help Steph get to the bottom of this, and if it came to it, make sure Miles relocated her again to a place of safety. The last thing Connie needed was another person's blood on her hands.

CHAPTER TWENTY-SEVEN

DI Wade

Friday 9 June

From the second-storey corridor window, Lindsay Wade stood and watched. She followed Connie Summers' unhurried entrance into the police building with interest and slight trepidation. She hoped involving her in the investigation as an expert advisor was the right call. It wasn't like she was independent of the case – it could backfire spectacularly. And the fallout of a screw-up wasn't one she wished to consider. She took her hands out of her trouser pockets and made her way down the stairs to the reception.

As Lindsay walked towards Connie, she did a quick appraisal of her. She looked younger than her thirty-seven years, with no visible wrinkles around the eyes, which were a pretty shade of green. She had a bright complexion – a far cry from the grey tone Lindsay's skin had taken on recently. Her trousers strained slightly on the thighs, accentuating her larger frame, but her face was slim – no sign of a double chin. Lindsay wondered if the weight gain was recent – a side-effect of her experience with Hargreaves and the prison last year. She'd mentioned time off sick. Lindsay would bet it had been stress-related – possibly an episode of depression.

'Thanks for coming in, Connie.' Lindsay offered her right hand and gripped Connie's. The shake was firm. Lindsay took it as a sign that Connie wanted to come across as assured and confident. Perhaps she was. Connie smiled, but her smile didn't reach her eyes: they told a different story – uncertain, flitting nervously around the reception area, not quite making contact with hers. Lindsay reached up and placed her hand on Connie's shoulder – she was a good three inches taller than Lindsay – and gently guided her towards the main incident room. The team had been prepped for Connie's arrival and were waiting for her professional insight.

Thankfully as they entered the room everyone was busy, so Connie's presence went largely unnoticed. Better than everyone stopping to stare at her. It would help put her at ease if she could slip in and join the briefing without too much fuss. Lindsay took her to her desk and pulled up a spare chair. Connie sat, scanning the room. The whiteboard held the photos of Hargreaves' post-mortem, the photos of the tattoos. And a photo of Connie. Lindsay noticed the flinch in her face as she clocked it. Her mouth twitched, but she said nothing.

'So, Mack tells me that he showed you the pictures of the tattoos yesterday.' Not much of an opening, but the best she could do to get the conversation going. She'd yet to consume her obligatory third coffee – her senses didn't fully come alive until that magic number.

'Yes, but they weren't the clearest, I'd like to see the originals.' Connie's gaze travelled back to the whiteboard.

'Sure, go ahead,' Lindsay said, indicating towards the back wall. 'Take your time. I'll give you a shout when the briefing is due to begin.'

Lindsay watched Connie walk up and down in front of the pictures for a few minutes, then turned her attention to her briefing sheet. Out the corner of her eye she spotted Mack approach Connie's side. It was hard not to openly stare; she kept her focus on the paper in her hands, periodically looking up. There was something weird about the way Mack acted around Connie. She'd mocked him and hinted at there being a history – but it was becoming less of a joke. Perhaps there really had been something. Mack was single. Kind of. Had been separated for so long from his wife that everyone classed him as single, even though they'd never even contemplated divorce. From the little Mack had told her, they'd married too young, had their kids too quickly, but were still the best of friends. Connie was single – by all accounts. Despite the disparity in age, perhaps their paths had crossed – it wasn't out of the realms of possibility, even if Lindsay did doubt it was Mack's style. If they had, though, Mack was doing a good job of keeping it to himself.

The sun streamed through the windows of the second incident room, the one they used for official briefings. The heat was already evident even though it was only 10 a.m. Lindsay hung her suit jacket over the chair and stood behind it, leaning forwards, placing both hands on the back. She waited for everyone to file in and take a seat. Connie was last inside the room.

'Morning, everyone. Forensic psychologist Connie Summers is joining us today. She'll be here to give any insight she has on Hargreaves.' The team – twelve officers of varying rank – mumbled their greetings and then settled. 'If you could perch here, Connie.' Lindsay pointed to the chair next to hers. 'Okay, so where are we up to, Mack?'

'Right. Firstly, Oscar Manning, ex-con who knew Hargreaves while inside. We found him, interviewed him – and found no evidence of him being in contact with Hargreaves once he was released. His probation officer said he'd kept all appointments and is working part-time in a garden centre six miles out of town. He doesn't have his own transport and relies on a co-worker for lifts to and from work. So, not looking hopeful as the person who helped Hargreaves escape. He wasn't forthcoming with any further info and, as we had nothing, we could only ask that he contact us if he thought of anything else.'

Lindsay stood straight, crossed her arms and began pacing. 'That's disappointing. What about the tattoos?'

'Clarke and I spoke to a number of the prison officers at HMP Baymead and not one of them believed any to be related to a particular gang – not well-known ones anyway. The prison governor is helping with enquiries and cooperating with the team by checking all rosters and working out who was on shifts on Hargreaves' wing the most, then cross-referencing with wing records. He should be able to see what contact certain officers had with Hargreaves in the lead-up to his escape – looking specifically at the two officers who escorted Hargreaves at the funeral, but not ruling anyone out at this stage.'

'That's good, and we've been given access to all Hargreaves' offending behaviour work carried out with Connie Summers.' Lindsay turned towards Connie. 'It would be good if you could also go through them – with a fresh pair of eyes – and look for anything relevant that could give us a clue as to why your name found its way on to his hand.' Lindsay noted a visible flinch on Connie's face, but continued. 'It can't be in relation to an upcoming appointment or anything of that nature, since Connie left the service a year ago.' The team murmured, and heads nodded in agreement.

'So, are we definitely ruling out Hargreaves writing this himself?' DC Anika Patel asked.

Connie leant forward and gave a small cough. 'He was left-handed, so it would be difficult for him to have written on his left hand . . .' She looked around at all the faces turned to hers. 'But, if you look closely at the way my name is written, there's a uniformity about it, don't you think? It's printed, in capitals. Almost like a stencil. In which case, there *is* a possibility he did it himself. Personally though, I feel it's more likely to have been done by the perpetrator.'

The officers looked thoughtful, and for a moment the room was quiet. Lindsay allowed the lull. She wanted her officers to process the information, come up with questions without her jumping in.

Anika leant across the table and directed her question at Connie. 'Why would it be a stencil, why not just write it?'

'It needed to be clear, no room for misreading?' Connie said, her voice lilting. 'Stencilling would ensure it could be read. Perhaps the person who wrote it had awful handwriting?'

'But if that was the case, why were the tattoos done freehand instead of using a stencil?'

'Perhaps he didn't *want* those to be clear. Wanted ambiguity – to screw with us,' Mack offered.

'That's certainly a possibility,' Connie said.

'It was important. He needed to make sure we could read the name, no mistake.'

Lindsay noticed Connie shift in her chair.

'Connie. We've had some thoughts as to why *your* name. You must have too?'

'My first thought, and, well, the one that horrified me, was that I was somehow the next target.'

'Why?'

'I wondered if the person doing this was related to Hargreaves' last victim. Perhaps someone seeking revenge for it. And if that was the case, then perhaps he wanted me to pay too – seeing as I was the one who was instrumental in Hargreaves' release. Although, I wasn't actually instrumental as such.' Connie's voice was now firm; confident. 'The parole board had various evidence at their disposal to make the final decision to release him. But the way it was reported at the time – you'd think it was all me, that I was the one who allowed Hargreaves to walk out and attack another woman.'

Lindsay caught the sharp turn of Mack's head in her direction; his eyes narrowed. 'This was something we'd considered briefly. Mack, perhaps you could follow this line of enquiry – check the boyfriend and family members of . . .'

'Katie Watson,' Connie added.

'Yes, Katie Watson, and see if all have solid alibis for the time of the funeral and the time of the body dump.' Lindsay paused, watching the scribble of notes; the look of indignation on Mack's face. He was annoyed with her. He'd been concerned Connie was a target and she'd been dismissive. She still had a gut feeling Connie was not 'next' but she should have ruled it out officially straight away. Not four days later. She brought her focus back to Connie. 'Any other ideas?'

'Once the initial shock wore off, I thought it was more likely that the person who wrote my name merely wanted you guys to know I had a link with either them, or the victim.' Connie paused, her eyebrows raised. 'Although, Kelly Barton made the link without the knowledge of my name on the dead man's hand.'

'A leak from within the prison? Someone keen to drag your name through the mud again?'

'Yes, something like that,' Connie said.

'We keep coming back to the *why*? Why was it so important to get us to notice your name?' Lindsay paced the room again, hands on her hips – the movement creating a welcome shift of air.

'I still like my theory, Boss.'

'Go on, Clarke.' Lindsay was glad of Clarke's interruption.

'You know – the secret admirer, or perhaps not so secret, who thought he was doing Connie a favour, getting even on her behalf. Getting rid of the scum who ruined her career.'

Connie's skin blanched.

Lindsay tapped her index finger on her lips, thinking. 'We could do with a list of people you have had relationships with, gone out with, or have had, or do have dealings with, or even that have shown an interest in you.'

'Really? How far back?' Connie's voice had raised an octave; her eyes were wide. Lindsay felt sorry for her – not the easiest thing to have to do, no doubt. Opening yourself up to a whole team, spilling how many relationships you'd had. It might have been better to have asked her privately. Too late now.

'I'd go back a year prior to your dealings with Hargreaves. To start with.'

Lindsay looked to Mack, his head was lowered.

She wondered if his name would appear on that list.

CHAPTER TWENTY-EIGHT

Connie

The day had been long. Connie'd been at the police station for eight hours – yet at the same time it had come as a shock when Lindsay had told her it was six o'clock and she should go home. Being with people other than clients had given her an energy she hadn't experienced for a while. Her blood had pumped harder; her mind had been sharper. She hated to admit it, but she'd enjoyed being part of the team, even if it had only been for a day.

Now Connie sat back on the sofa, Amber flopped on her lap, and pressed the phone to her ear. Her mum's voice was quiet – she sounded as though she were far away instead of a few miles.

'Mum, really, you shouldn't worry so much. I'm fine.'

'You always say that. *I'm fine.* Said it for as long as I can remember, especially when it wasn't true.'

Connie gave an exasperated sigh. Her mother wasn't going to let up. 'Okay, I'll come over and see you at the weekend.'

'Good, good. Tomorrow or Sunday? Or you can have your old room, it's still got your bed – and you can spend the whole weekend. Let me cook you some decent meals, look after you.'

Decent meals? Could her mother see the discarded plastic microwave meal containers, the empty pizza boxes in her bin? Her conscience tugged. Despite her mum living just ten miles away, she hadn't seen her for months, had only called sporadically. But, with the content of the memory stick so insistently on her mind, how would she stop herself from dragging up Luke's death if she spent the entire weekend in her mum's company? Her mum would be distraught if she pulled her back into the trauma of losing her son. They still spoke of Luke on important occasions, how bright he'd been, what a clever, talented seventeen-year-old – a young soul plucked from this earth way too early. But not the actual incident. That had never been discussed. Not since that dark day in 1995. She shouldn't really broach the subject, it was her dad she should talk to. If the content of the memory stick was to be believed, then he was the one in the know. But her mum was concerned – she'd just have to keep her questions about Luke to herself.

After agreeing to stay the whole weekend, Connie hung up, then texted Niall. She'd told herself she should. She'd contemplated asking him to meet her in town, at a bar – but actually, she couldn't be bothered going out now. Anyway, it was probably too late for him to come over tonight – it was unlikely he'd be around. But she tapped out a message nonetheless. Said she was free now, and if he came back with a 'no' – well, at least she'd tried.

The ping came within seconds of her sending the text. He'd be over in half an hour. *Wow. Keen. I wonder why?* A niggle inside of her. A warning voice. His sudden interest in her again could be to see what information she had about Hargreaves.

She was sounding paranoid, even to herself.

He wanted company, she needed company. Simple as that. *Don't read anything into it that's not there.* Connie gently pushed Amber off her on to the sofa cushion and headed for the shower.

She picked out a pair of linen trousers and a blue short-sleeved silky top. Nothing fancy. She didn't want to look like she was trying to impress him. A smatter of light make-up, to make her appear brighter than she felt.

The doorbell rang.

Why had her heart rate picked up?

She took a deep breath and answered the door with a smile.

'Hey, Niall. Long time no see.' She broke eye contact quickly, tucked her hair behind one ear and then stood aside to let him in.

Niall, dressed casually in a white T-shirt and jeans, stepped inside and bent to kiss her on the cheek. She caught the scent of Boss aftershave. He hadn't changed. Still the same aftershave, the same haircut – a grade two all over, which she knew was to disguise his balding at the crown – and still the same style of clothes. Looking at him now, it was hard to believe there'd been a year's gap since seeing him last.

'You look great.' His gaze lingered on her as he hovered in the hallway.

'Thanks.' Connie doubted he meant that. She looked down at herself self-consciously, knowing full well the last time he'd seen her she'd been a fit, slim size 12. 'Go on in, then.' She ushered him into the lounge. The awkwardness was palpable. She was beginning to regret her invitation; it wasn't as though they could just pick up where they'd left off; she held on to too much animosity for that. Why *did* she want him here? 'Tea, coffee?'

'Oh. Nothing stronger?'

'I assume you drove here?'

'No, actually – got a lift from a mate. So, you know—'

'So you could stay over?' she blurted.

'Er . . . nooo, so I could have a drink was what I was *going* to say.' He raised his eyebrows.

Connie made a face. 'Oh, right.' She gave an apologetic smile. 'Um, well, I have wine or lager then, in that case. And when's your mate picking you back up?'

'Lager, please. And when I text to say I'm ready.' He grabbed the TV remote, sat down heavily on the sofa, causing Amber to flee, then settled back and stretched his legs out. Connie bristled. *Make yourself at home.*

In the kitchen, Connie fiddled with the wine bottle. Should *she* have any alcohol? She'd let her guard down too easily if her defences were weakened through drinking. That was her usual behaviour. The reason she'd had one-night stands in the past. Her mind flipped to the idea of 'the list' and her stomach dropped. She didn't even know, or couldn't remember, all of the surnames of the men she'd been with during the past year. How would *that* look to the police? Niall, however, wasn't in that category. She knew all about him, and he was in the category labelled 'traitor'. And if she allowed something to happen between them she'd be really disappointed with herself in the morning. He'd let her down. Dumped her when she'd needed him most. She shouldn't even be giving him the time of day.

Yet, here he was.

She'd thought it a good idea to have company. Someone she knew, someone who knew her past.

Someone who could have easily spoken to a reporter and linked my name to Hargreaves.

'Where've you gone for the drink – Sainsbury's?' Niall's voice erupted from the other room.

Connie jolted out of her thoughts. She replaced the wine bottle in the fridge, took two cans of lager and returned to the lounge.

'Here.' She handed him one of the cans and sat at the other end of the sofa, snapping the ring pull from her own. One lager would be plenty. Enough to relax her, nowhere near enough to make her tipsy. She would stay in control.

But she had another six cans she could ply Niall with.

His tongue would loosen after those. She knew now why she'd wanted him to come to her house.

CHAPTER TWENTY-NINE

Then

Barton Moss Secure Care Centre, Manchester

Dear sis,

How are you? Hope all is good. I've been having some kind of therapy sessions. It was scary at first, didn't want to talk about what happened. Couldn't even remember that night really. I suppose I've blanked it. That's what Polly said too (she's my therapist, she's real nice). She said that my mind has done a good job protecting me. It's like my brain's shielding me by stopping my memory from seeing that night. She's clever, knows stuff. So, I've started talking now. I can't say much 'cos I don't see it yet. But I'm working on it – actually trying to remember now instead of blocking it.

So, that's progress, right? So you can come visit now. I'm sorry, Jenna. I'm so sorry you're mad at me. Please come see me. I need you.

Brett x

CHAPTER THIRTY

Connie

Saturday 10 June

To get to her mum's, Connie had to take the train to Teignmouth then a taxi across the bridge into Shaldon. What had once been their holiday home when they'd lived in Manchester had become their permanent home after Luke died. Back then, Connie hadn't been able to appreciate the serenity, the beautiful scenery, the idyllic cottage near the river. She'd been taken from her home, her friends – her memories of Luke. Her life had practically ended – she'd hated her parents for dragging her away just before she was due to take her GCSEs and plonking her in a pathetic little village in South Devon. It'd taken a long time before she'd felt thankful for it.

She watched as the now familiar scenery flashed past the train window, her eyes blurring with the motion. She closed them, and thought about her evening with Niall. Having only the one lager had definitely been the key; she hadn't succumbed to her usual tendency to get overemotional and 'cuddly', which would've ultimately led to sex. But, her intention of getting Niall talking freely about the prison, and specifically, Ricky Hargreaves, had hit a setback. When Connie had pushed for details surrounding the day Ricky absconded, Niall had merely sidestepped by saying that it wasn't good for Connie to talk about the prison. That she shouldn't revisit past traumatic events. He'd swiftly changed the subject each time she attempted to talk about it. Connie didn't know whether to get mad at him for it, or appreciate what he was trying to do. So they'd settled into safe-territory subjects.

The train pulled into the station, stopping any further musings about her evening with Niall.

When the taxi dropped Connie at the end of her mum's road, she stood for a while, her overnight bag hung on one shoulder, and stared out across the estuary of the River Teign. The warm weather had brought a horde of tourists – the beachside pub and the sandy stretch opposite were rammed already and it was only ten in the morning. It was something you got used to if you lived there permanently. The quiet winter months were preferable.

The net curtain twitched as Connie approached the gate, then seconds later the front door flung wide.

'Hello, my darling!' Her mum rushed out, arms outstretched, and caught her in a bear hug. She had an impressive agility and strength that Connie could only hope for at sixty-five. She was struggling even at thirty-seven.

'Hey, Mum. Good to see you.' She broke from the hug and kissed her. She smelled sweet – of baked goods. Connie noted her trademark floral pinny tied around her waist. Great. She'd probably cooked cakes and biscuits and apple pie – she could almost feel the pounds pile on her right there and then.

Connie followed her into the kitchen – the aroma filling the compact space was both familiar and comforting. It took her back to her childhood; the moments spent beating the wooden spatula in the sticky mixture, remembering the texture of the gloopy mess as she swept out the remnants in the bowl and licked it from her fingers. They'd baked a lot together after Luke died too. Connie thought that must've been one of her mother's coping mechanisms. Her dad's had been spending time at the pub, or 'gentleman's

110

club' as her mum used to call it. They'd each handled Luke's loss differently. They still did.

'I'll just finish up, then we can have a nice cup of tea and a warm biscuit.' Her mum swapped one baking tray for another in the oven.

'They smell delicious. I'll pop the kettle on.'

Connie went through to the lounge with the tray of tea, setting it down on the oak coffee table. She walked across to the sideboard and ran her fingertips over the photos in their silver-plated frames. The story of their life lined up in order. Her throat tightened. The toddler sat on the beach, his curly blond hair poking out under a baseball cap; the footballer in his kit, ball under one arm; the infant stood outside the house, proud in his oversized school uniform; the child with an awkward grin in an official school photo, his younger sister squirming beside him; the teenager on his bike with his cheeky grin – the sparkle in his intense green eyes. They had that in common, everyone told her that after he died: *you've got your brother's eyes.* She'd hated it. Once during a particularly bad bout of grief she'd wanted to get a spoon and gouge her eyes out. Later she'd settled for coloured contact lenses.

'Here we go, love.' Her mum placed a plateful of warm biscuits next to the tea tray. 'Come and sit down.'

'Where are the other photos?' Connie remained standing.

'Oh, you know – here and there. So, how's your new consultancy going? I want to hear all about it.' She patted the sofa cushion beside her.

Avoiding the question. That was usual, she realised. She'd never really addressed the way conversation was swiftly diverted to something else whenever Connie brought up Luke. She'd always assumed it was because it was too painful. She hadn't considered that it was because her mum and dad wanted to prevent Connie from digging. From finding out something that they'd kept from her. Had they thought she'd been too young to understand; too young to cope with the truth? And then, as the years had passed, decided to maintain things as they were, not alter any memories; her perceptions of what she'd been told. Had her parents lied to her? Were they going to continue to do so?

Or, as the material on the memory stick seemed to suggest, was it just her dad that knew something he didn't want her to know?

Connie's thoughts, her questions, swamped her brain. Before being given the memory stick, the story she'd grown up with was simple. Luke had been in the wrong place at the wrong time. It was a tragic accident. It wasn't meant to be Luke. He'd just got in the way.

Now someone had gone to the trouble of showing her an alternative explanation, she wasn't so sure. It had thrown everything she thought she knew into question. How could she have lived this long without querying it?

'Sit down, sweetheart,' her dad had said. His washed-out face, its serious, rigid expression, towering above her. 'We've got bad news. It's about Luke.'

Connie recalled the whimper, the tears from her mum huddled in the corner of the room, Aunt Sylvie's arms wrapped protectively around her. No one's arms wrapped around Connie. 'He, well . . . there was a fight. After the match. I . . . I couldn't—' His voice had cracked, his face crumpled.

Connie's eyes stung with the memories.

'Biscuits. Yes, let's see if you've still got the knack.' Connie smiled the tears away and took a bite out of the freshly baked ginger biscuit.

Had Luke's death been more than a random accident?

CHAPTER THIRTY-ONE

Connie

Monday 12 June

The weekend had been a mixed bag of emotions and two days in her mum's house had been too much. It wasn't that she didn't enjoy her mum's company, more the fact that she felt suffocated. Restricted. The many attempts at getting her mum to open up about Luke's death had hit barriers at every turn. She'd managed to get her to find the other photos though. They'd spent a couple of hours poring over them, laughing at remembered stories, crying for the ones that would never be. In each captured moment, Luke's bright green eyes stared out at her, seemed to penetrate her own. What had really happened to him? But details of that final day were still elusive. Connie had nudged for information; asked about where her dad had been when the fight broke out. *He'd got pushed aside in the crush . . . he couldn't get to him*, she'd said before picking up another photo and talking about that instead.

Why did the document on the memory stick refer to her dad? Whoever gave her the stick seemed to be pointing to her father keeping details about Luke's death from others. From her and perhaps even her mum. Whether that was to protect them from the true horror of that day or to hide something was not made clear in the content, but the very fact the memory stick had been given to her must've been so she'd question it. At the time of the incident, though, it had been reported as a case of wrong place, wrong time. No one had even been convicted of Luke's murder because of the lack of evidence; too many people in the crowds outside the football ground meant key people hadn't been identified, and no one had come forward with information. That's the story that'd been told for years afterwards, until they'd stopped mentioning it altogether. And that's what her mum had said at the weekend, when she'd been pushed into speaking about him. Connie had never questioned what she'd been told. Why would she? But having seen the articles with a new perspective – things just weren't adding up.

Today she was relieved to be back at work, immersing herself in her clients' problems rather than thinking about her own. And she was due to see Steph tomorrow, if she kept the pre-booked session, which would definitely keep her from her own thoughts. She'd also returned to a message from DI Wade, asking if she could spare them another day this week. A flutter of excitement broke loose inside her stomach. It was good to get the old adrenaline going again, to be part of something – part of a team. Something to challenge her skill set. The code she'd written down after Mack had left last Thursday had floated around her mind since. Nothing tangible had been grasped yet, but something would come to her, she was sure. She loved puzzles.

For lunch, Connie decided to walk down to the bottom of town and sit on the grass verge by the River Dart – watch as the riverboat took people out, and relax in the sunshine. She'd made a packed lunch to avoid having to hang around in any bakeries. She didn't want to risk another 'accidental' run-in with Kelly Barton.

It was surprisingly quiet given the warmness of the day. She checked her watch: 2 p.m. – a later-than-usual lunch. She'd hoped that by taking different lunch hours it would deter the annoying bitch of a reporter.

Connie's thoughts drifted; she let them. Although she was looking over the river, she wasn't really *seeing*. A squeal drifted across to her and pushed into her consciousness. On the other side, where the riverboat boarded and disembarked its passengers, next to the riverside café, there was a play area. The large wooden pirate ship there was the source of the sudden squeal – a child on the deck, his mother chasing him around. Connie held her hand up to her forehead to shield her eyes from the sun to gain a better view. They were a fair distance away, but she knew the figures. Steph and Dylan. How wonderful to see them like this – away from the glare of assessment, from judgement. They were like any other mum and child, playing and enjoying the moment. Steph's lightness and caring nature warmed Connie. She could tell that Steph was smiling at her son as she picked him up and swung him towards the sky. They laughed again; the happy, high-pitched giggles carrying on the air. Connie smiled. There was a carefree delight in their laughter. No worries. Not in that moment.

Realising the time, Connie got up to leave. She had to get back for her next client in half an hour and didn't want to have to rush up the hill. She balled up the empty paper bag which had held her ham and salad sandwich and deposited it into the bin at the water's edge. She looked up, a parting glance towards Steph and Dylan.

Her breath caught.

A man, wearing a baseball cap, black hoody and dark jeans, seemed to be looking in their direction too. But he was on their side of the river, hovering near the café, just feet away from the pirate ship. Was it Connie's imagination or did Steph's demeanour change? She watched helplessly as Steph grabbed Dylan, bundling him into her as they began making their way down the ladder of the ship to the ground. Was that panic, fear?

The man moved forward. Connie was too far away to get to them – she'd need to cross over the bridge and walk through the outskirts of a housing estate, it would take too long.

'Steph!' The shout left her mouth. But Steph didn't turn. Connie walked briskly along the raised path running alongside the river's edge, a good fifteen feet above the river bed, to position herself directly opposite the pirate ship. The man was getting closer to Steph, who'd now jumped down from the ladder and was reaching up to Dylan. She watched as Steph turned her head in his direction. It would be now that she'd notice if his presence was a real problem; she'd tell by Steph's reaction.

Steph didn't miss a beat, she immediately pulled Dylan from the step. Connie's breaths were coming rapidly; shallow and loud. She rummaged in her bag, trying to maintain the visual of the man as she did so. Her fingers clasped her mobile; she fumbled but managed to press the first nine. She hesitated, looked up. Steph had taken Dylan's hand and they were now running in the opposite direction to the man, heading down the road that led to the housing estate. Why didn't she run into the café, raise the alarm? Connie sidestepped along the edge of the river, squinting now at the retreating figures of Steph and Dylan. The man shouted something. Connie couldn't make it out. *What the hell is going on?* He stopped. Connie's grip on her phone loosened. Was it over? The man leant against the pirate ship, but he still seemed to be watching the two figures. Steph and Dylan disappeared out of Connie's line of sight. They must've been out of his sight, too. She breathed out. Her heart felt as though it was hitting against her ribs. Her chest hurt.

Was that Brett? Had he found her?

The man stayed propped against the pirate ship, not moving. Connie lifted her phone again to take a picture, but her fingers trembled and she couldn't seem to press the capture button. It was too far away for a clear image anyway, but it would have been better than nothing. Just in case.

Just in case what?

The man suddenly pushed away from the side of the ship. Connie looked away, began to move off, back towards the footpath.

She tilted her head slightly towards where he'd been. But he wasn't there. Connie scanned quickly along the edge, trying to locate him. He couldn't have gone far.

A chill consumed her stomach. He was dead opposite her.

He'd seen her. And now he was watching her, walking quickly, keeping up with her.

She quickened her steps and progressed diagonally across the grassy area towards the gateway leading back to the road. He couldn't catch up with her, she knew that, but her skin prickled with fear nonetheless. He didn't know her; he couldn't have known she'd been watching. There was nothing to be afraid of.

Think rationally, Connie.

But it was surprising how rational thought could leave you when someone was following you.

Connie's footsteps turned into a jog. It wasn't until she was back on the pavement near the busy road that she chanced a look back.

The man had gone.

She kept her mobile in her hand as she walked back up the hill, taking a look over her shoulder every few steps. She couldn't see him. He wasn't tailing her. She gave another furtive look around before she let herself into her building.

There was going to be a lot to cover with Steph in tomorrow's session.

CHAPTER THIRTY-TWO

DI Wade

Lindsay Wade reverse-parked the Volvo into the last available on-road parking spot, impressed with herself that she'd squeezed it into such a tight space. She'd been lucky; if she hadn't been able to park there, it would've meant driving around all the narrow side roads with little hope of being able to park close to 34, Fisher Road. Due to its proximity to the town, many people used these roads as free parking rather than the pay and display car parks in the town centre. They really should make it residents' parking only.

With DC Sewell by her side, they approached the terraced house. Two women seemed the best approach given the sensitivity of the situation. Going back over the past would be traumatic enough, without adding the complication of asking for alibis from Katie Watson and her family members – which openly hinted that the police were thinking they could be responsible for her attacker's death. It might be better coming from the two women, rather than Mack or any of the male officers. Lindsay was leaving the interviewing of the males of the family to them; she was happy to take the criticism – the inevitable sexist remarks that would fly her way.

Lindsay assumed the woman who opened the door and greeted them with a pallid complexion and red-rimmed eyes was Katie.

'Miss Watson?'

'Yes. Come in.' Her eyes darted around warily. She showed them into the kitchen. Two other women sat at a large, circular pine table. Katie, her small frame swamped by a black baggy T-shirt and jogging bottoms, introduced them as her mother, Anna, and sister-in-law, Jenny, then moved some chairs out and walked to the far side of the table, her movements jittery.

Lindsay and DC Sewell took the offered chairs. This was going to be difficult to approach. Lindsay wanted to speak to the family members separately, didn't want them playing off each other. But even suggesting that seemed inappropriate. They'd been through so much already, treating them like suspects now would certainly add to their distress. Part of her was glad the man who'd taken this young woman's confidence, her trust, was dead. Who wouldn't be? One less criminal; one less piece of scum on the streets. That's how the majority of the public saw this. But Lindsay was a detective, upholding the law. And whatever Hargreaves had done, his murder was a crime, and the perpetrator required punishment too. Hargreaves' killer needed to be brought to justice, and eliminating Katie and her family from enquiries was a step that had to happen.

'Tea? Coffee?' Anna asked, raising from her chair.

'We're good, thank you. Can I ask that we talk to Katie first?' Lindsay smiled. 'We need to speak to you separately, if we may.'

Lindsay noted Anna's body stiffen as she shot a look towards Katie.

'I'll be okay, Mum. Honestly.' Katie wrung her hands, but smiled confidently at Anna.

'We'll just be in there, you shout if you need us, won't you?' Anna shuffled towards the door leading to another room. 'Come on, Jenny, she'll be all right.'

Jenny gave Katie's hand a squeeze and then followed Anna, closing the door gently behind her.

'I'm sorry to have to visit you and ask this, Katie. As DC Clarke informed you in his call earlier, the man who attacked you was found dead – murdered – on Monday 5th June at approximately 7.15 in the morning. We need to ascertain people's whereabouts—'

'I know what you're here for. You think that because he attacked me and now he's dead, that one of my family did it. Out of revenge. And you want our alibis.' She sat back hard in her chair and crossed her arms.

'It's not quite like that, Katie. We do need to know where you were, so we can eliminate you from the investigation. But that's so we can be thorough.'

'Yep. I get it.' Tears swelled. 'I have to prove where I was when that . . . *he* . . . got what he deserved. Otherwise you're dragging me down the police station and probably arresting me for murder.'

'Like I said, I am sorry for causing you distress. Once we've spoken to you and your family, you can put this behind you. It'll be over.'

'It'll never be over.' Katie twirled a strand of her long, dull, brown hair around her index finger, twisting it until it was tight, like a piece of rope.

There wasn't anything Lindsay could say, no comforting words, no snippets of wisdom that would make Katie feel any better. She wanted this interview done so she could get out of this poor girl's house; her life. After all, how do you move on if people keep dragging you back?

For a moment, Lindsay's mind flipped to Tony. How many times had she attempted to drag him back? She wasn't letting him move on. Couldn't. Wouldn't. Why should he get a new chance at happiness – a fresh start, with another woman?

DC Sewell's voice infiltrated her thoughts.

'Were you with anyone at 7.15 on the 5th of June?'

Katie looked directly at DC Sewell. 'Not *with* anyone as such, no. I was here, my mum was here, but I slept in until ten-ish. I'd had a bad night. I dream a lot you see, you know, like nightmares. I spend a lot of each night in a cold sweat, lying awake staring at the ceiling. Until exhaustion takes over. I go into such a deep sleep, often until mid-morning. So, at that time I would've been in bed. Alone.'

'Can your mum corroborate this?' Lindsay's full attention was now on Katie, praying she was about to say 'yes'.

'She brought me a cup of tea at ten, like she usually does.' Her gaze fell to the table.

If Katie's mum hadn't seen Katie until ten, Lindsay guessed that Anna had also been on her own up until that point. This wasn't going well. But the time of Hargreaves' escape could still help eliminate them.

'Okay, what about the afternoon of Friday 2nd of June at 2.30?'

Katie tilted her head back, and took a deep breath in. 'A Friday? Then that would be the afternoon my support group meets. I don't miss those.'

'Yes, it was. That's great, thanks Katie. Who runs that, please?'

'Maddy. I've got her number, I can give it to you so you can check I'm telling the truth.' Her face reddened. 'You do know I don't blame Connie Summers for what happened to me, don't you?'

The question threw Lindsay. At no point had she mentioned Connie's name. And Katie had used her current name – not *Moore*. How did she know she'd changed it?

'That hadn't crossed my mind,' Lindsay said. 'Why did you think it had?'

'Everyone always assumes I blame her. I just wanted you to know that I don't. Typical how they tried to pin all the responsibility on one person – and a woman. Like she was the one who single-handedly released that evil excuse for a human being, instead of it being a joint decision by dozens of people. I don't hold any grudges against her.'

'Do you hold them against anyone else?'

She smiled. 'No. My support group is teaching me to let go of hatred, blame – all the negativity that eats away at your soul. The only way to get over this, eventually, is to forgive.'

If she was lying, she was very convincing.

'Have you had contact with Miss Summers at all?' It was niggling Lindsay that Katie had brought up Connie's name.

Katie's neck flushed pink. 'Erm . . . no, I haven't met her before, just seen pictures. You know, in the paper, on the local news and stuff.'

Lindsay pursed her lips and tapped her pen on the pad, looking straight at Katie. 'Only, you mentioned her by her new name, not the one that was in reports. I was just curious, that's all.' She smiled, wanting to play it cool; she didn't want to make Katie feel as though she was being interrogated.

Katie shrugged. 'I must've just heard it, or seen it – actually, I think someone told me a while back. I can't really remember. It's a small town, after all.'

'Yes,' Lindsay said, 'I guess it is.' She thanked Katie, and asked if she'd show her mother through next.

Anna's story confirmed Katie's, and Jenny had been at a school assembly on the 2nd and with her husband, in bed, on the 5th.

Lindsay and DC Sewell left the Watson women hugging each other in the kitchen.

'Let's hope that they really didn't have anything to do with Hargreaves' murder. It would be terrible if we had to pay them another visit.' DC Sewell closed their front door.

'Agreed. I wonder how the male Watsons fared?'

Lindsay's gut feeling was that they would all be in the clear.

But then, her gut *had* been wrong before.

CHAPTER THIRTY-THREE

Connie

Tuesday 13 June

Connie checked the time on her computer again.

Steph was late. She was never late. It was twenty minutes past her appointment. Connie's fingers drummed on the edge of the desk. Why wasn't she here? Perhaps she'd had issues with the pre-school; Dylan might be unwell. The only contact number Connie had was her landline, and she hadn't answered that.

She'd be here.

Her next client was due at eleven. Should she put him off? If Steph was any later, Connie wouldn't get the time she needed with her to cover everything she had in mind. If she cut Steph's appointment short, it might be detrimental. And Connie doubted whether asking her to come back later in the day would go down well. She put her head in her hands and pulled at her hair. What to do?

She strode to the window, checked the street, the market – no sign. Maybe she'd forgotten – that was a problem with pre-booked sessions. She ought to send reminder texts, like her dentist did. That's the only reason Connie never missed her own appointments.

Dammit.

Connie picked up the phone and dialled Paul. Hopefully she could reschedule him without causing him undue anxiety. He was reaching the end of his sessions with her – it would be a good indicator of how he was coping with everyday problems. Or that's what she convinced herself as she explained the need to alter his session.

Thinking it could well be a waste of time – and that Steph wouldn't show up at all today anyway – Connie set about writing notes about everything she wanted to discuss with Steph. Every few minutes she checked out the window. *Come on, Steph – where the hell are you?*

Could the man from yesterday have caught up with her? Should she call the police, or Miles, to go and check on her? Connie's heart fluttered erratically.

What if Brett had found her?

Connie reached for the phone again. Then stopped. She was blowing this out of proportion. Steph was just late. She replaced the receiver. She'd give it another ten minutes. Her attention was caught by the new mail icon flashing on her computer screen. She clicked on it.

You have received a new private message through your counselling directory page.

Distractedly, she scanned it. She usually got messages from people enquiring about her service – how many sessions, how much it cost – even though this information was already set out on the website. Really it was their way of reaching out; taking the first tentative step. They wanted to get a personal message from the person they were considering putting all their trust in. It was understandable.

But the new message was not someone reaching out in that way.

124

Connie read through the message twice to make sure she'd not misread it.

It's you who needs the counselling. No wonder, when you've had to keep secrets for 22 years. That stuff screws with your head. Or are you still claiming you know nothing about it all?

Don't you remember, Connie?

Your dad does.

He clearly doesn't care though, he's still carrying on like it was nothing to him.

He didn't learn the first time, maybe he needs another lesson.

She stared at the message in shock. Then her brain kicked in. Why would someone send a message like that through her website? They must *want* her to inform the police. Unless they believed she wouldn't involve them for fear of dragging her and her family into a horrible, stressful situation. The memory stick was one thing – that was telling her to wake up and see that Luke's death was no accident. It wasn't threatening. But *He didn't learn the first time* implied another 'lesson' was coming. These things couldn't be a coincidence, it must be from the same person who gave her the USB. This was more worrying.

Connie let out a long breath. With a shaky hand, she grabbed the receiver and began dialling DI Wade.

CHAPTER THIRTY-FOUR

Then

No matter how much air freshener she sprayed, or Shake n' Vac she scattered, the stench of weed, dirt and sweat seeped back through – the concoction of smells made her retch. For the five months she'd lived there, Jenna had never had time with Vince alone – his gang of mates practically lived there too.

She'd complained. Asked if they might have time without them, but Vince told her they were his family; he couldn't tell them to sling their hooks, because he owed them. Owed them what exactly, she didn't know, and he didn't offer any explanation. Judging by the drugs that changed hands, though, and the money that suddenly appeared at odd times, it wasn't hard to guess. What could she do? She'd made her bed – as her mum had often told her in the past, now she had to lie in the shitpit. And boy, had she made her bed.

If her mother could see her now. Would she even care? What kind of mother abandoned her only daughter? Things had never been amazing, she wouldn't have ever given her a 'Mother-of-the-Year' award, but after Brett's arrival they'd progressively worsened. Her mother had become snappy, quick to anger. She'd made it obvious she disliked Brett and the arguments she and Brett's dad had were almost always about him. Jenna was pushed out of the picture. She'd tried visiting her mum at the nursing home a few times after the fire, but as she'd been met with a wall of silence, a glazed look of indifference each time, she'd stopped. Couldn't bear to see the empty shell. How had her mother been so lucky? The sudden onset dementia meant she had no idea what it was like to live with the fallout. How convenient.

Her mum, like the rest of her family, was dead to her now.

CHAPTER THIRTY-FIVE

Connie

Connie gave a yelp of surprise and dropped the phone as the door swung open and banged against the wall.

'Sorry. Didn't mean to scare you.' Steph burst through, dragging little Dylan behind her.

Connie's chest rose and fell rapidly. 'No problem,' she managed. The call to Wade would have to wait.

'I'm late because I had an argument wi' the school 'cos I told 'em I'm not leaving Dylan there again today. He needs to stay wi' me.'

Connie opened her drawer and retrieved the colouring pencils and paper she'd given Dylan before.

'Hey, Dylan. How would you like to draw me a picture this morning?' Connie crouched down, smiling at him. He lowered his head and scuttled behind Steph, still clutching her hand.

'Go on.' Steph pulled him back around her and gave him a nudge towards Connie. 'Take 'em. You can do a nice happy picture. I'll put it on the fridge when we get home.'

Dylan edged forwards, his first two fingers of one hand jammed in his mouth. He chewed on them. Poor kid seemed really nervy. He hadn't been like that last time he'd been in her office. Connie smiled and placed the pencils and paper on the floor beneath the window. He'd go to them in his own time.

'Sit down, Steph.' Connie took her notebook and pen, then moved her chair to be beside Steph. A sickly-sweet aroma reached Connie's nostrils; she repositioned the chair slightly further away. She didn't want to appear rude, but the smell was overpowering. Was it cannabis? Surely not. 'Are you doing okay, Steph?'

'Been better.' Her eye sockets appeared sunken; dark puffy skin bulged underneath. 'Not slept the past few nights.'

'Have you been taking anything?' Connie thought she might as well be direct.

'What, like drugs you mean?' Her voice cracked.

'Yes, like drugs. Only I've got to say, I know you said you've not been sleeping, but your appearance is, well—'

'I took a bit of weed. That's it – to try and relax me. It wasn't much, nothing really.' Steph broke eye contact and looked over at Dylan, who was finally busy with his colouring.

Connie knew that cannabis had been an issue for Steph in the past, when she'd lived with her boyfriend. But to her knowledge, she hadn't used it since being relocated. She wondered where Steph had acquired it. It was a question for another time, though; her priority for today's session was finding out about any perceived or real danger Steph might be in. With the focus on her brother, Brett.

'Perhaps we'll talk about that a bit later, see if together we can come up with some more appropriate ways of dealing with stress and learning some relaxation techniques?'

'Yeah, whatever.'

'I'm going to write notes as we chat today, Steph. I feel we need to get some things straight and I want us to come up with a plan by the end of this session. Does that sound reasonable to you?'

'Fine. If you think that's gonna help, knock yourself out.'

'Don't *you* think it'll be helpful?'

'Depends.' She shrugged her shoulders. 'I guess. If the plans include moving me again, then that might work.'

Connie sat back in her chair. Steph must feel the threat to her was great if she was even thinking about that.

'I would imagine that would be a last resort for Miles and his team. They'd want to do what they can to ensure your safety here, first.'

'If you say so. Look, I know you mean well, and you're trying your best for me. But you can't save me. No one can.'

'What do you mean by that? Why do you believe you can't be saved?'

'It's written in the stars. Set in stone. My destiny – whatever. I wasn't meant to live, was I? Death . . .' Steph gave a quick sideways glance, lowering her voice to a hushed whisper. 'Death will come for me. I know it. I feel it.'

Connie shuddered. Steph's face was set, her jawline strong; defiant. Did she even want Connie to disagree, argue for the opposite? Say she was wrong? Her mind seemed made up. Resolute.

'No, Steph. Death will *not* come for you. The reason Miles brought you here under the protected persons scheme was to do just that – protect you. And Dylan. But to ensure your safety we need to know everything that's going on.'

Steph's eyes darted from Connie to Dylan and back again.

'Right, yes. I know. And I trust you, Connie. Whatever they're saying about you in the news.'

Connie lowered her head as a heat spread from her neck to her face. No time to deal with that right now.

'Have you had any further letters?'

'No, not letters.'

'Then, what?' Connie's brow creased.

'I had some calls. But when I picked up, no one spoke.'

'How many, and when?'

'I dunno. Three, not many. One a day for the last three days. All in the evening, about eight.'

'Just the last three days . . .' Connie ran her index finger over

130

her bottom lip. 'Yesterday, I went to the quay, for lunch.' Connie kept her eyes on Steph's. There was a flicker in them, she was sure.

'Yeah?'

'Yes, and I saw you and Dylan, playing on the pirate ship. I was a distance away, so you didn't hear me when I shouted to you.'

'No, well – my mind was elsewhere. I took Dylan out of school then too, so we were just having some fun.'

'It looked as though you were having fun, yes, and it was great to see you and him playing like that.' Connie smiled. 'But then I saw a man. He seemed to be hanging around.' She almost added 'watching you' but stopped herself.

'Yeah, some weirdo. Black hoody?' Steph bounced against the back of her chair.

'Yes, that's right. Weird how?'

'I think he was a druggy. Either that or an alky. Wanted a handout, that's all.'

'Ah, I see.' Connie wasn't convinced. But if Steph had been concerned it was Brett, she would've said, wouldn't she? Now, thinking about it, it was more likely that the bloke was who she got her weed from and perhaps he was touting for more business.

'I didn't want to hang around to find out, so I took Dylan and left.'

'And no other *weirdos* have approached you?'

'Nah. Just that one time. I'm still feeling like someone is watching, though. Get that creepy feeling where the hairs stand up on the back of my neck. I'm always looking over my shoulder, expecting Brett to be there.'

'Is it only Brett you're worried about?'

'I think the others from the gang might want to get hold of me. The ones who didn't get sent down. There were two who got off. But they didn't have a lot going for 'em; one wash short of a load, both of 'em. So I'm not sure they'd be able to find me. Can't rule it out, mind. Vince's lot would string me up if I was in

131

Manchester, I know it. But it's Brett. He's the one wi' the biggest grudge. And he's the one who threatened me.'

'But why do you think he holds such a big grudge?'

Steph paused for a long time, fiddling with a ring on her finger. Connie wondered if she was even going to answer. Finally, she sighed, and looked Connie straight in the eye.

''Cos he expected me to keep shtum about it. Stick up for him, I s'pose. Kept saying I was his big sis, I should protect him. And I didn't. First thing I said that night was, "It was him, he did it, he killed him". I remember it so clearly. His face, in the back of the cop car – the way his eyes looked through me; right inside to my core. He hated me in that moment.'

Connie placed a hand over Steph's. Such an awful experience, no wonder she was afraid now Brett was released. 'I've got Miles looking into it. He's going to check where Brett is.'

'You mean he actually took me seriously, that Brett is a threat?'

'Yes, he took it very seriously, Steph.' She didn't add that he'd said she didn't even have a brother, or that Steph was making a whole load of this stuff up.

'Surprises me. He wasn't interested when I told him before.'

'What, about your fear of Brett having found where you were?'

'Yeah. Flapped his hand, said not to worry, no one but the team knew my location.'

'And it was specifically Brett that you told him about. Your brother?'

'Yeah, why?'

'Just checking.' Connie took a while to recover. Why had Miles acted as though Brett was new information? She made a mental note to challenge him about it. 'Right, well, with Miles on the case and you being vigilant and reporting any incidents out of the ordinary, like anyone approaching you, for whatever reason – even if it's just to ask directions – I think we can keep you safe here. Don't you?'

'I guess.' She turned to look at Dylan. 'It's really hard to put mine and Dylan's lives into other people's hands. I thought I might get some control over what happens to me once I settled here. Stupid, aren't I?'

'Not at all. Of course you want to gain control, that's what these sessions are for, to give you the tools in order to achieve that. We'll get there, Steph.'

Steph smiled. 'I hope so, Connie. I really hope you're right *this* time.'

CHAPTER THIRTY-SIX

Connie

The lilac air freshener mixed with the scent of the fresh-cut grass diffuser as Connie sprayed it all around the room. Now it smelled of public toilets. *Oh, God*. Stepping over Dylan's pictures, she reached the window latch and threw the window open as wide as it would go. She sucked in the fresh air, then bent to pick up the paper and pens, shoving them all in her desk drawer before retreating from the room. She'd have a coffee and sit in the reception room, give it a bit of time to clear. Hopefully, by the time her next client arrived in about ten minutes, it would smell fine.

Poor Steph. For her to be using cannabis again meant she'd taken a big backwards step. Connie placed a cup under the coffee maker, the bubbling liquid replacing the smell of air freshener. Why did she have the sinking feeling that her sessions with Steph were only scratching the surface and what she really needed was more intense therapy? Certainly more than what Connie was currently offering. Perhaps she could take Steph on as a private client after the agreed sessions that the protected persons scheme had paid for concluded. Connie was engaged in Steph's life now, felt committed to helping her and ensuring her safety. She'd happily do them for a reduced rate – free even, seeing as Steph was surviving on state benefits.

For the time being she would have to carry on as planned. She hoped Miles would come back to her soon and she'd be able to confidently reassure Steph that Brett was not a threat. That he was still in custody, or at the very least under strict probation terms so that it was impossible for him to be here, in Totnes. One issue would be resolved, then Connie could concentrate on the next. Like the fact she'd now have to tell Miles about the man she'd seen watching Steph. If it was someone selling her drugs, then Miles should know about it – the last thing Steph needed was to get in with another set of drug users, or worse, dealers. One by one, though, Connie felt sure they could overcome, or manage, each of Steph's anxieties. For Dylan's sake, as well as her own, Steph needed to move forwards now and put her traumatic past behind her.

Connie gave a snort. Putting the past behind you. Like she had done? And what good had that done her? Now that very past was fighting its way back into her consciousness; her present. And not by her own doing. She'd never forgotten Luke, though. She'd chosen her profession *because* of what had happened to him. If she could do something to help others avoid going through the loss of their child, sibling, or friend, then something good would've come from his death. That's what she'd convinced herself.

Did she really believe that?

The phone rang in her office. She ran up the stairs, but it'd gone to answerphone before she reached it. She waited for the message.

'*Hello, love. It's your mum.*' Why did she always say that? Connie would obviously know who it was. The moment stretched; her mum silent. Connie shook her head, smiled. She knew her mum was waiting for an answer; she really didn't seem to get the whole answer machine thing. After every sentence, she paused, waiting for Connie to speak, even though she knew she wasn't actually speaking with her daughter.

'*Just been speaking with your dad, he was down this way, did you know?*' The pause was so great this time that Connie thought she must've put the phone down. She tutted, and picked up the receiver.

'Oh, you're there, dear.'

'Yes, sorry about that, Mum, the machine kicked in before I could reach the phone. You were saying, Dad is here?'

'Well, he *was* here. I thought he might've been in contact with you.'

'Nope. Heard nothing from him.' She yanked her hand through her hair, angrily. Typical. Her dad had been in Devon and couldn't be bothered to call her; pay her even a fleeting visit? 'But you said you'd just been speaking to him, and did I know! You clearly knew he hadn't been in contact if you'd been talking to him.' She regretted her harsh tone the second she spoke, but, really, why was she telling her this now?

'Um, well . . . I didn't really ask him. He was telling me all about his new project – he's going to *diversify* apparently – he seemed so excited, had to rush back to Manchester.'

'Right, fine.' Connie wasn't the slightest bit interested in what that meant, exactly. 'No time for his family, then.' Her mum had caught her in just the right mood. She was up for questioning her. 'Anyway, why did Dad run back to Manchester in the first place all those years ago, I thought he was meant to be retiring?'

'Ah. Well, you know your dad. Always wanting to be in the thick of things, this quiet life wasn't for him.'

'He's still working all the hours, then?' Connie's bitterness at her dad for spending more time building his antiques import and export business than sharing time with them wasn't ever far from the surface.

'He's got some new bloke, made him a partner – the idea being he'd take a back seat more, particularly with the foreign deals. He can't let go, though, Connie. Can't bear to hand over full respon-sibility to anyone else. Would've been different if he'd been able to pass the business over to Luke . . .' Connie noted how her mother's voice became hushed when she spoke his name. After a small pause, she continued, 'He said he needs to keep a close eye on things, make sure there are no mistakes. He was always the one to be in control. Certainly won't let go of the reins easily.'

'No,' Connie scoffed, 'they'll have to prise them out of his hands from his grave.'

'Connie!' Her mum's shock travelled through the wire. 'That's a terrible thing to say.'

'Sorry. Was only meaning it would take rather a lot for that. After all, if he couldn't let go for his family . . .' She let the rest of her comment slide. She'd got her point across. It wasn't her mum's fault; she shouldn't be taking it out on her. 'I need to speak to him, actually. What time did he leave?'

'Must have been around ten this morning.'

It would take him about five hours to drive back, give or take. By the time she'd finished for the day he should be back in Manchester, she'd call him.

It was time to confront the past.

CHAPTER THIRTY-SEVEN

DI Wade

'You okay?' Mack kept his eyes on the road as he drove towards the area they were informed the incident had taken place. Numerous 999 calls had been logged from tourists and walkers. This had the makings of a bad day.

Lindsay stared out of the passenger window. The bushes whooshed past a little too quickly, her stomach squirming in response. Together with the heat, the twistiness of the narrow roads and the apprehension of what was to come, she thought she might vomit.

'You're speeding a bit . . . making me feel sick. I should've driven.'

'That's not what I meant.'

She took a deep breath in through her nose. 'I know.' Her voice was almost a whisper. Lindsay cricked her neck, left then right, and repositioned herself to look forward. She had to get it together before they reached the scene. 'I used to love coming to the moors. A shame that doesn't work any more. Me and Dartmoor are no longer good bedfellows.' Her attempt at humour, a defence mechanism at times like these.

'Not all memories are bad ones, though, eh?' Mack gave her

one of his reassuring grins. 'Try and remember the good times you had here, not those to do with work.'

'Tell me that again when we're driving away.'

Their car began a sharp incline. At the top of this hill and round one more bend, the granite rocks of Haytor would come into sight.

A shiver jerked her body. Would she be able to handle this?

Mack looked at her again, his focus removed from ahead.

'Can you watch the road, please?'

'I know it's not much comfort, but at least this is a suicide, not a murder we're going to. This person had a choice.'

'Some would argue that Karen Finch had a choice too, she chose to stab herself moments before her husband killed their daughter's abductor.' The memory of that evening's events was as clear in Lindsay's head now as the day it occurred. Some cases never left you. What a mess that scene on the moors had been. What mess were they about to encounter now? A leap from the highest point of Haytor, crashing into rocks as they fell, would not be a pretty sight.

'There's media everywhere.' Mack's voice low, as Haytor loomed in front of them. There was a helicopter circling, camera crews in the lower car park, police vehicles scattered along the road leading to the tor. Lindsay's eyes flitted from the grey of the tor to the greens and browns of the rolling moorland, trying to take in the whole area of what appeared to be chaos. It wouldn't be, though. Each person there had a role to play; a job to do. Their car was ushered into a space at the bottom of the tor.

'Everyone loves a good suicide.' Lindsay shook her head, questioning the need for so much media interest. It was like a pack of animals skirting around their prey, waiting to pounce and rip it to shreds. She tutted. 'So sad. Bet they didn't envisage their death being such big news.'

Lindsay and Mack approached the police officer at the perimeter of the crime scene tape, gave their names so he could write them on his clipboard. Another uniformed officer called to them.

'Not a nice one, this,' he said.

'Are there ever nice suicides?' Lindsay frowned.

'Brace yourself for this, though, Detective Inspector Wade. It's not exactly your standard suicide.'

Those words hit her in the gut. Hard. She took a deep breath and headed for the white tent.

CHAPTER THIRTY-EIGHT

Connie

After a quick hello cuddle with Amber, Connie headed for the fridge and the cold lager she knew was waiting there. Her skin was clammy after the train journey and then the walk from the station. Or that's what she told herself. Not from the thought of calling her dad. She swigged straight from the bottle, the refreshing liquid hitting just the right spot, then went into the lounge. She stared at the phone for a long while, as though it were a deadly spider she didn't want to take her eyes off in case it moved. Then she picked it up and dialled.

His voice, assured and confident, bellowed in her ear. 'Darling, this *is* a surprise. How are you?'

'Me calling you is a surprise? Wouldn't you class the bigger surprise as you being in Devon but failing to come and see me, Dad?'

'I know how busy you've been, setting up your practice and working long hours.' His reply was quick. Practised? 'Chip off the old block and all that.'

Connie recoiled from the phone. Did he just compare her to him?

'Even so, I thought you'd make some time to squeeze in a visit with your only child.'

'I'm sorry, love.' His tone was lowered. Her comment had caught him. 'Maybe next month, I should be down again then. Couldn't leave Max in charge for too long, so much going on at the moment. Big deals on the horizon.' His deep, strong voice was back. Talking about his precious antiques business did that. Not like talking about his family.

'Anyway, Dad, I need to speak to you.' She wasn't sure how to broach the subject. Straight to the point? Or subtly?

'Sounds important. Do you need some business advice?'

'No. Nothing like that. It's about Luke.'

She heard a sharp intake of breath. Then nothing.

'Dad?'

'Look, darling. I don't really have time to reminisce, although I'd love to . . .'

'Not exactly reminiscing, more a case of you telling me what, exactly, went down that day. And why. I don't think you've been honest with me about it.' Once the words had left her mouth, the rest flowed. Years' worth of words that'd been unspoken, left strangled in her throat, unable to form. She glanced at the clock on the lounge wall. She'd been speaking, without stopping for a response, for several minutes. The release was immense, she felt lighter, almost woozy from the outpouring. The heavy silence at the other end signalled to Connie that the weight that she'd lost had just piled on to her dad. Had she even asked a question in all of that?

'Are you still there, Dad?'

'Yes. Yes, I'm here.' His voice was weak. Even though she'd been doing the talking, she'd drained him. Perhaps it hadn't been such a good idea, doing this over the phone. She needed to see him, his reactions, to fully assess the situation. Maybe this was too much for him all in one go. A release for her, but clearly not for him. She didn't want to give the old bugger a heart attack.

'Sorry. I realise this might feel as though it's all a bit sudden. And I guess it is. Things that have been happening here have brought it all to the forefront. And I realise how much I don't know. About Luke. And about you, Dad.'

'We need to get together, Connie, love. Have a good chat about it.'

'But I need answers now. Things are happening and I need you to help me.'

'What things? What's happening to you?' His words were laced with concern, as though for the first time during the conversation he realised it wasn't merely Connie being dramatic, or acting up. That there was a reason for her sudden outburst.

She paced up and down, the receiver firm to her ear, wondering how much to reveal. With an ongoing police investigation, which she was involved in both personally and professionally, she didn't want to give details that could get her in trouble. Because her dad *would* kick up a fuss and get involved himself, she was certain of that. And how would that affect her mum?

She took a deep breath. 'Things have been shown to me, articles that were written when Luke was killed. But there were also, well, accusations, I suppose, that it wasn't an accident. That Luke was a target.'

'That's nonsense, Connie. Whoever is telling you this?'

'That's just it. I don't know. It's anonymous.'

'Well, there you go, then. If they can't even be open about who they are then they clearly have nothing real to say. It'll be some random idiot who wants to dig up the past.'

'But what for? Why would they want to, and why now?'

'Who knows, darling. I wouldn't worry. There's been nothing more?'

'Well, actually, there was another message left on my counselling page on the internet. It came across as threatening.'

'What! What did it say?' Connie imagined her father getting hot and bothered, loosening his tie, wiping his brow with the back of his hand.

'That you didn't learn the first time.'

143

'Ah, well, it'll be someone I've crossed in business no doubt.' He sounded relieved. 'Don't know why on earth they're involving you. The fact is, Luke was killed because of a football crowd that got out of hand and he got caught in a fight. Bloody hooligans. Hooligans were responsible for his death . . . not me.'

'But how would they even link me with you, Dad? I changed my surname, remember?' Connie's attention was drawn to outside her front window. A dark blue Volvo had pulled up, and a woman was climbing out. She slammed the driver door and stood, hands in her trouser pockets, looking up at the house. Her dad's mumbling became inaudible.

'I've got to go, Dad. Speak later.' Connie brought the conversation to an abrupt end and went to the front door.

CHAPTER THIRTY-NINE

Then

Barton Moss Secure Care Centre, Manchester

Have you seen Mum? How is she? I know she probably hates me as much as you seem to, and obviously I'm not as close to her as you, but I thought she'd come and visit. You know, at least once, even if it was to scream at me, slap me – anything.

I've been dreaming about it. The fire. Every night for the last month, it's been the same dream, over and over. In it, I'm panicking, feeling sick that I can't get to them and help them out of their bedroom. I see them, their faces frozen in horror at what's about to happen. Then Mum gets out, leaving Dad on his own, stuck in the room with a wall of fire between him and the exit. The next thing, I'm stood in the road with you. You're shouting at me: 'It's all your fault. What have you done?' But I don't know what you're talking about, I'm dazed, confused. And even though it's just a dream, I can feel the heat from the fire. And I can feel the hatred. It's oozing from the house. From you. And me.

Each time I wake, I'm left with a taste in my mouth, like burnt charcoal from one of Dad's rubbish barbeques. I actually taste it; it stays on my tongue until the rank breakfast replaces it.

But no matter what I eat, there's still a horrible taste that stays with me. It's hate. And nothing seems to get rid of that.

CHAPTER FORTY

Connie

'What is it? What's the matter? Why are you here, at my house?' Connie greeted DI Wade before she'd made it through the gate. Lindsay's face – stern due to her hard jawline and grooves in her forever-frowning forehead – was ashen.

'Can I come inside, Connie?'

She was on her own. No sidekick today. Connie dropped back to allow her to pass into the hallway.

'Sorry to come to your home, but I know you're not happy about us coming to your office . . .'

'Well, that's mainly because of my clients, well, one of them anyway. It puts her on edge—' Something about Lindsay's expression stopped her. 'No matter, come on in.'

They stood, until Lindsay suggested she should sit. Connie's stomach fluttered, her heartbeat banging in her ears. What was this about?

'I'm really sorry, Connie.'

Connie swallowed hard. This moment – the feeling that was creeping inside her like death spreading its poison through her veins – sent her right back to the time she was told about Luke. Bile burned the back of her throat. What could possibly be coming?

'Why are you sorry – what's happened?'

'There's no easy way of saying this,' Lindsay sighed and put on a thin, sympathetic smile. 'I'm afraid we've just come from Haytor, on Dartmoor . . . where there's been a suicide.'

Connie shook her head. 'I'm sorry, that's terrible – they jumped?'

'I'm afraid so.'

Lindsay's usual sharp tone was replaced with a softer one. Was this her 'bad news' voice? There was something more to come; Connie could sense it.

'Why are you here, telling me this?' Her throat tightened as she spoke the words.

Lindsay's chest rose as she inhaled deeply. 'She was one of your clients.' She looked down briefly at her hands before re-establishing eye contact again. 'It's Stephanie Cousins.'

There was a bang deep in Connie's chest, like an explosion that sent shrapnel tearing into her organs. The room wobbled as tears flooded her vision. She could hear the words, *Oh my God, Oh my God*, over and over. Her voice. Lindsay's arm was around her, she had a vague sensation of its weight on her shoulder.

'Connie, Connie! Take some deep breaths.'

She did as she was instructed until she regained her natural breathing pattern.

'I don't understand. Why would she? She wouldn't, she just wouldn't. Where was she? I only saw her this morning! Oh, no. No. Where was her son? Where was Dylan?'

'You really need to try and remain calm, please, Connie.'

'But she wouldn't kill herself, she wouldn't leave Dylan.'

Lindsay removed her arm from Connie's shoulder and instead took both of her hands, gripping them tightly. 'She didn't leave him, Connie. I'm so sorry – she took him with her.'

Connie pulled her hands away, jumping up from the sofa. *No, no way. This isn't true.*

'I'll make some tea,' Lindsay said before disappearing into the kitchen, leaving Connie in stunned silence.

'It doesn't make sense. We spoke this morning.' Connie's hands burned, pins and needles pricking her palms where she'd held the hot mug of tea for far too long.

'What time did she leave you?' Lindsay opened her pocketbook, her pen poised ready to write.

Connie leant forward to place the mug on the coffee table. She stared at her hands, bright red from the heat, and rubbed them together. There was no feeling in them.

'She was late arriving, so she didn't stay for the full hour. By the time we'd finished I'd say it must've been about quarter to eleven? Give or take five minutes.'

'Did she mention anything about where she was going after?'

'No. She had Dylan with her, I assumed she'd be going back home.' She bit at the edge of her thumbnail. 'But I did see them at the pirate ship yesterday, the one by the river in Totnes. It might be somewhere they go regularly; she may have gone there afterwards.' The memory of the unknown man surfaced. Had he been selling Steph drugs? Or had he been harassing her? Had he been the catalyst for her actions?

'Okay, thanks. Is there anything else you remember her saying, any hint at her state of mind?'

Where should she start? How much was relevant? Connie didn't want to betray Steph's confidentiality, despite her being dead. *Dead.* Connie sighed. How hadn't she seen this coming? What kind of counsellor missed something this huge? Perhaps she hadn't, though. Was DI Wade absolutely sure it was suicide? Was she even sure it was Stephanie and Dylan?

'How do you know it was Steph, anyway? And that she was my client?'

'She had some ID on her, and one of the local officers recognised

149

her name. We made the link to you once we found out she was in the protected persons scheme.'

'Have you spoken to Miles Prescott, her handler, then?'

'We spoke briefly on the phone to confirm our suspicions as far as we could at that point. He'll do the formal identification, I'm sure . . . but I wanted to see you first, before you heard anything on the news.'

'Oh.' Connie slumped. It sounded definite – it was Steph. An icy sensation snaked through her veins. And she'd killed Dylan. Her mind attempted to grasp this, but failed. She shook her head, trying to disperse the image of his little face. What'd Steph been thinking?

Lindsay cleared her throat. 'Sorry, but to get back to my question . . . her state of mind when you talked to her?'

'Well, it's difficult to say. She'd been afraid of being found by her brother, and when I saw her and Dylan at the pirate ship there was a weird bloke hanging around there. She'd seemed alarmed, took hold of Dylan and hurried away. I think there was more to that encounter than she let on to me during our session. And then there were the inconsistencies between what Steph had told me and what was in the file Miles Prescott had given me. I mean, it might not have been suicide, Lindsay.' Connie's thoughts were coming fast, and disjointed – the likelihood Steph had taken her own and her son's life didn't sit well at all.

Lindsay nodded silently as she made notes in her pocketbook, the scrape of the pen on the paper the only sound. Then she looked up at Connie and spoke slowly, as if she was talking to a child.

'People saw her, not long before – no one saw anyone else with her, apart from Dylan. There was no evidence at the scene that suggested anything other than suicide.'

'How long is *not long before*?'

'We had sightings reported about fifteen minutes before they were found at the bottom of the tor.'

Connie buried her head in her hands: the vision of Steph and Dylan, broken at the foot of Haytor, too much.

'We can look into the guy at the pirate ship, though. Hopefully there's some CCTV that covers that area,' Lindsay continued.

'Well, it's near the café too, so there must be something,' Connie said, her voice flat.

'Would you recognise him again?'

'No. Probably not – I was on the other side of the river, he had a hoody on. I might be able to rule out people though. But why are you bothering if you are sure it was a suicide?'

'We want to retrace her last steps; he might be useful. We're putting out an appeal as well.'

'Oh.' Connie's head snapped up. 'Is that a good idea, her identity is meant to be protected.' She heard the panic in her own voice.

'No reason to protect her now.'

Connie recoiled. 'Christ. Just like that, her life now means nothing. No need to protect her.'

'Sorry, it sounds harsh, but it's the reality. Our job is to put together the pieces of the last moments of their lives. Ultimately, Stephanie Cousins committed murder. She has family that will want answers.'

'Really? What bloody family?' A heat blazed at her cheeks. 'Not one of them was bothered about her as far as I know – her mother has dementia, her dad is dead, or missing depending on who you believe, she has a good-for-nothing uncle, and her brother, well, according to Steph, he was in prison until recently. If he exists at all. Why will they ask questions?' She stared, wide-eyed, at Lindsay, not realising until this moment how messed up Steph's situation had been – and how little she, Connie, had actually managed to piece together.

'They still need to be informed, Connie. Stephanie's new identity was to protect her from her ex-boyfriend and the gang members she gave evidence against. I know that meant no contact with her family either, and they weren't privy to her new name or location, but now, given the circumstances, they need to know what's happened.'

'Well, good luck – it'll be interesting to see who you actually find to tell!' Connie got up and paced the lounge, her arms rigid at her sides, fists balled. 'There's got to be more to this. It doesn't feel right.'

'You're in shock, Connie. You need time for this to register. I know this is a difficult situation, and you've had a lot to deal with this week.' Lindsay offered a sympathetic smile as she stood.

'Yes, it seems I have.'

'Can I call anyone for you?' Her question seemed an afterthought, one she quickly added before heading out the front door.

Connie huffed. 'No. I'm fine, thanks.'

She was far from fine, but who would she call anyway? She had to be on her own to get her head around this; to figure out why Steph would've taken such drastic action so soon after their session. It wasn't how it was meant to be. They were working together, to create a new life for her and Dylan. Connie had listened, believed in her – attempted to dig deep to get to the cause of her fears. She'd thought they were getting somewhere.

Clearly Steph hadn't.

And poor little Dylan – totally innocent in this – his future now stolen. A heavy sadness settled in her stomach as the vision of his blond curls, his small, four-year-old body forced itself into her mind's eye again. His life had been cruelly, needlessly, snuffed out.

She rested her head against the closed door, her eyelids shut tight. The house, silent. She'd told Steph just before she'd left her office that morning: 'We'll get there.' Steph's last words now shot into her mind, loud; accusatory:

'I hope so, Connie. I really hope you're right *this* time.'

How could she have been so wrong?

CHAPTER FORTY-ONE

It won't be easy, but I have back-up. Course, getting the right ones onside, that was a challenge in itself. In here, you know everyone is dodgy; choosing those to trust is a real art form. I got used to reading the signs, though. Sussing out who the grasses were, the arse-lickers, the weak, the lost. Some of the lost ones are the best. They're dying just to have purpose, eager to please – be with the crowd that'll keep 'em safe.

I found the right one. Or he found me. Bloody spot-on – fell right in my lap. Sometimes, things are meant to be. Being celled up with him was like a gift from God. Not that I believe in God. How could I? But something, some 'force', is obviously on my side.

We've got links. Things in common.

I didn't let him know that, though. I need him to think I'm doing it all for him, that's one of the most important parts of the plan. He's more use to me if he's kept in the dark about my real reasons. Besides, I'll be making sure he gets what he wants from this.

He just won't know he's going to be complicit in murder too.

The staff, well, they took the longest. Trial and error – spent some time down the block, got a few adjudications in the process. But it was worth it.

I've chosen well I reckon.

You'd be proud.

CHAPTER FORTY-TWO

Connie

The house was so silent that she could hear her pulse in her ears. Like putting a shell to your ear and hearing the sea; a gentle whooshing and the feeling of calm. Only she wasn't calm. Her emotions were in turmoil: the past and the present colliding at high speed within her. Her mind couldn't separate the events, they fought for attention, getting more and more jumbled. A guilt-ridden mess. Hargreaves. Katie. Steph. The list seemed like one long list of cock-ups, which were her fault. Add into the mix the resurfacing of Luke's death, and the anxiety-fest was complete.

Connie's fingers were tapping out a text before she'd consciously decided she wanted company. When DI Wade had been in her lounge earlier, she'd had a strong urge to ask her to stay. Share a bottle of wine; chat about something mundane. She gave a burst of laughter, cracking the silence open. No, it seemed unlikely that Lindsay Wade would be the type to converse over a glass of wine. She always appeared so uptight – and whilst that *might* be her professional demeanour, Connie thought it was a strong possibility she was like that twenty-four/seven. As she waited for a reply from Niall, she allowed her mind to wander – to imagine what Lindsay's life was like outside of the police force. If she even *had* a life outside it. Was she married? She hadn't noticed a ring. Did she have children? She doubted that, somehow.

Her phone pinged.

I can get to you for 8. N x

She placed the phone on the coffee table and went to the kitchen, throwing the fridge door open so wide it hit the wall. The light illuminated a pot of yogurt, an out-of-date pack of pasties and, on its side on the middle shelf – the last lager. That was it. She blew out a large breath of air. When was the last time she'd done a proper shop? Connie snatched the bottle of lager, then closed the fridge. She wasn't hungry anyway. The drink would be enough. After flipping the lid off the bottle, she went back to the lounge, and sitting on the edge of the sofa, took two big swigs. Immediately, her head felt woozy, replacing the ache that had been there permanently since Lindsay had given her the news.

Woozy was good. Better.

She got her phone and sent another message to Niall.

On your way over can you pop into shop and pick up wine – and lager for yourself, ta x

Connie sent it. Then quickly wrote another:

PS You might want to grab some pizzas too, unless you've already eaten. x

*

At the sound of the doorbell, Connie jumped up, lager still in hand, and let Niall in. She drained the bottle as she walked into the lounge, then turned to him.

156

'You managed to get some supplies, then?' She motioned to the Sainsbury's bags in his hands.

'Yep, sounded as though you were running low on food, so I thought I'd get you stocked up,' he said as he headed to the kitchen.

Connie frowned. She'd only asked for pizzas and drink – not a whole week's worth of food. Why was he being this nice? It wasn't like he'd ever done her shopping before. She let it go. No doubt she'd find out later if he had an ulterior motive for his thoughtfulness.

'You remembered the wine, didn't you?'

Niall put the bags on the worktop and withdrew a bottle of white wine, then turned to Connie.

'Yes . . . but, do you think it's a good idea to drink—'

Connie pulled the wine from his grip without speaking. Why would he say that? He'd never questioned her before, why the hell would he now?

'Right. Okay, then.' Niall raised his eyebrows, but made no further comment about it. 'Bad day?'

'You could say that.' Connie rolled her head, trying to release the tension in her neck. After opening the bottle and pouring the wine, she settled on the sofa next to him. What started as a brief few sentences, her intention to summarise as quickly as possible and without detail, turned into an hour-long, in-depth breakdown of Steph and Dylan's story. Their deaths.

By the time she'd finished speaking, she'd also finished the wine.

The room was quiet. Connie was aware of Niall's hand lying lightly on her thigh, where he'd placed it in a comforting way while she'd been spilling her guts. Now, as he kept eye contact with her, he shifted it higher. Connie felt the warmth of his hand spread until it was between her legs. He waited, still staring into her eyes. He was waiting for the sign.

She gave it.

CHAPTER FORTY-THREE

DI Wade

Wednesday 14 June

It had come as a shock to Lindsay. She'd fully expected the suicide site to have a major impact on her, given the child, and the fact it was Dartmoor again. But she hadn't anticipated the emotional aftermath of her visit to Connie Summers' house. She'd delivered bad news before, and whilst she dreaded that part of her role, she always carried it out with professionalism and what she hoped was sensitivity. And afterwards, she usually came away feeling confident that she'd fulfilled her role to the best of her ability. Somehow, yesterday's experience had been different. It'd played on her mind all night; keeping her awake until the early hours. She'd felt redundant, useless, watching Connie's reaction, like she was merely on the sidelines watching a bad football game.

Connie had taken it badly. The very fact that Lindsay knew she'd already had a lot to deal with lately made it all the more difficult to offer the right level of comfort. Stephanie Cousins had been Connie's client, but Lindsay sensed that she'd felt more responsible for the young woman than was usual from a therapist–client relationship. She wondered if it was to do with the guilt from Hargreaves leaving the prison and attacking Katie. Whatever it was, Lindsay couldn't shake the uneasy feeling she had right now, as she sat in the car waiting for Mack to stop chatting to the officers at the police station entrance and get in. Connie's pale, waxy face would not shift from her mind. She'd left her too quickly. She should have stayed with her longer, talked through her concerns. And now, Lindsay was going to make matters even worse for her.

Lindsay reached across and slammed the heel of her hand on the centre of the steering wheel. The resulting blare had the desired effect. Mack spun around, his shocked expression turning to one of irritation: his eyes narrowing and forehead crinkling. He muttered something then slowly walked towards the car.

'Wow, someone's patient today,' he said as he folded his legs into the footwell of the driver's side.

'Wasting police time is an offence, you know.' Lindsay settled back in the passenger seat and drew the seatbelt sharply across her, clunking it in its holder with a heavy hand. Mack gave her a sideways glance and started the car.

'You going to tell me what's got your goat, then?' he asked, face forward as he drove out of the station car park.

'We need to go and see Connie Summers.'

'Oh? I thought you'd already done the deed?'

'I did, yes. I also told her that Miles Prescott would be making the formal identification of the bodies.'

'And?'

'Well, now he's not. Apparently he's stuck in Manchester and won't be back until the weekend. So . . .' Lindsay sighed, and ran her hands through her hair. 'We're going to have to ask the only other person who knew Stephanie Cousins and her son well enough.'

An awkward silence fell between them.

CHAPTER FORTY-FOUR

Connie

Miles Prescott was busy. Busy avoiding Connie's calls. She'd spoken to his colleagues four times since the news about Steph's death yesterday and none of those times had yielded any information. They weren't interested. She'd asked them to make sure he called her as soon as he was less busy, but she had the distinct feeling she'd be giving him another ring later. She wouldn't let him ignore her forever.

It'd been the longest day. Connie stretched back in her chair, clicked her neck. Thank God it was almost over, no more struggling through sessions. The memory of last night flashed in her mind. Was she wrong to have sought comfort in the arms of someone who'd abandoned her when she'd needed him most? Niall hadn't asked questions, and she'd been grateful for that. But when he'd left early that morning, he'd given her a quick kiss on the top of her head and left without conversation. It'd left her feeling empty. A moment of passion turned sour by a sheepish parting. Not how Connie had wanted to feel after giving herself to him. Again. Maybe it'd served its purpose, but something inside, a desire for something *more*, niggled at her and left her cold when he left. She realised now that she had wanted him to comfort her and talk things through. Had needed to share how she felt about everything going on. Wanted someone to make her feel loved.

She fiddled with the notes on her desk, shuffling them from one side to the other. The piece of paper underneath some session notes revealed itself. It was the code that Mack had shown her. The one she was meant to be deciphering to impress him.

Was that what she was trying to do? Impress Mack? She shook the thought away. Holding the paper in her hand, she sat back and studied the letters and numbers. *Come on, come on – what are you? What do you mean?* Her brain ached, she was trying too hard – looking for some complicated pattern. A cipher?

She pushed the paper away from her. Perhaps if she did something else, her brain would subconsciously work it out. Although that hadn't worked so far. Leaning forwards, Connie grabbed it again and opened the bottom drawer of her desk, ready to shove it into the darkness. A noise caught her off guard. The rolling of crayons. Connie's eyes blurred as she watched the gentle rocking motion of the coloured wax sticks. Her stomach pitched. Poor Dylan. She carefully pulled at the picture that lay beneath them. She swallowed hard, the lump in her throat feeling huge. Staring at the roughly drawn scene, Connie's heart thudded. Bless him. Blinking away the tears, she saw that there were three stick figures with big round heads. The one on the left had long hair, wide eyes and a big red smiling mouth. Steph. And she was holding the hand of the small figure, presumably Dylan. He too had big wide eyes, but he didn't have a mouth, the area where it should be left blank. But it was the figure standing to his other side that caused Connie's mouth to dry. The tall one. A man? This figure was entirely void of facial features. Dylan had instead filled in the large circle of his head with heavy scribbles of black crayon. Connie lowered the drawing and sat back. Not the usual picture for a four-year-old to draw. This would be creepy enough in usual circumstances, but now, given that Steph and Dylan were dead – from apparent suicide – this was straight-up unnerving. Why had Dylan drawn a picture like this? What could it mean?

Connie cradled her face in her hands. Who was the blacked-out figure? And what if this was not from Dylan's imagination? This stick man could be who Steph had been afraid of. She shuddered.

Brett.

The past sessions with Steph flew through her mind. She had never come across to Connie as being at danger of harming herself or Dylan. She just couldn't believe that Steph had committed suicide and killed her son in the process. Dylan was everything to Steph. She would've tried other options before taking such a devastating step, and even *if* suicide had crossed her mind, she would've spoken to Connie first. Wouldn't she? Even if she hadn't spoken about thoughts of ending it all, Connie would've sensed her mood shifting; picked up on the signs. And surely, if she'd been that scared, she would've been more forceful about getting Miles to relocate her.

Unless Connie had somehow missed the signals; misread her behaviour?

No, no, no!

She refused to believe that.

The sick, shaky sensation in her stomach told Connie that she didn't believe it was suicide at all.

Her gut was telling her that Steph and Dylan must've been pushed.

CHAPTER FORTY-FIVE

Then

He flicked the lighter and stared at the dancing flame.

He could hear them; they thought he was asleep, but he wasn't. It was 2.20 a.m. and he was wide awake, full of rage.

They hated him. That's what *she'd* said once before.

We need to do something; he's got out of hand.

The voices downstairs were muffled, but he knew the man and woman were talking about him. His own dad, *her*, how could they? She'd never wanted him; he just came as a package. It'd been clear from the beginning she only wanted half of it. And now he was causing problems. The school had expelled him – he was a nuisance.

A freak.

Perhaps he could bring them back together; be a real family. Make them love him.

His breaths were rapid as he bundled together the paper, screwing the pieces up into tight balls. Sitting on his bed, his back against the wall, he threw each ball in the direction of the waste-paper basket in the corner of his bedroom. They'd removed it once. But he'd found it, *and* the lighter. They were stupid if they thought he wouldn't look in the shed. That's where they always went for a fag. It was the most obvious place.

His stomach tensed. Why didn't she want him? Why couldn't she love him like she loved his dad? Because *she* hated him, he felt sure his dad was beginning to as well. He'd do anything to keep her happy. He was losing his dad to *her*.

He propelled himself off the bed and thrust his hand into the bin. He flicked the lighter again and again, touching it against each of the paper balls. The flame caught, and grew until the entire contents were engulfed with the bright orange glow.

He smiled as the heat reached his face.

And his heart rate reduced, along with the knot of anger in his stomach.

Fire always calmed him.

CHAPTER FORTY-SIX

Connie

The buzzer made her jump. Connie dropped the picture and reached across to the intercom.

'Hello?'

'Hi, Connie, it's Lindsay and Mack, can we have a moment of your time?'

Connie's head dropped. She hesitated, then pressed the button to release the door. The sound of their heavy footsteps on the stairs raised her heart rate. She rushed to the door, flinging it open just as they reached it.

'Glad you're here—'

'That makes a change,' Mack said, a frown creasing his forehead.

'Well, it's not an issue *now*, is it?' Connie couldn't hide the sarcasm in her voice.

Lindsay had placed her hand on Mack's arm; a warning to proceed with care?

'I'm afraid we need to ask something of you . . .' Lindsay looked reluctant, her body language closed.

What do they want now?

Fearing she was going to be asked something she might not like, Connie shot to her desk, picked up the crayon picture and thrust it in front of Lindsay.

'What do you make of that?'

'Er . . .' Lindsay gave Mack a sideways glance.

Connie could taste the tension. They wanted to talk to her, and she was making it awkward for them. So what? This was important.

'It was drawn by Dylan. Tuesday morning.' Connie raised her eyebrows, hopeful Lindsay would see it the way she had.

'Kids draw some weird things, don't they?' Lindsay passed it back to Connie. 'Look, Connie, I'm so sorry to have to ask you—'

'Don't you *see*?' Connie couldn't believe Lindsay was so dismissive of this possible evidence. 'Look at the figure he's drawn next to him, how he's blackened out the face with scribbles.' She held the picture towards her again, but when Lindsay didn't take it, she pushed it into Mack's hands instead. 'That's not right, is it? That figure has to be who Steph was afraid of.'

Mack smiled thinly, and took the picture. After studying it for a few seconds he lowered it, and made eye contact with Connie.

'We'll take it, it might be useful, thank you.'

Connie narrowed her eyes. Was he trying to placate her? Would they do anything with it, or just bury it in a file somewhere? Before she could question him, Lindsay spoke again, her voice loud, direct. She clearly didn't want to be interrupted again.

'Miles Prescott has been unable to confirm the identities of our suicide victims. You're currently the only other person who knew Stephanie and Dylan well . . .'

'Really? Are you kidding me? *Why* hasn't Miles been able to?' Connie felt her pulse bang in her neck. She moved around the desk, sitting heavily in her chair.

'He's away in Manchester on police business and won't be back until after the weekend. It's important we don't wait any longer for the official ID to be made,' Mack informed her.

That would explain why he hadn't returned Connie's calls. It would have been easy enough for his colleagues to tell her he was away, though. Unless he didn't want people to know. Manchester. Could he be looking into Brett's whereabouts? Perhaps he'd taken Steph and her concerns seriously after all.

'Right. Well. I guess I don't have a choice, then. Do I?' Connie directed this to Mack. He shrugged his shoulders.

'We could drive you now, if that's convenient.' Lindsay shifted her weight from one leg to the other, watching her, waiting for her to answer. To say it was fine.

Connie's head was heavy. It wasn't fine. Nothing about this situation was fine. The thought of seeing Steph and Dylan's lifeless bodies was too awful. This wasn't how she'd envisaged her day ending. All she wanted was to get home to Amber and have a long soak in the bath.

But, on the other hand, Connie couldn't bear to think of Steph and little Dylan, cold and alone, waiting for someone to identify them. She ran her hands through her hair and groaned.

'Okay. I'll do it. Let's go.' Connie bolted up from the chair so quickly that she felt dizzy.

'Thank you. We greatly appreciate you doing this, I realise it won't be easy.' Lindsay offered a steadying hand to Connie.

'No. It won't be. Not at all.'

The three of them left the office, Connie trailing behind Lindsay and Mack down the stairs. When they reached the front door of the building, Mack stooped to pick up some post. He held it out to Connie, and she threw it on to the tub chair. She'd deal with that tomorrow. Her mind was on the scene she was about to be subjected to. She'd never even seen a dead body before. Her dad had categorically refused to let her see Luke; she'd been too young, he'd said; her memories of him should be when he was vibrant and full of life. Not as he was on the cold slab. He'd said something similar to her mum. Connie remembered her putting up a fight; she'd wanted closure, felt the only way to get that was to see her son. But in the end her dad had succeeded in convincing her that she would regret it. It was just a shell. Luke was gone.

It looked as though her memories of Steph and Dylan were not going to enjoy the same protection.

CHAPTER FORTY-SEVEN

Connie

To distract herself from the task ahead, Connie bombarded Lindsay and Mack with questions during the car journey to the hospital morgue. But it wasn't just distraction. She needed to know more.

'Have you looked in her house – found anything suspicious?' She leant forward from the back, pushing her upper body between the front seats, looking from Mack to Lindsay.

'Can you put your seatbelt on please, Connie?' Lindsay took her eyes off the road ahead and shot Connie a harsh look.

She shuffled back and clunked in her belt.

'Well, have you? Was there anything on her answer machine, because she said she'd been getting weird calls?'

Lindsay shook her head – it was minimal, but Connie noticed. Why weren't they answering her questions? They wanted her opinion before. Now, suddenly, they weren't interested.

'The usual lines of enquiry have been completed, Connie, and no – there was nothing suspicious in her house, and as far as I'm aware, no strange messages on her answerphone.'

'As far as you're *aware*? So, you didn't check personally?'

Mack turned his head sharply to look back at her. 'Really. Everything has been covered, we promise. I realise you want this *not* to be suicide. But it is what it is. Sorry.' He turned back, his eyes darting to Lindsay before looking straight ahead.

Connie slumped in her seat. Had they missed something crucial because they had been searching the house for a suicide note, not clues, anything untoward? Their focus was too narrow. They'd made up their mind it was suicide and weren't seeing anything further. If there had been letters from Brett, they could have been removed prior to Steph's death. Had Brett been in and covered his tracks?

'Did you find a suicide note?' If Brett had wanted it to look like she'd killed herself, he would've made her write a note. Connie waited for an answer. None came. They hadn't heard her. 'I said,' she spoke loudly, 'did you find a suicide note?'

'My God, woman – you're like a dog with a bone, aren't you?' Mack's voice boomed in the confined space of the car. Connie reeled. She heard Lindsay chastise him.

'Sorry. I'm only trying to get to the bottom of it. I really do think someone else was involved,' Connie said, her voice quiet; wounded by his outburst.

'No, I'm sorry,' Mack said more softly. 'I know this is a difficult time for you, and as you've worked so closely with her it must be hard to fathom her reasoning. But, as far as our investigation goes, we've not uncovered a single thing to suggest anything other than plain old suicide.'

Connie smarted. 'Plain old suicide'. There was nothing plain about someone taking their life. There was also nothing plain about murder. Which she was sure this was. Perhaps she'd be better off talking to Lindsay alone. Mack clearly had no patience for her. It was as if she'd done something very wrong, and he was punishing her for it. Only, she had no clue what her offence had been. Her mind flipped back to some of the occasions she'd worked for the police as an independent psychologist. Had they crossed paths? Perhaps she'd offended him in a professional capacity at some point. If that was the case, then why didn't he spit it out, they could move on then. Maybe he wanted to play the game, get her to mention whatever it was first. Well, he was in for a long wait, because apart from a niggling memory she couldn't retrieve, the source of his inconsistent behaviour towards her was a mystery.

The tension was palpable by the time the car parked up, just outside the outpatients' department of Torbay Hospital. Connie's palms were slippery with sweat, as a result of the awkward journey in the car, or the impending identification process, she didn't know. How did it even work? She stayed immobile in the back seat, as the anxious grip that used to haunt her took hold once again.

As if reading her thoughts, Lindsay approached Connie's side of the car and opened the door. Crouching down to her level, she placed a reassuring hand on her arm.

'It'll be quick. The bodies are ready to be viewed. It's a case of going in the room, looking at each face in turn, and making a positive identification. Then we'll be out of there. Okay?'

Connie felt sick. And that was before seeing them. She sucked in a large gulp of air, and got out of the car.

'Let's get this over with,' she said as she fell in step with Lindsay.

It was bright – too bright; the false strip lighting harsh and unforgiving.

Each mark, every blemish and dark bruise was stark against the waxy skin of the young woman's lifeless face. Connie's legs shook, her stomach turning over as she stood, staring, unable to tear her eyes away. Her head was light, then heavy; a shadow moved across her vision, like a curtain drawing. She was going to faint.

Arms grasped her from behind. 'You want to sit down?' Mack held her up, and then made to move her towards the chair.

'No. No, I'll be fine,' Connie said, shaking his arms from her. 'It's just the shock, that's all.' It wasn't just shock, though. It was horror. And there was worse still to come. The motionless, smaller body lay on the gurney next to the woman. Connie closed her eyes, an attempt to put off the inevitable for a moment longer. She took slow, deep breaths. The smell, a mix of clinical products with what she guessed was the stale odour of death, overpowered her nostrils, and her stomach churned.

'Breathe through your mouth, not your nose,' the man's voice told her. She was afraid she'd taste it if she did that, but she did as instructed. When she was confident she wasn't going to faint, or throw up – and without Mack's aid – she moved around the metal gurney to reach the second body.

Tears pricked like tiny needles, her breathing shallowed.

The boy's pale white face, his misshapen head with his blond hair, dirty and matted with blood, was the last image she saw before she fell and hit the rough, grey floor of the mortuary.

'Drink, come on – take bigger sips,' Lindsay encouraged with her sharp tone and a gentle push.

Connie held the tea between her shaking hands, the hot liquid sloshing in the plastic cup. She lifted it slowly to her mouth and drank. It was sweet – they must've put at least three sugars in. Her mum had always advocated tea with lots of sugar as a counter for shock, too. Connie recalled the time she'd been ironing her dolls' clothes one day, her mum close by, keeping a watchful eye – when there was a loud bang. The iron had, in Connie's mind, blown up and she'd dropped it and ran screaming from the room. Her mum had sat her down, given her a mug of tea. Connie had gagged on the syrup-sweet drink, but her mum had insisted she finish it. *It'll help the shock.* Was that a real thing? Or just a very British thing: tea and sympathy. Had Lindsay's mum told her the same?

'I have to ask,' Lindsay said, her arm on Connie's, 'can you confirm the identities of the bodies for me, please?'

Connie winced at the words. *The bodies.* No longer people, just husks – like her dad had said about Luke.

'I can confirm the woman is Stephanie Cousins, previously known as Jenna Ellison. And the boy is Dylan Cousins, previously Dylan Ellison.' The words had a robotic quality to them. Her emotions were drained; the official identification was complete. Her memory now stained with the sight of her dead client and her son.

'Thank you.'

'Where's Mack?' Connie asked, looking around.

'He had to take an important call. Look, I know this was an awful thing for you to have to do. Trust me, if there'd been anyone else . . .'

'I know.' Connie mustered a smile. 'I didn't think you'd find any capable family member. I haven't experienced anything like that before, that's all, and seeing them both, like that.' Tears sprung again, this time she couldn't hold them back. 'I so wanted to help her, you know? Achieve a new life. That was the aim. Not to have it ended.' Lindsay's arm tightened around Connie's shoulders and she felt a squeeze.

'I'm sure you did your best for her. You can't save everyone.'

Connie's eyes widened, her head snapped around to face Lindsay's. 'I clearly can't save *anyone*, though, can I?' She hung her head again, staring at the tea. 'All I manage to do is mess up lives.'

'That's not true.' Lindsay straightened, her posture official again.

'The evidence is stacking up against me,' Connie said bluntly. Bad things happened around her. She was the common denominator – how could she not be to blame in some way? She was jinxed.

The double doors to the room swung open. Mack reappeared, his cheeks flushed red.

'We need to get back to the station,' he said as he approached Lindsay.

'Oh? We had a break?' Lindsay was off, heading for the exit

173

before realising that Connie was still sat, recovering. She swung back to face Connie. 'We'll have to get you home, quickly, sorry to rush you, but—'

'Sure. No problem.' Connie stood, wavered for a moment, and then steadied herself.

'Are you going to be okay? Can I call anyone for you, so that you're not on your own at home?' Lindsay said.

Connie snorted. 'Nope. I'll be good, there's not really anyone I want with me.'

'Oh, that reminds me.' Mack, still flushed, stood aside as he held the door open. 'We need that list from you, like ASAP, please.'

Connie noted that Lindsay's mouth fell open. She'd obviously had the same thought Connie had. Not the most appropriate time to drop that in. She blew out her cheeks.

'I haven't forgotten. I can email it through to the station later if you want it that desperately.' She hoped he caught the terse edge to her voice.

'Great. Thanks. Right, let's get you home.'

Connie followed, the sense of dread rising like a tidal wave in her stomach. Immediately after taking a call, Mack was asking for her list of people – men – that she'd had, or did have, contact with.

What was going on?

CHAPTER FORTY-EIGHT

DI Wade

Lindsay felt uncomfortable knowing she was dropping Connie home to an empty house. After what was clearly a traumatic experience for her, she really should have company. It was the second time Lindsay had felt wrong leaving her. What was that about? Why had Connie affected her so strongly? Was it that she saw similarities between them, related to their circumstances? Single woman, living on her own, successful – to a degree – yet with a black mark against her for a past poor judgement call, one which had caused others to question her ability, her skills as a professional.

Lindsay had fought hard against the backlash from her first murder case she'd been on as a DI. Her own judgement had been lacking, and as a direct result of that, a woman had died and a man had been murdered. A family had been left broken. For Connie, her apparently poor decision had resulted in a dangerous man being released from prison and a woman being attacked, raped in broad daylight, metres from her home. Then the man responsible had been murdered. Lindsay felt for Connie, though. As professional women who fought to gain their position in their chosen jobs, they should stick together – not every decision was necessarily going to be the right one; life wasn't as simple as that.

But now, as they drove away from Connie's house and Mack

relayed the phone conversation he'd had whilst they were at the morgue, Lindsay wondered if, yet again, her judgement had been off. Were her personal feelings causing her to narrow her focus?

There was clearly more to Connie Summers than she'd considered.

'Okay, guys! Some hush, please.' Lindsay perched on the edge of the melamine desk, scanning the room of officers. Everyone stopped talking and faced her.

'We have positive IDs on both bodies from Tuesday's suspected suicide. It's now confirmed, they are Stephanie Cousins and her four-year-old son, Dylan. We have no reason to believe the incident is suspicious or that anyone else is involved. I've prepared a report for the coroner and the post-mortems will be carried out now they have been identified. We expect the findings to be suicide for Stephanie and unlawful killing for Dylan.'

The room was silent. When a child was involved, especially in circumstances such as this, the mood of the team was often heavy. A number of the officers had children themselves.

'Moving on.' Lindsay lifted the briefing sheet from her lap, desperate to also lift the atmosphere. 'We've had a delivery.' She paused, looking out at the expectant faces. 'An anonymous envelope was left at reception.' A low mumble broke out. Lindsay could feel their excitement. The photos contained within the envelope were significant to the Hargreaves murder case. The officer who'd been in receipt of them had been extremely hyper when he'd called Mack to inform him of the latest development.

But Lindsay didn't share that excitement. As far as she was concerned, this was going to cause added grief, and it gave her an unpleasant taste in her mouth. As much as she wanted to stretch this out, prevent the disclosure for longer, she knew she had to update the team. The officers shuffled, muttering to each other, and Lindsay heard some tutting. She couldn't put it off any longer.

Putting on latex gloves, Lindsay reached for the evidence bag which lay on the desk beside her, and slowly retrieved a large A4 brown envelope. She was aware of how still the room had become. From the envelope she pulled a photograph: one of the two that had been included – she was holding the other one back, for now. She sighed, holding it up so everyone could see it. There was an outbreak of whispers, then louder comments.

'We don't know who took it.' Lindsay raised her voice above the others. 'But you might recognise one of the people in the photo.'

'It's Connie Summers,' Clarke said.

'Yes,' Lindsay tried to keep the disappointment from her voice, 'and the person she's with is ex-prisoner, Trevor Jones.'

'What's the significance, Boss?'

Lindsay stood, photo still in one hand. 'The photo is date-stamped 6th June, so the day after the body dump. And see here?' She pointed with a gloved finger at Connie's hand. 'She appears to have been handed something by Jones. She seems to be attempting to conceal it. But, whether she is or isn't taking something from him, our initial concern is,' she glanced over at Mack, 'that, despite having left the prison service, it's clear that Connie Summers is associating with ex-prisoners. And the burning question is, why would she be doing that?'

CHAPTER FORTY-NINE

He was always the one that everyone looked up to. When he spoke, everyone listened. You didn't mess with my old man. If you were brave enough, or, as he'd say, stupid enough to cross him, then look out.

He never forgot.

Never forgave.

He'd just bide his time until the right moment. It might be a day. A week. Even months or years. He was patient. Waited until the opportunity and the resources aligned.

Then WHAM.

He never left a trace.

And now it's down to me. I need to be the same.

CHAPTER FIFTY

Connie

Thursday 15 June

Getting out of bed had been a challenge. Connie had wanted nothing more than to pull the duvet over her head and lie there all day – not facing the world. That would've been the easiest thing to do. Her sleep had been fitful. Visions of Steph's and Dylan's bodies slammed her unconscious and jolted her awake, sweat-soaked and afraid. The fear kept her from settling back to sleep, so she'd switched the lamp on, taken her notebook and made a start on the list.

The damn list.

She stared at the thirteen names now, as she sat facing the wrong way on the train. Going backwards made her queasy. But it was that, or squashing up beside an obese man, whose body took up three-quarters of the empty seat next to him.

Thirteen names.

Connie imagined the look on Mack's face when he perused it. Would he question her about each man? She guessed he would – they needed to ascertain whether any of them could be a possible suspect for a revenge attack on Hargreaves. She still felt it was ludicrous to even consider that any of her 'acquaintances' would be bothered enough about her professional demise that they would take such extreme action.

But, as a psychologist, she had to admit she would be asking similar questions of someone else. There was a possibility that, if one of the men had certain traits, or a personality disorder, he might have taken far greater an interest in her and her life than she'd even realised. One of them might have felt compelled to act to 'save her' or 'even the score' by eliminating Hargreaves – the source of so much angst, depression and hurt. Scanning the names, some of which were only first names, she highly doubted any of them had such traits. But then, some of them she'd only known one night. What if they knew her better than she knew them?

Connie reached her building without having remembered the journey. She looked at the plaque to the side of the entrance – the one that a matter of days ago had brought such pride. Today, all she felt was emptiness, a strange detachment. Still with a sense of disinterest, Connie unlocked the door and walked into the reception room. The door failed to close behind her, snagging on the doormat.

'Christ's sake.' She bent down and yanked it back, then slammed the door. That's obviously what had happened the other day when her client had managed to enter the building without pressing the security buzzer. She should have had a sunken area for the doormat to fit snugly into. She made a mental note to call the builder she'd used for the interior refurbishment, get him to sort it. Snatching yesterday's post from the tub chair where Mack had left it, Connie made her way upstairs.

The nausea she'd felt the week before returned – the smell of cut grass hitting her senses as she walked into her office. Dropping the post on the desk, she went to the window and lifted the sash to breathe in the normal air. It was about time she got a new fragrance for the infuser. After a few deep breaths, Connie straightened. And that's when she saw him.

A figure across the street. A man in a black hoody.

180

He stood stock-still, staring up at her.

Connie jerked back instinctively. Was it the same guy she'd seen near the pirate ship with Steph?

Flattening herself against the wall, she edged towards the window again. Slowly, she turned her head to peep out. He hadn't moved. Was he waiting for Steph? Perhaps he thought she'd be having her usual session with Connie. And if that was the case, she could assume he had nothing to do with her death, couldn't she? She moved away from the window again. Then, without stopping to really think about what she was going to say, she bolted from the room, ran heavily down the stairs and flung open the front door ready to confront him.

He'd gone.

Panting from the exertion, Connie looked frantically up and down the street. Surely he couldn't have moved that fast, not so much as to be completely out of sight. He must've ducked into a shop. She took a few steps away from the entrance of her building, her eyes darting from shopfront to shopfront.

Nothing. No man in a black hoody.

The hand touching her arm made her shout out.

'Sorry. Didn't mean to startle you, are you okay?'

'Oh. Paul,' she said, her words now no more than a whisper: an exhalation of air and fear. Her heart jumped erratically; Connie put her hand to her chest, as if to prevent it escaping.

'I'm a bit early, sorry.'

'No problem.' Connie hadn't noticed her client's approach; her attention had been on the other side of the road. 'Come on in.' She forced a smile as she and Paul made their way inside. Connie closed the door, pushing it tight until she heard the reassuring clunk that indicated the lock had operated.

Paul stood watching.

For the first time since she'd set up the consultancy, Connie questioned her security measures. She hadn't wanted to be upstairs with a client, worrying about who could walk in, so the intercom system seemed the best idea. Without the buzzer system that allowed her to control who she let in, anyone could access the building. She needed to keep people out.

But now, with Paul staring blankly at her, she questioned why she hadn't installed anything that might offer protection from those she was inviting *inside*.

CHAPTER FIFTY-ONE

Connie

'You look really pale, Connie. Are you feeling all right?'

She considered the question for a few seconds before answering. In that time, she also asked herself whether she had any need to suddenly fear a man she'd been happily counselling for six weeks.

'Yes, yes. A bit tired, but I'm fine, thank you.' She could hear her mother's voice in her head: *You always say you're fine.*

'You're sure? I mean, if you don't feel well . . .'

'Honestly,' Connie started up the stairs, 'I'm good to go.'

'That's just as well,' Paul said, squinting, 'because this is our last session together. I wanted to make sure it was a good one.'

Her stomach tightened. It was probably her imagination, but those words seemed to have an edge to them. The way he'd said 'this is our last session together' sounded almost threatening.

Stop being melodramatic.

What was wrong with her? It *was* his last session. He was purely stating a fact, not threatening her. Having no sleep was clearly having a detrimental effect. She needed to get her act together and conduct Paul's session professionally.

He followed her up the stairs and into her room. Before she took her seat, Connie had a quick look outside. There was no sign of the man.

'Okay, Paul. Take a seat and let's get started.'

It took at least half an hour before she settled into the session. Half an hour to relax and stop mistrusting Paul. He'd given her no cause for concern before. And now he'd also got into full swing, he was his usual chatty self. When his hour was up, he thanked her and left. She heard the clunk of the front door lock hitting home and allowed her anxiety to melt away.

It was four o'clock. She still hadn't emailed her list of names to Mack as she'd said she would. Connie curled the top corner of the paper, staring at the column of names. Then she flipped it over, placing it face down on the desk. Perhaps she'd make a drink first, then write the email. She knew she was trying to find any reason to stall . . . prevent this disclosure for as long as possible.

The post. She should open it. It was already a day old; there might be something important that required dealing with urgently. Pushing the list aside, Connie set about opening the mail.

She sifted through it. Mostly it was junk. Then her breath caught.

The large brown envelope was addressed to *Connie Moore*.

She hadn't used that name since leaving the prison service.

With fumbling fingers, she ripped it open, pulling from it some photographs and a white sheet of paper. The photos were face down, but the typed words glared at her:

You can't escape your past by changing your name. It doesn't work like that.

Connie stared at the words, her pulse skipping. If she didn't turn over the pictures, if she threw them in the bin instead, she'd never have to know what they were of. She knew she couldn't do that, though. She'd never stop thinking about them, wondering what they showed. She slammed her elbows on the desk, and held her head in her cupped hands. What was going on? She wanted to scream, release the tension and anxiety that was building to unbearable levels inside her.

She sat back, locking her hands behind her head and bounced against the chair.

'*God's sake!*'

Connie flipped the photos over.

Her stomach flipped too.

CHAPTER FIFTY-TWO

DI Wade

The search for Eric Hargreaves' murderer had so far brought complications; twists and turns that even with their investigation management system, HOLMES2, made for a procedural nightmare. Lindsay's head was full of questions as she left her DCI's office. Despite the updates and new information, they were still lacking anything solid. The team had been working around the clock for the past ten days, following original leads, new ones, checking numerous CCTV feeds, trawling through statements, interviewing persons of interest.

But the latest information made Lindsay nervous.

Her instinct told her that Connie had been in the wrong place at the wrong time. The photo of her with ex-prisoner, Trevor Jones, proved nothing on its own. However, her team had disagreed, quickly jumping on the theory that Connie had been involved in getting Hargreaves taken out of the picture – used her past associations with criminals to her advantage, somehow getting them to carry out her act of revenge. Jones had been convicted of aggravated burglary – it wasn't such a huge leap, especially given his record of violent outbursts while in custody too, to think him capable of doing something on this scale.

It certainly threw a different light on Connie. And if she was in contact with one criminal, could there be more?

Mack and DC Clarke had left early to go fetch Jones, bring him in for questioning.

Lindsay hoped he gave them a plausible reason for him and Connie being together.

Sitting at her desk, her third coffee in one hand, Lindsay scrolled through her emails. The one with the subject heading 'POST-MORTEM RESULTS' stood out. Stephanie and Dylan. It was likely to be cut and dried; given the height from which Stephanie had jumped with Dylan, the cause of death was obviously going to be blunt force trauma.

The toxicology report would take longer, probably another six or so weeks. But, reading the report, Lindsay didn't think that would be of huge significance. She might have had drugs in her system – God knows Lindsay would've had to in order to even contemplate such an act – but ultimately the fall was what killed Stephanie and Dylan Cousins.

Goosebumps prickled on Lindsay's arms. The vision of the bodies lying at the bottom of Haytor was still vivid in her mind, refusing to shift. Such a terrible way to go. Selfish as far as she was concerned. At least Stephanie had had a choice in the matter. Her poor child hadn't.

How could someone, a mother, do that?

The literal 'how' also bothered her as much as the emotional. Had Stephanie pushed her son first then jumped herself? Their bodies had been close together, almost touching. Difficult to tell. They probably would never know – no one had come forward to say they'd witnessed the incident despite a huge public appeal. But another team had been tasked to piece together Steph's last movements; her own job was to continue the Hargreaves investigation. The niggling questions Connie had asked in the car yesterday about Stephanie's home and what had been found there, whether there'd been a suicide note, were the only things that prevented Lindsay shutting off from the suicide completely. It was strange that no note was found. But, she reminded herself, not *all* suicide victims left notes.

The door, swinging back and hitting the wall, jerked her out of her thoughts. Mack stormed through, his face stony.

'Eh up, what's the matter?' Lindsay stood and walked towards him.

'No sign of Mr Jones at his registered address.' He slumped on his chair. 'Waste of bloody time.'

'Is he still on licence?'

'Yep, tried his probation officer, too. She said she hadn't seen him for a week as he's now only on fortnightly sign-ins.'

'Okay, well we're bound to catch up with him sooner or later. If not before, then we can visit the probation offices next week.'

'A whole week, that's too long.'

'We'll be speaking to Connie about the pictures, so we'll be able to get her side of the matter. He can wait. Come on, Mack – not like you to be so negative.'

He shrugged, then turned to his monitor, saying nothing more.

Lindsay chewed the end of her pen while staring at Mack's turned back. They hadn't had a proper chat for a while. There was something up with him lately, and it was affecting him at work. She hadn't noticed anything untoward prior to this case. Prior to meeting Connie Summers.

What was it about her that brought out the worst in her DS?

And what was it about Connie Summers that was making Lindsay feel so unsettled?

CHAPTER FIFTY-THREE

Connie

Connie sat down at her desk and tried to get the events straight in her head. So, she'd been given a memory stick with a news article about Luke's death and a document that suggested her dad knew more than he'd ever let on to her and her mum about the circumstances that led to her brother being killed. She'd received a perturbing email via her consultancy web page, accusing her dad of not having learned the first time, and now she'd been hand-delivered an envelope containing two photos.

Acid burned Connie's throat.

The photos lay side by side on the desk. She regarded them with a mix of anger, fear and confusion.

The one on the left had been taken at the train station. On the bridge where, moments before this was captured, she'd been confronted by the stranger with the memory stick. In this image, though, the focus was on her and Jonesy. It was when he'd helped her after her legs had weakened and she'd all but collapsed. His hand was on her elbow, steadying her. But that's not what this looked like. This appeared to be a tender moment – a gentle hand on her arm; almost intimate.

Jesus. How could a scene be captured so wrongly? She hadn't even noticed anyone else close by, let alone someone with a camera.

The other picture perturbed her even more. The picture with Jonesy had been taken in a public place. This other one was not.

Her hand trembled as she picked it up again to study it.

How and why did someone take this photo? Connie stared at the two figures silhouetted in what she knew was the bedroom window of the terraced house. The light from the room was enough to enable her to identify herself and the man.

Remembering the list, Connie pulled it from under the photos and began the email, punching the keys on her laptop so hard the sound echoed in the room.

As she hit the send button, she sighed. The shit would soon hit the fan. She couldn't keep the photos to herself, it would be stupid of her not to disclose them. Who knew what the unknown sender was going to do next. The fact that the second photo showed her and one of the men she'd also had to name on the list was going to complicate things even more. She couldn't even remember the guy's surname, she'd blocked it from her mind for some reason – she only knew him as Gary. A heat spread across her cheeks. Not even knowing the full name of a man she'd slept with, and become pregnant by, did play on her mind. Her behaviour, particularly in the last year, had been questionable – the stress, the worry, had piled on, and her outlet had been meaningless one-night stands. Now that period of promiscuity was coming back to haunt her – again. As if it hadn't been a big enough wake-up call to fall pregnant and then be punished by suffering a miscarriage, it appeared she was going to continue to pay for it.

Was that why the mystery photographer had taken this one in particular? They couldn't possibly know, could they? Gary had no doubt told someone, though. He'd been very vocal when she'd informed him she was pregnant – even saying that he wanted them to be an item, make a future. She wished she hadn't bothered telling him at all now – but at the time, it felt the right thing to do. It'd taken a lot to shake him off – a few white lies she wasn't proud of – and in the end she'd got angry with him, told him to leave her alone. She was too old for him. He could do far better.

Connie tapped her pen against the edge of the desk, while simultaneously bouncing one leg, staring at the phone. Any minute now. Either Mack or Lindsay would've seen her email. They'd be calling. Wanting her to come into the station no doubt. All her nerve endings were jumping, her anxiety levels rising by the second. She could imagine what they were thinking, what they were assuming. She was going to add to the rather unsavoury picture the list painted her in by informing them of the photos. She would skim over the finer details of her and Gary, they didn't need to know about her pregnancy, and the photo of her and Jonesy could be easily explained. But would they believe her?

What was taking them so long?

To take her mind off the impending call, Connie turned to her computer to check her emails. She was behind with all her admin, and she hadn't listened to her phone messages either – she needed to keep sight of her own goals. Gaining new clients had been high on her list of priorities, and now, given she'd lost Steph, and Paul had completed his therapy, she desperately needed to build it up again. Her breath caught. She'd 'lost Steph'. She hadn't lost her, she'd been taken. And one way or another she had to make Lindsay believe there was more to it than suicide.

An email caught her attention.

From Miles. She took a deep breath. The bastard. Leaving her to identify the bodies, while he swanned about in Manchester. *This better be good.* She noted the subject heading:

PSYCHIATRIC REPORT – Jenna Ellison.

Right, so not about Brett. She'd given Miles too much credit, it seemed – his trip to Manchester was obviously unrelated to Steph's case. Connie skim-read the email to double-check he hadn't mentioned anything about Brett. Nothing. In fact, the only bit of text written by Miles which accompanied the attached file was:

I've had the report that was written on Stephanie (Jenna Ellison) redacted as necessary, but hope it's of some use – you'll note that she had a history of lying.

Miles had made his mind up about her. And he clearly wasn't interested in digging further. Particularly as now she was no longer his problem. He wouldn't want the mess that a murder investigation would bring, not so close to his retirement – his unblemished career to date, ruined. No. He'd want to brush all this under the carpet – forget about Stephanie and Dylan. And with the police writing their deaths off as suicide, she was on her own.

It was going to be down to her to ensure justice was brought for Steph and her son.

The phone's shrill ring gave her a start.

This was it. She'd have to tell them about the photos. Would she be able to convince Lindsay and Mack that her meeting with Jonesy was purely coincidental? How much would they want to know about the list of names she'd sent? This was going to be an uncomfortable conversation.

She picked up the phone, and with an unsteady hand, put the receiver to her ear.

CHAPTER FIFTY-FOUR

Then

I can't remember how I started the fire, where I set it – but I can guess. And Jenna told me, that night when she screamed at me. I remember that clearly. Her face, white and angry: her eyes popping, her mouth wide – spit hanging in long trails. She looked mad, like a vicious, drooling dog. She also wrote to me and explained how it had happened, how she'd heard me go downstairs after setting the fire outside Mum and Dad's room.

I was a freak, she'd said.

Everyone said that, so it must be true. It's why I started fires all the time. Because I was weird. The court reckoned I didn't really mean to kill my dad. I don't think I meant to either. If anything, it was more likely I was trying to kill *her* – my wicked stepmother – so I could have my dad to myself again.

But Polly said I should look through a new lens at my past.

I didn't get her at first, thought she was chatting shit. But then she explained better. She told me that I needed to wipe my mind of what I'd been told, and of what I *thought* I remembered about that night. That I should take this new lens (which wasn't a real thing, she said it was metaphorical, or something) and look through it – concentrating specifically on that day: start in the morning, and go through until I got to the end. I assumed she meant the end of that night, when I was taken away by the police for murdering my dad.

So I used the relaxing techniques she'd taught me, and emptied my mind. It was like meditation.

And it worked.

CHAPTER FIFTY-FIVE

Connie

The conversation was terse. Connie had opened her mouth, ready to tell Lindsay about the photos, but she'd jumped in first, and informed her that *they'd* been in receipt of a package containing photos of her and Jonesy. Her stomach lurched, so much so that she grasped it, holding on to it tightly. Whoever had sent the photos to her had also sent some to the police. What if they'd also gone to the papers – to Kelly Barton? When Lindsay had stopped talking, Connie told her she had photos, too. The call was brought to an abrupt end.

Connie took the envelope, shoving it roughly into her bag, and left her office.

She'd been summoned to the police station.

Her footsteps clacking along the train station platform sounded a tap dance. Why was she rushing? The train wasn't even there yet, but there was an urgency. She wanted to be on it, safely enclosed in a carriage. Not outside, in the open; vulnerable. The tannoy boomed – the distorted voice telling her the train was due in five minutes. Head lowered, Connie made her way to the waiting room, then, seeing a dark figure of a man sat inside, thought better of it. It was only five minutes; she'd be fine to wait outside. There was nothing to be worried about. She leant up against the building and, retrieving her work mobile from her handbag, scrolled through her texts. The last one was a message informing her she had one new voicemail.

With the phone pressed to her ear, Connie listened. She squinted in concentration, the line breaking up several times. It was an enquiry, she guessed, a new client wanting her services. Excellent. Good timing. She saved the message so she could decipher it when she was somewhere quieter and contact him to arrange an initial consultation.

'Hello, Miss.' The voice came from nowhere, and together with the accompanied tap on her shoulder, caused Connie to leap away from its source.

Now, *this* wasn't good timing. Not in the slightest.

Connie faced Jonesy, and without a thought, shouted, 'What the hell are you doing?'

The man in the waiting room briefly looked in her direction, then returned his attention to his newspaper.

'Sorry, didn't mean to make you jump.' Jonesy smiled, exposing a row of blackened teeth.

'Well, you did.' She craned her head so she could take in the rest of the platform, and checked the bridge, too. No one with a camera that she could see.

'What's up? You're jumpy.' Jonesy followed suit, looking furtively up and down the station. 'You trying to find someone or avoid them?'

'Look, I'm sorry to be rude, but I can't be seen with you.' Connie walked purposefully in the opposite direction. Jonesy followed, skipping along beside her. She stopped. 'Really. Please, you have to leave me alone.' Jonesy's face crumpled, and for a horrible moment it looked as though he was going to cry. But then Connie realised it was his 'confused face'. She recalled it from group sessions. He'd used it when she'd asked him uncomfortable questions in front of the other prisoners.

'I will, Miss. But if I'm honest, you're freaking me out here. What's going on? You seem afraid. I could help—'

196

'No! Well, you can help – by staying away. Please.'

The screeching of the train pulling into the station was one of the most welcome sounds Connie had heard in a while – besides the popping of cork from a bottle of prosecco. She ran to the platform edge, her toes going beyond the safety line, and as soon as the train stopped and the door released, she jumped on it. The relief oozed from her as she found a seat and sat with her shoulders turned so she couldn't see out of the window. Couldn't see Jonesy. Had she dodged him quickly enough, though? The whole encounter must've only lasted a minute, but might someone still have had the opportunity to take a photo of them together? How could she avoid him in the future? It was impossible; he just turned up, what could she do about that?

Possible reasons why he kept showing up jumbled in her mind. Despite varying her schedule, he still appeared, like a bad penny. Connie was aware her breathing was more rapid than it should be, her pulse raised. Her heightened anxiety was too much. He'd asked if she was avoiding someone. But did he already know who, and why? Perhaps she should've asked *him* a few questions. Like, did he know they'd been photographed together? Had he been approached by anyone who'd asked about her?

Or was it Jonesy who was behind all of this? If so, what was it he wanted to achieve?

What did he want from her?

CHAPTER FIFTY-SIX

Connie

The atmosphere was different; the noisy room she'd been in last time she'd assisted the investigation now uncomfortably quiet. Numerous pairs of eyes followed her as she made her way over to Lindsay, who was sitting, her face turned away, talking to Mack. Connie daren't look towards the whiteboard at the back of the room, the one she'd been fascinated with before. Because she knew the photos would be displayed there. The one of her and Jonesy. And the one with her and Gary. The man with no surname. Connie shivered. If she thought the atmosphere in the room was uncomfortable now, it would be unbearable after they'd grilled her.

Mack jumped up as she approached. Connie noted the paper in his hand. Her list.

'Sorry. Someone should've shown you straight to the interview room, not here.' He was abrupt, and didn't make eye contact. Connie's stomach dipped.

'Fine,' she said.

'Follow me, Connie.' Mack strutted off, his long strides meaning he was already halfway across the room before Connie had a chance to move. She walked quickly to catch up, checking over her shoulder to see where Lindsay was. She remained at her desk.

Why wasn't she going with them? *Please don't let it just be Mack interviewing me.*

Just as she thought she'd lose him if he kept up his pace, Mack stopped, his left arm outstretched. 'After you.'

Connie hurried to where he was, and entered a small, airless room. She pulled at the collar of her shirt. It was a lightweight cotton one, but suddenly it seemed heavy, restrictive. A layer of heat covered her skin. She sat down where Mack indicated and waited for him to begin. As well as the list, he'd brought a file with him. He shuffled through it now, his head bowed. Silent. Connie fidgeted with the silver wishbone ring on her right fourth finger, rotating it around and around. Still, Mack was quiet. Then he placed two photographs on the table between them. They looked to be the same size as those she had in her bag. Connie kept her eyes on Mack's face.

'You have a right to consult a solicitor if you wish,' he said, finally breaking the silence. Connie swallowed hard.

'Are you charging me with something? Do I need a solicitor?'

'You are not under caution, no, this is informal. At this point. But you can still have someone with you, or call a solicitor.'

'No. I'm good, thanks. I've done nothing wrong.' Connie reached down, taking her handbag, and retrieved her brown envelope. Mack frowned. She *had* told Lindsay that she'd received photographs, too. But Mack looked puzzled.

'So, we received two photographs from an unknown source,' Mack said, his eyes not making contact with hers. He separated the photos, turned them and pushed them towards her. Connie stared. The first one was no surprise; it depicted the same scene as the one she'd been given: her and Jonesy on the steps to the station bridge. She'd fully expected the other to be her and Gary. But it wasn't. Her shoulders fell.

It was her dad. In the photo, he was in what looked like a bar, shaking another man's hand. Why had the mystery photographer sent the police a photo of her dad?

'For the record, can you state who you see in each of these pictures?' Mack's voice was steady.

'Yes,' Connie attempted to keep the wobble in her voice under control, 'the one on the left is myself, and a man called Trevor Jones. And on the right is my father, Ian Moore. I don't know who he's with.'

Mack snorted. 'Are you sure about that?' He leaned forward, his upper body protruding over her side of the table.

She sat back heavily, her superficial composure now totally shaken. 'Yes, I'm quite sure. I don't recognise him. Why? *Should* I?'

Mack didn't answer. Instead, he reached for the envelope she had placed to the side of her elbow. She resisted the urge to slam her hand on top of it, preventing him from taking it. She had no desire to speak to him about the photo of her and Gary, for him to question her about who he was, what she was doing in his house, or anything else related to him. Her memory of Gary had been blighted by the aftermath of one night of drunken sex. Having to detail it to DS Mack was not something she wished to go through. Particularly as it appeared that he'd got over his one episode of being nice to her that day when he'd visited her at her consultancy, and was now back to his delightfully polite self.

'Is this the envelope I picked up at your office before we took you to identify the suicide victims?'

'They have *names*.' Connie tutted. 'Stephanie and Dylan, and yes, it is.'

'I take it your fingerprints are all over them.' Mack took a pair of gloves from his trouser pocket and pulled them on.

'Well, yes. As are yours.'

'Only on the envelope.' Mack shot her a warning glance before taking the photos out.

The first was the one of her and Jonesy, which Mack barely looked at, placing it carefully behind the second. He looked at the one of her and Gary, briefly, then his head snapped up and he glared at Connie.

'What? What is it?' Connie asked, alarmed at the look on Mack's face. His skin paled, his lips parted. He went to say something, then pushed his chair back. Holding the photos in his gloved hands, Mack rushed from the room.

CHAPTER FIFTY-SEVEN

DI Wade

Lindsay flinched as Mack stormed towards her.

'We need a chat, Boss.'

His momentum carried him forwards, and, not waiting for her response, he headed out of the double glass doors leading to the outside of the station. Lindsay jumped up to follow him. What on earth had just happened in that interview room?

'What's going on?'

Mack paced the enclosed courtyard area, the one usually used by the smokers, his head bowed.

'Well, you wanted the low-down on why things were a bit . . .' Mack flapped a hand dismissively, 'strained, you know, when I first saw Connie Summers.'

'*First* saw? Every time, really, Mack.' Lindsay leant back against the wall, hands in her trouser pockets, waiting for whatever revelation was coming next.

'Yeah, well.' He stopped pacing and held out the photo that had been grasped in his gloved hand since leaving the interview room. 'Don't touch it, just look.'

'I do know how to manage potential evidence, thanks.' Lindsay moved away from the wall and inched her face towards the photo. 'This was one of the ones sent to Connie, I take it?'

'Yep.' Mack's head was turned away, looking blankly at the wall ahead.

Lindsay regarded the photo. Two figures, one of which she assumed to be Connie, in a top window of a terraced house.

'Okay . . . so . . . who's that she's with?' Lindsay wasn't sure why Mack was reacting so strangely.

'Look closely, Boss. At the house.'

It was dark in the picture, but a nearby street light was illuminating the house. Black door. Miniature conifers lining the path.

'This is your house.' She looked up sharply. 'So what the hell is Connie doing in it?'

Mack closed his eyes for what felt like a long time. Lindsay wanted to push him along, get him to hurry up and explain. Had she been right about Mack being involved with Connie? She'd half been joking, teasing him. Mack slid the photo back in the envelope before she had a chance to study the other figure in the window more closely.

'When we asked Connie to make the list of names of men she'd been involved with, or had taken an interest in her, I knew what I was likely to see,' Mack said.

Here we go.

Mack shook his head. 'Here's the list. She sent it through earlier.' He handed it to Lindsay.

Lindsay snatched it, annoyed he hadn't shown her immediately. She skimmed the names.

'She didn't even know the surname.' Mack's voice was low, tight. 'Christ, she's something else.'

Lindsay saw the name. Gary.

'Ah, I see.' Lindsay couldn't keep the relief from her tone. 'Connie was involved with your son.'

'If you could call it involved. She's ten years older than him, she picked him up in a bar, he brought her home to our house, she used him and left. Left him in bits – I was witness to that, even though he didn't really speak about it.'

'Why? Because of a one-night stand? Sorry, Mack, but I'm pretty sure that happens all the time.'

'Yes. But not all of them end up in a pregnancy.'

'Connie's had Gary's baby?' She blurted it, loudly, then smacked her hand over her mouth.

'No, Lindsay.' Mack swung around, his eyes were wide. 'The heartless bitch terminated it, without even discussing it with him.' He brushed past Lindsay and went back inside. She stayed there, her mouth gaping. She hadn't seen that coming.

What further surprises did Connie Summers have for them?

CHAPTER FIFTY-EIGHT

She'd made herself an easy target.

People don't realise how much information we can find out.
Just because we're locked up, doesn't mean we're cut off. I have
a good network, both inside and out. And news of her cock-up
spread through the wings – one bloke had been transferred
here, she'd written a report about him, too. He kicked up an
almighty stink, wanting it done again, saying she was incom-
petent. She'd ruined his life. He was only jumping on the
bandwagon, but why not?

I was, too.

It hadn't taken long to realise who she was. And a few calls
confirmed it.

Sometimes the stars align perfectly.

She'll get hers, along with the others. The opportunity I
have now is priceless, so I guess it happened for a reason.

CHAPTER FIFTY-NINE

Connie

Mack's abrupt exit from the room left Connie stunned. She sat, brow creased, mentally running through the last few minutes of the interview. His response when he saw the picture seemed over the top – flying out like that, why?

Elbows on the table, her head in her cupped hands, a sudden jolt of memory hit her.

She had always thought Mack was familiar. But she'd assumed she'd come across him professionally. Now, she remembered. The morning after she'd slept with Gary, she'd crept downstairs, and, about to let herself out of the front door, had heard an exaggerated cough. She'd turned to see a man sitting at the kitchen table, newspaper in front of him, mug in hand – a look of disapproval plastered on his face.

Gary was Mack's son.

She could see it now – the height, the square jawline, the eyes. Damn. This was awkward. So that was the reason for his animosity towards her? Just because of a one-night stand? Hadn't *he* ever had one? And why was it her fault? It took two, after all. She had met Gary on a night out, where he was openly flirting with not just her, but half the bar, too. He was up for it. He hadn't thought of the consequences either. They were both irresponsible.

Her stomach fluttered. Did Mack know about her pregnancy?

Connie got her phone from her bag and checked the time. She'd already been at the station for an hour, and so far had made zero progress in finding out who the mystery photographer was. Now, sitting alone in the small room, she began to wonder if she'd been cut out of the loop. Maybe they didn't want her assistance now. They were looking at her through different eyes – she was in photos with an ex-con. That didn't look good. Yet Mack hadn't even asked her about it. As for the photo of her dad, well, that was weird. What was the point of that? How was she meant to know who some random guy in a photo with her dad was? He was always having meetings with various people, the man could've been anyone. Unless the police believed that the photo was meant as a threat, taken and sent to them as a sign that her dad would be harmed. But why? None of it made sense.

Connie got up and stretched. Was Mack even coming back, or should she leave the room and go and find him? She looked to the door, willing it to open. She'd much rather get this over with – dragging it out like this was torture. But that was probably what Mack was anticipating. He was enjoying making her as uncomfortable as he possibly could.

She thought about Jonesy. As he was in the photos with her, it was obviously not him taking them. But it was odd how he kept popping up, being in the same place she was. There was a possibility he was behind it, getting the photographer to take the photos. Connie mulled over the reasons he might have for doing this. Blackmail sprung to mind. If he'd been keeping up with the news, or had heard about Hargreaves through his contacts, he'd know that the last thing Connie needed was to be associated with ex-cons. He might be planning to ask Connie for money to prevent any further implications. But if that was the point, then surely he wouldn't have sent the photos to the police. There would be no need for Connie to pay him to keep them to himself if they were already in the hands of the law. As a drug user, perhaps the lengths he'd go to in order to fund his habit were more extreme than she'd imagined. Would he also go as far as killing Hargreaves for money?

If Jonesy was in any way responsible for Hargreaves' murder, then her being photographed with him was bad news. If Lindsay and Mack suspected that she had arranged for Jonesy to kill him, then these photos were highly incriminating. But they wouldn't find any further evidence that corroborated that theory. You couldn't find evidence where there wasn't any.

Unless that evidence was faked. Or, at the very least, manipulated.

Finally, the door opened. Connie sighed in relief – it wasn't Mack returning.

Lindsay, her face tired and drawn, entered and took the seat opposite Connie.

'Things seem to have taken an interesting turn,' she said.

'I'm not sure I'd agree with the interesting part.'

'First question I want answered is why were you with Trevor Jones?'

Connie shifted in her seat. 'I wasn't *with* Jones. When those photos were taken, I was at Coleton train station. I'd got off my usual train following my day at work in Totnes. I was literally halfway over the bridge, the one that goes across the tracks, heading for the exit, and I saw . . .' Connie faltered. She hadn't told them about the memory stick. As far as she was concerned it had nothing to do with them, with the investigation, so why should she? Now, though, in order to give credence to her account, she was going to have to tell Lindsay about the stick, and the man who'd given it to her. More questions would follow and she'd be getting deeper into the shit.

'Go on, please finish what you were saying.' Lindsay opened her hands, palms up, inviting her to keep going.

'I saw a man, standing against the railing of the bridge. For some reason, it scared me. No one else had got off the train and

I couldn't see anyone else around. He was wearing an overcoat, which was odd, because it had been such a warm day . . . anyway, he seemed to be waiting for me. I suppose I panicked, and I put my head down and continued forward. He moved too, in my direction – and that's when he bumped right into me. The shock took my breath from me. I was afraid, and I almost collapsed. I was hanging on to the rail when someone put their hand on my other arm and asked if I was okay. That someone was Jonesy.'

'So he appeared just after the guy bumped into you?'

'Yes. He helped steady me. That's what the photo captured.' Maybe she wouldn't have to tell Lindsay about the memory stick after all.

'Right.' Lindsay sat back, appearing to contemplate this information. 'That seems plausible . . .' she said, almost to herself. 'But,' she sat forward again, 'what did he give you?'

'Nothing.'

'In the photo it looked like you had something in your hand, an item that Jones had given you.'

Damn. Here we go, then.

'No. It wasn't Jonesy who gave it to me.'

'Oh, the man that knocked into you gave it to you. What was it?'

'I was unaware of what it was at the time – I was hiding it from Jonesy. I don't even know why. It wasn't until I was in the taxi that I realised it was a memory stick.' Connie kept eye contact with Lindsay, and quickly added, 'It has nothing to do with the Hargreaves murder, though. It was personal.'

'At this point, everything is to do with the murder case. You were seen with an ex-prisoner. Now, if we find that Jones has links with Hargreaves, then it really doesn't look good that a previously successful employee in the prison service, whose career was cut short because of our murder victim, is known to be associating with a criminal – revenge is sweet, as they say. And you may have got someone else to enact that revenge.'

'NO! Absolutely not. Look, I'd got on with my life. Yes, I'd been disgraced, and yes, my career *and* personal life took a dive. But I would not even consider taking any kind of revenge. Only that of showing him I could survive, that I could rebuild my life despite him. Why the hell would I risk further damage to my reputation, not to mention my health? Jesus, Lindsay, I'd suffered enough.' Connie's face burned; her chest tight.

'Calm down, Connie.' Lindsay stretched a hand across and touched Connie's. 'Shall we go and get a coffee?'

Connie pushed the chair back and stood up in a swift movement. 'Yes. I need to get out of this room.'

She was out of the door before Lindsay had responded. She needed breathing space, and some time, before the inevitable questions came about what information the memory stick contained.

CHAPTER SIXTY

Connie

'I was just outside here with Mack,' Lindsay said, as she passed a white polystyrene cup to Connie.

'Yeah? Talking about me, was he?' Her patience with Mack was wearing thin. Who was he to judge her?

Lindsay smiled, a straight-lipped one. 'He was pretty upset.'

'Because I slept with his son?' Her tone betrayed her disbelief.

Lindsay's eyebrows lifted. 'So you already knew that Mack was his father? Why didn't you say anything?'

'No. I didn't know. Not until just now. God, what a mess.' Connie threw her head back, looking skywards.

'Ah. Right. Well, yes – it is pretty messed up. But it was more than that, Connie. Apparently, Gary was pretty cut up about it all.'

'Oh, really! Well, not as cut up as I was. It might've only been a one-night stand, but he got away with more than me, didn't he? *He* didn't have to go to the hospital, *he* didn't have the repercussions to deal with.' Connie turned her face away from Lindsay, not wanting her to see the pain that still resided in her.

'That's a bit harsh, don't you think? I mean, he didn't even know about your pregnancy until it was too late for him to have a say?'

211

This was unreal. Who did Lindsay think she was, sticking her nose into this? It had nothing to do with her. Her anger flared, but then extinguished, Lindsay's words suddenly sinking in.

'Have a say? What "say" would he have liked?'

'I guess whether you kept the baby or not?'

'I didn't get the opportunity to discuss that with him. You do know I lost the baby, don't you?'

Lindsay took a step back. 'Oh. Um . . . I'm sorry, I – I thought you'd had it terminated.'

'That's what Mack told you?' Connie was livid again. 'No. I didn't terminate the pregnancy, I had a miscarriage. With the stress of everything going on . . .' Tears choked her, a tight band restricted her throat. She couldn't get any more words out.

She felt an arm around her shoulders.

'I'm so sorry, Connie. I jumped to conclusions.'

They were silent for a moment, the two of them semi-huddled in what was almost an embrace. Connie took some deep breaths, composing herself.

'It's okay. Easy enough to do, given the circumstances.' She wiped her eyes. 'You're doing your job, I know that.'

'Yes. I am. Which means I also need to ask you about the content of the memory stick you were handed.' Lindsay gave an apologetic smile.

'It really doesn't have relevance to the case, Lindsay. It's literally a couple of documents referring to something that happened over twenty years ago. A personal tragedy. Someone clearly wanted to hurt me, bring it all up again.'

Lindsay nodded. 'Well, we'll take a look anyway. Sometimes things don't always appear linked at first, but later down the line you get a eureka moment. Best to have it anyway. No stone unturned and all that.'

'Fine,' Connie conceded, not that she had much choice. 'I'll bring it in.'

'Thanks, I'd appreciate that.'

'Look, I am aware of how this all looks,' Connie said, 'but all I did was write a report, subsequently I was made a scapegoat and left the prison service, then I started my own business. I had absolutely no contact with anyone from the prison service, employees *or* prisoners. That is, until last week, when I first bumped into Jonesy at Coleton train station. That was the same day you and Mack turned up, and suddenly my name, yet again, became embroiled in a drama. Not long after, I got back into contact with a former colleague, Niall—'

'Was his name on the list?' Lindsay cut in.

'Yes. But I'd not heard from him in a year prior to him calling.'

'So, he got in contact with you just after Hargreaves' body was found?' Lindsay bit the corner of her bottom lip.

'Yes.' Her previous nagging thought came back to her. She'd considered whether Niall had been the one to give further details to the police about her links to Hargreaves. He hadn't known that her name was written on his dead hand, as the police kept that undisclosed. Therefore, why had he been so quick to give her name and get her involved in the investigation? A horrible thought occurred to her. Maybe he'd been the one who'd served Hargreaves up on a platter for her.

The idea was ridiculous. But, watching the look on Lindsay's face, she realised it wasn't ridiculous to her.

It was a plausible possibility.

CHAPTER SIXTY-ONE

DI Wade

She'd let Connie go home. Mack hadn't been impressed with that call, but Lindsay wasn't about to give her reasons in public; she would need to speak with him in private before he left the station. Worried that Connie had been upset and shaky following their discussion, Lindsay asked DC Clarke to drop her back to her house. She'd left without another word. Lindsay berated herself for jumping in feet first. Her gut told her that Connie had nothing to do with Hargreaves' death, not intentionally anyway. Treating her as a suspect felt wrong. She believed what Connie had told her about the photo of her and Jones. She couldn't help but feel sorry for her. Sometimes things weren't as they first appeared. That's how she thought about this situation: this whole thing might be someone pinning blame on Connie, as she had history. What better person to fit up for wrongdoing? Someone sending incriminating evidence to the police, anonymously, was suspicious in itself. They needed to find the mystery photographer.

At least they had a potential new lead. Niall Frazer, a former lover of Connie's and an employee at HMP Baymead. His timing in getting back into contact with her just after the murder certainly fit with one of the theories – that it'd been done as a revenge killing for Connie. As some macabre gift. As for the photos, he might even be behind those – had he been jealous of Connie's love life? He could've been following her, had the opportunity to take the one of Connie and Gary. But why would he have taken revenge for her, then tried to implicate her? That *didn't* fit. So the two might not be linked. A different person took the photos. But Niall was a possible culprit for the murder. They should look through his initial statement and interview transcripts again; they might glean something different, something they missed initially. At the time their main focus had been on Hargreaves' escape and who could have been involved internally. They'd been looking more closely at the statements given by the officers who'd had the most contact with Hargreaves.

Maybe they were looking in the wrong place.

She'd get Mack to go through it all – check again. That would also give him something to concentrate on, keep his mind off Connie. First, though, she needed to tell him what Connie had said.

'Mack.' She stood, looking in his direction. 'A word, please?' She raised her eyebrows and jerked her head in the direction of the spare office, located off the main incident room. Hopefully she could ease the animosity he felt towards Connie if she told him he'd been wrong about her. Or at least about the termination.

Lindsay sat on the desk's edge, awaiting Mack's entrance. He was taking his time. Sometimes he acted like a petulant child. Finally, he sauntered in.

'You sulking, Mack?'

He ignored the question.

'Look, I realise there's a personal level to this for you,' she crossed her arms, 'but you should've disclosed this straight away. Not sat on it, brooding like a child.'

Mack's head snapped up.

'Really? That's rich, Lindsay. You didn't brood one bit when your husband left you for another woman, did you?'

Lindsay's jaw tightened.

Mack held up his hands. 'Sorry, sorry, Boss.' His quick apology was a sign he knew immediately that he'd overstepped the mark. Lindsay should take him to task over it. But she wouldn't. How could she, when he was dead right?

'That's below the belt, Mack.'

'I know. Any chance you can forget I said that?'

'No. Actually, Mack, there's not. And I think you'll find my professionalism didn't waver throughout that time – only you knew about it.'

'I know. I'm really sorry, I've let this stuff get to me – I'm not even sure why. If I'm honest, I think I'm angrier at myself than I am with Connie. Anyway, I shouldn't be taking it out on you.' He lowered his gaze, staring at his feet.

'You do know you've put me in an awkward situation here, right? I should take you off the case—'

'No. Please don't do that. There's no need for that, really.'

'I don't *want* to. But you need to get your act together, or I'll have no choice.'

'Understood. I'm sorry, this is the last thing I wanted.'

Lindsay knew that. She also knew Mack was a good detective and she needed him. 'As punishment, you can trawl through all the evidence thus far relating to the prison officers, but taking particular interest in a Niall Frazer.'

Mack groaned, pinching his nose between a thumb and forefinger. 'Okay. But why?'

'Connie told me he'd got in contact with her just after the Hargreaves murder, hadn't spoken to her for a year prior. And his name is on her list.'

'Oh, yeah. And it's his *full* name. Lucky him.'

'Check his whereabouts at every crucial point, but if they check out, if he has an alibi – check *them* out thoroughly, too.'

Mack turned to leave.

'Oh, and Mack?'

'Yes, Boss.'

'You need to give Connie a chance to explain, I don't think you're in full receipt of the facts.'

'Meaning?'

'You said that she went ahead and terminated the pregnancy, without giving any thought to Gary's wishes.'

'Yeah.' His neck reddened, the anger returning.

'Well, you're wrong. She didn't have an abortion. She miscarried the baby.'

Mack paused by the doorway. 'And you believe that?'

'Yes, Mack. I do.'

'Why?'

'Women's intuition?'

'Huh. Don't give me that sexist bull, Boss.'

'Okay then. I just believe her.'

'I reckon she has some kind of hold on you, Boss.' He gave a wry smile, then turned and left.

CHAPTER SIXTY-TWO

Connie

Connie collapsed full length on the sofa, her hands interlocked and covering her face. Her body was weak, all energy sapped. She might stay there, not move, for days. Sod the new consultancy, her new life. What was the point? Every time she took a step forward, someone blocked it. Pushed her back. Her dad was right. She was a disappointment – Luke would've been successful. The perfect child would've transformed into the perfect adult. Not her. She was a disgrace. A let-down. Her life was a joke, and the fact she got to live it and Luke didn't *was* unfair. No wonder her dad wasn't interested, he couldn't bear to witness what a mess she was making. It hurt him to see her and not his perfect Luke.

Fuelled by an abrupt anger, Connie propelled herself up and paced the lounge. She *could* take control. For far too long she'd allowed herself to be a puppet, let others use and walk over her. Let herself be a scapegoat for anyone who could get away with it. If she was to ever feel any better about herself, give herself a chance to be anything, she had to stand up for herself. Others could only control her if she allowed them that power.

'Come on, Connie, take the damn control back,' she berated herself. Somehow it felt better to say it out loud.

Amber brushed up against her calf, almost knocking her over. 'Hello, baby.' She lifted her, snuggling into the long white fur. A cat supposedly had nine lives. Perhaps she did, too. Only one way to find out. She texted Niall. Asked if he would meet her for coffee. Although it was late afternoon he might still be at work. It depended which shifts he was doing this week. She said if he was free they should meet in town. She didn't want him to come to the house.

She needed to be certain there was nothing untoward about his contacting her after Hargreaves' murder. Clearly Lindsay had taken his appearance as some kind of suspicious timing. She didn't want to believe that. But, then, hadn't she also had her reservations about him? Either way, she'd rather be safe than sorry. The night they'd spent together had resulted in an awkward parting the next day, and now Connie was curious as to why. Yes, she was going to take control.

After sending the text from her personal phone, Connie picked up her work mobile. She should give that new client a call; she'd yet to respond to the voicemail he'd left. Sitting down with a pad of paper to take the details, Connie rang the voicemail box, listening, pen poised.

'*Hi, I want to arrange some sessions with you. I'm new in the area, and have a need for counselling . . .*' There was a long pause, then the voice started again, '*I've had a lot of trauma in my life and now it's essential I make a fresh start. For that to happen, I'll need extra help. Can I see you as soon as possible?*' His voice was soft, although the way he spoke immediately made Connie think he was reading from a pre-prepared script. It was stilted, the wording not as natural as a conversation would be. The caller left a number, which Connie scribbled down. A mobile. She dialled it.

'Hello, this is Connie Summers, psychologist, you left me a message to arrange an appointment?'

There was no response, but Connie could hear breathing.

'Hello, is this a bad line?' She held the phone out, checking the signal. She had four bars.

'No. The connection is fine.' His voice was flat. 'I can hear you clearly.' He fell silent again.

'Okay, good. I have spaces for an initial consultation next week, which day would you like?'

'Tomorrow?'

'Oh . . . er . . .' Connie could fit him in; she would rather have left it until next week, but he obviously was keen to get started. That was great, she needed the clients. And the money.

'Yes, I can do . . .' Connie checked her diary. 'Either ten a.m. or three thirty.'

'Ten is good, I'll see you then.'

'Um . . . wait a second.' Connie hadn't even got details and the man seemed ready to hang up. 'What's your name?'

Another pause. Had he gone?

'It's Brett. Brett Ellison.'

The phone went dead.

Connie's mouth gaped. Her hand containing the phone dropped limply in her lap as an icy grip seized her heart and immobilised her lungs. Then, as if she'd been immersed in water for several minutes, she gasped, hungry for air. Her heartbeat tripped and faltered. She placed a hand on it in an attempt to steady the rate.

Could it really be Steph's brother?

So, she'd been right, he had been released.

What was she meant to do with this information – call Lindsay and tell her? Conducting a counselling session with the man – the *boy* – she suspected killed Steph and Dylan seemed an impossible, not to mention risky, task. But it was one that ultimately she knew she'd manage. Her curiosity wouldn't allow for the alternative.

CHAPTER SIXTY-THREE

Brett

I waited a long time for this moment.

Today I am released.

Today, my life begins again.

I have unfinished business. Doesn't everyone?

I have to visit *her* first. I'm not expecting the truth, not anything remotely close to it. Her words will be lies. Ones she's told over and over. Like me, she's come to believe them, consciously at least. They will mean nothing to me. But her eyes. They will tell a different story. They will hold the truth.

Those eyes haven't seen me for eight years. Will they recognise me?

She won't look the same, either. The picture I have had for all these years has not aged; I have no reality to compare it to.

I'll know her when I see her, I am sure of that.

And when the reality dawns on her, the significance of my visit, she'll know it's time to pay.

It's *my* truth that matters now.

CHAPTER SIXTY-FOUR

Connie

Bubbles of white fluffy clouds hung in the dry air, hardly a breeze disturbing them, the cloud cover keeping the layer of heat trapped. Connie fiddled with her buttoned cuffs, un-popping them and roughly shoving her sleeves up her arms as the warmth pressed down heavily on her. It was difficult to tell if it was the heat or her anxiety that was making her sweat – either way, she wasn't looking forward to meeting Niall.

The café was quiet; only a few customers near the back remained. It was 4 p.m. and most people would be thinking about heading home after work. There was an hour before the café closed. If Niall was on time, that would be ample. Connie stared at the glass latte mug. Should she have called Lindsay, told her about Brett calling? Until she spoke with him, there was probably no point. She'd informed Lindsay and Mack of her fears; they'd not been unduly concerned. A thought occurred to her. How on earth had Brett managed to find her? Had the police found and contacted him? Lindsay had said they were going to inform Steph's relatives of what had happened. Perhaps that's why he was here, why he was 'traumatised'. She supposed it wouldn't have taken much effort to find counselling psychologists in the area, and it would have been just a matter of elimination until he got to her.

Her phone buzzed, the vibration informing her of a text. Great. Had Niall decided against meeting her after all? As she read the text, she was aware of a figure walking through the door. The message was from her mum. She was worried. Again. Connie would answer later – attempt the usual 'I'm fine, everything's fine' response. Niall threw himself in the chair.

'God! It's so bloody hot.'

'Yes, hello to you, too.'

'Good afternoon, Connie.' He grinned. 'Is that better?'

Connie scrunched her face, returning a sarcastic smile.

'Can't believe you've got a hot drink.' He got up, heading for the counter. As he turned away, Connie took in his T-shirt – a muscle-type sleeveless one, and she was about to shout 'Poser' after him – mock him – but the word failed to form. On his upper left arm, she saw a black tattoo. She hadn't noticed it the other night – although that was unsurprising given she'd had a few to drink and it was dark. Was it new? He was too far away now to decipher it. When he returned with a Coke can, she stared at it. Her pulse skipped.

It was a bird tattoo.

Niall looked down at his arm, following her stare. 'What?'

'Oh, just looking at that.' She pointed, trying to keep her voice casual. 'New, is it?' She picked up the spoon from her saucer and stirred her latte.

'Not really. But probably got it after we were, you know . . . together last year.'

'Oh, right.' Connie blew her drink, although it was already cool enough. 'What is it?'

'Wow. It's not that bad a tattoo, is it?' He laughed. 'It's a bird, Connie.'

'Any significance?'

He frowned. 'What? Why are you asking so many questions?'

'Just curious.'

'If you've asked me here to talk about tattoos, I think that's a gross misappropriation of my time.' He winked.

'Big word for you, Niall.'

The atmosphere calmed, but Connie's mind didn't. The image of the photos depicting Hargreaves' dead body, his tattoos, pushed to the forefront and nothing could replace them.

Or the thought that Niall's tattoo seemed remarkably similar.

CHAPTER SIXTY-FIVE

Connie

Friday 16 June

The anticipation had kept her awake; questions swamped her tired brain hour after hour. There was still time to call Brett and cancel the appointment for today. Give her more time to decide if seeing him was the right thing to do. But something was driving her on. It wasn't merely curiosity, it was wanting to face the fear – do something that was actually quite risky, be brave enough to do it. Since being outed as one of the people responsible for Hargreaves' release, Connie had shied away from doing anything remotely risky – instead playing it safe. Seeing Brett this morning was her way of taking back some control, being responsible for her own actions – and their consequences, again.

After shovelling a few mouthfuls of porridge in her mouth, Connie fled from her house and walked to the station quicker than she'd managed in weeks. She wanted to get the early train – one, to avoid Jonesy, and two, so she could be prepared for her ten o'clock appointment.

She shuddered at the thought.

How was she going to face this eighteen-year-old boy when she knew he'd not only killed his dad, but probably his sister and

225

nephew too? She'd worked with plenty of killers, but somehow, this was different. Personal. She'd left the prison service, leaving behind the perpetrators of crime to counsel those affected by a criminal act. Now, here she was, about to have a session with a possible murderer.

She barely noticed the walk to her building, she was on auto-pilot. Once inside she headed straight up the stairs and started the computer, bringing up all the information she had from Steph's sessions, plus the psych report she hadn't fully read yet. She scribbled some notes, points she wanted to cover with Brett. The question that burnt in her mind was – why had he chosen to consult Connie? There was no way it could be a coincidence. Somehow, he knew that Steph had been her client.

What did he want from her?

The report flashed up on the screen. Connie read each and every word, ensuring she took it all in. It was as if she were reading about another girl, not Steph. But she *had* been a different person then. Jenna Ellison. Sixteen years old, and prior to the fire that destroyed her house and her life, Jenna had a mum, dad and brother. Although, Brett was not mentioned by name in this report. The part he played in the fire was skimmed over, barely mentioned. Or blanked out. Miles had said the document would be redacted, and he wasn't kidding – huge chunks were black. Not for her eyes. She wondered what was so sensitive, so confidential, that she, as Steph's psychologist, was unable to see it. Above all, she wondered why, given Miles had access to this report, he'd kept the information about Steph having a brother to himself – was it a mistake on his part? One of many, it seemed. From what Connie could gather from between the many lines of blacked-out text, the main focus of this report was the mother. And Steph's feelings of aban-donment.

It made for very depressing reading.

Connie made a few notes; there wasn't much to go on. She dropped her pen as the noise of the buzzer blasted in her left ear.

Her finger hesitated over the door release button. This was it. Once she let him in, there was no going back. She looked to her phone, a last-second doubt surfacing. No, she'd be fine. She'd dealt with so much worse in the prison. She took a deep breath and pressed the button.

She stood up and moved away from her desk, ready to greet her new client.

The footsteps grew closer; Connie's heart banged hard against her ribs. The door swung open.

Brett strode in – assured, yet with an edge of vulnerability that flickered behind his eyes. He was tall, muscly and dark. His face had a hardness to it, one she'd seen many times from offenders who'd grown up in a prison environment; a deep scar ran from his temple to the top corner of his right eye. For a moment, they stared silently at each other. Each sizing up the other.

Connie was first to avert her eyes. She motioned to the chair she'd placed in front of her desk, and walked around to her own. She wanted to keep a barrier between them. Not her usual therapeutic style, but this was not her usual type of client. She'd positioned the phone close to her, in case she needed to make a 999 call. A large, heavy, metal hole-punch was also in reach. She blinked hard. She'd been alone with prisoners before. Murderers. Although in the prison, back-up had never been far away.

She'd been over and over this session in her head last night and this morning. Part of her knew she should've informed the police. But she had no evidence he'd done anything wrong since being released, neither did the police. And they'd given no weight to Connie's feelings on the matter, practically dismissing her theory out of hand. So for now she decided to assess the situation as it happened. And right now, her concern was with how she was going to play this. Ignorant? No mention of Steph – Jenna? Let him do the talking. He sat down, his legs crossed at the ankles, his knees splayed out wide, white kneecaps jutting from ripped holes in his black jeans. He leant back, resting his interlocked hands over his groin. Relaxed. In control. He seemed to be waiting. Connie's stomach knotted. This was going to be an uncomfortable hour.

'You seemed keen to see me. What's brought you here today?'

Brett stared, unblinking. He sat forward in his chair – his head and shoulders reaching across the desk, encroaching in Connie's space. She shifted, wriggling back in her seat to gain a few inches.

He smiled. 'I think you know.'

A prickle of fear began at the base of her neck. She rubbed at it with her hand, attempting to brush it away. Her earlier confidence that she was doing the right thing by seeing Brett before informing the police waned. She was alone with this young man. And now, seeing the intensity etched on his face, she felt foolish.

She swallowed. 'I'd prefer you to tell me. That's how I usually begin these sessions.'

'Fine. I'll tell you why I'm here.' His posture didn't change; his upper body remained forwards, his head uncomfortably close to hers – his gripped hands on the desk.

'Good, that's good,' Connie managed, though her throat felt tight, as if hands were clasped around it.

'I don't know what Jenna told you. But I can guess.' He sniffed hard, the sound of mucus being drawn up and into his throat making Connie want to gag.

'Do you mean Jenna Ellison, who, by the way, was Stephanie in her new life—'

The suddenness of his laugh stopped her. His head was thrown back and the booming sound echoed around the room.

'New life? Wow, wasn't she the lucky one?'

'I fail to see how she was lucky. You do know what happened, don't you?'

'I'm not here to convince you she was lucky, just know that she was, and is.'

'What's this got to do with you being here, then? I assumed

you'd be traumatised by her and Dylan's deaths.' Her voice was clipped.

'I am, I guess.' He shrugged. 'But no, that's not why I'm here. Not why I've come to you, Connie.'

Connie's heart took on a rhythm she wasn't sure was normal. She took some breaths in through her nose, silently, trying not to show her anxiety.

'Okay, so why are you here?'

'To tell my side. It's that simple. I want to be given the opportunity to tell everyone what she was like.' His honey-brown eyes focused intently on her. He didn't blink.

'I'm sorry, I'm not sure I can allow that. I think you'd be best off looking for a different counsellor. Steph was my client, and I don't think it's appropriate, given what I know—'

'Ah! That's just it, Connie. What you know is *not* the truth.' His dark eyebrows lifted high, disappearing beneath his fringe.

Connie got up and took big strides to the door, opening it and standing to the side.

'I'm sorry, I can't help you. If you wouldn't mind . . .' Connie waved her hand towards the exit, waiting for Brett to leave.

'But you can. You're probably the only one who can, now.' His eyes darkened, his body slouched. Was he going to refuse to leave? But, to her relief, he pushed up from the seat and made a move to the door. Connie's hands trembled. As he walked past her, he looked like a frightened young boy. But she knew differently. Brett Ellison was a killer.

He turned just as Connie was about to close the door, putting his hand against it to prevent her shutting it.

'I didn't do what she said.' His hand fell away.

Connie took advantage of this and slammed the door. She put her ear to it, she didn't hear movement. Then his voice again, loud. Urgent.

'It wasn't me who started the fire, Connie. She lied. You have to believe me.'

Connie leant hard against the door. Would he force his way back in? She listened intently, hoping to hear his footsteps descending the stairs. When she heard the front door slam she blew out the air she'd been holding. She rushed to the window and watched as Brett crossed the road and disappeared out of sight.

That wasn't the conversation she'd been expecting.

Of course he would deny everything that Steph had said; it was easy now, with her out of the way. No one to disagree. He had free rein.

Had that been his plan all along? Get rid of Steph, the only other person who truly knew what'd happened that night. Dementia had robbed their mother of the memories and their father seemed to have died in the fire.

Now Brett could rewrite his past.

But then why bother coming to Connie? To convince her he was innocent? Steph's death had been ruled a suicide, and the responsibility for the loss of Dylan's life was firmly placed on Steph. No one else was implicated. *Yet.* Connie was sure once she went to the police with the psychiatric report on Steph and told them about Brett's release prior to Steph's death, they might actually take her concerns more seriously. But did Brett somehow know that Connie thought he was involved?

Was he here to find out how much Connie knew?

And if she was willing to keep digging to find out the truth?

In which case, she needed to be careful. Young Brett might do anything to eliminate those who knew what he'd done.

CHAPTER SIXTY-SIX

Then

'What are you starin' at?'

The boy's face flushed, suddenly aware of his mistake. He'd watched as she towel-dried herself after showering and continued to stare as she began to dress; taking in the loose skin hanging from her upper arms, her squidgy, wrinkly belly. He quickly turned away from her, not wanting her to see his embarrassment, and moved away from the open bedroom door.

'How long you been watching me? You freak,' she hissed, lurching towards the door wearing only her bra and knickers, slamming it shut. The noise filled his ears, along with the echo of her words.

Why was she so cruel? He only wanted to talk to her.

He needed to know.

Was it him they'd been talking about in hushed whispers the other night, as he suspected? What were they planning on doing with him?

He sat on the bottom step of the stairs, his knees tucked up, his chin resting on them. He could hear her shrill voice even through the closed door. Shouting. She was on the phone. Talking to his dad? Telling him how she'd just caught the 'little freak' watching her naked again. 'He's not right in the head.' He hoped his dad might stick up for him, but he didn't usually. She carried on shouting down the phone. He was probably agreeing with everything she was saying. He wouldn't go against what his precious Rosie said. She meant more to his dad these days than he did.

He couldn't bear to listen to any more. His legs were heavy as he wandered outside. To the shed. To where he knew he could release the hard ball in his stomach.

Reaching in the tin marked 'tea', he took out the lighter.

His muscles relaxed. His heart rate settled, the pain in his chest evaporating.

It always ends in fire.

CHAPTER SIXTY-SEVEN

Connie

Connie was yet to sit down following Brett's exit, choosing instead to pace the room, arms crossed, a hard line creasing her forehead. What was she meant to do – allow him to come and trample over Steph's memory and replace it with accusations that she'd been lying?

But what if Brett was telling the truth? Her head throbbed.

Miles Prescott might have been right about Steph all along. Although he'd been wrong about her background; her family. Instead of becoming clearer, the whole situation was clouding, like a mist rolling in from the sea. Everything distorted by the haze.

Connie stopped walking and reached across to her laptop, pressing the music icon. Enya's ethereal tones filled the space. Anything was better than the sound of her own thoughts. She was the only person who believed the account Steph had given. Was she being naive – had she been taken in by Steph? She snatched her mobile phone and scrolled through her history until she found the number. It rang and rang. She was about to hang up when she heard a click.

'Yes?'

'I wanted to ask you to . . . er . . . come back,' she faltered, having to take a steadying breath, 'for a proper counselling session. I was, well, a bit surprised by what you said. I didn't give you a chance to talk it over.' Connie stopped talking. Waited. She heard Brett's breath – slow, steady, on the other end.

'Thank you, I'd appreciate that. I only want to be heard.'

'Yes, well, I can see you first thing Monday. Nine thirty?'

'Sure. That'd be great.'

She couldn't swear to it, but she sensed he was smiling when he spoke.

Probably laughing at her. Thinking he'd won her over.

He hadn't. Not yet, at least. She'd give him time to explain his side of the story, but she wasn't ready to give up on Steph and Dylan. She owed it to them to find out the truth. And the only person who could supply her with the evidence she needed to take to Wade and Mack was the murderer himself.

Content that she'd done the right thing, Connie settled at her desk to work. She had some client notes to type up and a session to plan for.

Her afternoon was clear. No more sessions. No new clients. As had become usual in these gaps during her working day, Connie's mind wandered. Tattoos had dominated her thoughts since seeing the bird on Niall's arm. She retrieved the paper with the code from her desk drawer, together with the sketches she'd done of what she recalled from the official police photographs. She studied them again, her eyelids squinting in concentration.

The code: U2X51 still stumped her: letters and numbers that had no significance yet. But a sudden spark of memory tugged on her consciousness when she looked at the drawing she'd done of the lines and crosses. *Relax your mind.* She closed her eyes, taking slow, deep breaths, digging deep and dredging her memories. She'd seen it, or something like it, before.

Her eyelids flew open. Yes. That was it.

She picked up the paper, staring at it again. It was missing the words, but that was it, she was sure. Not a random pattern, but part of an emblem.

Her dad's business emblem. The one he'd started when she and Luke were young, primary-school age. His first big venture. Around that time, Connie had become addicted to the game Scrabble. She recalled being shouted at because she'd used her dad's headed note paper to write their scores. 'You've got plenty of scrap paper, stop using mine,' he'd yell. It was an antiques business, the same as now, as far as she remembered. She'd check with her mum, rather than directly with her dad. She needed to call her anyway; she'd forgotten to return her text. Her mum would remember, was bound to. If she recalled correctly, there'd been many an argument when he'd begun that business. She'd assumed it was over money, the time spent away from his family – hours spent at the 'gentleman's club'. That's what most of the fallouts had been about.

Was that why the mystery photographer included a photo of him? Why, though? What the hell did her dad have to do with a murdered prisoner? Supposedly, the killer had left his handiwork as a clue. But to what? His intentions were far from clear, but this was beginning to look as though this was personal to her. Just like the memory stick. Was that linked to the investigation after all?

It was time to give Lindsay another call.

Connie hesitated, her finger poised over the button to dial. She'd want her to be alone when she visited. No Mack. No other officer. Just Lindsay. She sighed, and pressed it.

By the end of a slightly uncomfortable conversation, Connie had invited Lindsay Wade over for wine and an evening meal. And surprisingly, Lindsay had accepted.

Connie couldn't suppress her smile as she opened the door to Lindsay. Although she'd asked her over, she hadn't expected Lindsay to say yes. She came across as very 'by the book' and Connie had supposed, with the police's current interest in her, that Lindsay would feel obliged to decline. Mind you, it might not have been accepted with the same intent that it was offered. Maybe she had an ulterior motive for spending time with Connie. With a bottle in one hand and the other stuffed in a trouser pocket, Lindsay stepped over the threshold. She pushed the bottle towards Connie.

'Thank you, there was no need, though.' Connie tucked her freshly washed and straightened hair behind an ear and stood aside to let Lindsay through. Her outfit was no different from the one she wore to work. Wasn't this woman ever off duty? She didn't exactly seem relaxed, comfortable. Mind you, Connie *had* invited her over to discuss the latest development, so she wasn't going to give her a night off anyway. Leaving Lindsay sitting on the edge of the sofa, Connie went to the kitchen and opened the wine, pouring two large glasses.

'I wondered if you could get a taxi home? Or . . .' Connie called from the kitchen.

'Oh, er . . . no. It's a bit far to Plymouth by taxi. I thought I'd get one back to the station after, seeing as it's so close. I've lots to do. I can kip there and drive back home tomorrow.'

Connie walked in and handed the glass to Lindsay. 'Wow, you don't give yourself much time off, do you?'

She shrugged, but didn't offer anything further. For a long moment neither of them spoke, and Connie began to regret the invitation. She took the armchair nearest to the end of the sofa Lindsay was perched on.

'Thanks for agreeing to come over. I don't really *do* cooking, so I thought we'd get takeaway. Chinese? Indian?'

'I'm rather partial to Chinese.' Lindsay smiled.

'Excellent. Me too. I'll grab the menu.' She jumped up.

After choosing what they wanted and ringing it through, Lindsay settled back into the sofa. 'I'm guessing you didn't ask me here for purely social reasons?' She swigged from her glass.

'I did have an ulterior motive, yes. But let's not worry about that until after we've eaten. I was wondering, Lindsay, how long

236

have you and Mack worked together?' As far as idle chit-chat went, Connie realised that topic wasn't the best. Not for her.

'A fair few years now. He's a great officer, you know. Can be a bit old-hat at times, but he's good at his job. And he's kind, too.'

Connie let a sharp breath out through her nostrils. 'Sorry. Yes, I'm sure he is. I don't think I've witnessed that side of him yet. Given our *personal* issues, I am guessing I might not.'

'I know. You two didn't get off on the right foot. I'm sure he'll come around. When you're not in possession of the full facts, it's hard to make a proper judgement. Particularly when emotions are involved.'

'Yep. I know.' Connie lowered her head.

'You live on your own.' It wasn't a question. Obviously, Lindsay was already aware that she didn't live with a partner.

'No, I live with Amber.'

'Oh. Er . . . sorry, I had no idea, um—' Lindsay fumbled.

'My cat,' Connie jumped in. Had Lindsay thought she meant another woman?

'Ah-ha. Of course.'

'What about you, Lindsay? You married?' The question was out before she thought too much about it.

Lindsay gulped some wine – several mouthfuls – before she answered. 'Well. I am, I guess. I mean, officially.'

'Oh, I see. Sorry, I wasn't trying to pry.'

'No, don't be. It's fine. He's been gone well over a year. Moved in with another woman now. It's most definitely over.' She fiddled with the stem of the glass. 'Not sure I've moved on, though. I'm stalling on signing the papers. Not sure if it's because I'm hopeful he'll change his mind, or because I want to be a bitch – make his life more difficult.'

Connie laughed. 'I could hazard a guess.'

'Thanks!' Lindsay's smile seemed unsure at first, and Connie winced. She'd overstepped the mark. But then Lindsay gave a snort. 'So, you've noticed that about me then? That was quick, it usually takes a good few weeks of knowing me before people realise I'm a bitch.'

They both laughed, Connie relieved she hadn't caused offence.

After they'd shared out the Chinese and devoured almost all of it, plus opened another bottle of wine, the atmosphere became altogether more relaxed. Connie told Lindsay that she had seen one of the tattoos found on Hargreaves' body before, or at least something very similar to it. She explained about the emblem briefly, mentioning her dad's business as well. Then she felt comfortable enough to tell her about her brother's death, and handed over the memory stick.

'That must've been such a terrible time for you and your family,' Lindsay said. She'd let her speak, not interrupting up to then, but now appeared genuinely taken aback with Connie's story – not that she'd even given her all the details. It was enough for now to share the basics.

'It had a massive impact then – and continues to now. But, like I told you, what's on the stick has nothing to do with the Hargreaves case.'

'Okay, I appreciate you giving it to me though, thank you.'

When Connie went on to tell her about Brett's surprise call and subsequent visit, Lindsay's interest was clearly piqued and she was keen to hear all about it. She, too, was particularly struck by the discrepancies in the information held by the protected persons team, and what Steph and Brett had told Connie. They talked until after midnight, when Lindsay said she should get going.

'Thanks for coming over, Lindsay.' Connie wasn't sure quite how to say her farewell: a handshake, hug, air-kiss? Possibly because of the wine, she went in for a loose embrace – which Lindsay reciprocated. The main aim of the evening for Connie had been to get Lindsay to believe that Steph and Dylan had been killed, that it was not suicide.

As she saw Lindsay out and waved her off in the taxi, she wondered if she'd been successful.

CHAPTER SIXTY-EIGHT

DI Wade

The cool evening air was a relief after the mugginess of the taxi. Lindsay paused for a moment before entering the police station, breathing in the night. She'd always loved that smell. The smell of night had a particular kind of scent; comforting, somehow. She made her way to the office off the main incident room, passing a few officers who were on the late shift. Or early, depending on how you looked at it. Despite the people, the room held an altogether different mood. A subdued hush. Not the hub of frenzied activity it was during the day.

She had a lot to mull over. The evening with Connie had been an unexpected one. The things she divulged weighed on her mind. Everything was so confusing – nothing was piecing together in a straightforward manner. The very fact that Stephanie's brother, Brett, had found Connie and was telling her a different story to the one Stephanie had told was concerning. Connie was still so convinced that Stephanie and Dylan did not die by way of suicide, and Brett telling her that he was not, as she'd been led to believe by Steph, responsible for the fire, was falling on deaf ears with Connie. Why was she being so stubborn? Miles Prescott had told her there was no evidence that the brother had set the house on fire. In fact, according to Connie, Miles had denied all knowledge of a brother at first, then after finding a psychiatric report on Stephanie, changed this view and said instead that Brett had been responsible for a *school* fire, and it was that which he'd been sent to the secure home for. Miles had informed Connie, and Lindsay's team, that the police at the time were confident the house fire had been caused by a petrol bomb through the letter box. But Connie wasn't listening to reason. She'd got the bit between her teeth and was compelled to find out what she believed was the truth.

But at what cost?

If Connie carried on looking to implicate Brett in Stephanie and Dylan's deaths, wasn't she putting herself in a dangerous position?

If, in the unlikely event she was right, and she confronted Brett – the repercussions could be severe. Lindsay had told Connie this, hoping her words of warning would penetrate. But if Connie was as headstrong as she suspected, then it was a tall order to expect her to give up on her theory.

Maybe they *should* look into it further. Just in case. Lindsay opened the case files on her laptop, scrolling until she found the timeline she'd compiled. Connie had informed her that Brett had been released from the YOI on Thursday 1st June. Searching the timeline, she noted that was a day before Hargreaves' escape from custody at the graveside, and four days prior to his body being dumped. Coincidence? Why had he turned up on Connie's doorstep and how had he found her? The hairs on Lindsay's forearms bristled. Were there any other links? From what Connie had said, he wanted to put his side of the story forward, tell her that Stephanie had lied about him. It was strange he'd chosen Connie to unload this on to.

A nagging itch spread across her scalp. Had they been too quick to dismiss Stephanie as a suicide case?

Lindsay scanned the notes on the database. There were still no solid links between the timing of Hargreaves absconding from custody, the body dump and prison officers' rosters – but it had been Niall's day off. Yes, he'd given an alibi and it had obviously checked out because it hadn't been flagged. But someone might have lied for him. At the time, there'd have been no reason to be suspicious. Now though, the thought of a possible link between Niall Frazer and Brett Ellison crossed her mind. Both men had got in contact with Connie shortly after the deaths of Hargreaves and then Stephanie, which was either coincidental, or there was a reason for it. For Niall, it might have been purely because he wanted to offer comfort and had felt guilty for leaving it so long. Or he wanted to see how his handiwork had affected her, find out if it'd made her life better – how pleased she was with what he'd done.

Were he and Brett working together?

Lindsay shook her head. She was letting her mind get carried away. She'd allowed Connie's hysteria to rub off on her; she was getting swept along. Connie seemed to have an odd effect on her. She'd even confided in her about her husband. Now that was a surprise, even to her. Perhaps it was the counsellor in Connie that somehow made her more approachable, easy to talk to – after all, it had taken Lindsay months before she'd disclosed any personal details to Mack and she worked closely with him.

She needed to be logical now. The only way of cracking this case was to go over each small detail and find the evidence. It wouldn't do to fling theories around on the basis of one woman's say-so. Especially when there was still a possibility that that woman was central to the case and might have her own agenda. Lindsay questioned her own decision to accept Connie's invitation tonight – had she crossed a line? But although there was some evidence which could be taken as incriminating, whether that was enough to stop treating her as an expert advisor and more of a person of interest was doubtful. In Lindsay's mind at least. She had a feeling if her superior knew the situation fully, he might take a different view.

Lindsay clicked on the tattoo files. Connie had told her, almost as an aside, that Niall had a bird tattooed on his upper arm. Again, was this coincidence? Lots of people had bird tattoos, no doubt. Mack had taken pictures of them to a few local tattoo artists. None had recognised the work or could give a clue as to what they meant. Perhaps they were personal to the perpetrator, or Connie? The fact that Connie believed that one was similar to her dad's previous business emblem was curious. She hadn't come up with anything on the others. She had the memory stick now. And, as Connie had stated, it did seem unrelated to the current case. Worrying for her though – an unknown person purposely messing with her head, dragging up a past, painful event for no apparent reason. Lindsay would file the stick as evidence anyway, just in case more came of it at a later date.

Lindsay also had a team working on CCTV – seeing if the white van was spotted prior to or after the body drop. But there was literally nothing. It was as if it were a ghost van. The only thing they could gather from the lack of sightings was that he'd kept to lanes. He knew the area. Lindsay was sure he'd had help. But who? How many were involved in this? There were so many loose ends, it made Lindsay's head swim. Even the interviews with Hargreaves' final victim, Katie Watson, and her family had some inconsistencies. They couldn't be ruled out entirely, either.

Much to her annoyance, this case was proving to be more, rather than less complicated as it progressed.

CHAPTER SIXTY-NINE

Connie

Saturday 17 June

Her head was groggy; a fug from too much alcohol. Had it been a productive evening with DI Wade? Connie doubted it. She rolled on to her back, squinting against the brightness of the room, the sun's rays streaking across the ceiling like long fingers. Although Lindsay had listened, and even agreed in some part, Connie still thought that, ultimately, Lindsay believed Brett was telling the truth. That he didn't start the fire – and Steph was lying. As far as Lindsay was concerned, Brett's assertion fitted with Steph committing suicide. Steph had known the truth and, with the knowledge that Brett had been released, her lies were going to finally come to light. Her past had caught up with her. So, according to Lindsay's theory, Steph was frightened, but for a different reason than the one she'd given Connie.

Maybe Steph had been afraid that if the truth came out she would be in danger of being put in prison, of having Dylan taken into care? Connie flung the duvet off and slowly stood. Or had Steph been telling the truth about being scared that Brett was coming to find her? But not to finish what he started, as she'd said, but to exact his revenge for ruining his life. It might be that

243

Steph was telling a half-truth but, whatever her story, Connie still believed that her death was not a suicide.

And Brett had a motive to get rid of Steph in whichever version of the truth.

After swallowing two paracetamol, Connie fed Amber and then slumped on the sofa. It'd been nice to have female company last night. After the initial awkwardness, Lindsay had relaxed a bit, and had surprised her when she began telling her about her husband. Connie had the distinct impression that Lindsay was lonely. Her job clearly meant everything to her, and she'd also said she felt like she'd sacrificed a lot for it. Relationships had taken a major hit. Connie couldn't help feeling that Lindsay had forgotten how to apply some social skills, ones required to develop and sustain a healthy relationship. Connie hoped that now she'd made a move in the right direction with her, she'd continue to reach out. She liked the woman – her directness and honesty, the fact that what you saw was what you got – she could trust her. They might even become friends. Connie had to admit, they could both do with a female ally.

After a cool shower, Connie dressed in jeans and a white shirt, and, feeling refreshed and less headachy, decided to walk into Coleton to get something for lunch. Living meal-by-meal was becoming tiresome. What she really needed to do was a proper weekly shop; organise what meals she was going to have, to stop this pigging-out routine she'd got herself in. If she could lose a few pounds, well, a stone at least, she'd feel better, more like her old self. Her mum would stop worrying so much if she could see she was taking care of herself. Although, her mother would never stop worrying. If it wasn't about her health, she'd find something else to worry herself over.

It was only a ten-minute walk: past the park and then the train station, up takeaway alley and through the market walk to the supermarket. Which was fine on the way, when empty-handed, but when laden with bags, the walk back was far slower. Impeded by the throng of Saturday shoppers, Connie made slow progress. Plus, she had to keep stopping to rest and shift the bags to stop the plastic handles biting into her hands. She should've got a taxi home. As she leant against the wall of Sports Direct, facing the opposite side of the street, a familiar flash of purple hair caught her attention. Christ. Not now.

Connie gathered her bags and set off, head down, her pace as quick as she could manage.

'Ooh-ooh, Connie!' a high-pitched voice called.

Connie closed her eyes briefly, sighing loudly, but carried on moving. Perhaps Kelly would give up following.

'Connie, wait up.'

No. Of course she wouldn't give up. Connie stopped. Might as well let her have her usual dig, get it over, then she'd leave her be.

'What do you want, Kelly?' Connie turned sharply, Kelly almost bumping into her.

'Ah, well. I was wondering how things were, you know – things have been rotten for you. I heard the dreadful news about your client killing herself, murdering her beautiful child—'

'She did not kill herself, or her son!' Connie said, then instantly regretted her words. She'd played right into Kelly's hands.

'Oh, and why do you think that? Do you know something, Connie? If it wasn't suicide, then you must think she was killed. Do you know by who?' The woman tripped along beside Connie, her annoying voice, grating.

'I never said that. Don't put words in my mouth.'

'You said she didn't commit suicide. How else would you like me to take that?'

Connie didn't respond. They were level with the park. She didn't want Kelly following her any further, finding out where she lived. She walked to a free bench and placed her bags on it.

'Look, Kelly. I know you think there's some fabulous story here, one which will catapult you into stardom, or some such shit. But you're toying with people's lives. Using them. Does that feel good?

245

Knowing you're trampling on others to get up the rungs to the top of the ladder?'

'That's not what I'm doing. I'm simply seeking the truth. I've always endeavoured to find the real news, the nitty-gritty. Not some chocolate-covered candy version.'

'You just want to dig in the dirt. You're nothing but a pig, hunting for truffles.'

Connie was surprised to hear a laugh.

'Very good, Connie. I didn't know you were funny. Humorous is not one of the words I've heard others use to describe you.'

She was goading her again. Wanting her to ask who had said what in relation to her character. She wouldn't give her that satisfaction.

'Was there something you wanted to discuss, Kelly, or are you merely wanting to wind me up?'

Kelly sniffed, and readjusted her large shoulder bag. 'I guess what I really wanted to know was why you have been seen fraternising with ex-convicts?'

'Fraternising?' Connie shouted, instantly losing her cool. 'What on earth are you implying?'

Kelly reached into her bag and retrieved a camera.

Connie's chest tightened. She picked her bags up and pushed past Kelly. 'Fuck off, you horrible, irritating woman.' Her face was on fire. She hated this woman.

'What better way to get revenge on the man who ruined your career without having to get your own hands dirty – get a known criminal to do it for you. A bit lax of you, though, being seen in a public place together. I gave you more credit than that.'

Connie swung a bag around, hard, catching Kelly's knee.

'Ow!' She lifted the camera, clicking away as Connie turned away from her and walked towards the gap in the hedge. 'That's assault, that is,' Kelly shouted after her. 'Hit a nerve, did I? He was right about you.'

Connie wanted to stop and ask who? Who was right about her?

What did she mean? But, having already shown anger, she daren't hang around for another battle.

Once she was safe behind her closed door, Connie allowed the hot tears to course unheeded down her cheeks. Her breath escaped in shallow pants. Her limbs ached with the weight of the bags. Her headache was back.

The only person Kelly could have been referring to when she said 'He was right about you' was Niall. Niall must have given Connie's name to the reporter. Niall had something to do with those photos and had leaked the information about them to Kelly.

Niall was a back-stabbing, untrustworthy creep.

Maybe he was also a murderer.

CHAPTER SEVENTY

Connie

What should she do about Niall? She'd confided in Lindsay, so she was aware of the bird tattoo, and Lindsay had said that they were delving further into his story, his alibi. So, apart from avoiding any contact with him for the moment, she supposed there wasn't much else she could do.

Usually on a Saturday, Connie would relax, watch a movie, stuff her face with calorie-laden delights, read a book. But today her mind couldn't settle; it drifted as she watched TV. Whatever was on didn't stop her thoughts coming back to Steph. Rather than fight it, she got her laptop and loaded her client files. She always backed them up so they were on her work computer and her personal laptop – she didn't trust technology and certainly didn't want to lose all her valuable data.

Now, Amber draped beside her, Connie read through Steph's file, focusing on the redacted psychological report Miles had sent her. She'd already read it but it felt important to keep returning to it. Sometimes details could be missed in the first read. The more she read, the more she became unsettled by what was within the sentences, and what remained unsaid between the lines. Steph and her mum's relationship seemed to have been good prior to the fire. No real issues. But, afterwards, Steph's apparent feeling of abandonment went deeper than would have been expected of the situation. Something in the way the psychiatrist had worded the report niggled Connie. She seemed to be pointing to the fact that Steph – Jenna back then – held a grudge towards her mum. What stood out for Connie was the scribbled handwritten note in the margin: *Consider BPD due to amount of rage that Jenna demonstrates.*

Rage? The report showed evidence that Steph was angry at her mother, yes – but rage seemed a strong supposition. But then Connie only had access to the one report, and a redacted one at that. She could understand Steph's hurt at being left to cope with the aftermath of the fire, such a traumatic experience to go through alone. However, Connie herself had seen no evidence of rage during their sessions. Anger, yes. Naturally.

Connie's back tingled. The sensation prickled her skin, aggravating her nerve endings – like an itch deep inside her body. Unreachable. Something was off. She was missing something important. And it was to do with Steph's mum. How could she find out what it was? Maybe there was a clue to this somewhere in Steph's house. Connie slammed the laptop lid shut. Miles Prescott also knew more than he was willing to let on to Connie. That she was sure of. His sudden departure to Manchester the day Steph and Dylan were found, after Connie had relayed her concerns about Brett to him, was very suspect. He was avoiding talking to her, too. As yet, he'd been unable to give a satisfactory explanation about anything relating to Steph and the fire; her family. Brett. The whole thing felt wrong.

What was Miles covering up?

There was no way he'd respond to Connie on a weekend, so getting any answers from him would have to wait. But Connie might be able to get something from Steph's house. The police wouldn't have done a thorough search because as far as they were concerned it was a suicide. Any clues to what had been happening in the lead-up to Steph's death might be there somewhere, waiting to be unearthed.

And she would find it. Tonight, under the cover of darkness, Connie would get into Steph's house and conduct her own search.

She decided to catch the 6.20 p.m. train into Totnes, wait in her office until dark, then get a taxi to the end of Steph's road. She wasn't sure how she'd gain access to the property, it wasn't like she'd done this sort of thing before. Now would be the perfect time to 'fraternise' with ex-cons – like Jonesy. His expertise would come in handy. Her heart rate shot up. She was planning on breaking and entering. What was she thinking? What if she got caught, how would that look? She was in enough bother without purposely putting herself in a stupid position.

She had no choice. She had to see if there was something that would clear Steph's name. And prove Brett Ellison *and* Lindsay Wade and her team wrong.

After leaving the warmth of the taxi, Connie began to walk the length of Steph's road. She casually glanced at Steph's house as she approached it on her left, then swept her eyes around the estate, which contained roughly twelve houses: some terraced, some semi-detached. It had been ten o'clock when she hailed the taxi, and she supposed it'd taken about five minutes to reach the road she'd been dropped in. Lights shone in every house but Steph's. Connie's pulse jolted. A sadness swept over her.

Empty. The occupants dead. A void left behind.

What else had Steph left behind?

Nearing the pathway running to Steph's house, Connie's pace slowed. Then stopped altogether. Now she was close, she could see more clearly. Tears stung her eyes, a lump forming in her throat. Hundreds of tributes obscured the front wall of the house and littered the small, square garden. Damp, bedraggled teddy bears, candles, deflated silver helium balloons, bouquets of wilted flowers. Tributes – now as dead as those who once occupied the house.

Broken police tape, still partly attached to the metal railings and drainpipe, flapped gently in the breeze.

Maybe they did do a thorough search of the house, then. She should leave, be confident they did their job. There was a chance, though, that their search had been limited to finding something odd, out of place. What if the detail was ordinary, something easily missed by someone who didn't know Steph?

She had to go in.

Connie forced her legs to move. She checked around her to see if anyone had noticed her standing there. She couldn't see anyone. It seemed everyone was in their houses. If they'd seen her, they weren't bothered. They'd probably become accustomed to spectators over the last week and now ignored anyone hanging around. Connie moved on, turning the corner at the end of the row of houses. She walked back on herself, on the road that would take her past the rear of Steph's property.

She hesitated outside the large wooden gate at the back of Steph's house. Once she breached the perimeter, she'd be committed to carrying out her sweep of the house. No going back. She took a deep breath and lifted the gate latch. It creaked, loudly.

Christ.

After one last check around her, Connie stepped inside, closing the gate behind her. She crept up to the back of the house, searching for the best place to enter. It was secure. No open windows. What had she expected? Taking her backpack off, Connie rummaged inside it for the torch. Keeping it low, she scanned the back garden for a stone large enough to break the glass. Connie took off her jumper and wrapped it around her arm, the one holding the stone, and with a quick, sharp jab hit the middle panel of glass in the back door. The tinkling of shattering glass filled the quiet night air. She released her breath, then cautiously reached inside and opened the door.

She was in.

CHAPTER SEVENTY-ONE

Brett

She was going to take some convincing. He didn't know what he'd expected; had he really thought that she'd immediately agree with him, take him at his word? She'd been seeing Jenna for months, listening to her side. And Jenna really *was* convincing. She'd spent eight years telling herself the same story. Even she believed it. As he had done. Once.

Connie wasn't like he'd imagined her. She seemed younger, her skin pale and flawless, her eyes green like emeralds.

Green for envy.

He knew all about that.

Connie Summers was the only other person who might allow his story to be heard; acknowledged. The only person he could convince. Somehow it had become his focus. It felt important that someone in this world took his side.

He'd need something particularly good to persuade Connie he was right. That Jenna was a liar. And there was something that might do it.

Now, he just had to find it.

CHAPTER SEVENTY-TWO

Connie

Connie edged her way through the dark kitchen, her right hand outstretched, aiming the torch forwards. The yellow-tinged hue gave the place an eerie feeling; the beam wobbled with the shake in her hand. Moving through a doorway, she found herself in a long room. Obviously, this was used as both lounge and dining room; a square table with two chairs acted as a separator. At the far end, Connie could make out a sofa and coffee table. A large toy box stood underneath the front window. She kept the beam of light low, hoping no one would see it from outside.

A chill settled on her insides. Abandoned toys lay scattered around the open toy box, exactly how Dylan had left them. Gooseflesh prickled her skin. She was inside the house of a dead woman and child. The horror hit her hard, bile rising in her throat. She felt along the wall until she reached the sofa, and she sat, her breaths escaping her in ragged bursts.

What on earth was she thinking, coming here alone at night?

After a few moments to compose herself, Connie got up and began to search the room. There was a dresser in the alcove to the side of the fireplace, an old-fashioned-looking one, the kind Connie remembered had been in her own house when she was a child. It was as good a place as any to begin the search. If there had been letters from Brett, that's where Steph might've kept them. Holding the torch under her chin, she used both hands to riffle through the drawers. Mostly, they were full of utility bills, pictures Dylan had drawn and pre-school letters. Nothing that looked useful to poor Steph now. She swallowed down the urge to cry.

Apart from the letters from Brett that Steph had told Connie she'd received, what else was she hoping to find? The room was in disarray, and Connie wasn't sure if it was because that's how Steph had left it, or it was how the police had, following their 'search'.

The shadows created from the torchlight cast long patches of darkness across the walls. Each time one moved due to her directing the beam elsewhere, her heart leapt. This was ridiculous. When she was a teenager, she and Luke, along with a few of their older friends, had gone into a derelict house as a dare. They'd heard many stories of the house being haunted by The White Lady, and being only thirteen and fifteen were easily pumped and primed before they'd even entered. It had been exciting to start with, all fun and giggles. Until footsteps were heard overhead and a scraping noise filtered through the floorboards. They'd all screamed and ran, each pushing the other to be the first one outside, back to safety. That fear had stayed with her for months afterwards, causing many a nightmare, plus a lifetime avoidance of scary movies. Now, the memory of it flooded back. There were no friends to egg her on, no friends' reactions to feed off. But her mind was conjuring enough terrifying thoughts to make up for the lack of others' panic.

Connie couldn't see any other cupboards, or anywhere Steph might've kept any valuables or keepsakes. She'd have to venture upstairs. A ball of anxiety swelled inside her gut. An impulse to leave tugged at her. She gritted her teeth. She was here now – had come this far, it would be silly not to see it through. If she didn't try to find something that would convince the police that she was right, she'd always regret it and kick herself for failing.

Standing at the foot of the stairs looking up, the dark seemed even more chilling; malevolent – like something bad was up there, hiding, waiting for her. The tiny hairs on her arms and the back of her neck stood erect. Every muscle in her body, every sense, screamed at her to turn back, leave the house. Connie shut her mind to the warnings, and placed one foot on the first stair. One by one she climbed them, a creak sounding on each step, remarkably loud in the otherwise silent house. The first room she came to was a bathroom. The next had a double bed. Steph's room. She swept the torch around.

A figure caught in the circle of illumination.

Connie yelped, dropping the torch. She scrambled on the floor, hands patting all around her. Her fingers found the hard object and she picked it up, quickly directing it where she'd seen the figure. She let out a large breath. A mirror. She'd seen her own reflection.

Her hands trembled, her legs shaking as she stood again.

A nervous giggle erupted from her as she checked her reflection again, making sure it really was her own. A tiny shiver tracked down her back as she saw the green of her irises highlighted in the beam of light. Luke's eyes. 'Stupid woman, scaring yourself half to death,' she whispered. Even as a whisper, her words seemed loud. She shook her shoulders to loosen her rigid muscles. Regaining her composure, Connie looked around the room. A chest of drawers and a wardrobe were the only items of furniture apart from the bed. She'd try the wardrobe first. She stood on the bed, unsteady on the soft mattress, and shone the light at the top. Nothing. Opening both doors, she swept the hangers from right to left, the squeal of metal on the rail sounding like tiny screams. A cold shiver ran the length of her back, her unease heightened. One side of the wardrobe had a shelf, on it a few boxes: bought ones, patterned, pretty. Connie dragged them down one by one, placing them on the bed. She knelt on the floor beside them, not wanting to sit on Steph's bed. The second box contained letters.

'Bingo.'

A surge of adrenaline shot through her veins as she emptied out the box. These would prove that Steph hadn't been lying about Brett, might even prove that he was after her, and that her suicide was in fact murder. She fumbled with the envelopes, her fingers clumsy – she rested the torch on the duvet so she could pull out the folded paper from the envelopes.

She took the torch again, shining it on to the pages. Her heart dipped.

The letters were not from Brett.

They were not *from* anyone.

Connie flipped the envelope over, then frantically checked the others. All unsent – each addressed to the same person. She sank back, sitting on the floor. The letters slid from the bed, scattering around her. She wanted to scream. These were no use. She sighed, but took one of them anyway, curiosity getting the better of her, and began to read. With each word, her hopes for finding supporting evidence to clear Steph's name evaporated. She skim-read another. They were filled with anger, hurt. All of it directed at one person.

A tinkling of glass.

Connie froze. Below, a scraping. She strained her ears.

Footsteps.

Someone was in the house.

Move, Connie, move.

The person shifted through the house, their footsteps soft, yet audible, even above the whooshing noise of the pounding pulse in her ears. She must get up; hide.

Quickly gathering the letters and shoving them in her backpack, Connie cast her eyes around for a hiding place. The wardrobe was too small and too crammed with clothes. She lifted the duvet and cursed. It was a divan, no gap underneath.

Shit.

She snatched the torch and on shaky legs made her way out

on to the landing. A beam of light caught her eye, on the wall at the bottom of the stairs.

They were coming upstairs.

Connie crept as quietly as she could into the next bedroom, closing the door slowly behind her, but leaving it slightly ajar so as not to make more noise. Scanning the room, she was relieved to see that the single bed was at least a wooden one, with space underneath. Dylan's bed. She had no time to ponder on that now. Sliding her rucksack under first, Connie lay down, wriggling her body into the small space.

It was tight. Her back scraped across the wooden slats as she crawled on her stomach to get herself as far under the bed as possible. She berated herself for not having gone on the diet she'd been planning for the last six months.

Would she be seen?

The carpet was damp, the musty smell irritated her nose. *Don't sneeze.* Her head was at the foot of the bed, angled towards the door. She shuffled again, inching back, pushing herself hard against the wall. The pressure of the wooden slats squeezed the air from her lungs, she couldn't take deep breaths.

She felt like she was going to suffocate.

Light appeared at the crack of the door, widening and lengthening as the door pushed open.

Nothing to see in here, move on, please go away.

She had to quieten her breaths or they'd hear her.

Who was it?

There was only one name that came to Connie.

Brett.

He was the only one other than her who would want to come here.

Perhaps they were after the same thing.

He was in the room now. Although her instinct was to screw her eyes up tight, she kept them open, watching, waiting for Brett to turn around. Leave.

The feet didn't leave. Instead they made their way towards her, inches from the bed. *Shit, shit, shit.*

She should've been more careful. No one even knew where she was. If he found her here, what would he do with her?

She held her breath. The whooshing of blood in her ears was so loud she was scared he'd be able to hear that instead. She watched wide-eyed as a pair of boots came to a standstill near her head. Her eyes were going to burst, the pressure behind them increasing with each rapid heartbeat. He was going to find her. She was going to die in this house.

A shuffle.

Connie stifled a scream. The person lowered to the floor.

She was going to be found.

Screwing her eyes up tightly, she waited for the inevitable capture. The hopeful part of her held on to that old childhood belief that if you can't see them, they can't see you. The pain in her lungs reached an unbearable level, threatening to crush her chest. She couldn't hold her breath for much longer.

Even through her closed eyelids, she was aware of a darkness closing in.

Then breath tickling her face.

Brett.

CHAPTER SEVENTY-THREE

Connie

'And what do you think you're doing, eh?'

Connie's eyes sprang open at the sound of the voice, her breath rushing out. Tears bubbled and escaped; the fear releasing itself.

'Jesus Christ,' she managed, weakly. Every bit of strength had left her body the moment she'd felt the breath on her skin.

'I knew you wouldn't be able to leave this alone. Come on.' The outstretched hand reached under the bed. Connie grasped it, a film of sweat causing it to slip. 'Well, you've got yourself in quite a situation there, haven't you?'

'I guess you think it's funny!' Connie struggled to manoeuvre herself out from under the bed, and she knocked her back against the bed frame as Lindsay Wade helped pull her out.

'No, actually. I think it's incredibly stupid. I can't believe you've done this.'

Connie got herself into a sitting position and leant back against the bed. 'I think I might have to agree. I really thought I was done for then.' Her chest heaved with the effort of crawling out from under the bed, and from the fright Lindsay had given her.

'So, who were you expecting it to be?'

'Brett. I thought he might come here looking for the same thing I am.'

259

'Which is?'

'Evidence, Lindsay. Something that incriminates him, some-thing that'll prove to you that I'm right in thinking Steph did *not* commit suicide.'

Lindsay sighed. 'I thought as much after our conversation at yours last night. I knew you were still holding on to that, and nothing I said was going to change your mind. Was it?'

'You know what it's like, when you've got a gut feeling about something. I have taken on board the things you said, and I know everything points to Steph killing herself. And Dylan. But it all seems too easy. Neat. I'm convinced that there's more to it.'

'So you thought you'd come here, break and enter and get yourself in a whole heap of trouble?'

'I wasn't expecting to get caught. How did you know I was here – were you following me?'

'I had my suspicions. I wouldn't say I was *following* you, more like looking out for you.'

'Right, well, what are you going to do with me now? You already think I'm cavorting with criminals, and now I suppose I'm going to be charged with this.' Connie got to her feet, picking up her rucksack and torch ready to get out of the house.

'I'm going to pretend I didn't find you here. I'll put the broken glass in the back door down to teenagers, tell the landlord he needs to secure the property. Come on. Let's get out before we attract any unwanted attention.'

Lindsay led the way out of Dylan's room, back through the house and outside. Connie followed close behind. Wary of being seen, she kept looking behind, the feeling of being watched giving her the creeps.

'I'll drive you back to your house,' Lindsay said as she approached her car.

Connie climbed in, feeling like a naughty child caught up to no good. They drove for a few minutes in complete silence, the darkness pressing against the window as Connie rested her head against it.

'Thanks. For not reporting me,' Connie said.

'Hmm. I won't put my neck on the line for you again, though. Do you understand? So no more meddling, Connie. Promise me?'

Connie faced her and nodded.

'Right. That's good. I don't want to be worried about you, I've enough to think about.'

'Yeah, like what?' Connie straightened in the seat. Had there been a development?

'For starters, I came away from a conversation with Miles Prescott with a feeling that he wasn't sharing everything with me, that he was purposely being vague. His story sounded rehearsed. *Off.* I can't put my finger on it but I'm going to dig further into the team at the protected persons scheme, and Miles in particular. The fact that so much about Steph . . . Jenna's background, her family, was ignored and pushed aside, just so they could get a conviction on the boyfriend, seems wrong. Careless.'

'Why hide the fact they weren't thorough?'

'I don't know. Miles is coming up for retirement. I can't imagine an enquiry at this point would be welcomed. Or perhaps he felt guilty?'

'Huh. I can relate to that – you've no idea how much guilt I've experienced over the past year and a half.'

'I think you'll find I do, actually. It hangs over me like a veil – guilt for a mother's death, her family left behind, guilt for my failed marriage, because my focus was always elsewhere, guilt for bringing you in on this case . . .'

'Ah, well, you can cross that one off your list. It wasn't you who wrote my name on a dead man's hand, was it?'

Lindsay smiled. 'No, that wasn't me.'

'Maybe we should both stop giving ourselves a hard time.'

'Yeah, maybe,' Lindsay said.

'Anyway, back to Miles.' Connie needed to change the subject;

the car felt heavy with responsibility. 'I still wonder if he's covering his back. I think he knows more than we do, anyway. How are you going to get him to confess?'

'I'm not saying he's *deliberately* messed up,' Lindsay faltered. 'I probably shouldn't have mentioned it.'

'But you're clearly thinking he's hiding something, and you're going to investigate further?'

'Yes, like I said, I'll dig deeper, see what I can uncover. Oh, and by the way, I'm afraid Mack did some digging himself.'

Connie sighed. 'Great, now what?'

'Niall Frazer.'

Connie's pulse throbbed in her neck. Was she about to find out that Niall was involved in Hargreaves' murder?

'Go on, don't keep me in suspense.'

'I'd asked Mack to go back through statements, interviews and the like—'

'Get to the point, Lindsay.'

'All right, all right, patience. He has an alibi.'

'Yes, you said that before, you knew he had.'

'Yes, I knew that all the prison officers did, but after you mentioned the bird tattoo I thought they should be looked at again. And guess who gave your Niall an alibi?'

'He's not *my* Niall . . . but who?'

'One Kelly Barton.'

Connie's jaw dropped. No way. The sneaky rat.

CHAPTER SEVENTY-FOUR

Connie

Sunday 18 June

'I need to see you. Now.' Connie disconnected the call before her anger spilled over. She'd managed little sleep after Lindsay had dropped her home at midnight. She'd spent an hour sitting up in bed, poring over Steph's unsent letters – everything swimming around her head, nagging her, making her question things again, and again. The letters had all been written by Steph to her mother. Poor girl. She guessed they hadn't been posted because Steph knew her mum would never be able to read them, her dementia preventing that, or even any understanding if someone else read them to her.

Just as Connie had thought sleep might finally steal her, her mind conjured another face. That bastard, Niall. She'd been suspicious of the timing of him getting back in contact and she'd also allowed herself to think he might've been the one who'd given Kelly Barton her name in the first place, helped the despicable woman link Connie's name to Hargreaves. But she hadn't considered that Niall and Kelly were *together*.

Could Lindsay still be wrong? Yes, he had an alibi. But was it a trustworthy one? That lowlife Kelly would stoop that far just to get in on the action – be in the right place for a killer story. She could've lied for Niall, said she was with him in return for him giving her the juicy details; insider information.

Getting him to explain was likely to be futile. Wouldn't he continue to feed her lie after lie? She had to do something, though. Attempt to gain some form of explanation.

'Before you launch into me . . .' Niall thrust a garage-bought offering of flowers into Connie's hands. 'I'm sorry.' He stayed on the doorstep, head bowed. So, he thought he'd get in with a quick apology, try and diffuse her anger. That wasn't going to work.

'How could you do it to me?' Connie snatched the flowers from him, then thought better of it and threw them back at him. They hit his chest, then fell – a flurry of red petals floating to the ground.

'Flowers were a bad idea, then,' he said, his smile faltering.

'Deciding to come back into my life was a bad idea.' Her initial anger released, Connie stood back and invited Niall inside. He gingerly stepped over the threshold.

She closed them both inside.

'I assume you're not happy with me,' Niall stated casually.

'And I assume you know why!'

Niall cricked his neck from one side to the other, then sat down. His eyes were puffy, dark bags visible beneath them. He looked rough. The past year had clearly not been kind to either of them.

'I'll let you enlighten me. I don't think it's wise for me to guess why you're mad.'

'No, of course not. Because then if what I say isn't what you think it might be about, you'll be off the hook.'

'I'm not sure I follow—'

'Oh, enough, Niall.' Connie didn't want to play more games. 'I know about Kelly Barton, all right? *That's* why I'm mad at you.'

He gave a brief nod, didn't try the 'I don't know what you are talking about' spiel. He knew it was pointless, that he was defeated.

'In my defence, I *was* drunk.'

It was no good, she couldn't sit still – she had to pace.

'Haven't heard that excuse a hundred times, Niall. Although they've usually been from criminals.'

His head snapped up. 'I am not a criminal.'

'You're bloody acting like one.'

'I let a few things slip, big deal. You know what she can be like.'

'What do you mean, you let a few things slip?'

'A bit of background stuff, you know – about your . . . er . . . *issues* with Hargreaves.'

'Wow, you're a real friend.'

'I'm sorry. Really sorry. She was clever – she obviously knew where the prison officers went to drink and followed us to the bar one night. She lulled me into a false sense of security; she flirted with me, paid me attention—'

'And that's all it took.' Connie spat the words at him.

'She plied me with alcohol all night, knowing if I got drunk I'd talk openly.'

Connie smarted as she remembered her own plan the first night she'd invited Niall over a couple of weeks ago. Her idea to get Niall drunk, to loosen his tongue. The same as Kelly. Were they that very different, then – both taking advantage of a loose-lipped drunk to get what they wanted? Connie put her fingers to her temples and rubbed them.

'Are you still sleeping with her?'

'What? No. I never *slept* with the woman. Give me some credit.'

'But she was your alibi?' A creeping heat spread up her neck. 'She said you were together the night Hargreaves was murdered, and when his body was dumped outside the prison gates the following morning.'

'Well, I'd been there most of the night . . .' he mumbled.

'*Most* of it? So, she gave you a false alibi?' Connie couldn't believe what she was hearing.

'Well . . . it wasn't much, a few hours, tops. She asked for a favour in return, of course—'

265

'And I was that favour,' Connie snapped. 'Get information from me about the case. Ensure Kelly gets first crack at the whip. I suppose you told her where I'd be, places I'd go, so she could watch me, follow me. *Photograph* me.' She dug her nails into her palm, and attempted some steadying breaths. However, the question was, if Kelly *had* taken the photos of her at the train station, of her at Mack's house with Gary, the one of her dad, then why hadn't she used them in the papers? Why send them to her and the police?

A game. Some cruel, messed-up game. It had to be.

Would this god-awful woman ever leave her alone?

CHAPTER SEVENTY-FIVE

DI Wade

Monday 19 June

'Come on, people. Let's make today a good one. I want leads, no – I want more than leads; I want a suspect. Get me a suspect, preferably in custody by the end of the day, or don't bother coming back into this station.' Lindsay waved off her team, and they dispersed. Apart from one. Mack leant against a desk, his legs sprawled in front of him, arms crossed. His brow matched.

'If you're waiting for me,' Lindsay said, 'you'd best make yourself a bit more comfortable. I'm going to be half an hour.'

'I'll make us a coffee then.'

'Sure. Are you okay, Mack? You look peaky. You ill?'

'No time to be ill, Boss.' He pushed up from the desk and wandered off towards the coffee machine. 'Besides, I'm tired, that's all. Had a bit of a heart-to-heart with Gary last night,' he called over his shoulder.

'Oh? How did that go?' Lindsay faced her computer screen, checking her emails as she spoke.

'All right, in the end.' He filled two cardboard cups with a toffee-coloured liquid. 'It appears I've been a crap dad, when all's said and done, though.'

'You can't be with them all the time. And anyway, he's an adult, Mack, what is he – twenty-seven now? You can't hold his hand on all his dates.' Lindsay gave him a brief look, and laughed.

'It's not hand-holding he'd needed. It was his old dad to listen to him more. He'd told me that Connie was pregnant, that she went on to get rid of it, or so he thought. But I was so angry at her that I didn't listen to *him*. I didn't give him an opportunity to confide his feelings about it before now, I just saw how it affected him and acted on that.' He returned, placing the cups on the desk.

'You've been so busy; he knew you were there for him. All he had to do was ask, I'm sure.'

'That's not always what having a kid is about. As a parent, you're meant to know; sense when they need you, or want to talk. They don't always come to you outright, ask for something – unless it's money, then they're straight there, hands open in readiness. It's the important stuff I missed. When me and Barb stopped communicating, it seems that I stopped communicating with my kids, too.'

'I don't know what it's like having a child, I know that.' Lindsay sat back in her chair, facing Mack, giving him her full attention. 'But I do know what it's like having parents. And from what I can recall, they went through their own personal hell and had no time for me during the worst of the times. But when my dad finally came out of his man-made foggy cave after Mum buggered off, I knew I could count on him again. It's never too late to make up for it you know, Mack. It takes time and effort, but it's possible. He's confided in you now, and you've listened now – it's where you take it from here that's important.'

'Yeah, thanks, Boss. Sorry, getting all bleeding soppy on you. Old fool.'

'Don't be. Just don't wipe your tears on my shirt.' Lindsay gave his thigh a smack. 'Relationships are hard. All of them. We muddle along as best we can, each of us groping in the dark. So to speak.'

They laughed, the intensity of the sudden emotional sharing broken.

'Back to work then, slacker.'

'Hey, I'm waiting for you. What's your plan, anyway?' Mack moved his chair next to Lindsay's, sitting backwards on it and facing her.

'I was rather hoping you had one. Come on, Mack, I can't be the brains *and* the beauty of this operation. You need to put in your share, and as you're not that pretty . . .'

'Ah, you can't help but flatter me. Fine. If you want my honest opinion, I think we've missed something – something . . . ordinary. It's like I was saying about not listening to the kids when you've got all your own shit going on. I think this has been a bit like that – we've blocked the main noise in favour of the background noise. We need to listen to what's right here.' Mack balled his fist and hit it against his chest.

'That's your heart. If that starts speaking we've got more problems on our hands than we first thought.'

'Take the piss. But you'll see I'm right. We need to go to the beginning and listen afresh.'

'Okay. I'll humour you.' Lindsay cupped her chin in her hands and looked thoughtfully at Mack. 'So, oh wise one, what am I supposed to be listening to?'

'Connie Summers.'

Lindsay lifted a single eyebrow in a high arc. 'That's your big idea?'

'Yes, Boss. It begins and ends with our Ms Summers. We've just not been listening to the right bits of her story.'

CHAPTER SEVENTY-SIX

Connie

Connie fussed with the items on her desk, moving them, straightening them – anything to give her fingers a job – stop them trembling. She glanced at the clock. Still an hour before Brett arrived. After she'd called him, asked him to come back for a full session, Connie had made some enquiries. As per usual, Miles Prescott's team had been unhelpful. She'd tried the local probation office, her theory being that if Brett was newly released and staying in this area, he'd likely have a probation officer assigned to him. She couldn't see that someone like him, and at his age, would be released straight from the YOI with no licence.

She'd been in luck; she'd been able to get the details of Brett's probation officer and finally, this morning, she spoke directly with her. Laura, a new PO and therefore incredibly cooperative, had given Connie lots of information. If only Miles had taken a keener interest when it mattered, things would've turned out differently. But then, he was on the opposite end of the scale – knocking on the door of retirement – he couldn't have been less helpful if he'd tried.

Brett had been transferred from the youth offending team to probation services because he'd just turned eighteen. Laura had listed numerous incidents involving Brett while he'd been within the secure home and the YOI in Manchester. Mostly, they were fire-related, often occurring in the middle of the night. She went on to explain that Brett had been diagnosed as suffering with childhood pyromania, which was uncommon, but all clinical evaluations pointed towards it: revenge-seeking, social disorder – he'd been expelled from school and possibly had ADHD or adjustment disorder, although that had only been hinted at, never formally diagnosed. Perhaps he'd slipped through the net. But looking at it all now, everything ticked the box for pyromaniac. The exact underlying cause changed over the years. Different professionals each having their favoured theory. One thing agreed by all, however, was that Brett used fire as an impulsive act of stress-relief.

Everything Laura told Connie reinforced Steph's story, and it fitted well with the timing of the fire that devastated the family house. The fire that destroyed a family. The fire Brett had been responsible for, unlike Miles' assertion otherwise.

It seemed pretty cut and dried.

How did Brett expect her to believe he was innocent, that Steph had lied?

This and many other questions bombarded Connie's already battered brain as she fought to keep control of her own emotions this morning. Yesterday's admission from Niall, that he had been passing snippets of information to Kelly Barton, still grated. Hurt. Even though she'd had doubts about his intentions, deep down she hadn't really thought he'd sink that low. Somehow it felt like an element of karma was coming into play here. She was getting punished. Thing was, she wasn't at all certain what for, exactly, and who else was dishing it out.

Still playing for time, Connie headed downstairs to the reception room and made a coffee. Standing at the lower window, she watched the people that went by, all going about their business, largely unaware of others. Was the hoody-man out there somewhere, watching? She hadn't noticed anyone since the day after

Steph's death, so maybe he really had been waiting for her – had been the one supplying her cannabis. She was unlikely to ever find out who he was, or what he'd wanted now. The trail had ended; no new leads. She closed her eyes, an image of Steph and Dylan on the pirate ship that Monday lunchtime coming to her. How could it be that a day later they were gone? For a moment Connie was lost, her focus blurring as cars drove by.

It was surprisingly quiet inside the building, given that it was situated in the main shopping street of Totnes. It was an old building, the walls thick, so most of the noise was filtered. It was like being in a giant cocoon: quiet, comforting, and protective. Until Brett came in; he'd break the seal, crack open the shell and it wouldn't feel quite as safe. The bang of a door shutting upstairs startled her – a breeze from her open office window obviously blowing it closed, bringing her back to the moment. She quickly swallowed the last of the coffee and nipped to use the toilet off the reception room.

With both hands leaning on the small basin, Connie stared at herself in the mirror. Her face seemed swollen. Lack of sleep, lack of decent food, lack of hydration, all adding to a look of pallor, a dullness to her skin. She needed to visit a spa, go and get a facial or beauty treatment. Spoil herself. Would Lindsay go with her, so they could have a girly day together? Connie laughed out loud, and shook her head. Stupid thought. She'd like it, though. She'd spent more time with Lindsay than any other female friend for, well, she couldn't remember the last time. It'd definitely been over a year ago. And she couldn't really count the other women she'd worked with in the psychology department – they were different, not exactly friends, more colleagues. It was about time she made the effort to socialise, to make time for a proper friend – one who could be a constant in her life. Could Lindsay fit that role?

Connie took in a large breath. It was time to get organised for her client. Her stomach dipped violently, a mouthful of lukewarm coffee regurgitating into her mouth. She must call Lindsay, tell her that she was about to have a session with Brett, and that, if she didn't call back by eleven, to assume something had happened. Something bad, and she should send someone over.

With a slightly more confident step, Connie ascended the stairs and rang Lindsay.

'What is it you would like to gain from this session, Brett?' Connie sat in the chair opposite him, no desk as a barrier, no pad and pen. Just her and him. Counsellor and client. She needed to treat him the same as she would any other; be professional.

He regarded her in silence, his eyes locked on hers. She resisted lowering her own gaze.

'I can't get my missing years back. My childhood was lost to the system. I have no family. No job, or likelihood of gaining one. This session, the next one, or a million after it, isn't going to get me anywhere. In effect, my life is over. It ended in the street outside a burning house eight years ago.'

Connie wasn't sure where to go with this. He wasn't here for her help, not with cognitive behavioural therapy. He was here for something else. The realisation that it could be revenge chilled her. Had he already carried it out, did he want to talk about it – or was it still to come? And what part was she going to play in his plan? The therapist in her told her to avoid being drawn in to his negativity, to try a different tack.

'Your PO informs me that as a child you were diagnosed with the disorder pyromania.' Connie noted a twitch in Brett's eye as he shot forwards. She held his stare and continued quickly before he could interrupt her. 'In children, it's quite rare – and the desire and the need to set fires is thought to be as a form of release. Like from pent-up anger or tension. Can you remember when you first felt that compulsion to set a fire?'

He shrugged. 'I guess when I was about nine.'

'What was it about that time that had caused you stress, or anger?'

'It wasn't anger. Not then. But stress, yeah – it could've been that. We'd just moved in. Been there about a week I suppose, when I saw it. When I got the feeling she hated me.'

'Who hated you?'

'Mum.' His eyes seemed to darken and for a moment he was lost in a memory.

'You believed your mum hated you? What made you think that?'

'She was right pissed when she realised we came as a pair.'

Connie narrowed her eyes. 'I don't understand what you're saying – when you came as a pair? What do you mean?'

'She thought she was just getting my dad. Not another kid. She had one of them. Jenna. She said she had no money to support a benefit scrounger and his scraggly kid. From that day she treated me like shit. She was real mean, nasty. I hated her as much as she hated me. So that's when I started burning things.'

Connie sat back. Brett and Steph *weren't* brother and sister. Had that been why there was nothing in the background information, why Miles didn't believe Steph? Maybe Miles wasn't holding back relevant details from her, he simply didn't know himself. Steph had never offered up the fact that Brett was a stepbrother. What else had Steph failed to mention?

'How did family life progress from the way it was when you first moved in?'

'Got worse, basically. Mum clearly regretted her decision. I never once saw her and my dad kiss, cuddle, nothing. And as for Jenna, she went in on herself. Didn't speak, dressed real scruffy, didn't even wash.'

'And you remember this?'

'Yes. I worked a lot on my memories when I was inside.'

Connie raised her brow. It would be interesting to find out more about how they attempted to retrieve memories, delve into it all, but now wasn't the time. She had to keep up the pace. 'How about the fire-setting?'

'I used that to keep me calm. I never did anything too bad, was only ever paper, the odd pillowcase. Small stuff. And it always worked – when she did something, said stuff, burning things always stopped the ball in my gut getting any bigger.'

'So, you were angry, hurt, upset. All those emotions must've been so difficult for your ten-year-old mind to contemplate. It was an accident, Brett. I believe that. I don't think you would've deliberately set out to kill your dad, burn the house to the ground. When we're young the consequences of our actions aren't as easy to predict.'

'What are you on about?' He slapped his hands down on his legs. 'I didn't start the fire that night. I'm trying to tell you, Connie. I used flames to calm me, not to hurt anybody else. I never let the fire get out of control. Never.' He leant into Connie's space, his face almost against hers. 'I. Did. Not. Kill. My. Father.' He sat back.

Connie cleared her throat. Her pulse skipped with the added adrenaline rushing through her body. She had to be careful how she said what she wanted to say next. Use a tone that was curious, not accusational.

'All the evidence, in terms of your behaviour at the time, the opportunity and motive, all points to you, Brett—'

'Can't you see, Connie? I was the perfect scapegoat. Pin it on the ten-year-old pyromaniac. Perfect.'

Connie's blood chilled. Scapegoat. Yes, she could relate to that. Is that why he came to her?

'Why did you look me up?'

'I thought you, of all people, might understand what it's like to be blamed – I thought you'd give me a chance.'

'How did you find me?'

'Inmates talk. Your "case" was well known. Wasn't that hard to find you.'

But Connie had changed her name for that exact reason – so that it *wasn't* easy for anyone to find her: ex-prisoners, ex-colleagues, ex-anything. She let it slide for the moment, but the squirming doubt consumed her stomach – had he had help finding her? The usual suspects sprang to mind: Niall Frazer and Kelly Barton. Or had he merely followed the police trail? Had he been watching them? Was *he* the hooded figure she'd noticed? The thought lodged in her mind. Suddenly, she wanted this session to be over.

'Your time's up today, Brett.'

He gave a nod and stood up. Digging in his jeans pocket, he retrieved two scrunched-up twenty-pound notes and placed them on Connie's desk.

'That's right, isn't it?' He looked into her eyes.

Connie felt weird about taking his money, despite that being the point of private therapy. She had to take it, though, otherwise she'd give the wrong impression.

'Yes, thank you. Maybe you could discuss the arrangement with your probation officer, see if they can help with the cost of further sessions.' Connie spoke quickly. A part of her hoped he wouldn't return for another session. He'd found her. The suspicion of how would only grow from here.

Brett lingered, like he wanted to say something more. Connie walked around him to get to the door, opened it and stood aside, giving him his cue to leave.

CHAPTER SEVENTY-SEVEN

Connie

A dull ache throbbed at her temples. That had been an intense hour. Brett had seemed reluctant to leave, even after she'd ushered him to the door. She was relieved when he finally thanked her and walked out. It wasn't until she heard his feet descending the stairs that she realised her hands were shaking. She rested her head in her crossed arms on the desk, closing her eyes. What a tangled web. She didn't know what to make of Brett; he came across as genuine enough. Angry, yes – but a killer? As with Steph, she'd yet to scratch the surface of Brett's outer shell. They were similar in so many ways. Young, traumatised, damaged. The parents had a lot to answer for.

The more Connie thought about it, the more it was becoming clear the mother must hold the key. The letters Steph had written, the events Brett had spoken of – the mother was the common denominator. Connie turned to retrieve her bag from beside her desk – the zipped compartment was already open. She was sure she'd closed it properly. She tutted at her carelessness. Rummaging in her bag, she pulled out some of the letters, rereading them with a new perspective. The anger within the words was more directed, not only because she'd abandoned Steph after the fire, she could see it now. Steph *blamed* her mum for the whole thing. In their sessions Steph had only ever apportioned blame to Brett. Why, when these letters blatantly focused on the mother? And where did Brett's dad, Steph's stepdad, fit in to all of this?

How convenient the mother was ravaged by dementia. Maybe Connie should pay a visit to the home to find out how severe her condition really was. If she had lucid moments, then Connie might have a chance at uncovering the real story. Because there was more to this than she'd first thought. In a burst of energy she sat upright and found the number for the protected persons team. It took fifteen minutes of trying, but she came away with the address. The care home was a stone's throw from Salford, Connie's old stomping ground; the area she'd lived in when she and Luke had been youngsters. That was before her dad moved them to the 'decent' side of Manchester after Luke'd been killed.

Within seconds, Connie had formulated her plan. She'd phone the nursing home tomorrow, make the necessary arrangements, then go online to sort a train ticket. Amber could go to her mum's, she'd be delighted to have a bit of company, and Connie would tell her she had decided to make an impromptu visit to her dad. Which meant she really *would* have to go and see him. Not that he'd bothered to see her when he was in Devon. It would keep the cost of the trip down, though, if she didn't need to worry about accommodation. She needed to watch her expenditure. She didn't want to go cap in hand to her dad.

A creaking noise from downstairs brought her back to the moment. Had Brett not left?

Damn. She hadn't watched his departure out the window as she had before, too relieved he'd left the room. It didn't cross her mind that he'd hang around inside the building. She checked the clock on her laptop. He left over twenty minutes ago, surely he wouldn't have been inside for that long? She would've have heard him before now.

Slowly opening the desk drawer, Connie withdrew the only thing she could think might offer some protection. The large metal, double hole-punch. Armed with it, she tiptoed to the door, edging herself towards the top stair. She peered over the top of the banister.

Nothing.

Should she shout a warning from where she stood? Tell him she'd called the police? She strained to hear any movement.

A squeak – like a trainer on the lino flooring, reached her ears.

Someone was in the downstairs toilet.

Connie expelled the air she'd been holding in, lowering the arm wielding the hole punch. Brett must've just wanted to use the toilet before leaving.

But there was no sound of flushing. Hardly any sound at all, as if he was purposely attempting to go undetected. What was he playing at?

Another noise. A squeaking?

She descended the rest of the stairs and, raising the hole punch, approached the toilet door.

A blur of movement to her side caught her off guard. Something solid, a body, slammed against her shoulder. With the wind knocked from her, she fell to the floor, her head banging down, hard.

Pain shot from her shoulder to her head. As the room began to fade, darken, Connie heard the front door slam.

CHAPTER SEVENTY-EIGHT

DI Wade

When Lindsay walked through the upstairs office door, DC Clarke in tow, she found Connie, a wet tea towel pressed against her head, slumped over her desk.

'Jesus, Connie. You should see a doctor, get that checked over.'

'I'm fine, really. It wasn't that bad, the carpet cushioned my fall.'

'You could have a concussion.' Lindsay moved around the desk and put her hands either side of Connie's head.

'Ow!'

'Sorry. Look at me, Connie.'

Her pupils were even, she looked as though she was focusing on her face, and she could follow Lindsay's finger. That was a relief, at least.

'Stop fussing, I'm not suffering from concussion, I'm just pissed off – hurt pride and all that.' Connie pulled her head back from Lindsay's grip.

'What happened, who was it, did you see?'

'Blimey, Lindsay, is that how you question all your witnesses?'

Connie's call to the station had been vague – an intruder had pushed her to the ground and could Lindsay visit. She'd decided to take Clarke along, rather than Mack, and they'd rushed there, blue lights and all.

'Is there any CCTV covering your building?' Clarke asked, his notebook open ready to jot down the details.

'No. I didn't see the need for that as well as the buzzer system for the door. It *is* only Totnes. Meant to have one of the lowest crime rates in Britain, apparently.'

Lindsay gently shook her head. 'Lowest. Not non-existent. You should still take precautions.' She left Connie's side and asked Clarke to stay with her. She was going to do a sweep of the building. Although the intruder had gone – Connie said she'd heard him leave – she needed to make sure, check the perimeter, ensure he wasn't still hanging around outside. She'd also check around to see if he'd left any evidence behind.

'Where were they hiding, do you reckon?'

'Downstairs toilet. Could've sworn I heard noises in there when I was standing at the top of the stairwell. But he – I'm pretty certain from the force it was a man – came at me from my left, as I was facing the toilet, so he must've been hiding around that wall, leading to the kitchenette.'

'Okay, I'll have a look. You sure you don't need medical attention?'

'I'm sure.' Connie smiled up at her. She looked so vulnerable, yet she had a tough quality about her, too. She confused Lindsay a bit. Or perhaps she was merely confused by how Connie made her feel: one minute she wanted to chastise her, the next, protect her. Lindsay returned her smile, then headed to the lower floor.

The intruder had left no sign of forced entry; she'd checked all access points. It looked as though Connie had been right. It was Brett, and he'd stayed inside after their session. Waited.

But why?

If he'd wanted to attack her he could've done it immediately, there was no reason to wait. No one else had been in the building at the time.

Lindsay paced up and down, a thumbnail jammed between her teeth, biting down on it rhythmically. Connie said he'd come at her from her left, shoved her to the ground. Then run off without doing anything else? It was as if he hadn't wanted to hurt her; that hadn't been his goal. So what was? She walked back to the toilet door and cast her eyes inside. It was a tiny room, toilet and small handbasin. As she tucked her head around the door, she saw it.

A round mirror above the basin.

Now she was inside she could see it properly. Writing. She pulled the light cord and the word was displayed clearly.

'Connie!' Lindsay shouted up the stairs. 'Come look at this.'

She pushed her hands into her trouser pockets and stood back from the room.

'In there, on the mirror,' Lindsay motioned with her head.

'What the hell's that?' She heard Connie say from inside.

'I hoped you'd know.'

'No. Ah, hang on. Have you got a mirror, Lindsay?'

Lindsay scoffed, 'Er, no.' Did she look the type to carry a handbag with a compact inside? 'But it's *on* a mirror, Connie.'

Connie nudged past them and ran up the stairs, her heavy footsteps pounding on the staircase. Lindsay shrugged her shoulders in a return gesture to Clarke's raised eyebrows. What was Connie doing?

'The word looks weird because I think it's backwards,' Connie said as she came back down, out of breath. With a compact mirror in hand, Connie went back into the toilet and held it up against the wall mirror.

'Yep. There you are.'

'What? What does it say?'

'This is personal.' Connie's hushed tones filtered from the toilet.

'I'm pretty sure what is written isn't *that* long,' Lindsay said.

'Oh, haha. No, Lindsay. One word meant as two. Personal to me.'

Lindsay shuffled inside. Connie's eyes had reddened, her nose turned pink. She was going to cry. She laid a hand on her arm.

'It's FORLUKE backwards.'

Lindsay frowned.

'It's a message to me. *For Luke*.'

'Your brother? The one who died twenty-two years ago?' Lindsay couldn't contain her surprise. She watched as Connie slowly nodded, her eyes set on the mirror.

CHAPTER SEVENTY-NINE

Connie

Tuesday 20 June

She hadn't felt much like talking after the discovery of the writing on the mirror. Lindsay and DC Clarke had been really supportive and, although they'd asked questions, they hadn't pushed her for the details of Luke's death. They'd been keener to run through the timings – when Brett had left, to when she'd heard the noise, and who else had had access to the building that day. As Lindsay had pointed out, it would be difficult to prove it was Brett with no CCTV – it would be their word against his.

What was 'for Luke', exactly? Yesterday, in her shock that Luke's name had been brought up again, she'd been unable to process it. Now, after tossing theories around her head overnight, she'd come to the conclusion that it could be interpreted in a few ways: maybe it was to do with an act of revenge that had happened, or possibly was *going* to happen. Or it was a relatively harmless message intended to taunt her, to ensure she'd taken the documents on the memory stick seriously by reinforcing it. Either way, the fact that Brett seemed the likely author of the message appalled and puzzled her. What did he have to do with Luke, with her and her family? Nothing, as far as she could see.

284

Determined to keep to her plan of visiting Manchester, despite feeling afraid and unsettled, Connie carried on with the arrangements. The taxi was calling in at her mum's so she could drop Amber off, then it was taking her on to the train station. She'd be in Manchester by 3 p.m. According to his second-in-command, her dad had been 'unreachable' at the time she called, in a 'very important meeting', so she took it as read that it'd be fine to stay with him. Hopefully she'd give him the surprise of his life, turning up, bag in hand, informing him she was staying with him for the night. It would be nothing to the other surprise she had for him though. She tucked the memory stick inside her laptop case and put it with her overnight bag.

It was time she faced the past. Time to make her dad face it, too.

Long train journeys were always the perfect conduit for thinking. Strangely though, Connie spent most of the time sleeping. Not heavily, but fitfully – dropping in and out. The last few weeks had drained her. Emotionally and physically. That, coupled with the steady noise of the train on the tracks, made her eyelids heavy and her head woozy. Lindsay's face popped into her mind as she drifted. When Connie had told her she was taking a quick trip to Manchester, Lindsay had thought it a good idea. Said that having some breathing space after what happened would be beneficial. Funny how people came into your life, the way they enter it and why. Who'd have thought Hargreaves would've brought her a friend. He'd brought a whole heap of unwanted things too, though. His murder had opened a Pandora's box.

Nerves fluttered inside her like patters of tiny feet dancing against her stomach wall. Confronting her dad had seemed a great idea back in Devon. Now, standing on his doorstep with no clear idea of what she was going to say to him, how she was going to approach the matter of the memory stick, the message on the mirror, Connie wanted to turn back. A hotel would have been better anyway. She could have had a relaxing few hours before heading to the nursing home, no need to see her dad and get involved in what was likely to be a wasted one-sided conversation. She turned on her heel and began to walk back out down the gravel driveway, her shoes crunching and slipping on the chippings as she went.

'Darling! This *is* a surprise,' her dad's voice bellowed behind her.

She took a moment to put a smile on her face, then turned to greet him.

There was no going back now.

His expression – blank eyes, mouth slack, his jowls hanging still – had frozen. It didn't seem to be one of shock, horror, or anything emotional. It was neutral. Gave nothing away. Even the air was still. Quiet. Connie heard herself swallow, the spittle catching in her throat. He hadn't said a thing since she showed him the content of the memory stick. She was afraid to prompt him. She waited, her stomach clenched, for him to respond.

'And you don't have any idea who gave you this?' Finally, he spoke – although his face stayed the same, facing forwards, not looking at Connie.

'No. I was shocked at the time, too afraid to look directly at him, so I didn't take his features in.'

'Not at all? Nothing? Not hair colour, eye colour, anything?' His expression broke, his voice urgent.

Connie shook her head. 'No, sorry.'

'I don't know what to say.' Suddenly he got up and strode out of the room. Connie followed him.

'You could start by telling me why whoever made this memory stick is under the impression you are withholding information from me. From Mum.'

'I honestly have no idea, darling. Like I said before, it'll be someone I've inadvertently crossed in business who has an axe to grind, I expect. It'll blow over.'

'Dad. That's your answer to everything. It *won't* blow over. The man who left the message in my building, knocked me to the ground – he hurt me, and could've done worse. This isn't harmless. Someone wants to get to me.' Connie paused for breath. And then added, 'Or you.'

'If they wanted to get to me, they could. I don't know why they would want to play games, go all around the houses by frightening you first. That doesn't make sense.'

'No, no it doesn't.' Connie had to agree. 'So, it's for Luke then. Like they said.'

'You think it has something to do with the stabbing at the football ground, all those years ago? Why now?'

'I can't figure that out either, Dad. Who else would feel the need to get revenge for Luke?'

'I can't imagine anyone would. It was an accident – the coroner's inquest said as much.'

'Really, Dad? He returned an open verdict, actually. And that was because he was unable to come to a clear picture of the events that led to his death. Are you sticking with this story even now I've shown you the memory stick? Is it because you've told yourself that for so long you've come to believe it yourself?'

'I can't do this now.' Her dad checked his watch. 'I'm late for a meeting. There's plenty of food in the fridge, help yourself. Wine is in the garage.'

And he walked out.

Connie was no further forward. She rushed to the front window and watched him get in his car. He didn't drive off, though, he stayed in the driveway, mobile phone to his ear. Connie squinted, and with a finger, edged one of the vertical blinds to the side to get a clearer view. He seemed to be shouting – his actions were animated, his face red. Someone was getting an earful.

I wonder who?

CHAPTER EIGHTY

Connie

After a snoop around the house, Connie concluded there was nothing that would offer any clues to what had really happened with Luke that night. Her dad wasn't going to be stupid enough to leave something incriminating in the house. She stopped short. Incriminating? What was it she thought she'd find anyway? Did she honestly believe that her dad had something to do with Luke's death, that somehow, he was responsible? Had that been the intent of whoever had given her the memory stick – to drive a wedge even further between her and her dad? She had to admit, it was working. Maybe it was all a ruse.

As he so often did when there was any discontent, any hint of being put in a difficult situation, her father had walked away rather than face awkward questions. He was an expert. She might visit his offices later; he couldn't run from her forever. For now, she had another person to visit – someone else she suspected was in retreat from the truth.

The nursing home was basic. No unnecessary flourishes, no home comforts. Enough to fulfil the requirements; adequate but nothing more. Connie's heart sank as she walked through the corridors, catching sight of the building's occupants. Some of them looked like they'd had all their happy memories taken from them via horrific means – Connie was immediately reminded of *Harry Potter*, and the hideous Dementors who sucked the very souls from people's mouths. These poor people resembled empty shells; dummies.

What a depressing place to end your days. Connie slowed her breathing, trying not to take in the aroma of stale urine and that unique 'old-people' musty smell. Her hope for gaining answers from Mrs Ellison diminished as she progressed through the home. Finally, the care assistant who she'd been following slowed.

'She's in 'ere. But she won't speak to you, you know that, right?'

Connie smiled thinly. 'Yes, I understand. I just want to sit with her, talk to her.' She wanted to add, 'Because it doesn't look like she's had any human interaction for years,' but refrained. The emaciated woman, dressed in a flimsy nightie, sat in a Parker Knoll chair, hands limp in her lap, staring dead ahead – presumably out of the window. Connie followed her gaze. A high red-brick wall was her only view. She turned to the care assistant to give her a nod in the hope she'd leave them alone, but she'd already gone, the door swinging shut and banging in its frame. Connie shook her head.

She looked around the room. There was a single plastic chair in the corner, so she took it and positioned it next to the woman. Now she was beside her, Connie saw the pallor to her skin, the deep wrinkles at her eyes, her mouth creased and dry. She hadn't responded at all to Connie's entrance. Not a flicker of acknowledgement. Connie took the crocheted shawl that hung over the arm of the chair and gently moved Rosie Ellison forwards, draping it around her bony shoulders. Still nothing.

Connie resigned herself to the fact she wasn't going to find out anything about the fire. She wasn't going to find out anything about anything. Instead, she decided to just chat to her, talk about Steph – Jenna – and Dylan. Would she even know who Dylan was though? She'd probably never met him, heard his name even.

After Connie had been talking for what felt like an hour, her mouth dry from her constant one-way conversation, a head popped around the door to the room.

'How's it going, love?'

'Oh, you know.' Connie gave a shrug.

The nurse came in, and sat on the edge of the bed. 'She's a bit of an enigma, our Rosie.' She reached across and gave the woman's arm a gentle rub.

'How do you mean?'

'She's been here years, ever since I started working here. And that's far too long for anyone.' She laughed. Her face was kind, and she seemed as though she was actually interested in Rosie. 'And sometimes I catch her,' she whispered.

'Catch her?'

'Talking to herself. But not in a random way, muttering like I've known her to do in front of us. No, sometimes, when her eyes are focused and intense, rather than vacant, she says things that make more sense. As if she's having a proper conversation with an unseen person.'

'Does she ever have visitors – her son, for example?'

'She only has a daughter listed, but as far as I'm aware she hasn't visited for years, not since Rosie's first year here. And there's Brett, but he's not her son. He'd lived with them before the fire, as his dad was Rosie's husband. Second husband, I believe. Very sad.'

'What was sad?' Connie played dumb about her knowledge of the fire, of Steph.

'The fire. That's why Rosie's here.' She spoke quietly again, as if her words might upset Rosie. 'The husband died when Brett set the fire. On a bad day, Rosie mutters about it, not in a coherent way – the words are jumbled and she repeats certain words and phrases, but I have been able to piece stuff together, sometimes.'

'Like what?'

'Oh, like how it's all his fault, she shouldn't have trusted him.

290

How she's a stupid woman, he'd always let her down. Why would this time be different, that sort of stuff. I might be wrong, though, like I say – it's my interpretation of her muddled snippets of sentences.'

'But you also said she says different things, when she doesn't realise you're there?'

'Yeah, she has more lucid moments. That's when she seems to be saying the opposite, where she talks about how it all went wrong. She didn't like him, but it wasn't meant to have happened like that.'

Connie's blood cooled in her veins. That was weird. Was Rosie telling one story to others and another to herself?

'Thanks for taking the time to talk with me, it's been really helpful. I won't stay for much longer. I'll just finish chatting to Rosie then I'll be off. Don't let me keep you from your work.' Connie wanted to have another moment alone with Rosie, so she needed to get the nurse out of the room.

To someone who didn't know what Connie knew about the event, Rosie's words might not mean much; it was hard to connect it all and make sense of it. But, for Connie, it was beginning to make a little sense. She waited for the door to close, then went to Rosie. She pulled her chair around, away from the window, turning it to face her. She sat right opposite Rosie and got level with her eyes. What she was about to do was cruel, went against everything her training had ever taught her – but she didn't have much time. Or much choice. And if Rosie really had dementia, hopefully her actions wouldn't have an effect.

She took a deep breath.

'Rosie. Look at me. I'm Connie. I've come here to ask you some questions. About the fire.'

Nothing.

God forgive me for this.

'Rosie. Your daughter, Jenna, is dead. Brett killed her.' The words came out clearly, despite the shakiness of her voice.

291

Rosie's eyes widened. Her pupils – dark, big – moved and focused on Connie.

Christ. What had she done? What a terrible thing to do to this poor woman.

Rosie's lips parted. Connie held her breath.

'Ahhh, noooo.' It was almost a wail.

Connie froze. Was she going to scream, cry? She looked towards the door, hoping no one was nearby. But Rosie quietened again. Connie didn't know what to do, so she placed her hand over Rosie's. It was cold, waxy. Her mind conjured Steph and Dylan's dead bodies on the metal gurney in the morgue. Goosebumps prickled her arms.

'Poor . . . Jenna.' Rosie's eyes shone with tears.

'I'm so sorry.' But Connie had started this now, she felt compelled to continue. 'What happened in that house, Rosie, the night of the fire?'

'It wasn't . . . his fault.' Rosie's words sounded almost brittle. 'It was mine.'

Connie's hearing was temporarily drowned out by the banging pulse in her ears.

'Why was it your fault, Rosie?'

She stared into Connie's eyes. The coldness of Rosie's hand spread up Connie's arm. She took her hand away.

'It wasn't meant to happen like that.'

'How *was* it meant to happen?'

'Fucking Jimmy!' she shouted.

Jimmy? Connie scrambled about in her memory, she'd heard that name before. From Steph, she was sure.

'What did Jimmy do?'

'He didn't. He didn't. He . . . he fell *asleep.*'

This was getting confusing. Connie had to piece this together. How could she pull this back?

Rosie lurched forward, grabbing Connie's arm. 'I made a mistake,' she hissed. 'I couldn't face what I'd done.'

'You set the fire?' Connie blurted.

Rosie shook her head. Side to side, more and more violently. 'I made a mistake, I made a mistake.'

'It's okay, Rosie. It's all over now.'

'It'll never be over. Not until we *all* burn.'

'No. It's going to be okay, really.'

'He's been here. He hates me. He knows.'

'Brett? What does he know?'

'Jenna. Poor Jenna. She only wanted it to go back as it was before. Before that man and his wretched boy came. I shouldn't have asked her to lie.

'Jimmy was meant to save us. Get the ladder. GET THE LADDER, JIMMY!' Rosie's shouts made Connie jump. Tears streaked Rosie's face. Then she turned away, looking back towards the window.

'I looked for Jimmy, he wasn't there. He was supposed to be there. I panicked, the smoke was so thick. Black. I managed to get out. I left him there. He thought I was still in the room, he was shouting, shouting, *Rosie, Rosie, where are you?* I let him die. Banging at the window, screaming for help. I left him.' She faced Connie again. 'I only wanted to go back to what it was before. With Jenna's dad. We thought we'd arranged it well. It all went so wrong. So wrong. We only wanted the money. The money to leave – just me, him and Jenna. We never wanted anyone to get hurt. I didn't want him dead. I just wanted to be away from him.'

Oh, my God. Had the fire been set deliberately to get insurance money? It suddenly came together in Connie's mind. Jimmy – that was Uncle Jimmy, the drunk. He was meant to be there to get them from the fire. Rosie said he fell asleep. So, he hadn't been where he should've been, ready with a ladder to help them all escape. Why the hell had she gone that far for money? And with them all inside the house? That was an extreme measure to make it more realistic, believable. They must've assumed that people

293

wouldn't question it, wouldn't think it was arson – an act to defraud – if they were all in the house at the time of the fire.

And Steph had been in on the plan. That's why she was so angry at her mum, and had been for all those years. Because she'd been left, the plan completely ruined, no house, a dead stepdad, life *not* back to how she'd wanted it with her mum and real dad. Instead, she'd been left with useless Uncle Jimmy – knowing he'd been the one who let them down. Connie remembered Miles saying that Steph's dad's whereabouts were unknown. It made sense now – he'd obviously done a runner after the fire destroyed everything. Was he the one who took the insurance money? He needed to disappear so he didn't have to answer awkward questions, so he couldn't be implicated. Which left three others who knew the awful truth: Steph, who was carrying around her guilt; lecherous Uncle Jimmy, who was flat-out pissed all the time; and Brett, who until recently had been safely locked up in prison. Alone, confused, and believing *he* had started the fire. That was, until the therapist had worked with him, helped him recall the traumatic events of that night. Then he realised he had been set up to take the blame when the plan went so terribly wrong.

He had been the scapegoat. Just as he said.

Brett had been telling the truth. Why on earth hadn't he appealed his sentence when he'd unearthed his real memories? But, then, memories weren't evidence. What a terrible situation, how would he have been able to prove his innocence with so much stacked against him?

As quickly as Rosie had become lucid and cooperative, she switched off again. Her eyes returned to their dull, blank and staring state. Connie had heard enough anyway.

It was difficult, in that moment, not to despise the broken woman before her.

CHAPTER EIGHTY-ONE

Killing him had been the task that he'd been given – that had been his responsibility, but once the tattoo idea had begun formulating in his mind, it stuck – it had been so genius there was no way he could unthink it once he'd thought it. A lot of the plans had been outside of his remit – being in prison meant he'd had to rely on others. He'd been given the details, bit by bit over the year. It'd been a painstaking process, and one he'd had little say in – just instructions. But the tattoos were his contribution – although he'd still needed help to execute it.

Whatever. His part had been vital, he'd been needed.

It felt good to be needed.

And it wasn't over yet.

He'd got her key copied easy enough. He'd left a message for her while he was there. To toy with her. It couldn't hurt to have a bit of fun with her first.

Now he waited.

For part two.

CHAPTER EIGHTY-TWO

Connie

Wednesday 21 June

Connie replayed the visit with her dad and Rosie again and again as she travelled back to Devon on the overcrowded train. She hadn't been able to get a seat until Birmingham New Street and now her legs were hot, her feet swollen – the tight skin acting like rubber bands around her ankles. She massaged them, wishing she could be home already, taking a cool shower, opening a cold bottle of lager.

She wasn't sure what she'd expected when she decided to visit Steph's mum; what she'd *wanted* to hear. She guessed it was confirmation she was after, for Rosie to somehow convey that Brett had to be responsible for Steph's death. Connie had been so convinced she was right, that he'd killed her – because Steph couldn't possibly have jumped to her death, killing Dylan in the process. How had Connie been so wrong about that? She'd have to speak to Lindsay when she got home, tell her it looked as though she and Mack were right after all – Steph had killed herself and her son in a terrible act of fear. Fear that her lies were finally going to be exposed, that the hideous plan she'd helped her mum with and had kept secret all those years was coming out. She'd protected her mum until the end. No wonder she was so angry. As far as she believed, her mum had got away with it all – and dementia had taken all the bad memories of what she'd done. Steph had been left to carry all of the guilt.

As for Connie's dad, now there *was* something she was right about. He was most definitely holding something back. Lying. To protect himself? To protect her and her mum? Or to protect Luke's memory? She'd spent the rest of Tuesday night at his house, waiting for him to return after he walked out. When he came back it was like nothing had happened. He had brought takeaway home, and they sat watching TV while they ate and shared a bottle of wine. All very convivial. After her third glass, Connie told him about the photo the police had been given anonymously. Him in a bar. It turned out to have been taken while he was in Devon, the time he failed to see Connie. He'd shrugged it off, said it was just a business deal. No reason anyone should've taken a photo of them. Must've been merely to throw in a red herring, cause her to question him, he'd said. Connie couldn't be as flippant. It felt like more than that. When she thought about the other photos, each were taken for a reason: her and Jonesy – to throw suspicion on her activities and give them cause to question whether she might've paid an ex-con to carry out a revenge attack; her and Gary in the house – to piss DS Mack off and further disaffect her relationship with the police. So the one of her dad and the unknown man were for what?

However hard Connie had pushed, her dad deflected every attack, and countered every argument she put forward with a reasoned response. She'd wanted to scream at the man, he was so exasperating. His final word on the matter that morning, before she got in the taxi, was: 'That bastard Hargreaves messed your life up. Don't let someone else carry on where he left off.'

What was that supposed to even mean?

Connie's head throbbed. She didn't want to visit Manchester again any time soon. Finally, at almost 3 p.m. the train drew into Coleton station. Stiff and tired, Connie jostled her way off the carriage, her overnight bag and laptop case banging awkwardly against other passengers. She looked cautiously up and down the platform before heading to the taxi rank. Now would not be a good time to run into Jonesy.

She'd told her mum she would pick up Amber, but too tired now, Connie gave the driver her home address instead – the cold lager was calling to her and the taxi would have her there in five minutes. She couldn't wait.

The smell hit her first.

As soon as she swung her front door open, it assaulted her. She hadn't even stepped inside. She put her hand to her nose. What was that? Gone-off food? She'd not even been gone two days. Nothing could smell that bad in such a short time, surely? Connie poked her head further in, and gagged. If she'd been at all healthy, she might have considered it to be rotting vegetables – broccoli perhaps. She took a deep breath and held it, rushing through the hallway to the kitchen. She'd have to open the windows and spray a can-full of Oust.

She stopped short of the window.

A dark oblong-shaped lump was situated in the centre of the kitchen floor.

She let out her breath and, with her hand cupped over her mouth and nose, stepped closer to inspect it.

A dead rat.

Connie's stomach convulsed. She stepped over it and flung the window open wide. She threw her head out of it, gasping for fresher air. Amber had only ever brought a single field mouse inside the house before – how had she got this huge rat inside without her noticing?

Then she remembered.

Amber was at her mum's. She couldn't have left a rat in the

middle of the kitchen before they left the house on Tuesday, Connie would've seen it.

In which case, how had it got there?

A chill shot through her insides, causing her to shudder violently.

Someone must have been in her house.

CHAPTER EIGHTY-THREE

DI Wade

Wade walked up and down in front of the board where all their photographic evidence was displayed. Crime scene photos, murder victim in situ and post-mortem, the tattoos, and the Connie Summers photos – all linked by an invisible cord.

'Come on, come on – it can't be that complicated, there's a clue here somewhere. Come on, show yourself,' Lindsay said to herself.

'First sign of madness.' Mack had crept up behind her, making her jolt with surprise.

'Bloody hell, Mack.' Lindsay wiped at her shirtsleeve where her coffee had slopped over the rim of the cup.

'Sorry, Boss.'

'Anyway, I already exhibit a whole host of signs – talking to myself is the least scary one, I can tell you.'

Mack laughed. 'Point taken.'

'Apart from scalding your boss, did you have any other purpose for sneaking up behind me?'

'Yes, actually.' Mack gave a mock-superior look. Lindsay's eyes widened in anticipation. 'The teams didn't bring you suspects, I'm afraid. But they did find someone who remembers seeing the white van that was used to transport our victim.'

'Keep talking.'

'He was going for his morning newspaper, same time as he does every day, 7.15 a.m. He walks the two-mile round trip to the post office in Ashbury to keep himself fit – he's eighty-two years old—'

'I don't care about his exercise regime, Mack – or how old he is. Get on with it.'

'Sorry. The van came speeding around the corner, heading out of the village, towards West Ashbury.'

Lindsay waved her hands impatiently. 'And this is telling us what, exactly?'

'The road to West Ashbury goes to West Ashbury.'

'Oh my God, Mack. Stop talking in riddles, man.'

He smiled. Clearly, he was enjoying prolonging the tension.

'It only goes to West Ashbury, no further. It's a small hamlet off Ashbury. There are a few roads, but they are all no-through ones. If our driver went there, there's a strong possibility the van, full of lovely forensic evidence, is still there.'

'Fabulous. Oh, and thanks for wasting ten minutes dragging that out, just to showboat.' Lindsay grabbed her suit jacket from the back of her chair and headed for the door. She heard Mack mumbling as he followed.

'Oh, Ma'am,' DC Sewell called after her. Lindsay had given up asking her to call her Boss, or Guv like the others. 'There's a call for you.'

'Take a message. I'm on my way out.' Lindsay swung the door open.

'It's Connie Summers, Ma'am, she sounds a bit upset.'

Lindsay stopped dead, her stomach flipping. Now what had happened? Connie must've only just got back from Manchester, had she had another intruder? She let the door fall back, knocking into Mack, and took the call.

'Wade. How can I help?' She wanted to keep the call professional, not come across as a concerned friend. She didn't want the others thinking she'd gone soft.

'There's a dead rat in my kitchen.' Connie's voice sounded wobbly.

'Okaaay.' Lindsay frowned, while trying hard not to sing the lyrics to UB40's hit eighties song, 'Rat in Mi Kitchen'. What did she want her to do about that?

'It was here when I got back. When I left on Tuesday, it wasn't. Someone's been inside the house while I've been away, left it for me as some kind of . . . I don't know, a message. It stinks, Lindsay.'

Lindsay's lips twitched with the urge to laugh.

'Look, I understand why you're rattled. The incident at your office the other day has put you on edge. But I imagine your cat brought the rat in, or you just have a rat issue . . .'

'Amber isn't here. I took her to my mum's before I went to Manchester, and there was no rat when I left.'

'Amber probably brought it in prior to Tuesday, alive, then injured it and it died while you were gone. There's a perfectly good explanation. Have you checked around the house – is there anything else untoward, any windows or doors been forced that you can see?'

'No, nothing like that.'

'Then I'm sure it's fine. Just a rat. Horrible creatures, but at least it's dead. If it'd reassure you, make you feel better, I'll send a DC around?'

'No, no need to do that. It unnerved me, that's all. If you don't think it's anything to worry about . . . I might go over to Mum's and pick Amber up now. I was going to leave it as I'm so tired, but I think I want her here. I'm sorry for bothering you with this. You're clearly right. I'm being oversensitive, it's been a hell of a visit to Manchester.'

'Perhaps I'll bring over a bottle of wine tomorrow night and you can bring me up to speed?'

'Sure, that'd be good.'

Lindsay paused after she'd replaced the receiver. *Was* Connie being oversensitive? Or was Lindsay being too flippant about her

302

concerns? There had been someone in the downstairs toilet at Connie's consultancy – that was a certainty. Whether that person was Brett, or someone they'd not considered, was up in the air. Could that same person have got into her house? It seemed unlikely. Unless they had a key – as Connie said there was no sign of anyone having broken in. Lindsay was suddenly aware of eyes on her.

'Sorry, Mack. Let's go.' She strode towards him, and together they walked to the car. All the while, Lindsay was thinking about Connie. After they were done for the night and before heading back home to Plymouth, she'd pop over to Connie's house and check no one was hanging around. Ensure the house was secure. Put her own mind at ease. 'I assume we have all hands on deck for this?'

'I've done the necessary, Boss. I've got maps of the land, dwellings, barns and everything. There's a farm there with various outbuildings, I thought that'd be a good place to begin.'

'Sounds the perfect drop-zone, doesn't it? Let's hope our *friend* thought so too.'

CHAPTER EIGHTY-FOUR

Connie

Wednesday 21/Thursday 22 June

Connie held her breath as she wrapped the dead rat in newspaper, then rushed outside and deposited it into the wheelie bin. She shuddered as it hit the bottom of the empty bin with a thud. Back inside the kitchen she squeezed a handful of washing-up liquid into her palm and rubbed her hands together until the lather dripped down her arms. Disgusting disease-carrying creatures. She still had a tingle of concern travelling up and down her spine, but, as Lindsay wasn't unduly worried, then she shouldn't be either. Her explanation did make sense. Even so, Connie waived the ice-cold lager and bath, and phoned for a taxi to take her to Shaldon. She'd have an hour with her mum – having to concentrate on keeping from her all that was going on would definitely take her mind off this current rat situation. Then she'd return home with Amber. Any further rats would swiftly be dealt with by her. She hoped.

Connie awoke the following morning with a pain in her head that was already threatening to become a migraine. She popped some paracetamol from the blister pack beside her bed and swallowed them with the stale water from the glass on her dressing table, knowing full well she'd regret having them on an empty stomach. It was the lesser of two evils: hideous debilitating headache, or a queasy tummy. It was no surprise she was getting a migraine now. It'd been a tense few days, followed by a tense arrival home, followed by a tense visit to her mum's to retrieve Amber last night.

She'd managed to avoid detailed conversation about her visit to Manchester and her dad. Nothing that went deeper than 'we ate pizza and chatted about my plans for the consultancy'. She didn't share the recent events, either, not wanting to scare her. Not wanting to scare herself. Her sleep had been fitful – no longer than an hour at a time – her dreams plagued with dark figures and dead animals. Now, with a migraine and feeling like she'd been hit by a bus, Connie had to face work.

Despite her fuzzy head and lethargy, Connie remained alert on her journey, regularly turning to check behind her as she walked from Totnes station to her office, making sure she didn't have a follower. No man in a hoody, no Jonesy, no Brett. She passed by Halls, the butcher shop, waving up to the man inside – she was getting to know people by sight now – the regulars on her daily walk who gave her a nod or a wave. It was a lovely, warm community, she was lucky she'd been able to set up in this town. Her relief at having made it almost to the front door without incident drained when she saw a hunched-up figure sitting on the steps. She had a flashback of Steph waiting there for her barely two weeks ago.

Brett looked up as she approached, then stood aside to allow Connie to reach the door. She wasn't sure how she should approach this. On the one hand, some of her initial fears had been unfounded; she now felt sure he had been telling the truth. However, on the other hand, there was still the question of whether he was the one who'd hidden downstairs and knocked her to the floor on Monday. Had written 'for Luke' on her mirror. If so, why? She knew her curiosity would mean that she'd invite him in – all her hopes of a well-ordered morning evaporated.

'It's Thursday – you don't have an appointment, Brett. Is there something you wanted?' Connie kept him on the step for the moment.

'I'd hoped you might be free for another chat. I've been going over Monday's session in my head. You suddenly seemed real keen to get rid of me. It's because you're scared of me, isn't it?'

What should she say – yes, actually I am? Or play it cool? Maybe she should tell him that she believed him. That's what he wanted to hear anyway, wasn't it?

'I was, I suppose. A little.' She watched him for a reaction. He looked sad, his face losing hope. 'But I've come to think, or perhaps question, my assumptions – my original beliefs.'

His head shot up, a smile lighting up his face. 'What made you suddenly believe me?'

'Let's just say, certain evidence came to light that corroborated what you'd told me. And refuted what Steph, sorry – I mean Jenna – had.'

He sighed. 'Eventually. Someone who's opened their eyes to Jenna's lies.'

Connie's stomach tightened at the bitterness in his voice. This young man still held a lot of anger within him, and a niggle scratched away inside her head – was she colluding with a criminal? Her prison training had warned of the dangers of manipulation, coercion, conditioning. Just because she'd left that environment she shouldn't forget all of that. Brett had spent his entire adolescence in a secure unit. She must be careful, remain cautious.

What she couldn't ignore was how terrible it was that the stupid actions of Steph's mother and father had impacted so detrimentally on their children. Brett and Steph's lives had been over before they'd had any chance to flourish. An awful case of adults' behaviour, their selfish actions, forever imprinting on their children.

And in Steph's case, the end result had been her and Dylan's deaths. Was Brett's future any brighter?

'My first client is due soon, but you can come in.' Connie didn't have a client until eleven, but she wasn't going to let him know that.

After they'd settled, with Connie positioned opposite Brett, she began the session as she would any other. Brett continued to focus on the relief he felt that someone finally believed him, how it was like being reborn, but didn't ask why she'd reached the conclusion he wasn't guilty of setting the fire. He talked quickly; maybe he wanted to get it all out before the next client showed up, but part of her wondered if he'd taken something, he seemed so hyper.

'How are you coping, being back in the community after so long?' She wanted to know how he saw his future, rather than his past.

'It's all right. I'm at the hostel, in Paignton. It's near the sea. That's good. A massive difference from Manchester, the home, the YOI. It's like being on holiday. Only, I'm on my own, obviously.'

'That must be difficult. How is it that you came here? I'd have thought the probation team would've wanted you in your own area.'

He lifted a shoulder and screwed his nose up, like he'd smelt something bad.

'Some guy in the YOI – the offender supervisor inside, he arranged it with outside probation. Said it would be better to go far away from my red flags, and said seeing as I had no positive people – the green flags – in Manc, then I should start somewhere new. Even though I got no links in Devon, he suggested it.'

That struck Connie as strange. Devon had been plucked out of thin air as the best place to relocate? Where his stepsister had also been relocated only months beforehand? That was one hell of a coincidence. Could Miles have had anything to do with it? She shook the thought away for the moment.

'How do you manage your anger now? Still with fire?'

He relaxed back in his chair. Connie waited while he seemed to consider the question – was he working out how he *should* answer, give a response that he thought Connie would want to hear? He cracked his knuckles. Then spoke.

'I don't get as angry. Now. Most of the reasons for my anger are no longer a problem.'

The way he said that sent a shiver rippling across her skin. He'd meant Steph, she was sure. And now Steph was dead he didn't have to hold on to the anger. Connie didn't feel like probing any further. It was unlikely Brett had started the fire. His obsession with fire had given Steph the perfect opportunity to blame him; he was just a confused, hurting ten-year-old kid who'd witnessed his dad die in the flames. He'd been primed, and was at that point easily manipulated. Steph had been a very resourceful sixteen-year-old. Clever. Devious.

Which begged the question, why wouldn't she have tried every other avenue before killing herself and Dylan?

'You sent letters to Jenna when you were in the secure home. Did she reply?' Connie wasn't sure any more that Brett had ever written to Steph, she may well have lied about that too.

'I started off sending them to Jenna, but she only ever replied a few times. Later, when I was beginning to recall the actual events, I wrote . . . well, more angry letters I guess. But I never sent them.'

'Okay, so the letters you sent said what?'

'Mostly begging for her to come and visit me. I'd lost my dad, wasn't expecting *her* to visit, so I only had Jenna. I used to tell her stuff, too, like what it was like in the home, the therapy I had, that sort of thing.'

'Why didn't you send the ones that were angry? I'd have thought you'd want her to know your feelings, that you were remembering certain things more clearly about the fire?'

'I wrote those letters as part of my therapy. We all had to write to our victim, or someone who'd been affected by our crime. Well, almost all of us. There were some who got away with all that, like Flint – jammy bugger.'

'I see.' Connie knew that was a part of some of the rehabilitation programmes in prison. So it was entirely possible that Brett had never written to Steph and certainly not while she'd been in Totnes. Miles had been right.

She was about to bring his session to a close – get rid of him in time for her client – but the niggle that had become a regular sensation in her mind attached itself to something Brett'd said.

'Who is Flint?'

Brett's eyes narrowed, and for a split second, Connie thought she saw panic flash across his face.

'Just a lad I was inside with in the YOI.'

'A friend?'

'I guess. I never really connected with anyone much. But he had my back. Tried to help me integrate when I first got put in there. It was a big jump, secure home to YOI. It could be brutal in that place. Flint had respect from a lot of the inmates, and he was a bit like me, we both had a thing for fire – that's why he had the nickname, Flint. In return for his protection, I helped him with his programme work. I'd made the most of my time, you see – took every opportunity to learn, to better myself. I loved the education programmes and I enjoyed teaching others when I could.'

'Why didn't he have to do the victim letters, though?'

'He had this brain disorder or something, which meant he couldn't write things down. All he had to do was tell the facilitator stuff, one-to-one, and I'd help with some writing for the in-cell work after sessions.'

Connie sat up straight. 'Brain disorder?'

'Yeah. He got a bad bang to the head when he was a kiddy. An accident of some sort, can't remember what he said now. But it left him with lasting damage. I mean, he was okay, up there,' Brett tapped a finger against his temple, 'he just couldn't write things down the same.'

Her mouth dried.

'What do you mean, he couldn't write things down the same?'

'Weird as hell it was. Like it was nothing to him, he could do it perfectly.'

Connie's pulse raced, knowing what was coming, but asking anyway.

'What could he do perfectly?'

'Mirror writing. He wrote everything backwards.'

CHAPTER EIGHTY-FIVE

Connie

As soon as Brett left and she'd watched him from the window until he disappeared from view, Connie picked up the phone and dialled the station.

Someone she didn't recognise answered and said DI Wade and DS Mack were out on a call. *Damn.* There was no point leaving a message, she'd phone again when she got home. Connie's hands shook and her pulse rate was doubled, as if she'd had twenty cups of coffee. She'd tried not to show any reaction when Brett spoke about Flint's condition, attempting instead to sound interested in the phenomenon, rather than in Flint himself. But when Brett went on to tell her that Flint had been released prior to him, Connie was sure her face must've given away her shock. She was now convinced that the writing on the toilet mirror must've been done by Flint. He and Brett were in this together – Brett had let Flint in when he left after their session. It was obvious. Although the 'why' was less so.

The more she thought about it, the more definite she felt about her theory.

But, then, was she panicking, jumping to a hasty conclusion? Just because this Flint wrote backwards, that wasn't enough evidence to be certain it was him – it might be coincidence. There must be other people who had the same condition.

Or those who could emulate it.

What a perfect way to detract attention from yourself to another. Was Brett playing her?

She couldn't trust anyone.

After seeing her client at eleven, there'd only been one more in the afternoon. Connie's new business was suffering. She'd have to focus on building it up if she was going to make a success of it. Allowing what was going on to affect it so much was counterproductive; she had to get a grip or it was going to go under. Right now, though, her resolve was poor. Only 4 p.m. and she switched off her computer, deciding to call it quits for the day. She wanted to go home, catch up with Lindsay, who'd said she was going to call around tonight. That's what Connie felt she needed right now – someone to talk to, someone else who knew what was going on. Someone she *should* trust.

Instead of walking the direct route to the train station, Connie took a detour, turning right as she exited her building and carrying on up the hill. There was a delicatessen at the top of High Street that did the most delicious takeaway antipasti platter that would be perfect for her and Lindsay to have later over a bottle of wine.

With the platter carefully placed in the bottom of her bag, Connie crossed the road to the narrow cut-through leading to a steep, winding road that would get her to Station Road quicker than going back down the busy main street. It had a claustrophobic feel to it, the high walls either side of the road so close she could almost reach out both arms and touch each one. The lack of cars and people meant it was always quiet.

Apart from the footsteps she could hear behind her.

She turned to see the source of them and her heart missed a beat.

A man in a black hoody.

She quickened her step.

He quickened his.

Connie scanned the road ahead of her – there was a turning coming up about a quarter of the way down the hill. She couldn't remember if that took her back on to the main road again, or to houses, but either of those options was better than staying there – it was a few minutes before she'd reach Station Road. And that might be too long.

'Hey, Connie. Fancy bumping into you again.' The voice came at her as she approached the turning, causing her to give a startled cry.

'For Christ's sake, are you stalking me?'

On this occasion, Connie had never felt so relieved to see Kelly Barton and didn't care that she'd obviously been hanging around again. It was far too much of a coincidence, her turning up like this; she'd clearly capitalised on the fact she lived close by and was keeping a close eye for any development, meaning she'd get in first with her report. Her dislike for Kelly would need to be put aside right now. Connie grabbed her arm and carried on walking, her pace fast.

Kelly opened her mouth, about to protest, but then must have picked up on Connie's anxiety and kept in step with her.

'What's going on?' She looked behind them. 'Are you being followed?' The excitement in her voice was barely containable.

'Keep walking, Kelly. He's dangerous.'

'Good try, Connie.' She laughed.

'I'm not messing.' Connie chanced another look behind her. The hooded figure was still following. 'Shit, he's going to catch us up.'

'Bloody hell, you're serious.'

'Have you known me to joke? As you've apparently already been informed, I don't have much of a sense of humour.' Her previous run-in with Kelly had not been forgotten.

'Just stop, confront him, and ask him what he wants.' Kelly

313

broke from her, looking as if she was going to wait for the man to catch up.

Connie grabbed Kelly's arm again, yanking her onwards. 'No! That's a really bad idea. What if he's armed?'

Kelly's eyes widened. 'Are you mad? Why *would* he be? What have you got yourself mixed up with, Connie?'

Connie risked another look, praying he'd gone, or at least was far behind them now.

'Fuck, there's another one.' A second figure was a few strides behind the hoody-man, closely following.

'Shit, are we about to get jumped?' Kelly's voice finally sounded concerned.

'Keep walking.'

They were in a secluded part of Totnes, narrow road, high walls. If something happened to them here . . .

'We need to get back into the main town – quickly,' Connie said, her breath coming in short bursts, her legs shaking from the effort of walking so fast in her stupid high-heeled slip-on court shoes.

Kelly pulled her arm out of Connie's. She rummaged in her bag and took out her camera, turned and, still walking fast, started snapping away.

'What the hell are you doing? Great, let's give the dodgy men something to kill us for!'

'Don't be so dramatic.'

'Really? You've got photographic evidence now.'

Connie remembered the photos she'd been sent. Kelly always carried that camera everywhere with her. Connie's suspicion that she was the mystery photographer now seemed undisputable. No time to question her now, though.

They started jogging. The men did the same.

'When I say . . . take your shoes off . . . and run, Kelly.'

They briefly gave each other a wary look, both pale-faced and huffing. Only the adrenaline was keeping Connie moving.

'Okay . . . now!'

They both stooped, taking one shoe off at a time, discarding them as they went – then began running. Connie could only hear her own heart banging, her own laboured breathing. Her lungs hurt, her feet, too.

They weren't going to make it.

Were the men right behind them? She was afraid to check. It'd be better not to see it coming. How stupid to have taken this cut-through for the sake of a few saved minutes.

'Shit, look.' Kelly had fallen back. What was she playing at? She must keep running.

Connie slowed her run to a jog so she could follow Kelly's gaze. The men were on the ground, way behind them now. They looked to be fighting.

'What the hell?' Connie bent over, hands on her thighs, taking in deep gulps of air. She was going to be sick.

'Come on, let's not hang around for them to stop and continue after us.' Kelly took hold of Connie's arm and together they jogged on until they reached the last corner that led on to Station Road.

Out of breath, panting and with no shoes, the two women merged in with the other people who were walking calmly, going about their afternoon in ignorance of Connie and Kelly's near miss with a stranger in a black hoody.

'They were my favourite shoes,' Kelly said as they approached the train station.

'How can you think about that at a time like this?' Connie muttered. But then she remembered her antipasti platter. Would it be ruined?

'Who were they, Connie?'

They were standing waiting on the platform for the next train to Coleton, and Connie pretended she hadn't heard the question. She needed to speak with Lindsay – she couldn't share any more information with this reporter. As grateful as she was for the fact

315

Kelly had been with her during that frightening chase, she was still the enemy.

'I suggest you hand that camera's memory card over to the police ASAP, Kelly. It's evidence.'

'Sure.' Kelly smiled.

Connie bet she would make copies first.

CHAPTER EIGHTY-SIX

Connie

Ignoring Amber's cries for attention, Connie headed straight for the fridge and opened a bottle of lager, glugging quickly and noisily, draining it within seconds. She wiped her mouth with the back of her hand and stood leaning against the worktop, staring down at her dirty feet.

What a bizarre turn of events. Who would've thought Kelly Barton would turn out to be her saviour? Although, to be fair, it wasn't her who'd saved the day. She had the mysterious, unknown man to thank for that. Thoughts of Flint filtered into her mind. What Brett had said about his brain injury tugged at her consciousness, as if it was trying to make a link to something.

She slammed down the empty bottle and went to her paperwork on the shelf under the coffee table. She riffled through it, scattering sheets of paper in her haste. There they were. The drawings she'd done of the tattoos covering Hargreaves' body. She found the one of the code: U2X51.

Could it be?

Snatching it up, Connie ran back to the kitchen. She got her bag, took out the antipasti – which, surprisingly, did not appear to be ruined – and then emptied the rest of the contents of the bag on to the counter. Taking her compact, she held the mirror against the paper.

Her breath caught.

It was still not altogether clear because some of the letters could be numbers and vice versa – but it was a start. This could be it.

The code had been written backwards.

The person who'd done the tattoos was the same person who'd been in her toilet at work.

The killer.

Horror mixed with excitement, her blood rushing through her veins, making her giddy. Hargreaves' killer was after her, but at the same time, she knew Lindsay was going to be chuffed with this when she told her. A breakthrough. Finally, this might be coming to an end.

Connie rummaged in her kitchen drawers for paper and a pen.

She was going to crack this code.

The light had gone, now replaced with a shadowy dimness. Connie's eyes ached. She got up from her crouched position over her laptop to switch the light on. She'd been poring over the numbers and letters, searching for all possible meanings on the internet for the past two hours. Now she had the sudden realisation that the original 5, once mirrored, could be interpreted as a 2, and the number 2 an S. This gave her 12XSU as the mirror image of the original tattoo.

Taking a deep breath, she punched this in the search bar and closed her eyes. *Please give me something.* She opened them. Nothing. A page full of random results that meant nothing. She wanted to scream. Maybe that was too obvious – the mirror image would've needed to be more complex for it to be a puzzle, so it wouldn't be a straightforward code. She remembered one of her early thoughts about it – a cipher. A simple substitution cipher was worth a go. So, instead of 12 it would be the letter equivalent – L. X would be the number 24, S, 19 and U would be 21.

L241921

Connie typed it in.

Again, nothing.

She banged the table, cursing. It was so infuriating. She was so close, she felt sure. She tried it again, this time spacing the numbers into twos.

Her stomach flipped.

The top result was: Luke 24:19:21. A bible reference.

Another tattoo that was meant for her? She read the passage about Jesus of Nazareth being sentenced to death. Tears pricked her eyes. She went back to the search results and looked to see if it was a fluke. Underneath that reference was another, this time Leviticus 24:19:21. She relaxed. Good, there was a possibility it wasn't a personal message, then. The first hit being her dead brother's name was only a cruel coincidence.

But the next passage alarmed her.

Leviticus 24:19-21 New International Version (NIV)
[19] Anyone who injures their neighbour is to be injured in the same manner: [20] fracture for fracture, eye for eye, tooth for tooth. The one who has inflicted the injury must suffer the same injury. [21] Whoever kills an animal must make restitution, but whoever kills a human being is to be put to death.

This *was* to do with Luke. It was apparent that someone was purposely involving her in this for whatever reason. What had her dad been up to? He was clearly covering something up from years ago, as she'd suspected. The questions as to what, why, when and how would need answering. Whether he'd intended to or not, he'd put her life in danger.

Connie was a target.

She paced like a caged animal until she saw the headlights of Lindsay's car draw up outside. She opened the front door before Lindsay had stepped out of the car.

'Where've you been? I've needed to speak with you all day.' Connie's tone was unintentionally abrupt.

'Let me in and I'll tell you all about the latest development,' Lindsay said. She walked through into the lounge. 'What on earth has happened here? You had a break-in?' Her eyes were wide with concern.

'Er . . . no. That was me. I've got something interesting to tell you, as well. Well, two things, actually.' Connie was full of nervous energy.

They sat together on the sofa, Lindsay with her feet tucked up beneath her, the most relaxed Connie had ever seen her. They shared the day's events. It was a relief to talk to someone other than Amber, and even though she was afraid, beyond any fear she'd ever experienced, having Lindsay with her calmed her. She felt protected.

Before getting to the nitty-gritty of what happened, Connie grabbed them each a glass of white wine, in an attempt to calm her nervous energy. How would Lindsay react to what she was about to tell her? She smiled as she handed Lindsay her glass, then took a deep breath and began. Lindsay listened in muted silence as Connie retold the story of her being followed, bumping into Kelly, then another man following – all resulting in a chase through a back street of Totnes.

When Connie had finally finished, she saw that Lindsay was shaking her head. 'What's going on? Why would someone want to follow you – do you think it's scare tactics? I can't figure out what this has all got to do with you – it's driving me mad.'

This was a good time to tell her about the code.

'I've cracked it, Lindsay.'

'Cracked what?'

'The tattoo – well, the one that we thought was a code, anyway.'

Lindsay lowered her wine, her face brightening. 'Give it to me then, don't keep me in suspense.'

Connie jumped up, gathering the notes she'd made from the table and the laptop showing the results of her search.

Lindsay looked on with her mouth slightly gaping as Connie described her thought processes, and how she'd finally worked it out.

'That's so clever. How did this guy think of that?'

'Some people are good with puzzles. If it *is* this "Flint" guy – which I suspect it is – according to Brett his brain works differently since an accident, so perhaps this is another side effect of his condition?'

'Well, it sounds promising, but obviously we'd need more than that to confidently link him to your mirror writing and a murder.' Lindsay leant across, placing a hand on Connie's leg.

Connie felt her excitement about cracking the code slip. It wasn't enough. She bowed her head.

'We've had some positive leaps forward in the last two days, though,' Lindsay said brightly. Her obvious attempt at lifting Connie's mood back up. 'But they've come at a price.' Lindsay's expression became serious again, the look that Connie had become accustomed to. 'I'm glad today has had a better ending than how it might have done. You should've called 999, Connie. If I'd had any firm evidence that you were in danger . . .' Lindsay's head fell forwards. 'I'm sorry. Had I listened to Mack right at the start this could have been prevented – he did bring up the possibility you were at risk and I played it down.'

Connie laid her hand on Lindsay's. 'Don't be stupid, there was no real reason to think I was a target before. Up until now it was just me being paranoid. Anyway, what would you have done, put me into protective custody? No thank you.'

'We would've given you a DC to keep an eye on you, at the very least.' Lindsay rubbed the back of her neck.

'To be fair, you have been keeping an eye on me yourself – I've had the best of the best watching out for me. Anyway, enough of what might or might not have been the best thing to do, the question is, where do we go from here?' Silence fell on the room while both women drank some wine. Then, Lindsay stood and walked to the window.

'We found the white van used in Hargreaves' murder yesterday,' Lindsay said, 'and in following that up, today another lead has come good. That's where we were when you called.'

'That's excellent, Lindsay. Finally, eh? I hope the van proves fruitful.'

'Forensics have been all over it and we've seized enough evidence – a partial print and DNA – to be able to link it to a suspect. When we get a valid one to try for a match, that is. I'm certain we're getting close – this Flint character might be it. Up to now, there've been several people in the frame, but none have been anything other than hopeful. I mean, I think Niall is a creep, but I don't think he's capable of all this.' Lindsay leant back against the window ledge, her hands in her trouser pockets.

'No, me neither – not now. I think he's weak when it comes to women, and Kelly played on that, pulling his strings for her own gain. I'm wondering if the bird tattoo on Hargreaves' body was to make us *think* Niall was involved. A red herring.'

'Poor sap,' Lindsay said, making a face and rolling her eyes. 'And we've got his DNA on file, we took all the prison officers', so we'll be able to rule him out once we get the results back from the van. Although, I guess that only rules him out of the actual murder. It doesn't mean he didn't have *something* to do with it.' Her face looked tired, but her eyes sparkled.

'Oh!' Connie sat forward. How could she have forgotten. 'Kelly has photos, possibly, of the two men that were following me. Supposing they aren't blurry from the running.'

'Really? She's a canny one. I'll get on that. Before she prints them in the paper.' Lindsay sat back down next to Connie. 'You might be able to make a positive ID from the photo, then we'll have a solid enough reason to haul this Flint guy in, and then get a DNA sample. We could have our murderer locked up tomorrow, Connie.' She clinked her glass against Connie's. 'In the meantime, I'm staying over.'

Connie didn't argue.

322

CHAPTER EIGHTY-SEVEN

Then

He hid in the shadows, ducking between the sofa and dresser when he heard the footsteps. If he was caught out of bed at this time that would be bad enough, but if caught with the lighter too, then he'd be punished for days.

A soft glow illuminated a patch of hallway where the street lamp shone through the glass half of the front door. The footsteps stopped there. He dared to peek out from around the arm of the sofa. Was that her? The silhouette looked right. But why was she standing so still like that? He didn't know if she sleepwalked, he'd never seen her do it before. He wished she'd hurry up and move, go back upstairs to bed. He rubbed at the pins and needles in his feet. He was only short, and wiry-thin, but being crouched, tucked into a small space, was uncomfortable all the same. And now he needed to pee.

Typical, why had he chosen this moment to steal the lighter from its hiding place?

Another glow took his attention. Not from the street lamp. This light came from inside the house, in the hallway.

He recognised it immediately.

Fire.

His breathing shallowed. What was she doing? He watched, his eyes transfixed on the dancing flame. It was beautiful.

323

Then she was gone – he heard the soft padding of feet overhead.

He uncurled from his position and quickly ran towards the growing flame, a gentle crackling noise now accompanying the waving tendrils of flame. The smoke was thickening already, and it snapped him out of his trance.

His first thought was to get a bucket of water, but the flames were now creeping up the wall. Soon they'd be at the stairs, blocking anyone's exit. There was no time. He jumped past the ball of fire and took the stairs two at a time. He was aware of shouting, cries of 'Fire!' filling his head. His voice.

His dad was at the door, a look of terror on his sleepy face. He looked dazed.

'Dad, we have to get out!' The boy tugged at his arm, but he didn't move. What was wrong with his eyes – he wasn't looking straight; his eyelids were puffy and half-closed.

Suddenly he was being pulled backwards.

'Come on, hurry Brett.' Jenna was dragging him.

Cold soaked him. A wet blanket wrapped around him. They were in the back bedroom. *She* was there too. The window was open wide, she was half hanging out, screaming.

'He's not there, Jenna. The fucking gobshite isn't there!'

'We have to get out now, Mum, we'll have to try the stairs. Quick.'

Jenna was gone. The smoke was so thick, black, choking.

'Stay low, put the blanket to your mouth,' Jenna told him.

He liked fire, his small, beautiful fires, ones he could control, not like this. The heat was so bad, even through the wet blanket. He followed Jenna down the stairs, the flames leaping across one side of the stairwell. His pyjama bottoms touched the fire, he smacked them with part of the blanket.

'Where's Dad?' he shouted.

'He'll be behind us – Mum went back for him.'

They only just made it past the fireball into the lounge, then kitchen, then the black night air touched his face. They were out.

Jenna led him up the path at the side of the house to get to the front.

She hadn't come out of the house yet. Neither had his dad.

From the time it had taken them to leave the back door and walk around the front, the flames had taken hold – engulfing the top floor. How had it happened that quickly?

He wiped tears away with the back of his hand.

He could see his dad. Trapped. Jenna turned to him.

'You're so stupid, Brett. Why did you start it? You could've killed us and look what you've done to our house!' Jenna's face was red, her eyes bulging.

'I didn't do it.' He creased his forehead – why was she saying that?

As they stood at the front of the house looking up, and with the sounds of squealing sirens filling the quiet night, Jenna reached into the pocket of his soggy dressing gown.

She pulled out the lighter.

'You little freak. You did start the fire. You caused this.'

Everything went black in his head, like the wet blanket had been placed over it. His chest hurt. He never did anything right.

This *was* his fault. He should've stopped her. Jenna did this but he should have taken charge of it, stopped it.

He looked up at his stepsister as she stared open-mouthed at the upstairs window.

At his dad, screaming there.

CHAPTER EIGHTY-EIGHT

Connie

Friday 23 June

Waking up with the knowledge Lindsay Wade had slept in the spare room in order to protect her made Connie smile. For someone who had initially come across stern, uptight, hard to like – Lindsay was being incredibly soft right now. Her insistence that it should be her that offered the protection was reassuring.

Today, though, Lindsay was going to organise for DC Clarke to sit downstairs in the waiting room of her consultancy while she saw her two clients. One of them being Brett. After talking the case over last night, both she and Lindsay had decided that Connie should call Brett and ask to see him. As they were currently unaware of Flint's real name or his whereabouts, he was their best lead. Connie wanted her own answers to some things too, and with Clarke close to hand she wouldn't be so worried about asking awkward questions.

Today was going to be an interesting one.

Brett fiddled with the zip of his hoody, and at the same time bounced his leg up and down. The vibration of the movement together with his erratic zipping action put Connie on edge.

'Nothing to worry about, Brett. I only wanted to continue where we left off yesterday.'

'Who's the geezer downstairs?' He sniffed, and swiped his sleeve across his nose.

'He's a policeman. He's here because I had a break-in. Just after your session on Monday.' That wasn't strictly true, but she didn't want to get into details, she wanted to see his reaction.

'Oh, really? Why would anyone bother? Not as if you keep money or drugs here, is it?'

'I guess some people might think I do. You'd be surprised how many people mix up psychologist with psychiatrist.'

'Uh, yeah, I suppose.' His face remained neutral, he hadn't flinched at the mention of the police or a break-in. 'He wasn't here yesterday.' He gave her a quizzical look.

'Well, no – I didn't think I needed him. But since then . . .' Should she mention being followed yesterday? He might have been involved.

'Go on, since then, what?'

In for a penny. 'I was followed, and a few other minor things have happened which made the police believe they should keep a closer eye on me.'

'Wow,' he said, nodding. His eyes narrowed. 'I guess you think I have something to do with this?'

Immediately he had assumed he was being blamed. Connie wrestled with her conflicting feelings. This young man had been blamed for a fire and a death. So far, his entire short life had been filled with mistrust. She was treating him exactly the same as he'd always been treated. She felt bad now for even thinking he'd killed Steph and Dylan.

'No. But I think you might know who has.'

He raised one eyebrow high. 'Are you going to give me a clue?'

'You spoke yesterday about Flint.'

Brett's skin blanched. His Adam's apple bobbed noticeably as he swallowed hard.

'Look, what Flint does is his business. We haven't had contact since he left the YOI.'

'You said he'd helped you settle when you moved from the secure home to the YOI, and in return you helped him with writing. A lot of favours are carried out in prison, once you owe someone, they will expect payback. What did he expect from you?'

'As I said, the payback was that I helped him with in-cell work. That's it.' He sat upright, crossing his arms and legs. He was closing off.

'Can you remember anything about what he said, things he asked you to write, that could explain why he might be targeting me?'

'You're not getting me to grass, Connie, that's not cool.'

She sat back hard in her chair, running her hands roughly through her hair. It was prison code, you didn't grass on fellow inmates – that was the worst offence a prisoner could commit.

'You aren't in prison any more, Brett – you're in the real world now. And you have to get on in *this* world. If you're not careful, *you* are going to be implicated in this.'

'Are you threatening me?'

'No, I'm not threatening you. I'm trying to help you. There's a murder investigation going on and I have a suspicion that Flint is involved, and maybe, by association, you. Anything you can say that'll help figure this all out, then the better all round for everyone.'

'Who was murdered?'

'Eric Hargreaves. A prisoner from Baymead.'

'Shit.' Brett stood up and walked to the window. 'Look, I'll tell you what I know but it's just what I picked up here and there, from months of listening. He didn't tell me a lot – I think he wanted to keep me in the dark a bit, make me think he was doing this for me rather than for his own reasons.'

'Doing what for you?'

'Just let me tell it my way, please.'

Connie took a deep breath, motioning for him to carry on. She'd have to be patient.

'I knew Flint had this score he wanted to settle, for his dad – it went way back, like twenty years or more – something about his cousin, Jonny, who was shot dead in Salford. It wasn't gang-related stuff to start with, but gang members got involved. The kiddy had been used as a heavy for a dodgy deal by a bent businessman who wanted his shipment to come through with no hassle. Something went wrong and it was this bloke's fault. Nothing was ever done about it, never enough evidence in a lot of these cases apparently – no one's willing to talk, and some of the big guys have the filth in their pockets anyway, so evidence disappears.'

Connie wiped her palms on her trousers.

'Flint said his family knew who was responsible – they didn't have proof as such, but from the chatter after the shooting, they were certain enough to make their move. But this so-called businessman had everything tied up in his assets, and he had protection. It wasn't easy to make him pay through the usual channels. No one could get to him in his ivory tower.'

She was afraid to ask, but knew she had to. 'So, what did they do?'

'Best way to get to him was through his kid – his pride and joy. Like Jonny had been to his dad, Flint's uncle. By all accounts you don't mess with this family and get away with it. Anyway, he bided his time. Then, wham!' Brett smacked one closed fist into his other open hand.

Could her dad be the businessman he was talking about? It seemed like too much of a coincidence, Connie didn't want to believe it. She shut her eyes, pressing her fingertips against them. *Don't cry.*

She took a moment, not trusting her voice. 'They got revenge by killing this businessman's child?'

'Yeah, that seems to have been the outcome. As far as I know they did it in such a way that it looked like an accident – wrong time, wrong place kind of thing. A fight among rival fans at a football match, or something.'

Connie bit the inside of her cheek, hard. The metallic taste of blood trickled down her throat. The bastard. All these years her dad had known Luke died because of his dodgy business dealings. How could he live with himself?

The information flooded her brain, she struggled to comprehend it. If the revenge had been exacted though, then why wasn't Luke's death enough? Why come after her?

'If he got his revenge, why would Flint and his family still want to carry this on? Surely the debt was paid.'

'Not sure.' Brett moved away from the window, sitting back down opposite Connie. 'I heard this and that, like how the man continued doing business in the same way, even after his son's death. *Still* does. He uses other people to help him import dodgy stuff – puts their lives at risk for his own benefit. Never gets his own hands dirty, of course.'

'Drugs?'

'I don't know what he's into, but apparently he didn't learn his lesson. He crossed Flint's dad again years later, caused him more grief using one of his lads for a deal. They got banged up for it and he got away scot-free again. I guess they got pissed off with him. There was something else, another reason – one call mentioned that he'd royally fucked them over. Flint said things like, *Who did he think he was, taking them for fools, trying to pull the wool over their eyes?* I never knew the details of that, though. But it sounded like the final piss-take and they meant business then.'

'Why not kill him, the businessman?'

'Apart from the problem of getting to him? Too easy to trace I suppose. Flint's dad didn't want a direct trail that'd lead back to him, bringing trouble to his doorstep. Plus, better to watch the man suffer, no?'

Did Brett know she was the sister of the dead boy? The businessman's daughter – the one Flint wanted to get to?

'I don't understand what Hargreaves had to do with this, why he was murdered.'

'I can't say I do, either. I heard Flint on the phone – not the PIN one – his smuggled mobile, talking about a "*suitable messenger*". Brett made quotation marks with his fingers. 'They wanted someone to not only deliver the message, but to find their way to the right person, too,' Brett said. Shrugging, he added, 'I've no idea about the particulars of this part of the plan, I wasn't privy to it. I knew this guy was someone who you had a history with, though. That was common knowledge on the wings after it all blew up. I knew the name Connie Moore, because you'd done a favourable report for him – got him released. Then he'd raped someone.'

Connie winced. She'd no idea her reputation had spread as far as Manchester.

'How did Flint carry this out?' she asked.

'Obviously he had help on the outside – his dad was the one who got everything in place, linked it all up. The man had a lifetime of people who owed him favours. Or were scared to death of him. Flint didn't know I was aware of so much, he thought I was only interested in what he could do for me.'

'Which was?'

'You have to understand, I was due to be released within months and I had no one. All I ever wanted was to fit in, Connie, you know? I wanted a family. I'd heard on the grapevine that Jenna had helped put away some gang members – drug-related offences. I just wanted to find her. Be some kind of family again. Anyway, she was in witness protection and the hope of finding her, slim. *That* was Flint's side of the deal – get me to Jenna. And he knew the right people, had already made good contacts. A shame I was too late.' He turned his face away from her.

'Good contacts?'

'Yeah. Do you know how many prison officers, police, other officials take backhanders? How many are willing to take a cut to turn a blind eye, or get you information?'

There was no need to answer. While she'd been at Baymead a number of officers had been suspended for allowing prisoners to have contraband items; a few had even got prison sentences for smuggling in drugs and mobile phones. She could certainly believe there were corrupt officers both in the prison and police service – it was a problem that had been reported to be on the rise.

The pieces of the puzzle were slowly fusing together, creating the most hideous picture, with her at its centre. She didn't want to hear any more. It was the police's job to wrap this up.

'You have to tell the police this, and tell them where they can find Flint.' She stood up and opened the door, ready to call DC Clarke upstairs.

Brett's hands flew up. 'No way. I'm the last person who's going to drop someone else in the shit, send them to prison again and ruin their life, and on what evidence? My story? It's circumstantial, Connie. Look, I've been there. I'm not going to be a party to it. You won't get me to grass him up. If you want Flint for this, you'll have to fit him up yourself.'

Connie was sure that Lindsay would come through with the hard evidence to connect Flint to the murder. Her job was to get a name, address, a place to start looking for Flint.

'Okay, I understand that. Can you at least tell me his name, area he lives, anything?'

Brett chewed on the tip of a finger. 'His name is Aiden Flynn.'

'Thank you, Brett. I know you won't tell them all you've told me, but you are going to have to speak with the police. They need to rule you out of the murder investigation. It's likely that DC Clarke will want to take you in for questioning now.'

'Whatever.' He pushed up from the chair and stretched his arms high, his hands almost touching the ceiling. Connie got a flash of his torso, a tattoo evident on his right side. Was it a bird? She shook her head and smiled. Would she ever again look at someone with a tattoo and not immediately think they were involved with this case?

'I'm so sorry things didn't go the way you planned, Brett. Sorry, too, that your stepmum drew everyone into her lies. Don't blame Jenna, she was only young herself. She was trying to protect her mum.'

Brett frowned. 'What makes you think it was my stepmum lying?'

Perhaps she shouldn't have said that, he'd probably be angry that Connie had been to see her.

'Er . . . something she said. I was up that way, so I visited.'

'Really? That seems to be going beyond the duty of a psychologist. I'm surprised she said anything, she never did to me.'

'I think it was one of only a few lucid moments. She said she shouldn't have blamed you, that it was her fault. She'd planned the fire to get the insurance money and it'd gone horribly wrong. She never meant for your dad to die, or for Jenna to have to protect her by lying to the police.'

He snorted. 'Well, well. Right up to the end, eh?'

'What do you mean?'

Brett scratched his head. 'She was always going to protect her daughter over me, wasn't she? But I'm surprised she kept it up until the end. I guess she'll take that to her grave.'

'Take what?'

But Brett turned and walked out without further comment.

Connie sank back into her chair, closing her eyes against the brightness of the room. A headache throbbed at her temples; she rubbed her fingertips in a circular motion with no expectation of relieving it. Too much had just happened, the pain would only get worse. Better to go home before it progressed. Clarke would take Brett into the police station. She'd ring Lindsay, let her know about the conversation she'd had with Brett, and Aiden Flynn would be found.

Maybe this part of the nightmare was coming to an end.

CHAPTER EIGHTY-NINE

DI Wade

Lindsay watched as Clarke brought Brett Ellison into the station. Her overall impression of him was that he was a lanky child, unsure of himself, vulnerable. His face though, well, that told a different story – prematurely aged and hardened from his years in the system.

She'd let Clarke and Mack conduct the interview. Until they had Flint – Aiden Flynn – in custody, they didn't have any evidence to link Brett to the murder. When Mack returned an hour later, he filled her in. Brett had told them the bare minimum about his dealings inside the prison, as Connie had warned them he would. They'd got more from her when she'd phoned in; she'd filled in some of the gaps she knew Brett was unwilling to divulge. Perhaps he'd tell them more later – if Flynn started pinning stuff on Brett, she was sure he'd talk then. Unless he wanted to go back to a YOI.

'Who's with Connie now that Clarke's here? I thought you were meant to be taking over from him.' Mack walked over to Lindsay's desk, where a precariously placed pile of files wobbled on the far edge.

'Careful.' She reached across and placed a hand to steady the pile. 'I'm going in a sec, after I put these back.' She pointed to the files.

Mack craned his head around her to look at the time on her monitor. 'You've left her on her own for over an hour.'

Lindsay's shoulders dropped. 'Shit!' She shot up, swiftly grabbing the pile of files and ramming them into Mack's arms. 'Can you sort these? I have to run.'

She hadn't realised that much time had passed – she'd intended to leave the station and head to Connie's work as soon as Clarke arrived with Brett. Then she'd got sidetracked.

'Don't panic,' Mack shouted over the top of the files, 'we've got Brett here, and the others have got an address for Aiden Flynn, they're going there now. She'll be fine.'

Yes, she probably would. But still, Lindsay didn't want to leave her without protection until he was in custody, securely locked up. Better safe than sorry.

Her finger was dead from keeping it pressed on the buzzer. Connie wasn't responding. Lindsay dialled her mobile. No answer. She stepped back into the road to look up at the window. No movement. She must've decided to pack up for the day and go home. Lindsay walked back across the market square, under the town hall to the car park. She'd go straight to Connie's. Hopefully she'd be home by the time she got there.

During the drive she mulled over the case, mentally ticking off the evidence. They would get Aiden Flynn for the murder, she was sure of it – the evidence in the van, DNA and timings of his release would tie him nicely to that. There was also the strong circumstantial evidence of the brain injury linking him to the tattoos on Hargreaves' body. With further investigation, Lindsay hoped they could gather harder evidence on that strand. But there were loose ends. Bloody untidy ones. Who had helped him? Multiple people would've been required for his plans to work. It was a difficult operation breaking Hargreaves free, getting to Connie once she'd changed her name – he'd had accomplices for sure. And not just his dad and his henchmen on the outside. The insiders were still unknown. All Lindsay could hope for was that, upon questioning, Aiden Flynn would give some of them up.

That was doubtful, though. She'd have to accept that sometimes things didn't tie up neatly in a bow. There were so many variables in this case and coming out with all the answers was far too optimistic. They'd have to settle for the main guy, at least to begin with.

As Lindsay began driving up Connie's road, the hair on the back of her neck bristled. She pulled over at the bottom of the hill, parked and turned the engine off. Her scalp tingled. For a reason she couldn't fathom, she *knew* something was amiss.

She picked up the radio to request a back-up car. She was told to wait, that assistance would be there shortly. She didn't want to wait. What if Connie was in danger? She texted Mack: **Connie's house. Now.** It would only take five minutes or so for him to get here, Connie's house being only two miles from the police station, but those minutes could be vital ones. She'd only ever gone to Connie's through the front entrance, there was no side path to reach the back of the house. Looking at the other buildings, it seemed there was a back road that led to the rear of the houses. It'd probably be easier to gain access through the back. If that was needed.

Her heartbeat was rapid, her breathing shallow. What was she expecting? She found the right gate and slowly edged it open, squeezing through. With her back tight against the wall of Connie's house, Lindsay made her way to the kitchen window.

She stopped breathing.

A quick glance had revealed two males inside. This was worse than she'd thought. She assumed one was likely to be Aiden Flynn. Who was the second? Could it be Niall after all? She hadn't seen Connie. What had they done with her? Lindsay had to get in there. Stop this before it was too late.

Another peek through.

Connie's legs were splayed and motionless on the floor, her upper body obscured from view.

Please don't have killed her.

The men had their backs to the window and were closer to the lounge than the kitchen. The smaller of the two squatted down over Connie, pulling her hair. He lifted her head from the floor, then dropped it, a dull thud reaching Lindsay's ears. She should get in there, do something. But if she burst in she had no weapon – no way of restraining two men. No way of stopping them from hurting Connie. Her heart pleaded with her to go in, get Connie to safety. Her head screamed at her to wait for back-up. She screwed her eyes up tight. How much time had passed? Was the back-up going to be here now? Where was Mack?

Go in. If you don't, you'll regret it.

If you do, and you fuck up, like you did on Dartmoor, then lives could be lost.

She'd have to wait.

A scream burst from the house.

Lindsay kicked the door again and again until it splintered and fell open.

'Police!'

She heard scrambling footsteps heading away from her. As much as she wanted to check on Connie, she stepped over her still body and chased after the men with no plan in her head, just adrenaline coursing through her veins. She'd made the wrong call; they were going to easily outrun her.

As she gave chase down the road and across the park, Lindsay heard sirens. Then she saw two other men in front of the suspects, at the opposite end of the park, running towards them.

Her legs and arms pumped as she ran, but the gap was lengthening. She could make out that one suspect was slower, he was falling behind the other. She was catching him up. Her legs burned. The gap was closing. The faster suspect stopped abruptly and the two other men jumped on him. Excellent, the civilians had stepped in. Sometimes that was good, sometimes not. Today, Lindsay was grateful.

Lindsay was vaguely aware of police vehicles screeching up at the perimeter of the park. Her eyes were on her goal. The slower man bent over, heaving for breath. She caught up with him, reaching out and grabbing his T-shirt. Both of them were immobile for that moment, both gasping for air.

Mack ran up beside her, and, after shooting her a glare that clearly meant he was angry at her recklessness, apprehended the out-of-breath man.

Now that Lindsay had recovered sufficiently enough to look at him properly, a thud of recognition hit her.

'What a lowlife. How the hell can you call yourself a police officer?'

Miles Prescott simply turned his head away from her.

The other man, who'd been wrestled to the ground and pinned to it by the helpful public, was Aiden Flynn, as suspected. The relief that he'd been detained, that she hadn't entirely messed it up, was huge.

'Who do I have to thank for the excellent take-down?' she said as she approached the police officers at the far end of the park. A curious crowd had gathered; there were people everywhere.

'You'll never believe me, Boss.' DC Sewell emerged from behind the uniformed officers.

'Go on. Surprise me.'

'Our Mr Trevor Jones. Jonesy.'

Lindsay didn't know what to say. He did have a strange habit of being in the right place at the right time where Connie was concerned. As grateful as she was for his assistance, she made a mental note to keep an eye on him in future – a restraining order might be required.

'Who was your have-a-go-hero partner, then?' Lindsay laughed.

Jonesy shrugged. 'Not sure. I've seen him about, mind. Mostly when I've seen Connie, as it 'appens.'

'Right, well he seems to have disappeared for now.' Lindsay's eyes scanned the area, but she couldn't see him. 'Thanks for your help.'

Lindsay walked back to the police vehicle that now contained Aiden Flynn.

'You don't mind if I have a moment, do you?' Lindsay motioned to the arresting officer, jerking her head towards the car.

'Sure. He's been cautioned.'

Lindsay climbed in. She wanted to see the man who'd gone to such lengths for herself. Her mouth almost gaped in surprise. Aiden looked so young – his skin surprisingly soft-looking, plumped. Healthy. Not what she'd expected and in stark contrast to Brett Ellison's. He didn't appear innocent-looking, though. His face held an expression of smugness, not that he had reason to be, as far as she could see – he'd been caught after all. His dark eyes bore into Lindsay's.

'What you looking at?' He thrust forwards. Lindsay flinched, even though she knew he was restrained. 'Think you're clever, don't you?' Spit sprayed from his mouth. Lindsay drew back slightly, then smiled.

'We've got enough evidence to put you away, if that's what you mean?'

'Yeah, well,' he sniffed and tried to wipe his nose on the shoulder of his grey T-shirt. 'You might bang me up. But it's not the ones on the inside you should worry about, is it?'

'Meaning?'

'No comment.' He grinned, and then turned away.

This, added to the things Connie had told her, made Lindsay think that this was bigger than Aiden Flynn. There were more people involved in whatever this was – would they ever uncover the whole truth and bring them all to justice? Probably not in her time. Lindsay left the car, and Aiden, behind. For now. She'd get her moment with him, but right now she had more important people to worry about.

'Hey, Mack.' Lindsay looked up at him, struggling to find clues to his mood on his weary face. 'Any news about Connie's condition?' She held her breath, praying for the answer she desperately wanted to hear.

'Being treated for shock, a few bruises, and ligature marks . . .'

Connie sucked in air through her pursed lips. That sounded nasty.

'I wonder what would've happened, if I hadn't interrupted them?'

'But you *did*. And as much as I'm angry at you for putting yourself and others in danger – because it could've ended very badly – you made a judgement call which turned out to be right. So, drinks are on you later.' He nudged her and winked.

'I'd best come and help you process these two.' Lindsay searched Mack's eyes, hoping he'd be kind.

'Go on. I've got Clarke and Sewell. I can manage while you check on your *mate*. It would be better if it was you who took her statement anyway.'

'Thanks, Mack. I owe you,' Lindsay smiled and walked back to her car, her legs still unstable from the running. She wanted to be at the hospital to offer her support to Connie.

She wanted to know her friend was okay.

CHAPTER NINETY

Connie

Monday 26 June

Everything ached. Connie wriggled, trying to get herself comfortable between the cushions Lindsay had positioned for her on the sofa – each movement sending a shooting pain down her left side where Flint had repeatedly kicked her. The doctors had tried to keep her in the hospital for longer, but once she knew she had no internal injuries, only bruising, there was no way she was staying in that place.

Lindsay and Mack had collected her from the hospital and driven her home. The first thing she noticed when she walked through into the lounge was that it'd been tidied. The upturned furniture, the broken vase, the pictures he'd wrenched from the wall – all arranged as they had been, and a new, pretty, blue-coloured vase replaced the old one. The cream carpet had been cleaned – there was no sign of the blood which had burst from her nose when she'd been hit in the face. No one would have ever guessed anything untoward had occurred. A visitor would have had no idea Connie'd been bound and gagged, kicked and beaten on the floor of this room.

Her mum and dad had been contacted – Lindsay made sure they were aware of the facts of what had happened. She hadn't explained fully the 'why', saying that was best left to Connie. The phone lay on her lap – she was waiting for her dad to ring. She'd spoken to her mum, trying hard not to launch into an attack of her father, for the lies he'd fed them. How he was the one responsible for Connie's current state – and she'd been fortunate to escape with her life. It would need to be discussed when she was feeling stronger. When she could better manage the hurt and pain of his betrayal. Her dad was lucky, in most ways. When he wasn't merely giving 'no comment' answers, the evidence Flint gave the police was all circumstantial – nothing would stick in relation to her dad, she knew that. He'd taken care of all eventualities, no doubt.

Lindsay was apologetic. Upset knowing she'd left Connie alone for that hour. No matter how Connie tried to reassure her the fault was not hers, she'd remained pensive. Lindsay had come to her rescue; hopefully she'd take comfort from that once the dust had settled and she could look at her actions objectively. It had been Connie's fault for leaving the relative safety of her office and going home. Flint had let himself in her house, again – it had been him who had left the rat before. He said it was a reminder of her dad. He seemed to be one for leaving convoluted clues, with some deranged idea that he was clever. As it turned out, he hadn't been as clever as he imagined, and he'd made *mistakes.*

He'd been waiting in her lounge for her with a pretty annoyed, reluctant-looking Miles by his side. Seems as though the police retirement package hadn't been enough for Miles. He'd become embittered with protecting criminals – helping them make a new life, getting away with the parts they'd played in breaking the law just by making a deal to testify against other, bigger players. Why should they get away with their criminality, gain money from it, when he'd worked within the law all his life and was going to retire on what he saw as a pittance in comparison to the money they were making? Being his last year in the police force, he thought he'd be untouchable.

Connie's initial shock at learning he'd been taking bribes was soon replaced with anger. How dare he leak confidential information about her and Steph? She held him responsible for Steph and Dylan's deaths. His assertion that Steph had been lying all the time was likely to have been to cover his own arse. What else had he failed to reveal? What information had been manipulated where Steph was concerned? Whatever his involvement though, he clearly wasn't impressed that Flint had dragged him further into his plans. The arguments between those two had bought her time when she was on the floor, awaiting her fate. It appeared that Flint had threatened to expose Miles' corrupt practices unless he went with him to Connie's, to help him make her suffer. Apparently, harming Connie had been a step too far, though, an act too low even for a bent copper. That was something. At least the man still had an ounce of morality and sense of what was right and wrong.

Connie checked her mobile volume was turned up – she had a habit of forgetting to take it off silent. It was at full volume. She hadn't missed a call from her dad. Was he afraid of speaking to her? She gripped the phone tightly. He ought to be.

The irony was that justice had been done for Ricky Hargreaves, someone who in most people's eyes didn't even deserve it. The news, radio, and newspapers would run his story for weeks. He'd forever be remembered. Yet Steph and Dylan would be all but forgotten. Their story had been overtaken.

Questions remained for Connie. Whilst she believed Brett's story about the fire, there were other things that bothered her. She'd never know for sure, now. She'd have to accept she'd missed the signs that Steph was going to take her life. Maybe Lindsay and Mack were right, she'd simply had enough of hiding, running – enough of the guilt. For her, maybe there was only one solution. Connie had failed her. But trying to find a reason to stop her own guilt was not the best way to allow Steph to rest in peace.

Finally, her mobile rang. The caller ID – *Dad*.

She waited, taking a few deep breaths, then pressed the accept button.

CHAPTER NINETY-ONE

Connie

Wednesday 28 June

The bouquet of red carnations fluttered gently in the breeze. Connie bent to place her own on the mound of earth of the newly dug grave. A small wooden cross denoted who was buried beneath – Jenna Ellison, Dylan Ellison – written in black on a gold label. The dew and showers they'd had over the last week had caused the label to fade and curl at the edges.

Who would place the headstone when the time came? Brett? Was he the one who'd left the carnations?

A heaviness lay in the pit of her stomach. A feeling of incompleteness.

If only Steph had felt able to come clean, confide in her. Perhaps Connie could have helped lift some of her guilt. They could have worked through it. Guilt was a destructive emotion, she knew that all too well. Connie's dad had lived with it, though. With not much trouble it seemed. Those lacking in the ability to show guilt, or remorse, often presented with a personality disorder, or sociopathy. Did that describe her father?

Her dad, the sociopath.

Lindsay said she was being too hard on him, that he had his

reasons for keeping the truth from her and her mum, most of which were not necessarily to prevent them from discovering he was to blame for Luke's death, but to protect them.

That hadn't worked out well. Connie had hardly felt protected when she'd been tied and beaten because of his failures. Her dad was due from Manchester that afternoon; they were meeting at her mum's in Shaldon. He promised to be open, tell them what had happened to Luke, and why.

She wasn't holding her breath for the whole truth to be told.

Connie pulled her cardigan around her tightly, a shudder running through her body. Then heat travelled up her neck as she saw who was approaching.

'Sorry, don't get mad at me.' Kelly put a hand up in a defensive manner.

'Are you *still* following me?'

'Er. On this occasion, yes.'

'On *this* occasion, you have been on every one.' Connie backed away from the grave and stepped on to the path, shaking the soil from her shoes.

'I wanted to apologise,' she said. Connie raised her eyebrows. Kelly Barton, apologising? That was new. She played along.

'What for?'

'I meddled, as per usual, and by doing so I made your life more difficult than I intended. I'm sorry for that. And for following you – taking pictures. I obstructed the investigation, really, and I was lucky not to get charged.' Her voice was high-pitched, excitement oozing. Connie almost laughed. The woman was incorrigible.

'Okay, thanks.'

'Oh, and also—'

'Oh, great! There's more?' Connie was losing the will.

'Yeah, I'm sorry for dragging Niall into my plan to get a good story.' Kelly held both hands out, palms up. 'I think that's it.'

'Did you *get* a good story? Was it worth it?'

Kelly shrugged. 'Yeah. I reckon so.' She nodded, smiling. Connie

345

got the distinct impression that Kelly knew more than she'd let on. Maybe the fact a photo of her father had been among the ones sent to the police was evidence of that – that she also suspected him of dodgy dealings. Kelly would probably never stop digging for a story.

'Excellent. Now, if you don't mind, Kelly, I've got a train to catch.' Connie made to move, but Kelly put an arm out to stop her.

'Wait a second, I wanted to give you this.' She opened the bag she had with her and took out a large, brown envelope. Connie sighed.

'Now who've you snapped me with?' She held her hand out to take it.

'Oh, it's not like that. This is of the men that followed you – us – the other day. I downloaded it before the police took my memory card.'

'I *knew* you'd do that.'

'You'll be pleased I did, Connie. I had it blown up. You'll find it particularly interesting, I think.' Her voice held a hint of smugness.

'Perhaps we could keep in touch,' she said, but didn't wait for a response – turning her back and walking quickly away.

Connie watched her disappear out of the cemetery gate. An uneasiness filled her as she slowly pulled the content from the envelope. Flint's shape filled the forefront of the photo, his dark eyes matching the black hoody he wore. Behind him in the alleyway was the unknown figure who'd stopped Flint and fought him to the ground. The man who'd prevented Flint from continuing to follow Connie.

Kelly's zoomed-in picture perfectly captured the man's face.

And his piercing green eyes.

CHAPTER NINETY-TWO

Connie

She'd demanded to meet with her dad before they were due at her mother's. She needed to talk to him alone. Needed to shout, scream, tell him how much she hated him. She wasn't sure how she'd react when she saw him because, right now, waiting on the strip of beach opposite her mum's road, all Connie wanted to do was hit him.

When she saw him walking towards her, his face was ashen. He lowered his head.

He knew what was coming.

Connie's heart pounded, her fists were clenched in readiness.

Before he got level with her, she launched forwards.

His face crumpled as he caught hold of her raised hands, forcing them down. She screamed at him, but in that moment lost all power and sank into his chest, her large sobs muted as she wept into his shirt.

'I'm so sorry, Connie.'

Once she'd regained some element of composure, she let him talk. She didn't interrupt him, forcing herself to listen to his attempts at explaining what had gone wrong all those years ago in his business, as if that explained why these people had come after Connie now. He didn't mention Luke once. She couldn't bear to hear more of it.

'I'm not sure you understand what exactly I'm so angry at. Apart from finding out that my father is a corrupt businessman, of course, which is bad enough. No, it's the other lie that I hate you for, Dad. The biggest lie anyone could ever tell.'

She watched his brow furrow deeper. His eyes widened as it dawned on him that she knew. He lowered his head – an attempt to prevent seeing the hurt in her eyes – or maybe so she couldn't see the shame in his.

'What you've done is unforgivable, Dad.' Connie pulled the photo that Kelly had given her from her bag and thrust it into his hands. He took a sharp intake of breath, and stumbled a few steps backwards. He stood silently, shaking his head.

'Don't try and give me any bullshit, either. I know who that is. I'd recognise those eyes anywhere.'

His chest heaved with a sigh. 'He's not meant to have had any contact with any of us – with his old life.' His jaw slackened, the skin on his face seeming to loosen with the knowledge that his lies had unfurled. Connie turned away – not wanting to look at him – at the man she'd thought she knew. 'That was the deal – his protection counted on it. I've no idea why he's broken the rules now.'

'Broken the rules?' Connie shouted. 'He must take after you.'

'I understand your anger, but I did what I had to do.'

'But only because you fucked up so badly with your dodgy work ethic that you had to then cover your back. I'm not just angry, Dad – I'm ashamed.'

'Still, what's done is done.' His usual defences were coming up – his brusque attitude creating an armour. 'He shouldn't have come here, whatever the circumstances.'

Connie was finding it hard to get her head around all of this. For twenty-two years Luke had been dead to her. Now, everything she'd once believed had been challenged – the shocking truth shoved in her face. How had Kelly even known to give her the photo saying it was 'interesting'? Was it only Connie and her mum that were in the dark about Luke? Unless, of course, her mum *did* know, and it was just Connie left in the dark. No. Connie pushed the thought from her mind. There was no way her mum could've kept that to herself all these years.

'Maybe he was trying to protect me, stop this mess getting even more out of control.'

He shrugged. 'It's a possibility; if he's been keeping an eye from afar he could've seen your name being linked to that Hargreaves murder I suppose. Let's hope he doesn't break cover again now, though.'

'Oh yes, heaven help him if he reaches out to his own family.'

'He made the choice—'

'No, Dad. You made the choice. Luke was seventeen, how much say did he have in your decision?'

'I'm so sorry, love, I really am.'

'What would you have done this time – if the culprit hadn't been caught, Dad? Faked my death too?'

'Connie . . .' He reached a shaking hand towards her.

'No, don't.' She stepped back out of his reach. 'How did you even pull this off? How could you have convinced us, everyone, that he'd died? I can't believe it, there would've been so much red tape, you couldn't have done that alone.'

'At the time, I was very powerful in my line of work—'

'What? Antiques?' Connie snorted.

'Not exactly. I dealt with more than antiques . . .'

Connie didn't like where this was leading, but in her heart, she already knew.

'Right, so that was your cover, or something? Doesn't explain how you got away with this huge lie, this betrayal.' Her eyes clouded. Knowing her dad was involved was one thing, hearing him trying to explain away his part in it hurt her more than she could possibly have imagined.

'Let's say I knew the right people that could help me without alerting those that would cause trouble for me.' All at once the things Brett had said, the old arguments she remembered her mum and dad having – the time spent at the 'gentleman's club' – all came together. Her dad belonged to some kind of funny-handshake brigade, a secret society – perhaps even the Masons – full of powerful professionals, no doubt. Did they turn a blind eye to his dodgy dealings? Help him out when he was in trouble?

'Christ, Dad.' She ran her hands roughly through her hair and paced around in a small circle. 'Go on, what else?' She stopped, and glared at him.

'I did a deal with the police – I gave them info about one of the biggest drug importers on their hit list – and they put Luke into witness protection. It was the only way I could safeguard him. And you and your mum.'

The irony hit Connie. She'd been counselling someone in witness protection and all along her own brother had been forced into a similar situation of isolation and insecurity. Poor Luke, she could only imagine how being taken from your family at the age of seventeen would've affected him. How had her dad allowed things to get to that stage?

'Don't pretend you did any of this for us. You've ruined all of our lives and I'll never forgive you.'

'I know. But you *are* all alive. For me, your hatred of me is something I'm willing to bear for that.' He gave a small smile and turned, walking back towards the road, and her mother's house.

'That's it, Dad? What happens now?' She rushed forward, pulling at his sleeve, forcing him to face her.

'We ought to get in now, your mother will be waiting. We'll talk about this another time,' he said. Then he took hold of her upper arms and looked into her eyes. 'Don't worry your mum about any of this, will you? Sometimes you have to make decisions that aren't going to benefit a lot of people. Maybe just to protect one.'

Connie wiped her eyes. 'I can't go in there and lie to her. We have to tell her the truth.'

'No. There's no point now – she buried him, she grieved. She went through hell. I can't undo that. I'm afraid it'll kill her. She can't see him, he can't be part of this family now, it's not safe for him to suddenly come back. He knows that – why do you think he stayed in the background and didn't contact you directly? Nothing can come of this – he has to stay dead, Connie.'

What he said made some sense. If her mum knew, she'd go to any lengths to find Luke – possibly putting them all in danger. But Connie couldn't live with the knowledge he was alive and not tell her mum.

'Sorry, *Dad* – but you don't get to play God and make all the decisions any more.' She pushed past him, crossed the road and went through the front door of her mum's house without looking back at him.

CHAPTER NINETY-THREE

Connie

Monday 3 July

Connie stood on the threshold of her consulting room, looking in. It had only been ten days, but the room held a musty odour that she would've expected from somewhere that had been shut up for much longer.

Nothing in her room was different.

Yet everything was.

Dropping her bag on her desk, she went to the window and threw it open. A rush of cool, fresher air flooded in. She closed her eyes, allowing it to wash over her face. Voices of people in the street below filtered up to her. They would be her company today, as she didn't have any clients booked in. The few she had left on her list she'd had to put off while she recovered from the recent events. She hadn't felt ready to help others through their issues when she was still working through her own.

It wouldn't be long, though. It couldn't be. She couldn't afford to be self-pitying, she had to get back in the saddle and get her consultancy up and running again.

She reached inside her bag and got out the rectangular box, setting up her new aromatherapy reed-diffuser on the small table just inside the door. The immediate scent of orange and grapefruit infused the damp-smelling air. It was called *Uplifting*. She hoped it wasn't false advertising.

The ringing phone startled her. She'd let the answer machine take it.

'DI Wade calling for Connie Summers.' The tone was light, jokey. Connie smiled and ran to the phone.

'Hey, Lindsay. Is this an official call, or a checking-up-on-me call?'

'It's an official-checking-up-on-you call. I thought you might be feeling, you know, a little . . . odd. It's been a weird time, and getting back to work might seem like a good idea to stop you from your constant overthinking and analysing, but only if you have actual work to do. Otherwise you're just overthinking and analysing everything but in a different location to home.'

'Some speech.'

'Thank you. I'd rehearsed it.' Lindsay laughed. 'But, seriously, be productive, get on the computer and do some marketing, try and build your client list again. But stay busy. And no googling the case!'

Lindsay had clearly got to know Connie well over the last month.

'Yes, Boss,' Connie mocked. 'Is everything going okay with the case, though – is there enough to take to the CPS?'

'Connie, please. Enough. Trust that we will do our jobs. You concentrate on getting your life back on track. Leave the likes of Aiden Flynn behind you.'

Connie knew she was right. But she didn't like loose ends – and there were too many here to prevent her leaving this all behind entirely.

'I will, Lindsay, I promise. But what about this gang of Aiden's? What about Brett – where did he really fit in to this? Have you spoken with him since Aiden's arrest, was he involved, what about Steph—'

'Okay, okay. I get you have unanswered questions. So do we. I can't talk about it in detail, but you know a fair bit – Brett told you a lot of it. He was helpful when we questioned him, and there's nothing to suggest he had any part in Stephanie's suicide. No witnesses saw her with anyone on Dartmoor prior to hers and Dylan's deaths. According to his probation officer, Brett's going back to Manchester now there's nothing left to keep him here. And, from what we've heard so far from Aiden, which I admit is limited, Brett appears to have been spot on. The gang wanted their revenge, had been waiting a long time for it, and supposedly, the catalyst for their actions was finding out that Luke was still alive.'

This had all started because they found out that they'd been duped, then. They'd realised Luke was alive, that the death of Jonny hadn't, in fact, been avenged. Connie gave a long sigh.

It begged the question – was this really over?

'Right. Thanks Lindsay. I appreciate you calling, I really do.'

'Good. Because I'll be calling again in a few hours. Someone needs to keep you in check.'

'Hah! Yeah, I thought you might. Speak in a bit, then.'

If one good thing had come out of all this, it was her friendship with Lindsay. Despite the moral and ethical challenges Connie's involvement in the case had created, Lindsay hadn't allowed her usual 'by-the-book' approach to stop it from forming. And, if the phone call was anything to go by, she was keen to keep it going.

Connie walked to the window and stared out at the people going about their business. Was Luke still out there? Her dad had been angry that he'd broken cover – gone against the rules – had, in his mind, put himself and the family in danger. But Connie didn't think that way. He'd broken his cover to protect her.

Connie took comfort in the thought he might be watching over her.

Epilogue

A cool wind whipped the long grass as he walked across the moor and stung his face as it caught him head on. It was cold, but the sun was getting higher, and sweat began pricking under his armpits. He'd taken an hour to walk to the tor.

Haytor.

He'd read about the Devon moors when he was in the YOI. There was something fascinating about them. Dark. They held secrets.

It held his.

He climbed the granite rocks, reaching the top easily. He let the wind buffet him as he stood on the edge looking down at the sheer drop. If he leant over a bit more he'd be able to see the smaller rocks below.

How simple. One push and he'd be over the edge. One small leap and he'd be flying.

Joining his stepsister and nephew.

He took a step back. Crouching down, he retrieved a bottle from his rucksack and sat on the rock. A chill permeated his trousers. Unscrewing the lid, he swigged from the bottle, coughing as the harsh taste of vodka burnt the back of his throat. He swiped the back of his hand across his mouth.

He lifted his chin and shouted, 'Cheers, sis.'

Enough.

Scrambling to his feet, he made his way to the edge again.

But he wouldn't let her win.

He clambered back down the side of the tor, careful with his footing. A couple walking their dog came into view at the foot of the incline. He hoped they would hurry up and walk on by. He wanted to be on his own.

He waited until they were small blobs on the horizon, then made his way to the place. The exact spot where Jenna and Dylan had been found. Staring at the area they'd fallen on to, he could envisage their bent and twisted bodies.

She shouldn't have lied.

Tugging at his jeans pocket, he pulled out a crumpled photograph. He looked at it for a long while, then placed it into a crevice by the rocks where Jenna's body had fallen.

He sat down beside the photo – a smiling Jenna looking up at him from the only family picture that'd ever been taken of the four of them. Jenna on the left, then him, his dad slightly behind. With *her*. Taking his Zippo lighter, he flicked it, watching as the small flame danced. He shut the lid. Then flicked it open again. He continued with the motion until he felt ready.

Leaning forwards, he touched the flame against the photo. The left edge blackened, then caught. The flame licked the corner, then spread, obliterating her face.

'I forgive you, Jenna.' He watched until the photo was destroyed. He was calm now. 'You had to die, though. It was only right.'

He smiled as he watched the ashes of the photo lift and get carried along by the wind. 'I always told you it ends with fire.'

Author's Note

This novel is a work of fiction – however, there are some real locations mentioned. For example, I talk about the wonderful historic town of Totnes in Devon – a place I know well. While real, I've used it in a purely fictitious manner, and to this end, have slightly altered some of the geography to fit my story.

Acknowledgements

Huge thanks to my agent, Anne, and my editors Natasha and Rachel, who did a great job helping shape *Bad Sister*. Thanks also to Kate from Kate Hordern Literary Agency and everyone at Avon, HarperCollins for their enthusiasm and hard work. I'm thrilled to be part of such a fab team.

As ever, thank you to Doug, Danika, Louis and Nathaniel and the rest of my family who have continued to support me and put up with me. I know it's not always easy!

My grateful thanks to my friends and writing companions, Lydia and Libby, who read through various drafts of *Bad Sister* and whose insights and suggestions were a huge help. You both know how important you are – your daily support means everything to me.

I feel blessed to have great friends – so many have been part of my writing journey. A special shout-out to Nicci and James, who are always there for me and whose friendship and constant encouragement keeps me going. I'll always be your Maeve, James! (Although, I'll be surprised if you ever read this . . .) Thanks to Emma, who I don't see nearly enough – but I always know you're there. And thank you to Tracey, my best friend since we were three years old – you are my rock.

I've met, both virtually and in real life, some amazing book bloggers. I'm so grateful for the support I received for my debut novel, *Saving Sophie,* and for their continued support on social media. You're all stars. Special mention to Kaisha Holloway – you did a stellar job on the last paperback book tour, I will always be grateful for your enthusiasm and help. Many thanks to my book club girls: Charlotte, Izzy, Tara, Luisa, Laura and Lauraine. Our monthly meet-ups ensure I do get out of the house sometimes . . .

I also couldn't get by without my chats with fellow authors, Helen Cox, Cass Green, and Louise Jensen – and the brilliant support from the CSers (you know who you are).

I will have missed people – I forget my own children's names, so it's inevitable. But please know, even if I haven't mentioned your name, if you've helped or supported me in any way, then Thank You!

And of course, thank you dear readers. I hope you enjoy *Bad Sister.*

Your daughter is in danger.

But can you trust her?

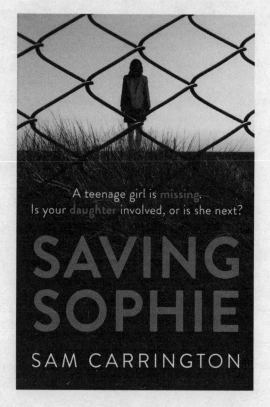

A teenage girl is missing.
Is your daughter involved, or is she next?

SAVING
SOPHIE

SAM CARRINGTON

Out now.